A TRAITOR TO MEMORY

One fateful night at Wigmore Hall, twenty-eight year old virtuoso violinist Gideon Davies lifted his violin to play in a Beethoven trio . . . and everything in his mind related to music was gone. Gideon suffers from a form of amnesia, the cure for which is an examination of what he can remember. And what he can remember is little enough until his mind is triggered by the weeping of a woman and a single name: Sonia. One rainy evening, a woman called Eugenie travels to London for a mysterious appointment. But before she is able to reach her destination, a car swoops out of nowhere and kills her in the street. In pursuing the killer of Eugenie, Thomas Lynley, Barbara Havers and Winston Nkata come to know a group of people whose lives are inextricably connected by a long-ago death, a trial, and a prison sentence handed down as retribution for a crime no one has spoken of for twenty years.

A TRAITOR
TO MEMORY
VOL 1

Elizabeth George

CHIVERS PRESS
BATH

First published 2001
by
Hodder and Stoughton
This Large Print edition published by
Chivers Press
by arrangement with
Hodder & Stoughton
2002

ISBN 0 7540 1793 1

British Library Cataloguing in Publication Data available

Printed and bound in Great Britain by
BOOKCRAFT, Midsomer Norton, Somerset

For the other Jones girl,
wherever she might be

'O my son Absalom,
My son, my son, Absalom!
Would God I had died for thee.'

Samuel II, *XIX*, 4

Maida Vale, London

Fat girls can do. Fat girls can do. Fat girls can do and do and do.

As she trod the pavement towards her car, Katie Waddington used her regular mantra in rhythm with her lumbering pace. She said the words mentally instead of aloud, not so much because she was alone and afraid of seeming batty but rather because to say them aloud would put further demands on her labouring lungs. And they had trouble enough to keep going. As did her heart which, according to her always sententious GP, was not intended to pump blood through arteries that were being fast encroached upon by fat.

When he looked at her, he saw rolls of flesh, he saw mammae hanging like two heavy flour sacks from her shoulders, he saw a stomach that drooped to cover her pubis and skin that was cratered with cellulite. She was carrying so much weight on her frame that she could live for a year on her own tissue without eating and, if the doctor was to be believed, the fat was moving in on her vital organs. If she didn't do something to curb herself at table, he declared each time she saw him, she was going to be a goner.

'Heart failure or stroke, Kathleen,' he told her with a shake of his head. 'Choose your poison. Your condition calls for immediate action, and that action is *not* intended to include ingesting anything that can turn into adipose tissue. Do you understand?'

How could she not? It was *her* body they were

1

talking about and one couldn't be the size of a hippo in a business suit without noticing that fact when the opportunity arose to have a glimpse at one's reflection.

But the truth of the matter was that her GP was the only person in Katie's life who had difficulty accepting her as the terminally fat girl she'd been from childhood. And since the people who counted took her as she was, she had no motivation to shed the thirteen stone that her doctor was recommending.

If Katie had ever harboured a doubt about being embraced by a world of people who were increasingly buffed, toned, and sculpted, she'd had her worth reaffirmed tonight as it was every Monday, Wednesday, and Friday when her Eros in Action groups met from seven till ten o'clock. There, the sexually dysfunctional populace of Greater London came together for solace and solution. Directed by Katie Waddington—who'd made the study of human sexuality her lifelong passion—libidos were examined; erotomania and -phobia were dissected; frigidity, nymphomania, satyrism, transvestism, and fetishisms were admitted to; erotic fantasies were encouraged; and erotic imagination was stimulated.

'You saved our marriage,' her clients gushed. Or their lives, or their sanity, or frequently their careers.

Sex is profit was Katie's motto, and she had nearly twenty years of approximately six thousand grateful clients and a waiting list of two hundred more to prove this true.

So she walked to her car in a state that was somewhere between self-satisfaction and absolute

2

rapture. She might be inorgasmic herself, but who was to know as long as she had success in consistently promoting happy orgasm in others? And that's what the public wanted, after all: guilt-free sexual release upon demand.

Who guided them to it? A fat girl did.

Who absolved them of the shame of their desires? A fat girl did.

Who taught them everything from stimulating erogenous zones to simulating passion till passion returned? A terminally hugely preposterously fat girl from Canterbury did and did and did.

That was more important than counting calories. If Katie Waddington was meant to die fat, then that was the way it was going to be.

It was a cool night, just the way she liked it. Autumn had finally come to the city after a boiling summer, and as she trundled along in the darkness Katie relived, as she always did, the high points of her evening's group session.

Tears. Yes, there were always tears as well as hand wringing, blushing, stammering, and sweating aplenty. But there was generally a special moment as well, a breakthrough moment that made listening to hours of repetitious personal details finally worthwhile.

Tonight that moment had come in the persons of Felix and Dolores (last names withheld) who'd joined EiA with the express purpose of 'recapturing the magic' of their marriage after each of them had spent two years—and twenty thousand pounds—exploring their individual sexual issues. Felix had long since admitted seeking satisfaction outside the realm of his wedding vows and Dolores had herself owned up to enjoying her vibrator and

3

a picture of Laurence Olivier as Heathcliff far more than the marital embrace of her spouse. But on this night, Felix's ruminations on why the sight of Dolores's bare bum brought on thoughts of his mother in her declining years was too much for three of the middle-aged women in the group who attacked him verbally and so viciously that Dolores herself sprang passionately to his defence, apparently washing away her husband's aversion to her backside with the sacred water of her tears. Husband and wife subsequently fell into each other's arms, lip-locked, and cried out in unison, 'You've saved our marriage!' at the meeting's conclusion.

She'd done nothing more than give them a forum, Katie admitted to herself. But that's all some people really wanted, anyway: an opportunity to humiliate themselves or their beloved in public, creating a situation from which the beloved could ultimately rescue or be provided rescue.

There was a genuine gold mine in dealing with the sexual dilemmas of the British population. Katie considered herself more than astute to have realised that fact.

She yawned widely and felt her stomach growl. A good day's work and a good evening's work meant a good meal as a reward to herself followed by a good wallow with a video. She favoured old films for their nuances of romance. Fading to black at the crucial moment got her juices flowing far more efficiently than close ups of body parts and a sound track filled with heavy breathing. *It Happened One Night* would be her choice: Clark and Claudette and all that delicious tension between them.

That's what missing in most relationships, Katie thought for the thousandth time that month. Sexual tension. There's nothing left to the imagination between men and women any longer. It's a know-all, tell-all, photograph-all world, with nothing to anticipate and even less left secret.

But she couldn't complain. The state of the world was making her rich, and fat though she was, no one gave her aggro when they saw the house she lived in, the clothes she wore, the jewellery she bought, or the car she drove.

She approached that car now, where she'd left it that morning, in a private car park across the street and round the corner from the clinic in which she spent her days. She found that she was breathing more heavily than usual as she paused on the kerb before crossing. She put one hand on a lamppost for support and felt her heart struggling to keep up its job.

Perhaps she *ought* to consider the weight loss programme her doctor had suggested, she thought. But a second later, she rejected the idea. What was life *for* if not to be enjoyed?

A breeze came up and blew her hair from her cheeks. She felt it cooling the back of her neck. A minute of rest was all she needed. She'd be fit as ever when she caught her breath.

She stood and listened to the silent neighbourhood. It was partly commercial and partly residential, with businesses that were closed at this hour and houses long ago converted to flats with windows whose curtains were drawn against the night.

Odd, she thought. She'd never really noticed the quiet or the emptiness of these streets after dark.

She looked round and realised that anything could happen in this sort of place—anything good, anything bad—and it would be solely left to chance if there was a witness to what occurred.

A chill coursed through her. Better move on.

She stepped off the kerb. She began to cross.

She didn't see the car at the end of the street till its lights switched on and blinded her. It barrelled towards her with a sound like a bull.

She tried to hurry forward but the car was upon her. She was far too fat to get out of its way.

Gideon

16 AUGUST

I want to begin by saying that I believe this exercise to be a waste of my time, which, as I attempted to tell you yesterday, is exactly what I do not have to spare just now. If you wanted me to have faith in the efficacy of this activity, you might have given me the paradigm upon which you are apparently basing what goes for 'treatment' in your book. Why does it matter what paper I use? What notebook? What pen or what pencil? And what difference does it make where I actually do this nonsensical writing you require of me? Isn't the simple fact that I've agreed to this experiment enough for you?

Never mind. Don't reply. I already know what your answer would be: Where is all this anger coming from, Gideon? What's beneath it? What do you recall?

Nothing. Don't you see? I recall absolutely nothing. That's why I've come.

Nothing? you say. Nothing at all? Are you sure that's true? You do know your name, after all. And apparently you know your father as well. And where you live. And what you do for a living. And your closest associates. So when you say nothing, you must actually be telling me that you remember—

Nothing important *to me. All right. I'll say it. I remember nothing that I count as important. Is that what you want to hear? And shall you and I dwell on what nasty little detail about my character I reveal with that declaration?*

Instead of answering those two questions, however, you tell me that we'll begin by writing what we do remember—whether it's important or not. But when you say we, *you really mean* I'll *begin by writing and what* I'll *write is what* I *remember. Because as you so succinctly put it in your objective, untouchable psychiatrist's voice, 'What we remember can often be the key to what we've chosen to forget.'*

Chosen. *I expect that was a deliberate selection of words. You wanted to get a reaction from me. I'll show her, I'm supposed to think. I'll just show the little termagant how much I can remember.*

How old are you, anyway, Dr Rose? You say thirty, but I don't believe that. You're not even my age, I suspect, and what's worse you look like a twelve-year-old. How am I supposed to have confidence in you? Do you honestly think you're going to be an adequate substitute for your father? It was he I agreed to see, by the way. Did I mention that when we first met? I doubt it. I felt too sorry for you. The only reason I decided to stay, by the way, when I walked into the office and saw you instead of him, is that you looked so pathetic sitting there, dressed all in black as if that could make you look like someone competent to

7

handle people's mental crises.

Mental? you ask me, leaping on the word as if it were a runaway train. So you've decided to accept the conclusion of the neurologist? Are you satisfied with that? You don't need any further tests in order to be convinced? That's very good, Gideon. That's a fine step forward. It will make our work together easier if, difficult though the acceptance may be, you've been persuaded that there's no physiological explanation for what you're experiencing.

How well spoken you are, Dr Rose. A voice like velvet. What I should have done was turn straight round and come back home as soon as you opened your mouth. But I didn't because you manoeuvred me into staying, didn't you, with that, 'I wear black because my husband died' nonsense. You wanted to evoke my sympathy, didn't you? Forge a bond with the patient, you've been told. Win his trust. Make him suggestible.

Where's Dr Rose? I ask you as I enter the office.

You say, I'm Dr Rose. Dr Alison Rose. Perhaps you were expecting my father? He had a stroke some eight months ago. He's recovering now, but it's going to take some time, so he's not able to see patients just now. I've taken over his practice.

And away you go, chatting about how it came about that you returned to London, about how you miss Boston but that's all right because the memories were too painful there. Because of him, because of your husband, you tell me. You even go so far as to give me his name: Tim Freeman. And his disease: colon cancer. And how old he was when he died: thirty-seven. And how you'd put off having children because you'd been in medical school when you first got married and when it finally came time to think of

8

reproducing he was fighting for his life and you were fighting for his life as well and there was no room for a child in that battle.

And I, Dr Rose, felt sorry for you. So I stayed. And as a result of that, I'm now sitting at the first floor window overlooking Chalcot Square. I'm writing this rubbish with a biro so that I can't erase anything, per your instructions. I'm using a loose-leaf notebook so that I can add where necessary if something miraculously comes to me later. And what I'm not doing is what I should be doing and what the whole world expects me to be doing: standing side by side with Raphael Robson, making that infernal ubiquitous nothing between the notes disappear.

Raphael Robson? I can hear you query. Tell me about Raphael Robson, you say.

I had milk in my coffee this morning, and I'm paying for it now, Dr Rose. My stomach's on fire. The flames are licking downward through my gut. Fire moves up, but not inside me. It happens the opposite, and it always feels the same. Common distension of the stomach and the bowels, my GP tells me. Flatus, he intones, as if he's offering me a medical benediction. Charlatan, quack, and fourth-rate sawbones. I've got something malignant devouring my intestines and he calls it wind.

Tell me about Raphael Robson, you repeat.

Why? I ask. Why Raphael?

Because he's a place to start. Your mind is giving you the place to start, Gideon. That's how this process is going to work.

But Raphael isn't the beginning, I inform you. The beginning is twenty-five years ago, in a Peabody House, in Kensington Square.

9

17 AUGUST

That's where I lived. Not in one of the Peabody Houses, but in my grandparents' house on the south side of the square. The Peabody Houses are long gone now, replaced by two restaurants and a boutique the last time I checked. Still, I remember those houses well and how my father employed them to fabricate the Gideon Legend.

That's how he is, my father, always prepared to use what comes to hand if it has the potential to get him where he wants to go. He was restless in those days, always full of ideas. I see now that most of his ideas were attempts to allay my grandfather's fears about him since in Granddad's eyes, Dad's failure to establish himself in the army presaged his failure at everything else as well. And Dad knew that's what Granddad believed about him, I suppose. After all, Granddad wasn't a man who ever kept his opinions to himself.

He hadn't been well since the war, my grandfather. I supposed that's why we lived with him and Gran. He'd spent two years in Burma as a prisoner of the Japanese, and he'd never recovered from that completely. I suspect that being a prisoner had triggered something inside him that would have remained dormant otherwise. But in any event all I was ever told about the situation was that Granddad had 'episodes' which called for his being carted off for a 'nice countryside holiday' every now and again. I can't remember any specific details about these episodes as my grandfather died when I was ten. But I do remember that they always began with some fierce and frightening banging about, followed by my grandmother weeping, and my grandfather shouting,

10

'You're no son of mine' at my father as they took him away.

They? you ask me. Who are they?

The goblin people is what I called them. They looked like anyone else on the street, but their bodies were inhabited by snatchers of the soul. Dad always let them in. Gran always met them on the stairs, crying. And they always passed her without a word because all the words they had to say had already been said more than once. They'd been coming for Granddad for years, you see. Long before I was born. Long before I watched from between the stairway balusters, crouched there like a little toad and frightened.

Yes. Before you ask, I do remember that fear. And something else as well. I remember someone drawing me away from the balusters, someone who peeled off my fingers one by one to loosen my grip and lead me away.

Raphael Robson? you're asking me, aren't you? Is this where Raphael Robson appears?

But no. This is years before Raphael Robson. Raphael came after the Peabody House.

So we're back to the Peabody House, you say.

Yes. The House and the Gideon Legend.

19 AUGUST

Do I remember the Peabody House? Or have I manufactured the details to fill in an outline that my father gave me? If I couldn't remember what it smelled like inside, I would say that I was merely playing a game by my father's rules to be able to conjure the Peabody House out of my brain at a time like this. But because the scent of bleach can still

11

transport me back to the Peabody House in an instant, I know the foundation of the tale is true, no matter how much it has been embroidered over the years by my father, my publicist, and the journalists who've spoken to them both. Frankly, I myself no longer answer questions about the Peabody House. I say, 'That's old ground. Let's till some fresh soil this time round.'

But journalists always want a hook for their story and, limited by my father's firm injunction that only my career is open for discussion when I'm interviewed, what better hook could there be than the one my father created out of a simple stroll in the garden of Kensington Square:

I am three years old and in the company of my grandfather. I have with me a tricycle on which I am trundling round the perimeter of the garden while Granddad sits in that Greek-temple affair that serves as a shelter near the wrought iron fence. Granddad has brought a newspaper to read, but he isn't reading. Instead he's listening to some music coming from one of the buildings behind him.

He says to me in a hushed voice, 'It's called a concerto, Gideon. This is Paganini's D Major concerto. Listen.' He beckons me to his side. He sits at the very end of the bench and I stand next to him, with his arm round my shoulders, and I listen.

And I know in an instant that this is what I want to do. I somehow know as a three-year-old what has never left me since: that to listen is to be but to play is to live.

I insist that we leave the garden at once. Granddad's hands are arthritic and they struggle with the gate. I demand that he hurry 'before it's too late'.

'Too late for what?' he asks me fondly.

12

I grab his hand and show him.

I lead him to the Peabody House which is where the music is coming from. And then we're inside, where a lino floor has recently been washed and the air stings our eyes with the smell of bleach.

Up on the first floor, we find the source of the Paganini concerto. One of the bed-sitting rooms is the dwelling place of Miss Rosemary Orr, long retired from the London Philharmonic. She is standing in front of a large wall mirror, and she's got a violin under her chin and a bow in her hand. She isn't playing the Paganini, though. Instead, she's listening to a recording of it with her eyes closed and her bow hand lowered and tears coursing down her cheeks and onto the wood of her instrument.

'She's going to break it, Granddad,' I inform my grandfather. And this rouses Miss Orr who starts and no doubt wonders how an arthritic old gentleman and a runny-nosed boy come to be standing at the door to her room.

But there is no time for her to voice any consternation, for I go to her and take the instrument from her hands. And I begin to play.

Not well, of course, for who would believe that an untrained three-year-old no matter his natural talent could possibly pick up a violin and play Paganini's Concerto in D Major the first time he's heard it? But the raw materials are there within me—the ear, the inherent balance, the passion—and Miss Orr sees this and insists that she be allowed to instruct the precocious child.

So she becomes my first violin instructor. And I remain with her until I am four and a half years old, at which time it is decided that a less conventional manner of instruction is required for my talent.

13

So that is the Gideon Legend, Dr Rose. Do you know the violin well enough to see where it lapses into fantasy?

We've managed to promulgate the legend by actually calling it a legend, by laughing it off even as it is told. We say, Stuff and nonsense, all of it. But we say that with a suggestive smile. Miss Orr's long dead, so she can't refute the story. And after Miss Orr, there was Raphael Robson, who has limited investments to make in the truth.

But here's the truth for you, Dr Rose, because despite what you may think concerning my reaction to this exercise in which I've agreed to engage, I am interested in telling you the truth.

I am in the garden of Kensington Square that day with a summer play group sponsored by a nearby convent, populated by the infant inhabitants of the square, and directed by three of the college students who live in a hostel behind the convent. We are collected daily from our individual houses by one or another of our three keepers and we are led hand-in-hand into the central garden where, it is hoped and for a nominal fee, we will learn the social skills that are engendered through cooperative play. This will stand us in good stead when we take our places at primary school. Or so the plan is.

The college students occupy us with games, with crafts, and with exercise. And once we are set busily to whatever task they've chosen that day, they—unbeknownst to our parents—repair to that same Greek temple affair where they chat amongst themselves and smoke cigarettes.

This particular day is earmarked for biking although what passes for biking is actually tricycle riding round the perimeter of the garden. And while I

14

trundle round and round on my tricycle at the tail end of the small pack, a boy like myself—although I don't remember his name—takes out his willie and urinates openly upon the lawn. A crisis ensues, during which the malefactor is marched directly home amidst a thorough telling off.

This is when the music begins, and the two college students who remain after the child has been removed haven't the slightest idea what it is that we're listening to. But I want to go to that sound and insist with a force so unusual that one of the students—it's an Italian girl, I think, because her English isn't very good although her heart is big—says that she will help me track it down. And so we do, to the Peabody House where we meet Miss Orr.

She is neither playing, pretending to play, nor weeping when the student and I find her in her sitting room. Rather she is giving a music lesson. She ends every lesson—I learn—by playing a piece of music on her stereo for her student. Today she is playing the Brahms concerto.

Do I like music? she wants to know.

I have no answer. I don't know if I like it, if what I feel is liking or something else. I only know that I want to be able to make those sounds. But I'm shy and say nothing of this, and I hide behind the Italian girl's legs, until she clutches my hand and apologises in her broken English and shoos me back to the garden.

And that's the reality.

You want to know, naturally, how this inauspicious beginning to my life in music metamorphosed into the Gideon Legend. How, in other words, did the discarded weapon left—shall we say?—to collect one hundred years of lime deposits in a cave become

15

Excalibur, the Sword in the Stone? I can only speculate, as the Legend is my father's invention and not my own.

The children from the play group were taken to their homes by their student keepers at the end of the day, and reports were given on each child's development and comportment. What else were the parents spending their money on if not to receive hopeful daily indications that a suitable level of social maturity was being achieved?

God knows what the display in public of what should have been a private bodily function earned the willie waver that afternoon. In my case, the Italian student reported on my meeting with Rosemary Orr.

This would have occurred in the sitting room, I dare say, where Gran would have been presiding over the afternoon tea that she never failed to make for Granddad, enveloping him in an aura of normalcy as a hedge against the intrusion of an episode. Perhaps my father was there as well, perhaps we were joined by James the Lodger, who helped us make ends meet by renting one of the vacant bedrooms on the fourth floor of the house.

The Italian student—although let me say now that she might as easily have been Greek or Spanish or Portuguese—would have been invited to join the family for refreshment, which would then have given her the opportunity to tell the tale of our meeting with Rosemary Orr.

She says, 'The little one, he wants to find this music we are listening, so we trail it up—'

'She means "hearing" and "track it down," I think,' the lodger interposes. His name is James, as I've said, and I've heard Granddad complain that his English is 'too bloody perfect to be real' so he must be

16

a spy. But I like to listen to him anyway. Words come from James the Lodger's mouth like oranges, plump and juicy and round. He himself is none of that, except for his cheeks which are red and get redder still when he realises everyone is listening to him. He says, 'Do go on,' to the Italian-Spanish-Greek-Portuguese student. 'Don't take the slightest notice of me.'

And she smiles because she likes the lodger. She'd like him to help her with her English, I expect. She'd like to be friends with him.

I myself have no friends—despite the play group—but I don't notice their absence because I have my family, and I bask in their love. Unlike most children of three, I do not lead an existence separate from the adults in my limited world: taking my meals alone, entertained and exposed to life by a nanny or some other child minder, making periodic appearances in the bosom of the family, spinning my wheels until such a time as I can be packed off to school. Instead, I am of the world of the adults with whom I live. So I see and hear much of what happens in my home and if I don't remember events, I remember impressions of events.

So I recall this: the story of the violin music being told and Granddad plunging into the midst of the tale with an expatiation on Paganini. Gran's used music for years to soothe him when he's teetering on the edge of an episode and while there's still a hope of heading it off, and he talks about trills and bowing, about vibrato and glissandi with what sounds like authority but is likely, I know now, delusion. He's big and booming in his grandiloquence, an orchestra in and of himself. And no one interrupts or disagrees when he says to everyone but in reference to me, 'This boy shall play,' like God declaring Himself for light.

17

Dad hears this, attaches to it a significance that he shares with no one, and swiftly makes all the necessary arrangements.

So it is that I come to receive my first lessons in the violin from Miss Rosemary Orr. And from these lessons and from that report from the play group, my father develops the Gideon Legend which I've dragged through life like a ball and chain.

But why did he make it a story about your grandfather? you want to know, don't you? Why not just keep the central characters but fudge on the details here and there? Wasn't he worried that someone would step forward, refute the story, and tell the real tale?

I give you the only answer I can, Dr Rose: You'll have to ask my father.

*　　　*　　　*

21 AUGUST
I remember those first lessons with Rosemary Orr: my impatience locking horns with her devotion to minutiae. 'Find your body, Gideon dear, find your body,' she says. And with a one-sixteenth tucked between my chin and my shoulder—for this was in the days when that was the smallest instrument one could obtain—I endure Miss Orr's perpetual adjustments to my position. She arches my fingers over the fingerboard; she stiffens my left wrist; she grips my shoulder to prevent its intrusion into the bowing; she straightens my back and uses a long pointer to tap the insides of my legs to alter my stance. All along while I play—when she at last allows me to play—her voice rings out above the scales and arpeggios that are my initial assignments: 'Body up,

18

shoulder down, Gideon dear.' 'Thumb under this part of the bow, not on the silver part, please, and not on the side.' 'The whole arm *up-bows.' 'Strokes are big and detached.' 'No, no! You use the* fleshy *part of the fingers, dear.' Continually, she has me play one note and set up for the next. Over and over we engage in this exercise until she is satisfied that all body parts which exist as extensions of the right hand—that is to say the wrist, the elbow, the arm, and the shoulder blade—function along with the bow like an axis and wheel, with the body parts keeping the bow on course.*

I learn that my fingers must work independently of each other. I learn to find that balancing point on the fingerboard which will later allow my fingers to shift as if through air alone from one position to the next on the strings. I learn to listen for and to find the ringing tone of my instrument. I learn up bow and down bow, the golden mean, staccato *and* legato, sul tasto *and* sul ponticello.

In short, I learn method, theory, and principle, but what I do not learn is what I hunger to learn: how to rupture the spirit to bring forth the sound.

I persevere with Miss Rosemary Orr for eighteen months, but soon I tire of the soulless exercises that dominate my time. Soulless exercises were not what I heard issuing forth from her window that day in the square, and I rail against having to be part of them. I hear Miss Orr excuse this to my father, 'He is, after all, a very small child. It's to be expected that, at such a young age, his interest wouldn't be held for long.' But my father—who is already doing two jobs to keep the family at Kensington Square—has not attended my thrice-weekly lessons and thus he can't perceive the manner in which they're bleeding life from the music I love.

My grandfather, however, has been there all along because during the eighteen months that I have been with Miss Orr, he has not experienced anything resembling an episode. So he's taken me to my lessons and he's listened from a corner of the room, and with his sharp eyes absorbing the form and the content of my lessons and his parched soul thirsty for Paganini, he has drawn the conclusion that his grandson's prodigious talent is being held back, not nurtured, by well-meaning Rosemary Orr.

'He wants to make music, damn it,' Granddad roars at my father when they discuss the situation. 'The boy's a bloody artist, Dick, and if you can't see that much when it's painted in front of you, you've got no brains and you're no son of mine. Would you feed a thoroughbred from the pig trough? I don't bloody think so, Richard.'

Perhaps it is fear that garners my father's cooperation, fear that another episode will be forthcoming if he does not acquiesce in Granddad's plan. And it is a plan that my grandfather makes immediately apparent: We live in Kensington, no great distance from the Royal College of Music, and it is there that a suitable violin instructor shall be found for his grandson Gideon.

So it is that my grandfather becomes my saviour and the trustee of my unspoken dreams. So it is that Raphael Robson enters my life.

22 AUGUST

I am four years and six months old, and although I know now that Raphael would only have been in his early thirties at the time, to me he is a distant, awesome figure who commands my complete

20

obedience from the first moment we meet.

He isn't pleasing to behold. He sweats copiously. I can see his skull through his baby-fine hair. His skin is the white of river fish flesh and it is patched with scales from too much time in the sun. But when Raphael picks up his violin and plays for me—for that is our introduction to each other—his looks fades to insignificance, and I am clay for him to mould. He chooses the Mendelssohn E minor, and he gives his entire body to the music.

He doesn't play notes; he exists within sounds. The allegro excitement he produces on his instrument mesmerises me. In a moment he has been transformed. He is no sweating patchy-skinned milksop but Merlin, and I want his magic for myself.

Raphael doesn't teach method, I discover, saying to my grandfather who interviews him that 'It's the work of the violinist to develop his own method.' Instead he improvises exercises for me. He leads and I follow. 'Rise to the opportunity,*' he instructs me over his own playing and watching mine. 'Enrich that vibrato. Don't be afraid of* portamenti, *Gideon. Slide. Make them flow.* Slide.*'*

And this is how I begin my real life as a violinist, Dr Rose, because all that has gone before with Miss Orr was a prelude. I take three lessons a week at first, then four, and then five. Each lesson lasts three hours. I go at first to Raphael's office at the Royal College of Music, Granddad and I on the bus from Kensington High Street. But the extended hours of waiting for me to finish my lessons are tiresome to Granddad and everyone in the house is afraid that they will provoke an episode sooner or later without my grandmother there to contend with it. So eventually an arrangement must be made for Raphael

Robson to come to me.

The cost is, of course, enormous. One does not ask a violinist of Raphael's calibre to commit vast stretches of his teaching time to one small student without recompensing him for his travel, for the hours lost from instructing other students, and from the increased time he will be spending on me. Man does not, after all, live on the love of music alone. And while Raphael has no family to support, he does have his own mouth to feed and his own rent to pay and the money must be raised somehow to see to it that he wants for nothing that would make it necessary for him to reduce his hours with me.

My father is already working at two jobs. Granddad gets a small pension from a Government grateful for the wartime sacrifice of his sanity, and it has been in the course of preserving that sanity that my grandparents have never moved to less expensive but more trying surroundings in the postwar years. They've cut back to the bone, they've let out rooms to lodgers, and they've shared the expense and the work of running a large house with my father. But they have not allowed for having a child prodigy in the family—and that is what my grandfather insists upon calling me—nor have they budgeted for what the costs will be in nurturing that prodigy to fulfil his potential.

And I don't make it easy for them. When Raphael suggests another lesson here or there, another hour or two or three with our instruments, I am passionate about my need for this time. And they see how I thrive under Raphael's tutelage: He steps into the house and I am ready for him, my instrument in one hand and my bow in the other.

So an accommodation must be made for my lessons, and my mother is the one who makes it.

22

CHAPTER ONE

It was the knowledge of a touch—reserved for him but given to another—that drove Ted Wiley out into the night. He'd seen it from his window, not intending to spy but spying all the same. The time: just past one in the morning. The place: Friday Street, Henley-on-Thames, a mere sixty yards from the river, and in front of her house which they'd exited only moments before, both of them having to duck their heads to avoid a lintel put into a building in centuries past when men and women were shorter and when their lives were more clearly defined.

Ted Wiley liked that: the definition of roles. She did not. And if he hadn't understood before now that Eugenie would not be easily identified as his woman and placed into a convenient category in his life, Ted had certainly reached that conclusion when he saw the two of them—Eugenie and that broomstick stranger—out on the pavement and in each other's arms.

Flagrant, he'd thought. She *wants* me to see this. She wants me to see the way she's embracing him, then curving her palm to describe the shape of his cheek as he steps away. God damn the woman. She wants me to see this.

That, of course, was sophistry, and had the embrace and the touch occurred at a more reasonable hour, Ted would have talked himself out of the ominous direction his mind began taking. He would have thought, It can't mean *anything* if she's touching a stranger out in the

23

street in public in a shaft of light from her sitting room window in the autumn sunshine in front of God and everyone and most of all *me* . . . But instead of these thoughts, what was *implied* by a man's departure from a woman's home at one in the morning filled Ted's head like a noxious gas whose volume continued to increase over the next seven days as he—anxious and interpreting every gesture and nuance—waited for her to say, 'Ted, have I mentioned that my brother—' or my cousin or my father or my uncle or the homosexual architect who intends to build another room onto the house—'stopped for a chat just the other night? It went on into the early hours of the morning and I thought he'd never leave. By the way, you might have seen us just outside my front door if you were lurking behind your window shades as you've taken to doing recently.' Except, of course, there was no brother or cousin or uncle or father that Ted Wiley knew of, and if there was a homosexual architect, he'd yet to hear Eugenie mention him.

What he *had* heard her say, his bowels on the rumble, was that she had something important to tell him. And when he'd asked her what it was and thought he'd like her to give it to him straightaway if it was going to be the blow that killed him, she'd said, Soon. I'm not quite ready to confess my sins yet. And she'd curved her palm to touch his cheek. Yes. *Yes.* That touch. Just *exactly* like.

So at nine o'clock on a rainy evening deep in November, Ted Wiley put his ageing golden retriever on her lead and decided that a stroll was in order. Their route, he told the dog—whose arthritis and aversion to the rain did not make her the most cooperative of walkers—would take them

24

to the top of Friday Street and a few yards beyond it to Albert Road where if by coincidence they should run into Eugenie just leaving the Sixty Plus Club where the New Year's Eve Gala Committee were still attempting to reach a compromise on the menu for the coming festivities, why that's what it would be: a mere coincidence and a fortuitous chance for a chat. For all dogs need a walk before they kipped down for the night. No one could argue, accuse, or even suspect over that.

The dog—ludicrously albeit lovingly christened Precious Baby by Ted's late wife and resolutely called PB by Ted himself—hesitated at the doorway and blinked out at the street, where the autumn rain was falling in the sort of steady waves that presaged a lengthy and bone-chilling storm. She began to lower herself determinedly to her haunches and would have successfully attained that position had Ted not tugged her out onto the pavement with the desperation of a man whose intentions will not be thwarted.

'Come, PB,' he ordered her, and he jerked the lead so that the choke chain tightened round her neck. The retriever recognised both the tone and the gesture. With a bronchial sigh that released a gust of dog breath into wet night air, she trudged disconsolately into the rain.

The weather was a misery, but that couldn't be helped. Besides, the old dog *needed* to walk. She'd become far too lazy in the five years that had passed since her mistress's death, and Ted himself had not done much to keep her exercised. Well, that would change now. He'd promised Connie he'd look after the dog, and so he would, with a new regime that began this very night. No more sniffing round the back garden before bedtime, my friend, he silently informed PB. It's walkies and nothing else from now on.

He double checked to make sure the book shop's door was secure, and he adjusted the collar of his old waxed jacket against the wet and the chill. He should have brought an umbrella, he realised as he stepped from the doorway and the first splash of rain water hit his neck. A peaked cap was insufficient protection, no matter how well it suited him. But why the hell was he even *thinking* about what suited him? he pondered. Fire and ice, if anyone wormed a way inside his head these days, it would be to find cobwebs and rot floating there.

Ted harrumphed, spat in the street, and began to give himself a pep talk as he and the dog plodded past the Royal Marine Reserve, where a broken gutter along the roof erupted rainwater in a silver plume. He was a catch, he told himself. Major Ted Wiley, retired from the Army and widowed after forty-two years of *blissful* marriage, was a very fine catch for any woman, and don't you forget it. Weren't available men scarce as uncut diamonds in Henley-on-Thames? Yes. They were. Weren't available men without unsightly nose hairs, overgrown eyebrows, and copious ear hairs scarcer still? Yes and yes. And weren't men who were clean, in possession of their faculties, in excellent health, dexterous in the kitchen, and of an uxorious disposition so rare in town as to find themselves victims of something akin to a feeding frenzy the very moment they chose to show themselves at a social gathering? Damn right, they were. And he was one of them. Everyone knew it.

Including Eugenie, he reminded himself.

26

Hadn't she said to him on more than one occasion, You're a fine man, Ted Wiley? Yes. She had.

Hadn't she spent the last three years willingly accepting his company with what he *knew* was pleasure? Yes. She had.

Hadn't she smiled and flushed and looked away when they'd visited his mother at the Quiet Pines Nursing Home and heard her announce in that irritating and imperious way of hers, I'd like a wedding before I die, you two. Yes, yes, and yes. She had, she had.

So what did a touch on a stranger's face mean in light of all that? And why could he not expunge it from his mind, as if it had become a brand and not what it was: an unpleasant memory that he wouldn't even have *had* had he not taken to watching, to wondering, to lurking, to having to *know,* to insisting upon battening down the hatches in his life as if it weren't a life at all but a sailing vessel that might lose its cargo if he wasn't vigilant?

Eugenie herself was the answer to that: Eugenie whose spectral-thin body asked for nurture; whose neat hair—thickly silvered though it was with grey—asked to be freed from the hair slides that held it; whose cloudy eyes were blue then green then grey then blue but always guarded; whose modest but nonetheless provocative femininity awakened in Ted a stirring in the groin that called him to an action he hadn't been capable of taking since Connie's death. Eugenie *was* the answer.

And he was the man for Eugenie, the man to protect her, to bring her back to life. For what had gone unspoken between the two of them these past three years was the extent to which Eugenie had

27

been denying herself the very *communion* of her fellow men for God only knew how long. Yet that denial had declared itself openly when he'd first invited her to join him for a simple evening glass of sherry at the Catherine Wheel.

Why, she's not had a man ask her out in *years*, Ted had thought at her flustered reaction to his invitation. And he'd wondered why.

Now, perhaps, he knew. She had secrets from him, had Eugenie. *I have something important I want to tell you, Ted.* Sins to confess, she'd said. Sins.

Well, there was no time like the present to hear what she had to say.

At the top of Friday Street, Ted waited for the traffic lights to change, PB shivering close at his side. Duke Street was also the main thoroughfare to either Reading or Marlow, and as such it carried all manner of vehicles rumbling through town. A wet night like this did little to decrease the volume of traffic in a society that was becoming depressingly more reliant upon cars and even more depressingly desirous of a commuter lifestyle defined by work in the city and life in the country. So even at nine o'clock at night, cars and lorries splashed along the soaked street, their headlamps creating ochroid fans that reflected against windows and in pools of standing water.

Too many people going too many places, Ted thought morosely. Too many people without the slightest idea of why they're rushing headlong through their lives.

The traffic lights changed and Ted crossed over, making the little jog into Greys Road with PB bumping along next to him. Despite the fact that they'd not walked even quarter of a mile, the old dog was wheezing, and Ted stepped into the shallow doorway of Mirabelle's Antiques to give the poor retriever a breather. Their destination was almost in sight, he reassured her. Surely she could make it just a few more yards up to Albert Road.

There, a car park served as courtyard for the Sixty Plus Club, an organisation attending to the social needs of Henley's ever-growing community of pensioners. There, too, Eugenie worked as Director. And there Ted had met her, upon relocating to the town on the Thames when he could no longer bear in Maidstone the memories of his wife's lengthy death.

'Major Wiley, how lovely. You're on Friday Street,' Eugenie had said to him, reviewing his membership form. 'You and I are neighbours. I'm at number 65. The pink house? Doll Cottage? I've been there for years. And you're at . . .'

'The book shop,' he'd said. 'Just across the street. The flat's above it. Yes. But I'd no idea . . . I mean, I've not seen you.'

'I'm always out early and back late. I know your shop, though. I've been in many times. At least when your mother was running it. Before the stroke, that is. And she's still well, which is lovely. Improving, isn't she.'

He'd thought Eugenie was asking, but when he realised she wasn't—indeed, she was merely *affirming* information that she already had—then he also realised where he'd seen her before: at Quiet Pines Nursing Home where three times each week Ted visited his mother. She did voluntary work there in the mornings, did Eugenie, and the patients referred to her as 'our angel'. Or so Ted's

29

mother had informed him once as together they watched Eugenie entering a cubicle with an adult-sized nappy folded over her wrist. 'She hasn't any relatives here, and the Home don't pay her a penny, Ted.'

Then *why*, Ted had wanted to know at the time. Why?

Secrets, he thought now. Still waters and secrets.

He looked down at the dog, who'd sagged against him, out of the rain and determined to snooze while she had the chance. He said, 'Come along, PB. Not much farther now,' and looked across the street to see through the bare trees that there was not much more time either.

For from where he and the dog stood sheltered, he noticed that the Sixty Plus Club was disgorging its New Year's Eve Gala committee. Raising their umbrellas and stepping through puddles like neophyte high wire artists, the committee members called out their goodnights to one another with enough good cheer to suggest that a compromise on comestibles had been finally achieved. Eugenie would be pleased at this. Pleased, she'd no doubt be feeling expansive and ready to talk to him.

Ted crossed the street, eager to intercept her, his reluctant golden retriever in tow. He reached the low wall between the pavement and the car park just as the last of the committee members drove away. The lights in the Sixty Plus Club went out and the entry porch became bathed in shadow. A moment later, Eugenie herself stepped into the misty penumbra between the building and the car park, working upon the tie of a black umbrella. Ted opened his mouth to call her name, sing out a hearty hello and make the offer of a personal escort back to her cottage. No time of night for a lovely lady to be alone on the streets, my dearest girl. Care for the arm of an ardent admirer? With dog, I'm afraid. PB and I were out for a final recce of the town.

He could have said all this and he was indeed drawing breath to do so when he suddenly heard it. A man's voice called out Eugenie's name. She swung to her left, and Ted looked beyond her where a figure was getting out of a dark saloon car. Back lit by one of the street lamps that dotted the car park, he was mostly shadow. But the shape of his head and that gull's beak nose were enough to tell Ted that Eugenie's visitor of one in the morning had returned to town.

The stranger approached her. She remained where she was. In the change of light, Ted could see that he was an older man—of an age with Ted himself, perhaps—with a full head of white hair scraped back from his forehead and falling to touch the turned-up collar of a Burberry.

They began to talk. He took the umbrella from her, held it over them, and spoke to her urgently. He was taller than Eugenie by a good eight inches, so he bent to her. She lifted her face to hear him. Ted strained to hear him as well but managed to catch only, 'You've *got* to' and 'My knees, Eugenie?' and finally, loudly, 'Why won't you *see*—' which Eugenie interrupted with a rush of soft conversation and the placement of her hand on his arm. '*You* can say that to *me*?' were the final words Ted heard from the man before he jerked himself away from Eugenie's grasp, thrust the umbrella upon her, and stalked to his car. At this, Ted breathed a cirrus of relief into the cold night

31

air.

It was a brief deliverance. Eugenie followed the stranger and intercepted him as he yanked open the door to his car. With the door between them, she continued to speak. Her listener, however, averted his face, and cried out, 'No. *No,*' at which point she reached up to him and tried to curve her palm against his cheek. She seemed to want to draw him to her despite the car door that continued to act like a shield between them.

It was effective as a shield, that door, because the stranger escaped whatever caress Eugenie wanted to bestow upon him. He dived into the driver's seat, wrenched the door closed, and started the engine with a roar that resounded against the buildings on three sides of the car park.

Eugenie stepped away. The car reversed. Its gears ground like animals being dismembered. Its tyres spun wickedly against wet pavement. Rubber met Tarmac with a sound like despair.

Another roar and the car was speeding towards the exit. Not six yards from where Ted watched in the shelter of a young liquidambar tree, the Audi— for now it was close enough for Ted to see the distinguishing quadruple circles on its bonnet— swerved into the street without so much as a moment's pause for its driver to determine if any other vehicles were in his way. There was just enough time for Ted to catch a glimpse of a profile that was twisted with emotion before the Audi veered left in the direction of Duke Street and there turned right for the Reading Road. Ted squinted after it, trying to make out the number plate, trying to decide if he'd ill-chosen his moment to happen upon Eugenie.

He didn't have much time to select between scarpering for home and pretending he'd just arrived, however. Eugenie would be upon him in thirty seconds or less.

He looked down at the dog, who'd taken the opportunity of this respite from their walk to deposit herself at the base of the liquidambar, where she now lay curled, with the apparent and martyred determination to sleep in the rain. How reasonable was it, Ted wondered, to suppose he could coax PB into a fast trot that would take them out of the immediate area before Eugenie reached the edge of the car park? Not very. So he would offer Eugenie the pretence that he and the dog had just arrived.

He squared his shoulders and gave a tug on the lead, preparatory to rounding the wall and entering the car park. But as he was doing so, he saw that Eugenie wasn't heading his way at all. Instead, she was walking in the opposite direction, where a path between buildings offered pedestrians access to Market Place. Where the blazes was she going?

Ted hastened after her, at a brisk pace that PB didn't much care for but couldn't avoid without serious risk of strangulation. Eugenie was a dark figure ahead of them, her black raincoat, black boots, and black umbrella making her an unsuitable ambler on a rainy night.

She turned right into Market Place, and Ted wondered for the second time where she was going. Shops were closed at this hour, and it wasn't in Eugenie's character to frequent pubs alone.

Ted endured a moment of agony while PB relieved herself next to the kerb. The dog's capacious bladder was legend, and Ted was certain that, in the lengthy wait for PB to empty a pool of steaming urine into the gutter, he'd lose Eugenie to Market Place Mews or Market Lane when she crossed over halfway down the street. But after a quick glance right and left, she continued on her way, towards the river. Passing by Duke Street, she crossed into Hart Street at which point Ted began thinking that she was merely taking a circuitous route home, despite the weather. But then she veered to the doors of St Mary the Virgin, whose handsome crenellated tower was part of the river vista for which Henley was famous.

Eugenie hadn't come to admire that vista, however, for she swiftly ducked inside the church.

'Damn,' Ted muttered. What to do now? He could hardly follow her into the church, dog in tow. And hanging about outside in the rain wasn't an appealing idea. And while he could tie the dog to a lamppost and join her at her prayers—if praying was what she was doing in there—he couldn't exactly maintain the pretence of a chance encounter inside St Mary the Virgin after nine in the evening when there was no service going on. And even if there *had* been a service, Eugenie knew he wasn't a churchgoer. So what the hell else could he do now except turn tail for home like a lovesick idiot? And all the time seeing seeing still seeing that moment in the car park when she touched him again, again that touch . . .

Ted shook his head vigorously. He couldn't go *on* like this. He had to know the worst. He had to know tonight.

To the left of the church, the graveyard made a rough triangle of sodden vegetation bisected by a path that led to a row of old brick almshouses, whose windows winked brightly against the darkness. Ted led PB in this direction, taking the time that Eugenie was inside the church to marshal his opening statement to her.

Look at this dog, fat as a sow, he would say. We're on a new campaign to slim her down. Vet says she can't go on like this without her heart giving out, so here we are and here we'll be nightly from now on, making a circumvention of the town. May we toddle along with you, Eugenie? Heading home, are you? Ready to talk, are you? Can we make this the *soon* you spoke to me about? Because I don't know how much longer I can hold on, wondering what it is that you want me to know.

The problem was that he'd decided upon her, and he'd reached the decision without knowing if she'd reached it as well. In the last five years since Connie's death, he'd never had to *pursue* a woman since women had done the pursuing of him. And even if that had demonstrated for him how little he liked to *be* pursued—damnation itself, when had women become so flaming aggressive? he wondered—and even if what evolved from those pursuits tended to be a pressure to perform under which he had consistently wilted, yet there had been an intense gratification in knowing that the old boy still had It and It was highly in demand.

Except Eugenie wasn't demanding. Which made Ted ask himself whether he was man enough for everyone else—at least superficially—but for some reason not man enough for her.

Blast it all, *why* was he feeling like this? Like an adolescent who'd never been laid. It was those failures with the others, he decided, failures he'd never once had with Connie.

35

'You should see a doctor about this little problem of yours,' that piranha Georgia Ramsbottom had said, twisting her bony back from his bed and donning his flannel dressing gown. 'It's not normal, Ted. For a man your age? What are you, sixty-five? It's just not normal.'

Sixty-eight, he thought. With a piece of meat between his legs that remained inert despite the most ardent of ministrations.

But that was because of their *pursuit* of him. If they'd only let him do what nature intended every man to do—be the hunter and not the hunted—then everything else would take care of itself. Wouldn't it? *Wouldn't* it? He needed to know.

A sudden movement within one of the squares of light from an almshouse window attracted his attention. Ted glanced that way to see that a figure had come into the room that the window defined. The figure was a woman and as Ted looked curiously in her direction, he was surprised to see her raise the red jumper that she was wearing, lifting it over her head and dropping it to the floor.

He looked left and right. He felt his cheeks take on heat, despite the rain that was pelting him. Peculiar that some people didn't know how a lit window worked at night. They couldn't see out, so they believed no one could see in. Children were like that. Ted's own three girls had to be taught to draw the curtains before they undressed. But if no one ever taught a child to do that . . . peculiar that some people never learned.

He stole a glance in her direction again. The woman had removed her brassiere. Ted swallowed. On the lead, PB was beginning to snuffle in the grass that edged the graveyard path, and she

36

headed towards the almshouses innocently.

Take her off the lead, she won't go far. But instead Ted followed, the lead looped in his hand.

In the window the woman began brushing her hair. With each stroke her breasts lifted and fell. Their nipples were taut, with deep brown aureoles encircling them. Seeing all this, his eyes fixed to her breasts as if they were what he'd been waiting for all evening and all the evenings that had preceded this evening, Ted felt the incipient stirring within him, and then that gratifying rush of blood and that throb of life.

He sighed. There was nothing wrong with him. Nothing at all. Being *pursued* had been the problem. Pursuing—and afterwards claiming and having—was the sure solution.

He tugged PB's lead so the dog walked no farther. He settled in to watch the woman in the window and to wait for his Eugenie.

*   *   *

In the Lady Chapel of St Mary the Virgin Eugenie didn't so much pray as wait. She hadn't darkened the doorway of a house of worship in years, and the only reason she'd done so tonight was to avoid the conversation she'd promised herself that she'd have with Ted.

She knew he was following her. It wasn't the first time she'd come out of the Sixty Plus Club to see his silhouette under the trees on the street, but it *was* the first time she wouldn't allow herself to talk to him. So she hadn't turned in his direction when she could have done, at the natural moment to offer an explanation to what he'd witnessed in the

37

car park. Instead, she'd headed for Market Place with no clear idea of where she was going.

When her gaze had fallen upon the church, she'd made the decision to slip inside and adopt an attitude of supplication. For the first five minutes in the Lady Chapel, she even knelt on one of the dusty hassocks, gazed on the statue of the Virgin, and waited for the old familiar words of devotion to spring into her mind. But they would not. Her head was too filled with impediments to prayer: old arguments and accusations, older loyalties and the sins committed in the name of them, current importunacies and their implications, future consequences if she made an ignorant misstep now.

She'd made enough missteps in the past to devastate thirteen dozen lives. And she'd long ago learned that an action taken was the same as a pebble dropped into still water: The concentric rings that the pebble effects may lessen in substance, but they do still exist.

When no prayer came to her, Eugenie rose from her knees. She sat with her feet flat on the floor and studied the face of the statue. You didn't make the choice to lose Him, did you? she asked the Virgin silently. So how can I ask you to understand? And even if you did understand, what intercession can I ask you to give me? You can't turn back time. You can't unhappen what happened, can you? You can't bring back to life what's dead and gone because if you could, you would have done it to save yourself the torture of His murder.

Except they never say it was murder, do they? Instead, it's a sacrifice for a greater cause. It's a giving of life for something far more important

38

than life. As if anything really is . . .

Eugenie put her elbows on her thighs and rested her forehead in the palms of her hands. If she was to believe what her erstwhile religion taught her to believe, then the Virgin Mary had known from the start exactly what would be required of her. She'd understood clearly that the Child she nurtured would be ripped from her life in the flowering of his manhood. Reviled, beaten, abused, and *sacrificed*, He would die ingloriously and she would be there to watch it all. And the only assurance she would ever have that His death had a greater meaning than what was implied by being spat upon and nailed up between two common criminals was simple faith. Because although religious tradition had it that an angel had appeared to put her in the picture of future events, who could really stretch their brains to fit around that?

So she'd gone on blind faith that a greater good existed somewhere. Not in her lifetime and not in the lifetime of the grandchildren she would never have. But there. Somewhere. Quite real. There.

Of course, it hadn't happened yet. Fast forward two thousand brutal years and mankind was still waiting for the good to come. And what did she think, the Virgin Mother, watching and waiting from her throne in the clouds? How did she begin to assess the benefit against the cost?

For years newspapers had served to tell Eugenie that the benefits—the good—tipped the scales against the price she herself had paid. But now she was no longer sure. The Greater Good she'd thought she was serving threatened to disintegrate before her, like a woven rug whose persistent unravelling makes a mockery of the labour that went into its creation. And only she could stop that unravelling, if she chose to do so.

The problem was Ted. She hadn't intended to draw close to him. For so very long, she hadn't allowed herself near enough to anyone to encourage confidence of any kind. And to feel herself even *capable* now—not to mention deserving—of establishing a connection to another human being seemed like a form of hubris that was certain to destroy her. Yet she wanted to draw close to him anyway, as if he were the anodyne for a sickness that she lacked the courage to name.

So she sat in the church. In part because she did not want to face Ted Wiley just yet, before the way was paved. In part because she did not yet possess the words to do the paving.

Tell me what to do, God, she prayed in the quiet. Tell me what to say.

But God was as silent as He'd been for ages. Eugenie dropped an offering in the collection box and left the church.

Outside, it was still raining relentlessly. She raised her umbrella and headed towards the river. The wind was rising as she reached the corner, and she paused for a moment to wrestle against it as it struck her umbrella with more force than she expected and turned it inside out.

'Here. Let me help you with that, Eugenie.'

She swung round and Ted was standing there, his old dog droopily at his side and rainwater dripping from his nose and his jaw. His waxed jacket glistened brightly with damp, and his peaked cap clung to his skull.

'Ted!' She offered him the gift of her spurious surprise. 'You look positively drowned. And poor

40

PB! What are you doing out here with that sweet dog?'

He righted her umbrella and held it over both of them. She took his arm.

'We've begun a new exercise programme,' he told her. 'Up to Market Place, down to the churchyard and back home four times a day. What're *you* doing here? You haven't just come out of the church, have you?'

You know I have, she wanted to say. You just don't know why. But what she said was, lightly, 'Decompressing after the committee meeting. You remember: the New Year's Eve committee? I'd given them a deadline to decide on the food. So much to be ordered, you know, and they can't expect the caterer to wait forever for them to make up their minds, can they?'

'On your way home now?'

'I am.'

'And may I . . . ?'

'You know that you may.'

How ridiculous it was, the two of them in such an idle conversation, with volumes of what needed saying deliberately going unsaid between them.

You don't trust me, Ted, do you? Why don't you trust me? And how can we foster love between us if we have no foundation of trust? I know you're worried because I'm not telling you what it was I said I wanted to tell you, but why can't you let the wanting *to tell you be enough for now?*

But she couldn't risk anything that would lead to revelation at the moment. She owed it to ties far older than the tie she felt to Ted to put her house in order before burning it down.

So they engaged in insignificant chat as they

41

walked along the river: his day, her day, who'd come into the book shop and how his mother was getting on at Quiet Pines. He was hearty and cheerful; she was pleasant albeit subdued.

'Tired?' he asked her when they reached the door of her cottage.

'A bit,' she admitted. 'It's been a long day.'

He handed her the umbrella, saying, 'Then I won't keep you up,' but he looked at her with such open expectation in his ruddy face that she knew her next line was supposed to be to ask him in for a brandy before bed.

It was her fondness for him that prompted the truth. She said, 'I've got to go into London, Ted.'

'Ah. Early morning, then?'

'No. I've got to go tonight. I've an appointment.'

'Appointment? But with the rain, it'll take you at least an hour . . . Did you say an *appointment*?'

'Yes. I did.'

'What sort . . .? Eugenie . . .' He blew out a breath. She heard him curse quietly. So, apparently, did PB because the old retriever raised her head and blinked at Ted as if with surprise. She was soaking, poor dog. At least, thank God, her fur was thick as a mammoth's. 'Let me drive you in, then,' Ted said at last.

'That wouldn't be wise.'

'But—'

She put her hand on his arm to stop him. She raised it to touch his cheek but he flinched and she stepped away. 'Are you free for dinner tomorrow night?' she asked him.

'You know I am.'

'Then have a meal with me. Here. We'll talk then, if you'd like.'

He gazed at her, trying—she knew—and failing to read her. Don't make the attempt, she wanted to tell him. I've had too much rehearsal for a rôle in a drama you don't yet understand.

She watched him steadily, waiting for his reply. The light from her sitting room came through the window and jaundiced a face already drawn with age and with worries he wouldn't name. She was grateful for that: that he wouldn't speak his deepest fears to her. The fact that what frightened him went unspoken was what gave her courage to contend with everything that frightened her.

He removed his cap then, a humble gesture that she wouldn't for all her life have had him make. It exposed his thick grey hair to the rain and removed the meagre shadow that had hidden the rubicund flesh of his nose. It made him look like what he was: an old man. It made her feel like what she was: a woman who didn't deserve such a fine man's love.

'Eugenie,' he said, 'if you're thinking that you can't tell me that you . . . that you and I . . . that we aren't . . .' He looked towards the book shop across the street.

'I'm not thinking anything,' she said. 'Just about London and the drive. And there's the rain as well. But I'll be careful. You've no need to worry.'

He appeared momentarily gratified and perhaps a trifle relieved at the reassurance she meant to imply. 'You're the world to me,' he said simply. 'Eugenie, do you know that? You're the world. And I'm a bloody idiot most of the time, but I do—'

'I know,' she said. 'I know you do. And we'll talk tomorrow.'

'Right then.' He kissed her awkwardly, hitting

his head on the edge of the umbrella and knocking it askew in her hand.

Rain dashed against her face. A car raced up Friday Street. She felt heavy spray from its tyres hit her shoes.

Ted swung round. 'Hey!' he shouted at the vehicle. 'Watch your bloody driving!'

'No. It's all right,' she said. 'It's nothing, Ted.'

He turned back to her, saying, 'Damn it. Wasn't that—' But he stopped himself.

'What?' she asked. 'Who?'

'No one. Nothing.' He roused his retriever to her feet for the last few yards to their front door. 'We'll talk, then?' he asked. 'Tomorrow? After dinner?'

'We'll talk,' she said. 'There's so much to say.'

*   *   *

She had very few preparations to make. She washed her face and cleaned her teeth. She combed her hair and tied a navy blue scarf round her head. She protected her lips with a colourless balm, and she put the winter lining into her raincoat to give herself more protection from the chill. Parking was always bad in London, and she didn't know how far she would have to walk in the cold and storm-stricken air when she finally arrived at her destination.

Raincoat on and a handbag hooked over her arm, she descended the narrow staircase. She took from the kitchen table a photograph in a plain wooden frame. It was one of a baker's dozen that she usually had arranged round the cottage. Before choosing from among them, she'd lined them up like soldiers on the table and there the rest of them remained.

She clasped this frame just beneath her bosom. She went out into the night.

Her car was parked inside a gated courtyard, in a space she rented by the month, just down the street. The courtyard was hidden by electric gates cleverly fashioned to look like part of the half-timbered buildings on either side. There was safety in this, and Eugenie liked safety. She liked the illusion of security afforded by gates and locks.

In her car—a second-hand Polo whose fan sounded like the wheezing of a terminal asthmatic—she carefully set the framed photo on the passenger seat and started the engine. She'd prepared in advance for this journey up to London, checking the Polo's oil and its tyres and topping up its petrol as soon as she'd learned the date and the place. The time had come later, and she'd balked at it at first, once she realised ten forty-five meant at night and not in the morning. But she had no leg to stand on in protesting, and she knew it, so she acquiesced. Her night vision wasn't what it once had been. But she would cope.

She hadn't counted on the rain, however. And as she left the outskirts of Henley and wound her way northwest to Marlow, she found herself clutching the steering wheel and crouching over it, half-blinded by the headlamps of oncoming cars, assailed by how the blowing rain diffracted the light in spearheads that riddled the windscreen with visual lacerations.

Things weren't much better on the M40 where cars and lorries put up sheets of spray with which the Polo's windscreen wipers could barely keep pace. The lane markings had mostly vanished beneath the standing water, and those that could be seen seemed to alternate between writhing snakelike in Eugenie's vision and side-stepping to border an entirely different traffic lane.

It wasn't until she reached the vicinity of Wormwood Scrubs that she felt she could relax the death hold she had on the steering wheel. Even then, she didn't breathe with ease until she'd veered away from the motorway's sleek and sodden river of concrete and headed north in the vicinity of Maida Hill.

As soon as she could manage it, she pulled to the kerb at a darkened Sketchley's. There, she let out a lungful of air that felt as if it had been held back since she'd made the first turn into Duke Street in Henley.

She rooted in her handbag for the directions she'd written out for herself from the *A to Z*. Although she'd escaped the motorway unscathed, another quarter of the journey still had to be negotiated through London's labyrinthine streets.

The city at the best of times was a maze. At night, it became a maze ill lit and in possession of a nearly laughable paucity of signposts. But at night in the rain, it was Hades. Three false starts took Eugenie no farther than Paddington Recreation Ground before she got lost. Wisely, each time she returned the way she'd come, like a taxi driver determined to understand just where he'd made his first mistake.

So it was nearly twenty past eleven when she found the street she was looking for in northwest London. And she spent another maddening seven minutes circling round till she found a space to park.

She clasped the framed photo to her bosom again, took up her umbrella from the back seat of the car, and clambered out. The rain had finally abated, but the wind was still blowing. What few autumn leaves had remained on the trees were being wafted through the air to plaster themselves on the pavement, in the street, and against the parked cars.

Number Thirty-two was the house she wanted, and Eugenie saw that it would be far up the street, on the other side. She walked along the pavement for twenty-five yards. At that hour, the houses she passed were mostly unlit, and if she hadn't been nervous enough about the coming interview, her state of anxiety was heightened by the darkness and by what her active imagination was telling her could be hidden there. So she decided to be careful, as a woman alone in a city on a rainy night in late autumn ought to be careful. She ventured off the pavement and proceeded on her way in the middle of the road, where she would have advance warning should anyone want to attack her.

She thought it unlikely. It was a decent neighbourhood. Still, she knew the value of caution, so she was grateful when lights swept over her, telling her that a vehicle had turned into the street behind her. It was coming along slowly, the way she herself had come and doing what she herself had been doing, looking for that most precious of London commodities: a place to park. She turned, stepped back against the nearest vehicle, and waited for the car to pass her. But as she did so, it pulled to one side and flashed its lights, telling her that the way was hers.

Ah, she'd been mistaken, she thought, resettling

her umbrella against her shoulder and going on her way. The car wasn't waiting for a parking space at all, but rather for someone to come out of the house in front of which it sat. She gave a quick glance over her shoulder when she reached this conclusion, and as if the unknown driver was reading her thoughts, the car's horn beeped once abruptly, like a parent who'd come calling for an unresponsive child.

Eugenie continued walking. She counted the house numbers as she passed. She saw Number Ten and Number Twelve—she'd gone barely six houses from her own car—when the steady light behind her shifted then went out altogether.

Odd, she thought. You can't just park in the street like that. And thinking this, she began to turn. Which was, as it happened, not the worst of her mistakes.

Bright lights blazed on. She was instantly blinded. Blinded, she froze as the hunted often do.

An engine roared and tyres screeched.

When she was hit, her body flew up, her arms flung wide, and her picture frame shot up like a rocket into the air.

CHAPTER TWO

J.W. Pitchley, aka TongueMan, had experienced an excellent evening. He'd broken Rule One—*never* suggest meeting *anyone* with whom one has engaged in cybersex—but it had all worked out, proving to him yet again that his instincts for picking fruit past its prime but all the juicier for having hung disregarded on the tree so long were as finely honed as a surgical tool.

Humility and honesty forced him to admit that it hadn't been that much of a risk, however. Any woman who called herself CreamPants was as good as advertising what she wanted and if he'd had any doubts, five meetings on-line that had had him coming into his Calvin Klein jockeys without the slightest handshake of the organ on his part should have set his mind at rest. Unlike his four other current cyberlovers—whose spelling skill was, alas, often as limited as their imagination—CreamPants had a capacity for fantasy that cooked his brain and a natural ability to express that fantasy that stiffened his cock like a divining rod the moment she logged on the net.

Creamy here, she would write. *R U rdy 4 it, Tongue?*

Oh my. Oh yes. He always was.

So he'd taken the metaphorical plunge himself this time instead of waiting for his cyberspondent to do so. This was wildly out of character for him. Usually, he played along cooperatively, always there at the other end of on-line encounters when one of his lovers wanted action, but never venturing into the arena of embodiment unless or until his partner suggested it. Following this pattern, he'd successfully transformed exactly twenty-seven Super Highway encounters into twenty-seven intensely satisfying trysts at the Comfort Inn in Cromwell Road—a wise and cautious distance from his own neighbourhood and night-clerked by an Asian gentleman whose memory for faces took a far back seat to his abiding passion for videos of old BBC costume dramas.

49

Thus, only once had he found himself the victim of a practical cyberjoke, agreeing to meet a lover called DoMeHard and discovering two spotty-faced twelve-year-olds dressed like the Kray brothers waiting for him instead. No matter, though. He'd sorted them out quickly enough and he was fairly certain they'd not be trying *that* little caper on-line again.

But CreamPants had got to him. *R U rdy 4 it?* She had him wondering almost from the first if she could do in person what she could do with words.

That was always the question, wasn't it? And anticipating, fantasising, and securing the answer were part of the fun.

He'd worked very hard to bring CreamPants round to suggesting that they meet. He climbed to new and dizzying heights of descriptive licentiousness with the woman. To develop more ideas in the carnal vein, he'd spent six hours over a fortnight browsing through the paraphernalia of pleasure in those windowless shops in Brewer Street. And when he finally found himself spending his daily commute into the City wrapped up in lustful visions of their sated bodies inextricably twined on the hideously hued counterpane of a Comfort Inn bed—this, instead of reading the *Financial Times,* that daily staple of his career—he knew that he had to take action.

So *Want it 4 real?* he'd finally written to her. *R U rdy 4 a rsk?* She'd been ready.

He made the suggestion that he always made when his cyberlovers requested a meeting: drinks at the Valley of Kings, easy enough to find, just a few steps away from Sainsbury's in Cromwell Road. She could come by car, by taxi, by bus, or by tube.

50

And if upon first sight they found they didn't actually appeal to each other . . . just a quick martini in the bar and no regrets, okay?

The Valley of Kings possessed the same priceless quality as the Comfort Inn. Like the vast majority of service-oriented businesses in London, its waiters spoke virtually no English and to them every English person looked alike. He'd taken all twenty-seven of his cyberencounters to the Valley of Kings without the *maitre d'*, the waiters, or the bartender so much as blinking an eyelash in recognition of him, so he was confident that he could take CreamPants there as well without any of its employees betraying him.

He'd known who she was the moment she walked into the restaurant's saffron-scented bar. And he was gratified to see that yet again he'd somehow instinctively known who and what she would be. Fifty-five years old if she was a day, well-scrubbed, and wearing just the right amount of scent, she wasn't some slag out on the pull. She wasn't a Mile End shag bag trying to better herself or a Scouse-come-south in the hope of finding a bloke who'd raise her standard of living. She was instead exactly what he'd assumed that she'd be: a lonely divorcee whose kids were grown-up and who was facing the prospect of being called *Gran* about ten years sooner than she wanted. She was eager to prove to herself that she still had a modicum of sex appeal despite the lines on her face and her incipient jowls. And never mind that he had his own reasons for choosing her despite the dozen years of difference between their ages. He was happy enough to supply her with the validation that she required.

Such validation took place in room 109, first floor, perhaps ten yards away from the roar of traffic. Being on the street—a request he always made *sotto voce* prior to securing the room key—obviated the necessity of staying the night. It would be impossible for anyone in possession of normal hearing actually to *sleep* in any of the rooms that faced Cromwell Road. And since spending the night with a cyberlover was the last activity on his mind, being able to say, 'God, what a din,' at one point or another usually sufficed as prelude to a gentlemanly exit.

So everything had gone according to plan: drinks had segued into a confession of physical attraction which had led to a stroll to the Comfort Inn, where vigorous coupling had resulted in mutual satisfaction. In person CreamPants—whose real name she coyly refused to reveal—was only slightly less imaginative than she was on the keyboard. Once all the sexual permutations, positions, and possibilities had been thoroughly explored between them, they fell away from each other, slick with sweat and other bodily fluids, and listened to the roar of lorries grinding up and down the A4.

'God what a din,' he groaned. 'I should have thought of a better spot than this. We'll never sleep.'

'Oh.' She took her cue. 'Not to worry. I can't stay anyway.'

'You can't?' Pained.

A smile. 'I hadn't actually planned on it. After all, there was always the chance that you and I wouldn't have made the same sort of connection in person as we did on the net. You know.'

How he did. The only question now as he drove

home was What next? They'd gone at it like beavers for two solid hours, and they'd both enjoyed themselves immensely. They'd parted with promises made on both sides of 'staying in touch' but there had been ever so slight an undercurrent in CreamPants' farewell embrace that belied her casual words and suggested to him that the course of wisdom called for steering clear of her for a time.

Which was ultimately, after a long aimless drive in the rain for sexual decompression, what he decided to do.

He yawned as he turned into his street. He'd have an excellent night's kip after his exertions of the evening. There was nothing like spirited sex with a relative stranger of advancing years to set one up for slumber.

He squinted through the windscreen as the wipers lulled him with their steady rhythm. He cruised up the incline and flicked on the indicator for his driveway—more out of habit than necessity—and was thinking about how much longer it would be before LadyFire and EatMe each suggested a meeting when he saw the heap of sodden garments lying next to a late model Calibra.

He sighed. Wasn't society crumbling round his ears? Beneath a thin protection of their epidermis, people were becoming little more than pigs. After all, why on earth should *anyone* drop his jumble at Oxfam when he could *just* as easily toss it into the street? It was pathetic.

He was about to drive past when a flash of white within the mass of soaked material caught his eye. He glanced over. A rain-drenched sock, a tattered scarf, a limp collection of women's knickers?

53

What?

But then he saw. His foot plunged wildly on the brake.

The white, he realised, was a hand, a wrist, and a short length of arm which itself protruded from the black of a coat. Part of a mannequin, he thought resolutely, to still the hammering of his heart. Someone's pea-brained idea of a joke. It's too short to be a person, anyway. And there're no legs or head. Just that arm.

But he lowered his window in spite of these reassuring conclusions. His face spattered with the rain, he peered at the shapeless form on the ground. And then he saw the rest.

There *were* legs. There was a head as well. It merely hadn't seemed so upon an initial glance through the rain-streaked window because the head was bowed deeply into the coat as if in prayer and the legs were tucked completely under the Calibra.

Heart attack, he thought in spite of what his eyes told him otherwise. Aneurysm. Stroke.

Only what were the legs *doing* under that car? Under it, when the only possible explanation for *that* was . . .

He snatched up his mobile and punched in 999.

*   *   *

DCI Eric Leach's body was screaming flu. He ached everywhere it was possible to ache. He was sweaty on the head, the cheeks, and the chest; he had the chills. He should have phoned in ill when he first started feeling like crap in a basket. He should have gone to bed. There, he would have gleaned a double benefit. He would have caught up on the sleep he'd been missing since trying to reorganise his life post-divorce and he would have had an excuse when the phone call came through at midnight. Instead, here he was dragging his sorry shivering bum from an inadequately furnished flat into the cold, the wind, and the rain where he was no doubt risking double pneumonia.

Live and learn, DCI Leach thought wearily. Next time he got married, he'd damn well stay married.

He saw the blue flashing lights of police vehicles as he made his final left turn. The hour was drawing on towards twenty past twelve, but the rising road in front of him was as bright as midday. Someone had hooked up floodlights and these were complemented by the lightning bolt hiccups of the forensic photographer.

The activity outside their houses had gathered a hefty collection of gawkers, but they were being held back by the crime scene tape that had been strung along the length of the street on both sides. Additional tape as well as barriers blocked the roadway at either end. Behind these, a number of press photographers had already gathered, those vampires of the radio waves who continuously tuned in to the Met's frequency in the hope of learning that fresh blood was available somewhere.

DCI Leach thumbed a Strepsil out of its packet. He left his car behind an ambulance whose waterproof-shrouded attendants were lounging against its front bumper, drinking coffee from Thermos lids in an unhurried fashion that indicated which one of their services was going to be required. Leach nodded at them as he hunched his shoulders against the rain. He showed his

55

warrant card to the gangling young PC who was in charge of keeping the press at bay, and he stepped past the barrier and approached the collection of professionals who were gathered round a saloon car halfway up the street.

He heard snatches of neighbourhood conversation as he wearily trudged up the slight incline. Most of it was murmured in the reverential tones employed by those who understood how impartial the reaper was when he sauntered by to do his grim business. But there was also the occasional ill-considered complaint about the confusion that ensued when a sudden death in the open demanded police examination. And when one of those complaints was spoken in *just* the sort of pinched-nose I-smell-something-decidedly-unpleasant-and-it's-you tone that Leach detested, he turned on his heel. He stalked in the direction of the protest, which was concluding with the phrase, '. . . one's sleep being disturbed for no *apparent* reason other than to satisfy the baser inclinations of the tabloid photographers' and found its source, a hair-helmeted ghoul with her entire life savings invested in a plastic surgery job that needed redoing. She was saying, 'If one's council taxes cannot protect one from this sort of thing . . .' when Leach cut her off by speaking to the nearest constable guarding the scene.

'Shut that bitch up,' he barked. 'Kill her if you have to.' And he went on his way.

At the moment, the crime scene action was being dominated by the forensic pathologist who, beneath a makeshift shelter of polythene sheets, was wearing a bizarre combination of tweeds, Wellingtons, and upmarket Patagonia rain wear.

56

He was just completing his preliminary examination of the body, and Leach got enough of a look to see they were dealing with either a cross dresser or a female of indeterminate age, badly mangled. Facial bones were crushed; blood seeped from the hole where an ear had once been; raw skin on the head marked the areas where hair had been ripped from the scalp; the head hung at a natural angle but with a highly unnatural twist. It was just the thing to have to look upon when one was already light-headed with fever.

The pathologist—Dr Olav Grotsin—slapped his hands on his thighs and pushed himself to his feet. He snapped off his latex gloves, tossed them to an assistant, and saw Leach where the DCI stood, attempting to ignore his own ill health and assessing what could be assessed from his position of less than four feet from the corpse.

'You look like hell,' Grotsin said to Leach.

'What've we got?'

'Female. One hour dead when I got here. Two at the most.'

'You're sure?'

'What about? The time or the sex?'

'The sex.'

'She's got breasts on her. Old but there. As for the rest, I don't like cutting off their knickers in the street. You can wait till the morning on that, I presume.'

'What happened?'

'Hit and run. Internal injuries. I'd venture to guess she's ruptured everything that could be ruptured.'

Leach said, 'Shit,' and stepped past Grotsin to squat by the body. It lay a scant few inches from the driver's door of the Calibra, on its side with its back to the street. One arm was twisted behind it, and the legs were tucked beneath the Vauxhall's chassis. The Vauxhall itself was unblemished, Leach noted, which hardly surprised him. He couldn't see a driver hotly seeking a parking space and running over someone lying in the street in order to get it. He looked for tyre marks on the body and on the dark raincoat she wore.

'Her arm's dislocated,' Grotsin was saying behind him. 'Both legs are broken. And we've got a bit of candy floss as well. Turn her head and you'll see it.'

'The rain didn't wash it off?'

'Head was protected under the car.'

Protected was an odd choice of word, Leach thought. The poor cow was dead, whoever she was. Pink froth from her lungs may well have indicated that she didn't die instantly, but that was not much help to them and no help at all to the hapless victim. Unless, of course, someone had come upon her while she still lived and managed to catch a few critical words as she lay dying in the street.

Leach got to his feet and said, 'Who phoned it in?'

'Right over there, sir.' It was Grotsin's assistant who replied, and she nodded across the street where for the first time Leach saw that a Porsche Boxster was double parked with its hazard lights blinking. Two police constables were guarding this vehicle at either end, and just beyond them a middle-aged man in a trench coat stood beneath a striped umbrella and anxiously alternated his gaze from the Porsche to the broken body that lay some yards behind it.

Leach went over to examine the sports car. It would be a short night's work if the driver, the vehicle, and the victim were forming a neat little triad here on the street, but even as he approached the car, Leach knew that this would not be likely. Grotsin would hardly have used the words *hit and run* if only the first term applied.

Still, Leach walked round the Boxster carefully. He squatted in front of it and examined its front end and its body. He went from there to the tyres and checked each of these. He lowered himself to the rain-washed pavement and scrutinised the Porsche's undercarriage. And when he was done, he ordered the car impounded for the crime team's analysis.

'Oh, I say. That can't be necessary,' was the complaint made by Mr Trench Coat. 'I stopped, didn't I? As soon as I saw . . . And I reported it. Surely you can see that—'

'It's routine.' Leach joined the man as a PC was offering him a cup of coffee. 'You'll have the car back quick enough. What's your name?'

'Pitchley,' the man said. 'J.W. Pitchley. But see here, this is an expensive car, and I see no reason . . . Good God, if I'd hit her, the car would show the signs.'

'So you know it's a woman?'

Pitchley looked flustered. 'I suppose I thought . . . I did go over to it . . . to her. After I rang nine-nine-nine. I got out of the car and went to see if there was anything I could do. She might have been alive.'

'But she wasn't?'

'I couldn't actually tell. She wasn't . . . I mean, I could see she was unconscious. She wasn't making

59

a sound. She might have been breathing. But I knew not to touch . . .' He gulped his coffee. Steam rose from the cup.

'She's a fair enough mess. Our pathologist concluded she's a woman by checking for breasts. What did you do?'

Pitchley looked aghast at the implication. He glanced over his shoulder to the pavement, as if worried that the collection of onlookers standing there could hear his exchange with the detective and would draw erroneous conclusions from it. 'Nothing,' he said in an undertone. 'My God. I didn't do anything. Obviously, I could see that she was wearing a skirt beneath her coat. And her hair's longer than a man's—'

'Where it's not been ripped from her skull.'

Pitchley grimaced but went on. 'So when I saw the skirt, I just assumed. That's it.'

'And that's where she was lying, is it? Right there by the Vauxhall?'

'Yes. Right there. I didn't touch her, didn't move her.'

'See anyone on the street? On the pavement? On a porch? At a window? Anywhere?'

'No. No one. I was just driving along. There was no one anywhere except her, and I wouldn't have noticed her at all except her hand—or her arm or something . . . white, this was—caught my eye. That's it.'

'Were you alone in your own car?'

'Yes. Yes, of course I was alone. I live alone. Over there. Just up the street.'

Leach wondered at the volunteered information. He said, 'Where were you coming from this evening, Mr Pitchley?'

'South Kensington. I was . . . I was dining with a friend.'

'The friend's name?'

'I say, am I being accused of something?' Pitchley sounded flustered rather than concerned. 'Because if phoning the emergency services when one finds a body is grounds for suspicion, I'd like a solicitor with me when I . . . Hello, there. *Do* keep your distance from my car, would you please?' This last was directed towards a swarthy constable who was part of a fingertip search ongoing in the street.

More constables combed the area surrounding Pitchley and Leach, and it was from this group that a female PC presently emerged, a woman's handbag in her latex-gloved grip. She trotted towards Leach, and he donned his own gloves, stepping away from Pitchley with instructions to the man to give his address and phone number to one of the policemen guarding his car. He met the female constable in the middle of the street and took the handbag from her.

'Where was it?'

'Ten yards back. Beneath a Montego. Keys and wallet are in it. There's an ID as well. Driving licence.'

'Is she local?'

'Henley-on-Thames,' the constable said.

Leach unfastened the handbag's clasp, fished out the keys, and handed them over to the constable. 'See if they fit any of the cars in the area,' he told her and as she set off to do so, he took out the wallet and opened it to locate the ID.

He first read the name without making a connection. Later he would wonder how he'd failed to twig her identity instantly. But he was feeling so much like trampled horse turds that it wasn't until he'd read not only her organ donor card but also the name imprinted on her cheques that he realised who the woman actually was.

Then he looked from the handbag he was holding to the crumpled form of its owner lying like so much discarded rubbish in the street. And as his body shuddered, what he said was, 'God. Eugenie. Jesus Christ. *Eugenie.*'

*   *   *

Far across town, Detective Constable Barbara Havers sang along with the rest of the party-goers and wondered how many more choruses of jolly-good-fellowing she was going to have to live through before she could make her escape. It wasn't the hour of the night that bothered her. True, one in the morning meant that she was already cutting critically into her beauty rest, but since even doing a Sleeping-Beauty wouldn't make an inroad into her general appearance, she knew that she could live with the knowledge that if she managed to get four hours' kip at the end of the night, she was going to be one lucky bird. Rather, she was bothered by the reason for the party, exactly *why* along with her colleagues from New Scotland Yard, she'd been crammed into an overheated house in Stamford Brook for the last five hours.

She knew that twenty-five years of marriage was something worth celebrating. She could count on the digits of her right hand the couples she knew who'd attained that hallmark of connubial longevity, and she wouldn't even have to use her thumb. But there was something about this particular couple that didn't strike her as right, and try as she had done from the moment she'd first stepped into the sitting room where yellow crepe paper and green balloons made a brave attempt to camouflage a shabbiness that had more to do with indifference than with poverty, she'd not been able to shake the feeling that the guests of honour and the company assembled were all taking part in a domestic drama for which she—Barbara Havers—had not been given a script.

At first she told herself that her disconnected feeling came from partying with her superior officers, one of whom had saved her neck from the professional noose nearly three months earlier and one of whom had attempted to knot the rope himself. Then she decided her discomfort came from arriving at the party in her usual state—partnerless—while everyone else had a companion in tow, including her fellow and favourite detective constable, Winston Nkata, who'd brought along his mother, an imposing woman six feet tall and dressed in the Caribbean colours of her birth. Finally, she settled on the simple fact of celebrating *anyone's* marriage as the source of her uneasiness. Jealous cow, I am, Barbara finally told herself with some disgust.

But even that explanation couldn't withstand much serious scrutiny, because under normal circumstances Barbara wasn't given to wasting energy on envy. True, there were reasons aplenty all round her for her to feel that barren emotion. She was standing in a crowd of chattering couples—husbands and wives, parents and children, lovers and companions—and she herself was spouseless, partnerless, and childless without a single prospect on her horizon for changing those conditions. But having engaged in her usual reaction to this state of affairs by browsing the buffet table for edible distraction, she'd quickly won herself over to considering all the freedoms afforded her unattached status, and she'd dismissed any disquieting emotions that threatened to undermine her peace of mind.

Still, she didn't feel as bonhomous as she knew she ought at an anniversary party, and as the guests of honour took an overlarge knife in their clasped hands and began to assail a cake whose icing was decorated with roses, ivy, twined hearts and the words *Happy Twenty-fifth, Malcolm and Frances,* Barbara surreptitiously stole glances round the crowd to see if anyone besides herself was giving more attention to his wristwatch than to the waning moments of the celebration. No one was. Each and every person was focused on Detective Superintendent Malcolm Webberly and his uxorial companion of a quarter of a century, the redoubtable Frances.

This evening represented Barbara's first encounter with Superintendent Webberly's wife, and as she watched the woman feeding her husband a forkful of cake and laughingly accepting her own forkful in turn, Barbara realised that she'd been avoiding any prolonged consideration of Frances Webberly for the entire evening. They'd been introduced by the Webberlys' daughter Miranda in her rôle of hostess and they'd made the sort of polite conversation one always made with the spouse of a colleague: *How many years have you known Malcolm?* and *Do you find it difficult working in a world with so many men to contend with?* and *What drew you to homicide investigations in the first place?* Still, throughout this conversation, Barbara had found herself itching for an escape from Frances, despite the fact that the other woman's words were kindly spoken, her periwinkle eyes fixed pleasantly on Barbara's face.

But perhaps that was it, Barbara decided. Perhaps the source of her uneasiness lay in Frances Webberly's eyes and what was hidden behind them: an emotion, a concern, a sense of something not quite as it should be.

Yet exactly what that something was Barbara couldn't have said. So she gave herself to what she earnestly hoped were the final moments of the shindig, and she applauded along with the rest of the company as the concluding 'and so say all of us' was sung.

'Tell us how you've done it,' someone from the crowd called out as Miranda Webberly stepped in to relieve her parents at the cake.

'By having no expectations,' Frances Webberly said promptly and clasped both hands round her husband's arm. 'I had to learn that early, didn't I, darling? Which is just as well since the only thing I actually *gained* from this marriage—aside from my Malcolm—is the two stone I've never been able to lose from carrying Randie.'

The company joined her lighthearted laughter. Miranda merely ducked her head and continued cutting the cake.

'That sounds a fair bargain.' This was said by Helen, the wife of DI Thomas Lynley. She'd just accepted a plate of cake from Miranda, and she touched the girl fondly on the shoulder.

'Spot on,' Superintendent Webberly agreed. 'We've got the best daughter on earth.'

'Oh, you're right, naturally,' Frances said, shooting Helen a smile. 'I would be nowhere without Randie. But just you wait, Countess, till the day arrives when that slender body of yours starts to bloat and your ankles swell. Then you'll know what I'm talking about. Lady Hillier, may I offer you cake?'

There it was, Barbara thought, that something not right. *Countess.* And *Lady.* She was several beats off, was Frances Webberly, giving those titles a public airing. Helen Lynley never used her title—her husband was an earl as well as a detective inspector but he'd go to the rack before mentioning that fact and his wife was just as reticent—and while Lady Hillier might indeed be the wife of Assistant Commissioner Sir David Hillier—who himself would go to the rack before *failing* to make his knighthood known to anyone within hearing distance—she was also Frances Webberly's own sister, and using her title, which Frances had done all night, seemed to be an effort to underscore for everyone differences between them that might otherwise have gone unremarked.

It was all very strange, Barbara thought. Very curious. Very . . . off.

She gravitated towards Helen Lynley. It seemed to Barbara that the simple word *countess* had driven a subtle wedge between Helen and the rest of the party, and as a result the other woman was tucking into her cake alone. Her husband appeared oblivious of this—typical man—since he was engaged in conversation with two of his fellow DIs, Angus MacPherson who was working on his weight

66

problem by ingesting a piece of cake the size of a shoebox and John Stewart who was compulsively arranging the remaining crumbs from his own piece of cake in a pattern that resembled a Union Jack. So Barbara went to Helen's rescue.

'Is her countess-ship thoroughly chuffed by the evening's festivities?' she asked quietly when she reached Helen's side. 'Or haven't enough forelocks been tugged in her direction?'

'Behave yourself, Barbara,' Helen remonstrated, but she smiled as she said it.

'Can't do that. I've got a reputation to maintain.' Barbara accepted a plate of cake and tucked into it happily. 'You know, your slenderness,' she went on, 'you could at least *try* to look dumpy like the rest of us. Have you thought about wearing horizontal stripes?'

'There *is* that wallpaper I got for the spare room,' Helen said thoughtfully. 'It's vertical but I could wear it on its side.'

'You owe it to your fellow females. One woman maintaining her appropriate body weight makes the rest of us look like elephants.'

'I'm afraid I won't be maintaining it for long,' Helen said.

'Oh, I wouldn't go to Ladbrokes to put five quid—' Barbara suddenly realised what Helen was saying. She glanced at her in surprise and saw that Helen's face bore an uncharacteristically bashful half smile.

'Holy *hell*,' Barbara intoned. 'Helen, are you really . . .? You and the inspector? Hell. That's bloody *brilliant*, that is.' She looked across the room at Lynley, his blond head cocked to listen to something that Angus MacPherson was saying to

67

him. 'The inspector hasn't said a word.'

'We've only just found out this week. No one actually knows yet. That seemed best.'

'Oh. Right. Yeah.' Barbara agreed, but she didn't know what to think about the fact that Helen Lynley had just confided in her. She felt a sudden warmth swell over her and a quick pulsing in the back of her throat. 'Gosh. Hell. Well, never fear, Helen. Mum'll be the absolute word at this end till you tell me otherwise.' And as she realised her inadvertent pun, Helen did also and they laughed together.

It was at this moment that Barbara caught sight of the caterer tiptoeing along the side of the dining room from the direction of the kitchen, a cordless phone in her hand.

'A call for the superintendent,' she announced, but she managed to sound apologetic about the fact, and she added, 'Sorry,' as if there had actually been a chance in hell that she could have done something about it.

'Here comes trouble,' DI Angus MacPherson rumbled as 'At *this* hour?' Frances Webberly asked. She said anxiously, 'Malcolm, good heavens . . . You can't . . .'

A sympathetic murmur rose from the guests. They all knew either first or second hand what a phone call at one in the morning meant. So did Webberly. He said, 'Can't be helped, Fran,' and he put a hand on her shoulder as he went to take the call.

*   *   *

Detective Inspector Thomas Lynley wasn't

68

surprised when the superintendent excused himself from the party and climbed the stairs with the cordless receiver pressed to his ear. He *was* surprised, however, at the length of time that his superior officer was gone. At least twenty minutes passed during which the superintendent's guests finished their cake and coffee and made noises about heading for their respective homes. Frances Webberly protested at this, casting more than one vexed glance at the stairs. They *couldn't* leave just yet, she told them, not before Malcolm had the chance to thank them for being part of their anniversary party. Wouldn't they wait for Malcolm?

She didn't add what she would never say. If their guests left before her husband had completed his phone call, common courtesy suggested that Frances step into the front garden to bid farewell to the people who'd come to honour her marriage. And what had long gone unmentioned between Malcolm Webberly and most of his colleagues was the fact that Frances had not put a toe outside her house in more than ten years.

'Agoraphobia,' Webberly had explained to Lynley on the single occasion when he'd spoken about his wife. 'It began with simple things that I didn't notice. By the time they had a tight enough hold on her to get my attention, she was spending all day in the bedroom. Wrapped in a blanket, would you believe it. God forgive me.'

The secrets men live with, Lynley thought as he watched Frances fluttering among her guests. There was an edge to her gaiety that no one could miss, a hint of the determined and the anxious to her pleasure. Randie had wished to surprise her parents with an anniversary party at a local

69

restaurant where there would be more room, even a dance floor for the guests. But that hadn't been possible considering Frances's condition, so the venue was restricted to the family's disintegrating old house in Stamford Brook.

Webberly finally descended the stairs as the company were making their farewells, ushered to the door by his daughter, who wrapped her arm round her mother's waist. It was a fond gesture on Randie's part. It served the double purpose of reassuring Frances even as it prevented her from tearing away from the door.

'Not leaving?' Webberly boomed from the stairs, where he'd lit a cigar that was sending a blue cloud in the direction of the ceiling. 'The night is young.'

'The night is morning,' Laura Hillier informed him, fondly pressing her cheek to her niece's and saying her farewells. 'Lovely party, Randie. You did your parents proud.' Her hand clasped in her husband's, she went out into the night, where the rain that had been falling heavily all evening had finally stopped.

Assistant Commissioner Hillier's departure gave the rest of the company permission to go, and people began to do so, Lynley among them. He was waiting for his wife's coat to be unearthed from somewhere upstairs when Webberly joined him at the door to the sitting room and said in a low voice, 'Stay a moment, Tommy. If you will.'

There was a drawn quality to the superintendent's face that prompted Lynley to murmur, 'Of course.' Next to him, his wife said spontaneously, 'Frances, have you your wedding pictures anywhere at hand? I won't let Tommy take me home till I've seen you on your day of glory.'

Lynley shot Helen a grateful look. Within another ten minutes, the remaining guests had departed and while Helen occupied Frances Webberly and Miranda helped the caterer clear away dishes and serving platters, Lynley and Webberly repaired to the study, a cramped room barely large enough for a desk, an armchair, and the bookshelves that furnished it.

Perhaps in deference to Lynley's abstemious habits, Webberly went to the window and wrestled with it to give some respite from his cigar smoke. Cold autumn air, heavy with damp, floated into the room.

'Sit down, Tommy.' Webberly himself remained standing, next to the window where the dim ceiling light cast him mostly in shadow.

Lynley waited for Webberly to speak. The superintendent, however, was chewing the inside of his lower lip, as if the words he wanted to say were there and he needed to taste them for their fluency.

Outside the house, a car's gears ground discordantly while inside the doors to kitchen cupboards banged shut. These noises seemed to act like a spur upon Webberly. He looked up from his musing and said, 'That was a bloke called Leach on the phone. We used to be partners. I haven't talked to him in years. It's rotten to lose touch that way. I don't know why it happens, but it just does.'

Lynley knew that Webberly had hardly asked him to remain behind in order to hear the superintendent wax melancholy on the state of a friendship. One-forty-five in the morning was hardly the hour to be discussing one's former mates. Still, to give the older man an opportunity to confide, Lynley said, 'Is Leach still in the force, sir?

I don't think I know him.'

'Northwest London police,' Webberly said. 'He and I worked together twenty years ago.'

'Ah.' Lynley thought about this. Webberly would have been thirty-five at the time, which meant he was speaking of his Kensington years. 'CID?' he asked.

'He was my sergeant. He's in Hampstead now, heading up the murder squad. DCI Eric Leach. Good man. Very good man.'

Lynley studied Webberly thoughtfully: faded thin straw-coloured hair hastily brushed across his forehead, natural ruddiness of complexion muted, neck holding the head at an angle that suggested too much weight on his shoulders. Everything about him spoke of bad news—and a single source—the phone call.

Webberly roused himself but didn't move from the shadows as he spoke. 'He's working on a hit and run up in West Hampstead, Tommy. That's why he called. It happened round ten, eleven tonight. The victim's a woman.' Webberly paused, seemed to be waiting for Lynley to make a response of some kind. When Lynley didn't do anything other than nod—unfortunately, hit and runs happened with a distressing frequency in an urban environment in which foreigners often forgot which side of the street they were supposed to be driving on and in which direction they ought to be looking if they were pedestrians—Webberly studied the tip of his cigar and cleared his throat. 'From the state of things, Leach's crime scene people are guessing that someone knocked her down, then deliberately ran over her. And then got out, dragged her body to one side, and drove on his way.'

'Christ,' Lynley murmured reverently.

'Her handbag was found nearby. Car keys and driving licence were in it. The car itself wasn't far, right there on the street. Inside, on the passenger seat, was a London *A to Z*, along with specific directions to the street where she was killed. And an address was there as well: Number Thirty-two Crediton Hill.'

'Who lives there?'

'The bloke who found the body, Tommy. The very same bloke who happened to drive up the street within an hour of her being hit.'

'Was he expecting the victim at his home? Had they an appointment?'

'Not that we know of, but we don't know much. Leach said the bastard looked like he'd swallowed an onion when they told him the woman had his address in her car. All he said was, "No. That's impossible," and phoned his solicitor.'

Which was, of course, his right. But there was certainly something suspicious about that being someone's first reaction to learning a murder victim was carrying his address.

Still, neither the hit and run nor the oddity of its discovery could explain to Lynley why DCI Leach had phoned Webberly at one in the morning or why Webberly was reporting that phone call to him now.

He said, 'Sir, is DCI Leach in over his head for some reason? Is something wrong with the murder squad in Hampstead?'

'Why did he phone, you mean? And more importantly, why am I telling you?' Webberly didn't wait for a reply before he sank into his desk chair

73

and said, 'Because of the victim, Tommy. She's Eugenie Davies, and I want you involved. I want to move heaven and earth and hell, if I have to, to get to the bottom of what happened to her. Leach knew that the moment he saw who she was.'

Lynley frowned. 'Eugenie Davies? Who was she?'

'How old are you, Tommy?'

'Thirty-seven, sir.'

Webberly blew out a breath. 'Then I suppose you're too young to remember.'

GIDEON

23 AUGUST

I didn't like the way you asked me the question, Dr Rose. I was offended by your tone and the implication. Don't try to tell me there was no implication because I'm not that much of a fool. And don't make allusions to the 'real meaning' behind a patient's drawing inferences from your words in the first place. I know what I heard, I know what happened, and I can summarise both for you in a sentence: You read what I've written, saw an omission in the story, and pounced on it like a criminal barrister with a mind so closed as to be virtually useless.

Let me repeat what I said in our session: I made no mention of my mother until that final sentence because I was attempting to fulfil your assignment to me, which was to write what I remember, and I was writing what I was writing as it came into my mind. She did not come into my mind before then: before

74

Raphael Robson became, virtually, my full time instructor and companion.

But the Italian-Greek-Portuguese-Spanish girl did come into your mind? you ask me in that insufferably quiet calm placid manner of yours.

Yes, she did. What's that supposed to mean? That I have a heretofore unmentioned affinity for Portuguese-Spanish-Italian-Greek girls, arising from my unacknowledged indebtedness to an unnamed young woman who unknowingly started me on my path to success? Is that it, Dr Rose?

Ah. I see. You give me no answer. You keep a safe distance in your father's chair and you fix your soulful eyes on me and I'm meant to take this distance between us as the Bosporus waiting for me to swim. Plunge into the waters of veracity, it suggests. As if I'm not telling the truth.

She was there. Of course she was there, my mother. And if I mentioned the Italian girl instead of my mother it was for the simple reason that the Italian girl—and why can't I remember her blasted name, *for God's sake?—figured in the Gideon Legend while my mother did not. And I* thought *you instructed me to write what I remembered, going back to the earliest memory I could recall. If that's not what you instructed me to do, if instead you wished me to manufacture the salient details of a childhood that is largely fiction but safely and antiseptically regurgitated in such a way that you can identify and label where and what you choose—*

Oh yes, I am angry, before you point that out to me. Because I do not see what my mother, an analysis of my mother, or even a superficial conversation about my mother has to do with what happened at Wigmore Hall. And that's why I've come

75

to see you, Dr Rose. Let's not forget that. I've agreed to this process because there on the stage in Wigmore Hall, in front of an audience paying mightily to benefit the East London Conservatory—which is my own charity, mind you—I mounted the platform, I rested my violin on my shoulder, I picked up my bow, I flexed my left hand's fingers as usual, I nodded to the pianist and the cellist . . . and I could not play.

This wasn't stage fright, Dr Rose. This wasn't a temporary block against a single piece of music, which, by the way, I'd spent the last two weeks rehearsing. This was a total, utter, complete, and humiliating loss of ability. Not only had the music itself been ripped from my brain but how to play the music was gone as well. I may as well not ever have held a violin, let alone have spent the last twenty-one years of my life performing in public.

Sherrill began the Allegro, and I heard it without the slightest degree of recognition. And where I was supposed to join the piano and the cello: nothing. I neither knew what to do nor when to do it. I was Lot's son incarnate had he and not the man's wife been the one to turn and observe the destruction.

Sherrill covered for me. He feinted. He improvised, God help him, with Beethoven. He worked his way round to my entrance again. And again there was nothing. Just silence like a vacuum, and the silence roared like a hurricane in my head.

So I left the platform. Blindly, body shivering, vision tunnelling, I walked. Dad met me in the Green Room, crying, 'What? Gideon. For God's sake. What?' with Raphael only a step behind him.

I thrust my instrument into Raphael's hands and collapsed. Babble all round me and my father saying, 'It's that bloody girl, isn't it? This is down to her. God

76

damn it. Get a grip, *Gideon. You have obligations.'*

And Sherrill, who'd left the platform in my wake, asking, 'Gid? What happened? Lose your nerve? Shit. It happens sometimes.'

While Raphael set my violin on the table saying, 'Oh dear. I was afraid this would happen eventually.' Because like most people he was thinking of himself, of his own countless failures to perform in a public venue like his father and his father before him. Every member of his family has a high-powered career in performance music save poor sweating Raphael, and I expect he's secretly been biding his time, waiting for disaster to befall me, making us official brothers in misery. He was the one who cautioned against climbing aboard the swift acceleration that occurred in my career after my first public concert when I was seven. Evidently, now he thinks the chickens of catastrophe, born of that acceleration, have come home to roost on my shoulders.

But it wasn't nerves that I felt in the Green Room, Dr Rose. And it wasn't nerves that I felt before, in front of that audience out in the hall. It was instead some sort of shutdown, which feels irrevocable and complete. And what was odd about it was that despite the fact that I could hear all their voices—my father's, Raphael's, and Sherrill's—quite clearly, all I could see in front of me was white light shining on a blue, blue door.

Am I having an episode, Dr Rose? Just like Granddad, am I having an episode that a nice calm countryside visit can cure? Please tell me because music is not what I do, music is who I am and if I don't have it—the sound and the sheer chivalry *of sound—I am nothing but an empty husk.*

So what does it matter that in recounting my

introduction to music, I made no mention of my mother? It was an omission of sound and fury, and you'd be wise to account its significance accordingly.

But to omit her now would be deliberate, you tell me. You say, Tell me about your mother, Gideon.

<u>25 AUGUST</u>
She went to work. She'd been a constant presence for my first four years but once it became clear that she had a child of exceptional talent that needed fostering, which was going to be not only time consuming but hideously expensive, she took a job to help out with the costs. I was given into the care of my grandmother—when I was not practising my instrument, having lessons with Raphael, listening to the recordings he brought for me, or attending concerts in his company—but my life had altered so appreciably from what it had been before that day I first heard the music in Kensington Square, I hardly noticed her absence. Prior to that, however, I do remember accompanying her—it seemed like every day—to early morning Mass.

She'd struck up a friendship with a nun at the convent in the square, and between them they'd arranged that my mother could attend the daily mass that was said for the sisters. She was a convert to Catholicism, my mother. But as her own father was an Anglican minister, I wonder now how much her conversion had to do with devotion to a different dogma and how much it had to do with slapping her father in the face. He wasn't, as I was given to understand it, a very nice fellow. Other than that, I don't recall him.

This is not the case for my mother, but she's a

78

shadowy figure for me because she left us. When I was nine or ten—I can't remember which—I arrived home from a concert tour of Austria to find that my mother had quit Kensington Square, leaving not a trace of herself behind. She took every article of clothing she possessed, each one of her books, and a number of family photographs. And off she went, like a figurative thief in the night. Except it was the day, I've been told. And she called a taxi. She left no note and no forwarding address, and I never heard from her again.

My father had been with me in Austria—Dad always travelled with me, and Raphael often accompanied us as well—so he was as much in the dark about where Mother had gone and why she had gone as I myself was. All I know is that we came home to find Granddad having an episode, Gran weeping on the stairs, and Calvin the Lodger trying to find the appropriate phone number with no one to help him.

Calvin the Lodger? you ask me. The earlier lodger—James, is that right?—he was gone?

Yes. He must have left the year before. Or the year before that. I don't remember. We had a number of lodgers over time. We had to, in order to make ends meet, as I've already noted.

Do you remember them all? you want to know.

I don't. Just those who figure large, I suppose. Calvin because he was there that night when I first learned my mother had gone. James because he was present when everything began.

Everything? you ask.

Yes. The violin. The lessons. Miss Orr. Everything.

26 AUGUST

I associate everyone with music. When I think of Rosemary Orr, I think of Brahms, the concerto that was playing the first time I met her. When I think of Raphael, it's the Mendelssohn. Dad is Bach, the solo violin sonata in G minor. And Granddad will always be Paganini. The twenty-fourth caprice was his favourite. 'All those notes,' he would marvel. 'All those perfect notes.'

And your mother? you ask me. What about her? Which piece of music do you associate with your mother?

Interestingly, I can't attach an actual piece of music to Mother the way I can with the others. I'm not sure why. A form of denial, perhaps? Repression of emotion? I don't know. You're the psychiatrist. Explain it to me.

I still do this with music, by the way. I still associate a person with a piece. Sherrill, for example, is Bartók's Rhapsody, which is what he and I initially played together in public, years ago, at St Martin's in the Fields. We've never played it since and we were teenagers then—the American and the English wunderkind *together made excellent press, believe me—but he'll always be Bartók when I think of him. That's just how it works in my mind.*

And it's the same for people who aren't musical in the least. Take Libby, for instance. Have I told you about Libby? She's Libby the Lodger. Yes, like James and Calvin and all the others except she's of the present, not of the past, and she lives in the basement flat of my house in Chalcot Square.

I hadn't thought of letting it till she turned up at my door one day, ferrying a recording contract that my agent had decided had to be signed at once. She

80

works for a courier service, and I didn't know she was a girl till she handed me the paperwork, took off her helmet, and said with a nod at the contracts, 'Don't be bugged by this, okay? I just gotta ask. You a rock musician or something?' in that excessively casual and friendly fashion that seems to plague the native Californian.

I replied, No. I'm a concert violinist.

She said, 'No way!'

I said, Way.

To which she produced such a blank expression that I thought I was dealing with a congenital idiot.

I won't ever sign contracts without having read them—no matter what my agent claims this reveals about my lack of trust in his wisdom—and rather than have the poor urchin—for so she seemed to me—wait on the front step while I read through the document, I asked her in and we climbed to the first floor; which is where the music room overlooks the square.

She said, 'Oh wow. Sorry. You *are* somebody, aren't you?' as we climbed because she noticed the artwork for the CD covers hanging along the staircase. 'I feel like a real dope.'

I said, 'No need,' and walked into the music room with her on my heels and my own head buried in clauses about accompanists, royalties, and timelines.

'Oh, this is awesome,' she intoned while I went to the window seat where even now I'm writing in this notebook for you, Dr Rose. 'Who's this guy you're with in the picture? This guy with the crutches? Geez. Look at you. You look seven years old!'

God. He's possibly the greatest violinist on earth and the girl's as ignorant as a tube of toothpaste. 'Itzhak Perlman,' I told her. 'And I was six at the time,

81

not seven.'

'Wow. You actually played with him when you were only six?'

'Hardly. But he was kind enough to listen to me one afternoon when he was in London.'

'Very cool.'

And as I read she continued to wander, murmuring from her rather limited vocabulary of exclamations. She took particular pleasure—so it seemed—in an examination of my earliest instrument, that one-sixteenth that I keep in the music room on a little stand. I also keep the Guarneri there, the violin that I use today. It was in its case, and the case was open because when Libby arrived with the paperwork for me, I'd been in the midst of my morning practice. Obviously unaware of the trespass she was committing, she casually reached down and plucked the E-string.

She might as well have shot a pistol in the room. I leapt up and bellowed, 'Don't touch that violin!' and so startled her that she reacted like a child who's been struck. She said, 'Oh my gosh,' and she backed away from the instrument with her hands behind her and her eyes filling. And then she turned away in embarrassment.

I set my paperwork aside and said, 'Look. Sorry. Didn't mean to be a swine, but that instrument's two hundred and fifty years old. I'm rather careful with it, and I usually don't allow—'

Her back turned to me, she waved me off. She took several deep breaths before she shook her head vigorously which made her hair puff out—have I mentioned that her hair is curly? Toast coloured, it is, and very curly—and she rubbed at her eyes. Then she turned round and said, 'Sorry about that. It's okay. I shouldn't have touched it and I totally wasn't thinking. You were right to tell me off, you really were. It's just that, like, for a second you were so totally rock, and I freaked.'

Language from another planet. I said, 'Totally rock?'

She said, 'Rock Peters. Formerly Rocco Petrocelli and currently my estranged husband. I mean, as estranged as he'll let us be since he holds the purse strings and he's not exactly into loosening them to help me get established on my own.'

I thought she looked far too young to be married to anyone, but it turned out that, despite her looks and what appeared to be a rather charming prepubescent plumpness, she was twenty-three years old and two years married to the irascible Rock. At the moment, however, I said, 'Ah.'

She said, 'He's got, like, this hair-trigger temper among other things, such as not knowing monogamy is usually part of the marriage deal. I never knew when he was going to blow a fuse. After two years cowering round the apartment, I called it quits.'

'Oh. Sorry.' I admit that I felt uneasy with her unburdening of personal details. It's not that I'm unused to such displays. This tendency to confession and contrition seems peculiar to all the Americans I've ever known, as if they've somehow become acculturated to disbosoming themselves along with learning to salute their flag. But being used to something isn't exactly akin to welcoming it into your life. What, after all, is one to do with someone else's personal data?

She gave me more of it. She wanted a divorce; he did not. They continued to live together because she could not come up with the money to break away *from him. Whenever she came close to the amount she needed, he simply withheld her wages until she'd spent whatever nest egg she'd managed to accumulate. 'And why he even wants me there is, like, the major mystery of my life, you know? I mean the man is totally governed by the herd instinct, so what's the point?'*

He was, she explained, a womaniser without peer, an adherent to the philosophy that groups of females—'the herd, get it?—' should be dominated and serviced by a single male. 'But the problem is that the entire female sex is the herd in Rock's mind. And he's got to hump them all just to keep them happy.' Then she clapped her hand over her mouth and said, 'Oh. Sorry.' And then she grinned. And then she said, 'Anyway. Gosh. Look at me. I'm, like, totally running off at the mouth. Got those papers signed?'

Which I hadn't. Who'd had an opportunity to read them? I said I'd sign them if she wouldn't mind waiting. She took herself to a corner and sat.

I read. I made one phone call to clarify a clause. I signed the contracts and returned them to her. She shoved them into her pouch, said thanks, and then cocked her head at me and asked, 'Favour?'

'What?'

She shifted her weight and looked embarrassed. But she plunged ahead and I admired her for it. She said, 'Would you . . . I mean, it's like, I've never actually heard a violin in person before. Would you please play a song?'

A song. She was indeed a philistine. But even a philistine is educable, and she'd asked politely. What would it hurt? I'd been practising anyway, working on Bartók's solo sonata, so I gave her part of the Melodia, *playing it as I always play: putting the music before myself, before her, before everything. By the time I'd reached the end of the movement, I'd forgotten she was there. So I went on to the* Presto, *hearing as usual Raphael's words: 'Make it an invitation to* dance, *Gideon. Feel its quickness. Make it flash, like light.'*

And when I was finished, I was brought back to an abrupt awareness of her presence. She said, 'Oh wow. Oh wow. Oh wow. I mean, you are so totally excellent, aren't you?'

I looked her way to see that sometime during the playing she'd begun to cry because her cheeks were wet and she was digging round in her leathers, looking—I presume—for something on which to wipe her dribbling nose. I was pleased to have touched her with the Bartók, and even more pleased to see that my assessment of her educability had been on target. And I suppose it was because of that assessment that I asked her to join me in my regular cup of midmorning coffee. The day was fine, so we took it in the garden where, under the arbour, I'd been creating one of my kites on the previous afternoon.

I haven't mentioned my kites, have I, Dr Rose? Well, there's nothing to them, actually. They're just something I do when I feel the need to take a break from the music. I fly them from Primrose Hill.

Ah yes. I can see that you're searching for meaning there, aren't you? What does creating and flying kites symbolise in the patient's history and in his present life? The unconscious mind speaks in all our actions. The conscious mind merely has to grasp the meaning behind those actions and wrestle it into comprehensible form.

Kites. Air. Freedom. But freedom from what? What need do I have to be free when my life is full and rich and complete?

I say that there is danger in digging too deeply for meaning when something can be so simply explained: As a child and once my talent became apparent, I was not allowed a single activity that might injure my hands. Designing and creating kites . . . My hands are quite safe from harm.

But you do see the relevance of an activity associated with the sky, don't you, Gideon? you ask me.

I see only that the sky is blue. Blue like the door. That blue blue door.

Gideon

<u>28 AUGUST</u>

I did what you suggested, Dr Rose, and I've nothing to report apart from the fact that I felt a real fool. Perhaps the experiment would have turned out differently had I cooperated and done it in your office as you asked, but I couldn't get my mind round what you were talking about, and it seemed absurd. More absurd, even, than spending hours at this notebook when I could be practising my instrument as I used to.

But I still haven't touched it.

Why?

Don't ask the obvious, Dr Rose. It's gone. The music is gone.

Dad was here this morning. He's only just left. He came round to see if I'd improved at all—for that you can read Have I tried to play again?—although he was good enough not to ask the question directly. But then, he didn't actually need to ask it since the Guarneri was in the position he'd left it when he brought me home from Wigmore Hall. I haven't even had the nerve to touch the case.

Why? you ask.

You know the answer. Because at the moment I lack the courage: If I can't play, if the gift, the ear, the talent, the genius or whatever else you wish to call it is moribund or gone from me entirely, how do I exist? Not how do I go on, Dr Rose, but how do I exist? How do I exist when the sum and substance of who I am and who I have been for the last twenty-five years is contained in and defined by my music?

Then let's look at the music itself, you say. If each person in your life is indeed associated in some way with your music, perhaps we need to examine your music much more carefully for the key to unlock what's troubling you.

I laugh and say, Did you intend that pun?

And you gaze at me with those penetrating eyes. You refuse to engage in levity. You say, So that final Bartók you were writing about, the solo sonata . . . Is that what you associate with Libby?

Yes, I associate the sonata with Libby. But Libby's nothing to do with my present problem. I assure you of that.

My father found this notebook, by the way. When he came round to check on me, he found it on the window seat. And before you ask, he wasn't nosy parkering. My dad might be an insufferably single-minded bastard, but he isn't a spy. He's merely given the last twenty-five years of his life to supporting his only child's career, and he'd like to see that career stay afloat and not go swimming down the plughole.

Not his only child for long, though. I'd forgotten all

about that in these last few weeks. There's Jill to consider. I can't imagine having a new brother or sister at my age, let alone a stepmother less than ten years my senior. But these are the days of elastic families, and the course of wisdom suggests that one stretch with the changing definitions of spouse, not to mention of father, mother, and sibling.

But yes, I think it a little odd, *this bit about my father and his production of a new family. It's not that I expected him to remain a divorced single man forever. It's just that after nearly twenty years in which he never to my knowledge even had a date with a woman—let alone a relationship whose depth might suggest the sort of physical intimacy that produces children—it's all come as something of a shock to me.*

I'd met Jill at the BBC when I was previewing a rough cut of that documentary they filmed at East London Conservatory. This was several years ago, just before she produced that outstanding adaptation of Desperate Remedies—*Did you see it, by the way? She's quite a Thomas Hardy buff—and she was working in their documentary division then, if that's what it's called. Dad must have met her as well at that time, but I don't recall ever seeing them together and I can't say at what point they became partners. I do recall being invited round to Dad's flat for a meal and finding her there in the kitchen, stirring away at something on the cooker, and while I was surprised to see her, I simply assumed she was there because she'd brought along a final copy of the documentary for us to preview. I suppose that might have been the start of their relationship. Dad became slightly less available to me after that evening, now I come to think about it. So perhaps everything began that night. But as Jill*

88

and Dad have never lived together—although Dad says that's being arranged shortly after the baby's birth—I really had no reason to conclude there was anything at all between them.

And now that you know? you ask me. How do you feel? And when did you learn about them and the baby? And where?

I see the direction you're taking. But I have to tell you it's something of a non-starter.

I learned about my father's situation with Jill some months ago, not on the day of the concert at Wigmore Hall, not even during the week or the month of the concert, in fact. And there was no blue door anywhere in sight when I was given the news about my future half sibling. You see, I knew where you were heading, didn't I?

But how did you feel? you persist in asking. A second family for your father after all these years—

Not a second family, I hasten to tell you. A third.

His third family? You look at the notes you've been taking during our sessions and you see no reference to an earlier family, before my own birth. But there was one and there was a child from that family, a girl who died in infancy.

She was called Virginia, and I don't know exactly how she died or where or how long after her death my father ended his marriage to her mother or even who her mother was. In fact, the only reason I know about her existence at all—or about my father's earlier marriage—is that Granddad began shouting about it during one of his episodes. It was in the same vein as his 'you're no son of mine' curses as he was being taken from the house. Except this time it was along the lines of Dad's not being any son of Granddad's because all he could ever produce was freaks. And I suppose I was given a hasty explanation by someone—Was it mother who told me or was she gone by then?—since I must have assumed that, in shouting about freaks, Granddad meant me. So Virginia must have died because there was something wrong with her, a congenital condition perhaps. But I don't actually know what it was, because whoever it was who told me about her in the first place didn't know or wouldn't say and because the subject never came up again.

Never came up? you query.

But you know the dance, doctor. Children don't mention topics that they associate with chaos, tumult, and contention. They learn quite early the consequences of stirring a pot best left alone. And I assume you can make the leap from there yourself since the violin was my sole concentration, once I was assured of my grandfather's esteem, I thought no more of the subject.

The blue door, however, is something else entirely. As I said when I began, I did exactly as you asked me to do and as we tried to do in your office. In my mind I recreated that door: Prussian blue with a silverish ring in its centre serving as a knob; two locks, I think, done in silver like the ring; and perhaps a house number or a flat number above the knob.

I darkened my bedroom and stretched out on my bed and closed my eyes and visualised that door; I visualised my approach to it; I visualised my hand grasping the ring that served as its knob and my fingers turning keys in the locks, the lower lock first with one of those old fashioned keys with large and easily duplicated teeth, the upper lock next, which is modern, burglar proof, and safe. With the locks disengaged, I put my shoulder against the door, gave a slight push, and . . . Nothing. Absolutely nothing.

There is nothing there, Dr Rose. Do you see? My mind is a blank. You want to make interpretive leaps based on what I find behind that door, or what colour it is, or the fact that it has two locks, not one, and a ring for a knob—Could he be fleeing from commitment? you ask yourself—while I'm inspired by this exercise to tell you bloody sod all. Nothing has been revealed to me. Nothing lurks ghoul-like behind that door. It leads to no room that I can conjure up, it merely sits at the top of a staircase like—

Staircase, you leap. So there's a staircase as well?

Yes. Which, we both know, means climbing, rising, elevating, clawing out of this pit . . . What of it?

You see the agitation in my scrawl, don't you? You say, Stay with the fear. It won't kill you, Gideon. Feelings won't kill you. You are not alone.

I never thought that I was, I say. Don't put words in my mouth, Dr Rose.

2 SEPTEMBER

Libby was here. She knows something's not right since she hasn't heard the violin in weeks and she generally hears it for hours on end when I'm practising. That's largely why I hadn't let the basement flat once the original tenants left. I thought about it when I first bought and moved into this house in Chalcot Square, but I didn't want the distraction of a tenant coming and going—even by a separate entrance—and I didn't want to have to limit my hours of practice out of concern for someone else. I told Libby all this when she was leaving that day, when she'd zipped herself into her leathers, returned her helmet to her head just outside my front door, and

91

caught sight of the empty flat below through the wrought iron railings. She said, 'Wow. Is that for rent or anything?'

And I explained that I left it empty. There was a young couple living there when I first bought the building, I told her. But as they weren't able to develop a passion for the violin at odd hours of the night, they soon decamped.

She cocked her head. She said, 'Hey. How old are you anyway? And do you always talk like a bottle's in your butt? When you were showing me the kites, you sounded totally normal. So what's up? Is this about being English or something? Step out of the house and all of a sudden you're Henry James?'

'He wasn't English,' I informed her.

'Well. Sorry.' She began to fasten her helmet's strap, but she seemed agitated because she had trouble with it. 'I got through high school on Cliff's Notes, bud, so I wouldn't know Henry James from Sid Vicious. I don't even know why he popped into my head. Or why Sid Vicious did, for that matter.'

'Who's Sid Vicious?' I asked her solemnly.

She peered at me. 'Come on. You're joking.'

'Yes,' I said.

And then she laughed. Well, not laughed actually. It was more like a hoot. And she grabbed my arm and said, 'You, you,' with such an inordinate degree of familiarity that I was both astounded and charmed. So I offered to show her the basement flat.

Why? you ask.

Because she'd asked about it and I wanted to show her and I suppose I wanted her company for a while. She was so absolutely un-English.

You say, I didn't mean why did you show her the flat, Gideon. I meant why are you telling me about

92

Libby.
Because she was here, just here, just now.
She's significant, isn't she?
I don't know.

3 SEPTEMBER

*'It's Liberty,' she tells me. 'God, isn't that, like, totally
the* worst? *My parents were hippies before they were
yuppies, which was way before my dad made, like, a
billion dollars in Silicon Valley. You* do *know about
Silicon Valley, don't you?'*

*We are walking to the top of Primrose Hill. I have
one of my kites. Libby's talked me into flying it this
late afternoon, sometime last year. I ought to be
rehearsing since I'm due to record Paganini—the
second violin concerto, this is—with the
Philharmonic in less than three weeks and the*
Allegro maestoso *has been giving me some trouble.
But Libby's returned from a confrontation with the
acidulous Rock about wages he's withheld from her
again, and she's reported his response to her request
for her money: 'The jerk said, "Fly a kite, bitch," so I
thought I'd take him up on it. Come on, Gideon,
you're working too hard anyway.'*

*I've been at it for six hours, two increments of three
with an hour's break to walk over to Regent's Park at
midday, so I agree to the plan. I allow her to choose
the kite, and she selects a multi-level affair that spins
and requires just the right wind velocity to show its
best stuff.*

*We head off. We follow the curve of Chalcot
Crescent—more gentrification sourly remarked upon
by Libby who appears to prefer London decaying to
London renewed—and dash across Regent's Park*

Road and thence into the park, where we set off up the side of the hill.

'Too much wind,' I tell her, and I have to raise my voice because the wind gusts fiercely against the kite and the nylon slaps against me. 'You've got to have perfect conditions for this one. I don't expect we'll even get it in the air.'

That proves to be the case, much to her disappointment because it seems that she 'just totally wanted to put it to Rock. The creep. He's threatening to tell whoever it is that gets told—'this with a wave of her hand in the vague direction of Westminster, by which I assume she must be talking about the Government—'that we were never really married in the first place. I mean physically married like in doing the deed with each other. Which is, like, just such a crock of shit that you wouldn't believe.'

'And what would happen if he told the Government that you weren't really married?'

'Except that we were. We are. Geez, he makes me nuts.'

As it turns out, she's afraid that her status in the country will change if her estranged husband has his way. And because she's moved from his doubtless— to my imagination—insalubrious home in Bermondsey to the basement flat in Chalcot Square, he's afraid that he's losing her for good, which he apparently doesn't wish to do despite his continued womanising. So they've had yet another row the end of which was his directive to her about kite flying.

Sorry not to be able to accommodate her, I invite her for a coffee instead. It's over coffee that she tells me the name for which Libby is merely a diminutive: Liberty.

'Hippies,' she says again of her parents. 'They

94

wanted their kids to have totally far out *names—' this with a mock inhalation of an imaginary cannabis cigarette—'My sister's is even worse: Equality, if you can believe it. Ali for short. And if there'd been a third kid in the family . . .'*

'Fraternity?' I say.

'You got it,' she rejoins. 'But I should be excessively glad they went for abstract nouns. I mean, God, it could be totally worse. My name could be Tree.'

I chuckle. 'Or perhaps just a type of tree: pine, oak, willow.'

'Willow Neale. I could get behind that.' She fingers through the packets of sugar on the table to find the dieters' sweetener. She is, I have discovered, a chronic dieter whose pursuit of bodily perfection has been 'the rip tide in the otherwise peaceful ocean of my existence', she said. She dumps the sweetener into her non-fat café latte and says, 'What about you, Gid?'

'Me?'

'Your parents. What are they like? Not former flower children, I bet.'

She hadn't yet met my father, you see, although he had seen her from the music room late one afternoon when she returned home from work on her Suzuki and parked it in her accustomed place on the pavement, right next to the steps that lead down to the basement flat. She roared up and gunned the engine two or three times, as is her habit, creating a ruckus that caught Dad's attention. He went to the window, saw her, and said, 'I'll be damned. There's an infernal cyclist actually chaining his motorbike to your front rails, Gideon. See here . . .' and he began to open the window.

I said, 'That's Libby Neale. It's fine, Dad. She lives here.'

95

He turned slowly away from the glass. 'What? That's a woman *out there? She lives here?'*

'Below. In the flat. I decided to let it out. Did I forget to tell you?'

I hadn't. But my failure to mention Libby and the flat hadn't been so much a deliberate omission as a subject that hadn't come up. Dad and I talk every day, but our conversations are always about our professional concerns, like an upcoming concert, a tour he might be organising, a recording session that hadn't gone well, a request for an interview or a personal appearance. Witness the fact that I didn't know a thing about his relationship with Jill until not mentioning it became more awkward than mentioning it: The sudden appearance of an obviously pregnant woman in one's life will demand some sort of explanation, after all. But otherwise, we've never had a chummy father-and-son relationship. We've both been absorbed with my music since my childhood, and this concentration on both our parts has precluded the possibility—or perhaps obviated the necessity—of the sort of soul-baring that appears to be the hallmark of closeness between people these days.

Mind you, I don't regret for an instant that Dad and I have the sort of connection with each other that we have. It's firm and true, and if it's not the sort of bond that makes us want to hike across the Himalayas together or paddle up the Nile, it's still a relationship that strengthens and supports me. Truth be told, if it were not for my father, Dr Rose, I would not be where I am today.

4 SEPTEMBER

No. *You will not catch me with that.*

Where are you today, Gideon? you ask me blandly.

But I refuse to participate. My father plays no part in this, in whatever this is. If I cannot bring myself to even pick up the Guarneri, it is not my father's fault. I refuse to become one of those gormless pulers who lay the blame for their every difficulty at the feet of their parents. Dad's life was rough. He did his best.

Rough in what way? you want to know.

Well, can you imagine having Granddad for a father? Being sent off to school when you were six? Growing up with a steady diet of someone's psychotic episodes to feed you when you were at home? And always knowing that there was never a hope in hell that you could fully measure up no matter what you did because you were adopted in the first place and your father never let you forget it? No. Dad's done the best he could as a father. And he's done better than most as a son.

Better than yourself as a son? you ask me.

You'll have to get that information from Dad.

But what do you think about yourself as a son, Gideon? What comes first to your mind?

Disappointment, I say.

That you've disappointed your father?

No. That I mustn't. But that I might.

Has he let you know how important it is not to disappoint him?

Never once. Not at all. But . . .

But?

He doesn't like Libby. I somehow knew that he wouldn't like her or at least wouldn't like her being there. He would consider her a potential distraction or, worse, an impediment to my work.

You ask, Is that why he said 'It's that girl, isn't it?'
when you had your blackout in Wigmore Hall? He
leapt right to her, didn't he?

Yes.

Why?

It's not that he doesn't want me to be with
someone. Why wouldn't he? Family is everything to
my father. But family is going to be stopped short if I
don't marry someday and have children of my own.

Except there's another child on the way now, isn't
there? The family will continue anyway, no matter
what you do.

Yes, it will.

So now he can disapprove of every woman in your
life without fearing the consequences of your taking
that disapproval to heart and never marrying, can't
he, Gideon?

No! I will not play this game. This is not about my
father. If he doesn't like Libby, it's because he's
concerned about the impact she could have on my
music. And he's well within his rights to be
concerned. Libby doesn't know a bow from a kitchen
knife.

Does she interrupt your work?

No, she doesn't.

Does she display an indifference to your music?

No.

Does she intrude? Ignore requests for solitude?
Make demands upon you that violate the time you've
set aside for your music?

Never.

You said she was a philistine. Have you discovered
that she clings to her ignorance like a badge of
accomplishment?

No. I haven't.

But still your father doesn't like her.

Look, it's for my own good. He's never made a move that wasn't for my good. I'm here with you because of him, Dr Rose. When he understood what had happened to me in Wigmore Hall, he didn't say, 'Buck up! Get a grip! You've a God damn audience who've paid to see you!' No. What he said was, 'He's ill,' to Raphael. 'Make our excuses,' and he spirited me out of there. He took me home and he put me to bed and he sat next to me all night and he said, 'We'll handle this, Gideon. Just sleep for now.'

He instructed Raphael to find help. Raphael knew about your own father's work with blocked artists, Dr Rose. And I came to you. Because my father wants me to have my music, I came to you.

5 SEPTEMBER

No one else knows. Just the three of us: Dad, Raphael, and I. Even my publicist isn't clear what's going on. Under a doctor's care, she's given out, telling the world that it's merely exhaustion.

I assume the interpretation given to that story is one variation or another of The Artist Piqued, and that's fine with me. Better the assumption that I stalked off the platform because I did not like the Hall's lighting than the truth reach public consumption.

Which truth is that? you ask me.

Is there more than one? I want to know.

Certainly, you say. There's the truth of what's happened to you and the truth of why. What's happened is called psychogenic amnesia, Gideon. Why it's happened is the reason for our meetings.

Are you saying that until we know why *I have this*

. . . this . . . what did you call it?

Psychogenic amnesia. It's like hysterical paralysis or blindness: Part of you that's always worked—in this case your musical memory, if you'd like to call it that—simply stops working. Until we know why you're experiencing this trouble, we won't be able to change it.

I'm wondering if you know how I recoil from that information, Dr Rose. You impart it with perfect sympathy, but still I feel like a freak. And yes, yes, I know how that word resonates in my past, so you needn't point that out to me. I still hear Granddad howling it at my father as they drag him away and I still apply that word to myself every day now. Freak, freak, freak, I call myself. Finish the freak off. Put an end to the freak.

Is that what you are? you ask me.

What else could I be? I never rode a bicycle, played rugby or cricket, hit a tennis ball, or even went to school. I had a psychotic grandfather, a mother who would have been happier as a nun and probably ended up in a convent for all I know, a father who slaved at two jobs till I was established professionally, and a violin instructor who shepherded me from concert tours to recording engagements and otherwise never let me out of his sight. I was coddled, catered to, and worshipped, Dr Rose. Who would emerge from conditions like that as anything other than a bona fide freak?

Is it any wonder that I'm riddled with ulcers? That I puke my guts out before a performance? That my brain sometimes pounds like a hammer in my skull? That I haven't been able to be with a woman in more than six years? That even when I was able to take a woman to bed, there was neither closeness, joy, nor

100

passion in the act but merely a need to have done, have it over, have my paltry release, and then have her gone?

And what is the sum of all that, Dr Rose, if not a sure fire genuine freak?

7 SEPTEMBER

Libby asked this morning if something was wrong. She came upstairs in her usual leisure attire—denim dungarees, a T-shirt, and hiking boots—and she seemed about to head out for a stroll because she was wearing the Walkman she usually takes with her when she's engaging in one of her diet hikes. I was in the window seat, doing my duty with this journal when she turned and saw me watching her. Up she came.

She's trying a new diet, she told me. The No-White-Diet, as she calls it. 'I've tried the Mayo diet, the cabbage soup diet, the Zone diet, the Scarsdale diet, the you-name-it-diet. Nothing's worked, so I'm on to this.' This, she tells me, consists of eating whatever she wants as long as it isn't white. White foods unnaturally altered with food colouring count as white as well.

She is, I have learned, obsessed with her weight and this is a mystery to me. She isn't fat, as far as I can tell, which admittedly isn't very far since she's always garbed either in her leathers for the courier service or in her dungarees. She doesn't appear to have any other clothes. But even if she does look slightly podgy to some people—and mind you, I'm not saying that she looks slightly podgy to me—it's probably because her face is round. Don't round faces make one look plump? I tell her this but it's no consolation. 'We live in skeletal times,' she says.

'You're lucky to be naturally skinny.'

I've never told her the cost of this emaciation that she seems to admire. Instead, I've said, 'Women are too obsessed with their weight. You look perfectly fine.'

On one occasion when I say this, she responds with, 'So if I look so perfectly fine, take me on a date, why don't you?'

And this is how we begin to see each other. What an odd expression that is, 'to see each other', as if we're incapable of seeing another person until we're socially involved. I don't much like it—'seeing each other'—because it smacks of a euphemism where one isn't needed. Dating, on the other hand, sounds so adolescent. And even if that weren't the case, I wouldn't call what we're doing dating.

So what are you doing with Liberty Neale? you want to know.

And you mean, Are you sleeping with her, Gideon? Is she the woman who's managed to melt the ice in your veins?

I suppose that depends on what you mean by sleeping with her, Dr Rose. And there's another euphemism for you. Why do we use a term like sleeping when sleeping is the last thing we intend to do when we climb into bed with the opposite sex?

But yes, we are sleeping together. Now and again. But by sleeping, I mean sleeping, not sex. We're neither of us ready for anything else.

How did this come about? you want to know.

It was a natural progression. One night she made a meal for me at the end of a particularly exhausting day of rehearsals for a concert at the Barbican. I fell asleep on her bed where we'd been sitting, listening to a recording. She covered me with a blanket and

102

joined me under it, and there we remained till morning. Now and again we sleep together still. I suppose we both find it comforting in some way.

Nurturing, you say.

In that it feels good to have her there, yes. Then it's nurturing as well.

Something that was missing during your childhood, Gideon, you point out. If everyone's concentration was on your growth and performance as an artist, it wouldn't be unusual for other more essential needs to have gone both unrecognised and unfulfilled.

Dr Rose, I insist upon your accepting what I say: I had good parents. As I've said, my father worked endlessly just to make ends meet. Once it became clear that I had the potential, the talent, and the desire to be . . . let's call it who I am today, my mother went out and found a job as well to help cover all the expenses incurred. And if I didn't see my parents as often as I might have done because of this, I had Raphael with me for hours each day and when he wasn't there, I had Sarah-Jane.

Who was she? you ask.

She was Sarah-Jane Beckett. I don't quite know what to call her, actually. Governess is too anachronistic a term and Sarah-Jane would have sorted you out in fairly short order had you ever called her a governess. So I suppose we'd have to call her my teacher. As I noted earlier, I never attended school once it became apparent that the violin would be my life because regular school hours conflicted with my schedule of lessons. So Sarah-Jane was employed as my teacher. When I wasn't working with Raphael, I was working with her. And because we fitted in lessons where and as we could, she lived with us. In

103

fact, she lived with us for years. She must have arrived when I was five or six—once my parents saw how impossible it was going to be for me to be educated in a traditional fashion—and she stayed until I was sixteen, at which time my education was complete and my schedule of concerts, recordings, rehearsals, and practice periods precluded any further courses of study. But until that point, I had daily lessons with Sarah-Jane.

Was she a surrogate mother? you want to know.

Always, always *it comes back to my mother. Are you looking for Oedipal connections, doctor? How about an unresolved Oedipal complex? Mother trots off to work when son is five, leaving him incapable of laying to rest his unconscious desire to bed her? Then mother disappears when son is eight or nine or ten or however old he was because I do* not *remember nor do I care to, and she is never heard from again.*

I remember, though, her silence. Odd. It's just come to me now. My mother's silence. And I remember waking up one night while she was still with us and finding her lying in bed with me. She's holding me and it's very difficult to breathe because of the way she's holding me. It's difficult because her arms are round me and she's got my head somehow . . . Never mind. I don't remember.

How is she holding you, Gideon?

I don't remember. Just that I can't breathe very well but I can feel her breathing and it's very hot.

Her breath is hot?

No. Just the feeling. Where I am. I want to escape.

From her?

No. Just escape. Run, actually. Of course, this could all be a dream. It was so long ago.

Did it happen more than once? you want to know.

I see where you're heading, and I refuse to pretend that I remember what you seem to want me to remember. The facts are these: My mother is beside me in my bed, I am held by her, it is hot, I smell her perfume. And there's a weight on my cheek as well. I do feel that weight. It's heavy but inert and it smells of perfume. Odd, that I would recall that smell. I couldn't tell you what it was—her perfume, Dr Rose—but I expect that if I ever smelled it again, I would know it at once and it would remind me of Mother.

I expect she was holding you between her breasts, you tell me. That's why you would both feel the weight and smell the perfume. Is it dark in your bedroom or is there a light?

I don't recall. Just the heat, that weight, the scent. And silence.

Have you lain that way with anyone else? With Libby perhaps? Or whoever preceded Libby?

God, no! And this is not about my mother! All right. Yes. Of course *I know that her desertion of me—of us—looms large. I'm not an idiot, Dr Rose. I come home from Austria, my mother is gone, I never see the woman again, never hear her voice, never read so much as a sentence in her handwriting addressed to me . . . Yes, yes, I know the song: This is a Very Big Incident. And since I never heard from her again, I also see the logical connection that I would make as a child: It was my fault. Perhaps I make that connection when I am eight or nine or however old I was when she left, but it is not a connection that I recall making and it's not a connection that I make now. She simply left. End of story.*

What do you mean end of story? you ask.

Just that. We never spoke of her. Or at least I never

105

spoke of her. And if my grandparents and father did, and if Raphael or Sarah-Jane or James the Lodger—

He was still there when she left?

He was there . . . Or was he? No. He couldn't have been. It was Calvin, wasn't it? Didn't I say earlier it was Calvin? Calvin the Lodger trying to phone for help in the midst of Granddad's episode after Mother left us . . . So James had long ago decamped as well.

Decamped, you say. There's a secrecy implied in decamped, you tell me. Was there secrecy behind James the Lodger's leaving?

There is secrecy everywhere. Silence and secrecy. That's how it seems. I walk into a room and a hush falls on it and I know they've been talking about my mother. And I am not allowed to speak of her.

What happens if you do?

I don't know because I never test the rule.

Why not?

The music is central. I have my music. I still have my music. My father, my grandparents, Sarah-Jane, and Raphael. Even Calvin the Lodger. We all have my music.

Is this rule stated? The rule about not asking after your mother? Or is it implied?

It must be . . . I don't know. She's not there to greet us when we return from Austria. She's gone but no one acknowledges that fact. The house has been wiped so clean of her that it's as if she never lived there in the first place. And no one says a word. They don't pretend she's taken a trip somewhere. They don't pretend she's suddenly died. They don't pretend she ran off with another man. They act as if she never existed. And life goes on.

You never asked about her?

I must have known that she was one of the subjects

that we just didn't talk about.

One? There were others?

Perhaps I didn't miss her. I don't actually recall missing her. I don't even remember much about what she looked like. Except that her hair was blonde and she covered it with head scarves, the sort you always see the Queen wearing. But this would have been in church. And yes, I do remember being with her in church. I remember her crying. Crying in church at morning mass with the nuns lined up in the first few pews of that chapel of theirs in Kensington Square. They're on the other side of this rood screen affair, the nuns, except it's not really a rood screen but more like a fence to keep a separation between them and the rest of the public except there's no one else there to be the rest of the public at early morning Mass. There's just Mother and I. And the nuns are in front in those special pews giving responses, and one of them is dressed in that old way, in a habit, but all the rest are done up normally but very plain and with crosses on their chests. And during Mass, my mother kneels, always kneels, with her head resting on her hands. She weeps the whole time. And I don't know what to do.

Why is she weeping? you want to know, of course.

She is always weeping, it seems. And this one nun—the one dressed in the old way—comes up to Mother after communion but before the end of Mass and she takes us both to a sitting room of some kind in the convent next door and there she and Mother talk. They sit in one corner of the room. I am in the other corner, the far corner, where I've been given a book to read and told to sit. I'm impatient to be back home, though, because Raphael's assigned me a set of exercises to master and if I master them to his

107

liking, we're to go to the Festival Hall as a reward. A concert. Ilya Kaler will be performing. He is not yet twenty years old but already he has won the Grand Prize at the Genoa Paganini Competition and I want to hear him because I intend to be far greater than Ilya Kaler.

How old are you? you want to know.

I must be six. Seven at the oldest. And I am impatient to go home. So I leave my corner and I approach my mother and I pull on her sleeve and say, 'Mum. I'm bored,' because that's what I always say, that's how I communicate. Not: I've got to practise, Mum. But: I'm bored and it's your duty as my mother to deal with my boredom. But Sister Cecilia—and yes, that's her name, I've remembered her name!— disengages my hand from my mother's sleeve and leads me back to the corner and says, 'You'll be staying right here till you're called for, Gideon and no nonsense about it' and I'm surprised because no one ever talks to me that way. I'm the prodigy, after all. I am—if there can be degrees of it—more unique than anyone within my universe.

The surprise of being disciplined in such a way and by such a woman in such a costume is perhaps what keeps me in my corner for another few minutes as Sister Cecilia and my mother huddle together at their end of the room. But then I begin kicking at a bookshelf to entertain myself and I kick too hard and books topple to the floor and a statue of the Virgin falls and breaks on the lino. We leave soon afterwards, my mother and I.

I excel at my lesson that morning. Raphael takes me to the concert as he's promised. He's arranged for me to meet Ilya Kaler and I've brought my violin and we play together. Kaler is brilliant, but I know I'll exceed what he has accomplished. Even then, I know this.

    And what happens to your mother? you ask.

    She spends much of her time upstairs.

    In her bedroom?

    No. No. In the nursery.

    In the nursery? Why?

    And I know the answer. I know *the answer. Where has it been for all these years? Why have I suddenly remembered now?*

    My mother's with Sonia.

8 SEPTEMBER

There are gaps, Dr Rose. They exist in my brain like a series of canvases painted by an artist but incomplete and coloured only black.

    Sonia is part of one of those canvases. I remember the fact *of her now: that there was a Sonia, and that she was my younger sister. She died at a very early age. I remember this as well.*

    So that would be why my mother was weeping all those mornings at early Mass. And Sonia's death must have been one of the subjects we did not speak about. To speak about her death would be to bring on a new torrent of Mother's terrible grieving and we wished to spare her that.

    I've been trying to conjure up a picture of Sonia, but nothing is there. Just the black canvas. And when I try to summon her up to take part in a specific memory—Christmas, for instance, or Guy Fawkes Night, or the annual taxi ride with Gran to Fortnum and Mason for a birthday lunch in the Fountain . . . anything . . . anything at all . . . nothing is there. I don't even remember the day that she died. Nor do I recall her funeral. I know just the fact *that she died because suddenly she wasn't there any longer.*

Just like your mother, Gideon? you ask me.

No. This is different. This must *be different because this feels different. And all I know for certain is that she was my sister, that she died young. Then Mother was gone. Whether she left us soon after Sonia died or whether it was months or years later, I couldn't say. But why? Why can't I remember my sister? What happened to her? What do children die of: cancer, leukaemia, cystic fibrosis, scarlet fever, influenza, pneumonia . . . what else?*

This is the second child to die, you point out to me.

What? What do you mean? The second child?

The second child of your father's to die, Gideon. You've told me about Virginia . . . ?

Children die, Dr Rose. That's what happens sometimes. Every day of the week. Children fall ill. Children just die.

CHAPTER THREE

'I don't really see how the caterer managed to cope in here, do you?' Frances Webberly asked. 'Of course, it's quite good enough for us, this kitchen. I can't see that we'd actually use a dishwasher or a microwave even if we had one. But caterers . . . They're used to all the mod cons, aren't they? What a surprise it must have been for the poor woman to arrive and find us living practically in the Middle Ages.'

At the table, Malcolm Webberly made no reply. He'd heard his wife's deliberately cheerful words, but his mind was elsewhere. To deflect a potential conversation that he didn't want to have with anyone, he'd set about polishing his shoes in the kitchen. He assumed that Frances, having known him for more than thirty years and thus being well aware of his aversion to doing two things at once, would see him at this modest industry and leave him to himself.

He very much wanted to *be* left to himself. He'd wanted that from the instant he'd heard Eric Leach say, 'Malc, sorry it's so late, but I've got some news,' and go on to tell him of Eugenie Davies' death. He needed the time alone to sort through his feelings, and while a sleepless night with his wife snoring lightly beside him had given him a number of hours to consider how the words *hit and run* actually affected him, he'd found that all he'd been able to do was to picture Eugenie Davies as he'd last seen her: with the river wind tossing her bright blonde hair. She'd covered that hair with a scarf the moment she'd stepped from her cottage, but during their walk the scarf had loosened and it was while she removed it, refolded it, and replaced it on her head that the wind flicked locks of hair round her shoulders.

Quickly, he'd said to her, 'Why not leave it off? The light in your hair makes you look . . .' What? Beautiful? he'd wondered. But she'd never been a great beauty in all the years that he'd known her. Young? They were both a decade past their prime. He'd supposed the word he wanted was actually *peaceful.* The sunlight in her hair made an aureole round her head, which reminded him of seraphim, which spoke of peace. But as those thoughts came to him, he'd become conscious of the fact that he'd never seen Eugenie Davies truly at peace and that at the moment—despite that trick of the halo created by light and wind—she was not at peace still.

These thoughts in his mind once again, Webberly smeared polish industriously on his shoe. As he did so, he became aware that his wife was still talking to him. '. . . a lovely job, though. But thank heavens it was dark when the poor woman arrived because Lord knows how she would have functioned had she got a good look at our garden.' Frances laughed ruefully. ' "I'm still holding out for my pond and my lilies," I told our Lady Hillier last night. She and Sir David are actually thinking of putting a jacuzzi in their conservatory. Did you know? I told her a conservatory jacuzzi is perfectly well and good if you like that sort of thing, but as for me, a little pond is all I've ever wanted. "And we'll have it someday," I told her. "Malcolm says we'll have it, so we will." Naturally, we'll have to find someone to scythe through the weeds and cart off that old lawn mower out there, but I didn't mention that to our Lady Hillier—'

Your sister Laura, Webberly thought.

'—as she'd hardly understand what I was talking about. She's had that gardener of hers since . . . I don't know how long. But when the time's right and the money's there, you and I will have our little pond, won't we?'

'I expect so,' Webberly said.

Frances eased behind the table in the cramped little kitchen and gazed from the window into the garden. She'd stood there so often in the past ten years that she'd worn a shoe-sized place in the lino, and there were finger grooves in the window sill

112

where she'd spent hours clutching onto the wood. What did she think as she stood there hour after hour every day? her husband wondered. What did she try—and fail—to do? A moment later he had his answer:

'The day looks quite fine,' she told him. 'Radio One claimed there's going to be more rain by this afternoon, but I think they've got it wrong. You know, I believe I'll go out and do some work in the garden this morning.'

Webberly looked up. Frances, apparently feeling his eyes on her, swung round from the window, one hand still on the sill and the other tight on the lapel of her dressing gown. 'I think I can do it today,' she said. 'Malcolm, I think I can do it.'

How many times had she said that before? Webberly wondered. One hundred? One thousand? And always with that same mixture of hope and delusion. She was going to work in the garden, Malcolm, she was going to walk to the shops this afternoon, she would definitely sit on a bench in Prebend Gardens or take Alfie for a romp or try the new beautician that was so well-spoken of . . . so many good and honest intentions coming to naught at the final moment when the front door stood implacably in front of Frances and, try as she might and God knows she tried, she couldn't force her right hand up far enough to grasp onto the knob.

Webberly said, 'Frannie—'

She cut in anxiously. 'It's the party that's made all the difference. Having our friends in . . . being surrounded like that. I feel as right as . . . well, as right as can be.'

Miranda's appearance at the kitchen door saved

Webberly from having to reply. With an 'Ah. Here you are,' she dropped her trumpet case onto the floor along with a weighty rucksack, and she went to the cooker where Alfie—the family's Alsatian mix—was having a lengthy post-party lie in on his blanket. She gave the dog a brisk rub between his ears, which he responded to by rolling over and offering his stomach for her ministrations. She cooperated, pausing to plant a kiss on his head and to accept a wet dog kiss in return.

'Darling, that's terribly unhygienic,' Frances said.

'That's doggy love,' Miranda replied. 'Which, as we know, is the purest kind. Isn't it, Alf?'

Alfie yawned.

Miranda said, over her shoulder to her parents, 'I'm off then. I've two papers to hand in next week.'

'So soon?' Webberly set his shoes to one side. 'We've had you barely forty-eight hours. Cambridge can wait another day, can't it?'

'Duty calls, Dad. Not to mention the odd exam or two. You still want me to try for a first, I take it?'

'Hang on, then. Let me finish with these shoes and I'll drive you up to King's Cross.'

'No need. I'll go by tube.'

'Then I'll run you up to the underground.'

'Dad.' Her voice was a model of patience. They'd walked this path often in her twenty-two years, so she was well-used to its twists and turns. 'I need the exercise. Explain it to him, Mum.'

Webberly protested. 'But if it begins to rain on your way—'

'Heavens, Malcolm, she's not going to melt.'

But they do, Webberly countered, in his mind. They melt, they break, they disappear in an instant. And always when melting, breaking, or

114

disappearing is the very last possibility in your head. Still, he knew the wisdom of compromise in a situation in which two females were beginning to join forces against him. So he said, 'I'll walk a bit with you, then.' And he added, 'Alf needs his morning toddle, Randie,' when Miranda rolled her eyes and looked ready to remonstrate against the idea of a father chaperoning his adult daughter down the street in broad daylight as if she were incapable of using a zebra crossing on her own.

'Mum?' Miranda glanced at her mother for support. Frances said with a regretful shrug, 'You've not taken Alfie yet yourself, have you, darling?'

Miranda surrendered with good-natured exasperation. 'Oh, come along then, you twit. But I'm not waiting for the shoe polish routine to be done.'

'I'll see to the shoes,' Frances said.

Webberly fetched the dog's lead and followed his daughter out of the house. Outside, Alfie rooted an old tennis ball from the shrubbery. He knew the routine when Webberly was on the other end of the lead: It would be a stroll to Prebend Gardens, where his master would unhook the lead from his collar and throw the tennis ball across the grass, whereupon Alfie would dash after it, refuse to return it, and run wildly around for at least quarter of an hour.

'I don't know who has less imagination,' Miranda said as she watched the dog snuffle through the hydrangeas, 'you or the dog. Just look at him, Dad. He *knows* what's up. There's not the least bit of surprise in store for him.'

'Dogs like routine,' Webberly told her as Alfie

emerged triumphant, a hairy old ball in his jaws.

'Dogs, yes. But what about you? Do you *always* take him to the gardens, for God's sake?'

'It's my walking meditation twice a day,' he told her. 'Morning and night. Won't that do?'

'Walking meditation,' she scoffed. 'Dad, you're such a fibber. Really.' They set off to the right once beyond the front gate, following the dog to the end of Palgrave Street, where he made the expected left turn that would take them up to Stamford Brook Road and Prebend Gardens that lay just on the other side of it.

'It was a good party,' Miranda said, linking her arm through her father's. 'Mum seemed to like it. And no one mentioned . . . or wondered . . . at least not to me . . .'

'It was fine,' Webberly said, squeezing his arm to his side to hold her closer. 'Your mother enjoyed herself so much she was talking about working in the garden today.' He felt his daughter looking at him but he kept his own eyes resolutely forward.

Miranda said, 'She won't. You know she won't. Dad, why don't you insist she go back to that doctor? There's help for people like Mum.'

'I can't force her to do more.'

'No. But you could . . .' Miranda sighed. 'I don't know. Something. *Some*thing. I don't understand why you won't take a stand, why you've never taken a stand with Mum.'

'What d'you have in mind?'

'If she thought you meant to . . . well, if you said, "This is it, Frances. I'm at my limit. I want you to go back to that psychiatrist or else."'

'Or else? What?'

He could feel her deflate. 'Yes. That's just it,

116

isn't it? I know you'd never leave her. Well, of course, how could you and live with yourself? But there's got to be something you—we—haven't thought of yet.' And then apparently to spare him from having to answer, she noted that Alfie was eyeing a cat up ahead of them with too much interest. She took the lead from her father and said, 'Don't even *think* of it, Alfred,' with a little jerk.

At the corner, they crossed and there they parted fondly, Miranda heading to the left which would ultimately take her in the direction of Stamford Brook underground station and Webberly striding onward along the green iron railing that formed the east boundary of Prebend Gardens.

Inside the wrought iron gate, Webberly took the dog off his lead and wrested the tennis ball from his jaws. He flung it as far as he could down the length of the green and watched as Alfie raced after it. Once the ball was in the dog's possession, Alfie did his usual: He loped to the far end of the lawn and began to race round the perimeter of the green. Webberly watched his progress from bench to bush to tree to path, but he himself remained where they'd entered, moving only to the paint-chipped black bench a short distance from the notice board on which announcements of coming events in the community were posted.

These he read without actually assimilating them: Christmas fêtes, antiques fairs, and car boot sales. He noted with approval that the phone number of the local police station was prominently displayed and that a committee hoping to organise a Neighbourhood Watch programme was going to assemble in the basement of one of the churches. He saw all this but he couldn't have testified to any of it later. Because although he perceived those six or seven pieces of paper pinned behind the glass of the notice board, and although he went through the motions of reading each one of them, what he actually observed was Frances standing at the kitchen window while his daughter said kindly and with absolute faith in him, *Of course you'd never leave her . . . how could you?* That last especially seemed to reverberate round his skull like an echo with a killing sense of irony. How could you leave her, Malcolm Webberly? Indeed, indeed, how could you leave her?

Leaving Frances had been the last thing on his mind that night he'd got the call to go to Kensington Square. The call had come via the Earl's Court Road station where he was a recently promoted detective inspector with a newly assigned sergeant—Eric Leach—as his partner. Leach did the driving down Kensington High Street, which in those days was moderately less jammed than it tended to be now. Leach was new to the borough, so they overshot the mark and ended up winding through Thackery Street, with its small-village feel so at odds with a huge city, and coming into the square from its southeast end. This put them directly in front of the house they were seeking: a red brick Victorian affair with a white medallion at the gable's peak giving the date of construction: 1879, relatively new in an area where the oldest building had been erected nearly two hundred years earlier.

A panda car, a tandem arrival at the scene along with the ambulance men when the emergency call

118

had first come through, still sat at the kerb although its lights were no longer flashing. The ambulance men themselves were long since gone as were the neighbours who had doubtless assembled as neighbours will do when sirens scream into a residential area.

Webberly shoved open his door and walked to the house, where a low brick wall surmounted by black wrought iron fenced in a flag stone area with a central planter. An ornamental cherry tree grew there, and at that time of year it created a roseate blossom pool on the ground.

The front door was closed, but someone inside must have been waiting for them because no sooner had Webberly put his foot on the bottom step than the door swung open and the uniformed constable who'd placed the call to the station admitted them into the house. He looked shaken. This was his first call to a child's death, he told them. He'd arrived in the wake of the ambulance.

'Two years old,' he informed them in a hollow voice. 'Dad's been giving her kiss of life and the medics tried everything they could.' He shook his head, looking stricken. 'No chance. She was gone. Sorry, sir. I've a baby at home. Makes you think . . .'

'Right,' Webberly said. 'It's okay, son. I've a little one myself.' He needed no reminding how fleeting life was, how vigilant a parent needed to be against anything that might snuff that life out. His own Miranda had just turned two.

'Where'd it happen?' Webberly asked.

'In the bath. Upstairs. But don't you want to talk to . . . ? The family're in the drawing room.'

Webberly didn't need a young PC to tell him his

119

business, but the boy was rattled, so there was no point sorting him out right then. He looked at Leach instead. 'Tell them we'll be with them shortly. Then . . .' He jerked his head towards the stairs. He said to the constable, 'Show me,' and he followed him up a staircase that curved round an ornate oak plant stand from which an enormous fern drooped fronds towards the floor.

The nursery bathroom was on the second floor of the house along with the nursery, a loo, and another bedroom that was occupied by the other child in the family. The parents and grandparents had rooms just below on the first floor. The top floor was occupied by the nanny, a lodger, and a woman who . . . well, the constable supposed she'd be called a governess although the family didn't call her that.

'She teaches the children,' the constable said. 'Well, perhaps just the older one, I expect.'

Webberly raised his eyebrows at the oddity of a governess in this day and age, and he went into the bathroom where the tragedy had occurred. Leach joined him there, his duty done in the drawing room below. The constable returned to his post by the front door.

The two detectives surveyed the bathroom somberly. It was a mundane location for sudden death to make its mark. And yet it happened so often that Webberly wondered when people would finally learn not to leave a child unattended for even a second when it came to so much as an inch of water anywhere.

There was more than an inch of water in the tub, however. At least ten inches remained inside, cool now and with a plastic boat and five yellow ducklings floating motionless on its surface. A bar of soap rested on the bottom near the drain, and a stainless steel bath tray with worn rubber ends bridged the width of the tub and held a limp flannel, a comb, and a sponge. All of it looked perfectly normal. But there was also an indication that both panic and tragedy had been recent visitors to the room.

To one side, a towel rack lay overturned on the floor. A soaked bath mat was crumpled beneath a wash basin. A rattan wastepaper basket had been caved in. And across the white tiles were the footprints of the paramedics whose last concern would have been to keep the room neat and tidy as they attempted to revive a child.

Webberly could picture the scene as if he'd been there because he *had* been there before while on uniformed patrol: no panic among the medics but rather intense and what seemed like inhumanly impersonal calm; checks for pulse and respiration, for reaction from the pupils, the immediate initiation of CPR. They would know she was dead within moments but they would not say those words to anyone because their job was life, life at any cost, life at every cost, and they would work upon the child and whisk her from the house and continue to work upon her all the way to the hospital because there was always the chance that life could be wrung from the limp tatter that remained when the spirit left the body.

Webberly squatted by the wastepaper basket and used a pen to right it, having a look inside. Six crumpled tissues, perhaps half a yard of dental floss, a flattened tube of toothpaste. He said to Leach, 'Check the medicine cabinet, Eric,' while he

121

himself went back to the tub and looked long and hard round its sides, round its taps and its spigot, along the grout that edged it, and into its water. Nothing.

Leach said, 'Baby aspirin in here, cough syrup, some prescriptions. Five of them, sir.'

'For who?'

'Made out for Sonia Davies.'

'Note them all, then. Seal off the room. I'll speak to the family.'

But it was more than the family he met in the drawing room because more than the family lived in the house, and more than only the house's inhabitants had been present when the tragedy supervened in their evening rituals. Indeed, the drawing room seemed to be bursting with people although there were but nine individuals present: eight adults and a small boy with an appealing fall of white blond hair across his forehead. Chalky-faced, he stood in the protective circle of the arm of an old man who was, presumably, his grandfather and whose necktie—a souvenir of some college or club by the look of it—the boy grasped and twisted in his fingers.

No one spoke. They looked in shock, and they seemed to be grouped to offer each other what support they could. Most of this was being directed at the mother, who was sitting in one corner of the room, a woman in her thirties like Webberly himself, but whey of complexion with large eyes that were haunted and seeing again and again what no mother ever ought to see: her child's limp body in the hands of strangers who fought to save her.

When Webberly introduced himself, one of the two men who were hovering near the mother rose and said he was Richard Davies, the father of the child who'd been taken to hospital. The use of the euphemism was clear when he gave a glance in the direction of the little boy, his son. Wisely, he didn't wish to speak of the other child's death in front of her brother. He said, 'We were at the hospital. My wife and I. They told us—'

At this a young woman—seated on a sofa accompanied by a man of her own age with his arm round her shoulders—began to cry. It was a horrible, guttural weeping that grew to the sort of sobs that lead to hysteria. 'I do not *leave* her,' she keened, and even through her lamentation Webberly could hear her heavy German accent. 'I swear to God almighty that I do not leave her for even a minute.'

Which begged the question of how she had died, of course.

They all needed to be interviewed, but not simultaneously. Webberly said to the German girl, 'You were responsible for the child?'

At which the mother said, 'I brought this down upon us.'

'Eugenie!' Richard Davies cried, and the other man who'd been hovering over her, his face shining with a patina of sweat, said, 'Don't *talk* like that, Eugenie.'

The grandfather said, 'We all know who's at fault.'

The German girl wailed, 'No! No! No! I do not leave her!' while her companion held her and said, 'It's *okay*,' which it patently was not.

Two people said nothing: an elderly woman who kept her eyes glued onto Granddad and a tomato-haired woman in a neat pleated skirt who watched

123

the German girl with undisguised dislike.

Too many people, too much emotion, growing confusion. Webberly told them all to disperse, save the parents. Remain in the house, he directed them. And someone stay with the little boy.

'I'll do that,' Tomato-hair said, obviously the 'governess' about whom the young PC had spoken. 'Come along, Gideon. Let's have a look at your maths.'

'But I'm to practise,' the boy said, looking earnestly from one adult to another. 'Raphael did tell me—'

'Gideon, it's all right. Go with Sarah-Jane.' The sweat-faced man left the mother's side, going to squat before the little boy. 'You're not to worry about your music just now. Go with Sarah-Jane, all right?'

'Come along, lad.' Grandfather stood, the little boy in his arms. The rest of the group followed him from the room till only the parents of the dead child remained.

Even now in the garden in Stamford Brook, with Alfie barking at the birds and chasing the squirrels and waiting for his master to call him back to the lead, Webberly could see Eugenie Davies as she had been on that long ago evening.

Dressed simply in grey trousers and a pale blue blouse, she didn't move an inch. She didn't look at him or at her husband. She only said, 'Oh my God. What's to become of us?' And even then she spoke to herself, not to the men.

Her husband said, but rather to Webberly and not in answer to her, 'We went to the hospital. There was nothing they could do. They didn't tell us that here. At the house. They didn't tell us.'

'No,' Webberly said. 'That's not their job. They leave that to the doctors.'

'But they knew. While they were here. They knew then, didn't they?'

'I expect so. I'm sorry.'

Neither of them wept. They would, later, when they realised that the nightmare they were currently experiencing was no nightmare at all but rather an extended reality that would colour what remained of their lives. But at the moment, they were dull with trauma: the initial panic, the crisis of frantic intervention, the invasion of strangers into their home, the agonising wait in a casualty ward, the approach of a doctor whose expression undoubtedly had said it all.

'They talked about releasing her later. The . . . her body,' Richard Davies said. 'He said we couldn't take her, couldn't make any arrangements . . . Why?'

Eugenie's head lowered. A tear dropped onto her folded hands.

Webberly drew a chair over so that he was on the same level as Eugenie and he nodded to Richard Davies to sit as well, which he did, next to his wife whose hand he took. Webberly explained to them as best he could: When an unexpected death occurred, when someone died who was not under the care of a physician who could sign a death certificate, when someone died in an accident— like a drowning—then a post mortem examination was required by law.

Eugenie looked up. 'Are you saying they'll cut her up? Cut her open?'

Webberly skirted the question by saying, 'They'll determine the exact cause of her death.'

'But we know the cause,' Richard Davies said. 'She . . . My God, she was in the bath. And then there was shouting, the women screaming. I ran upstairs and James came tearing down from—'

'James?'

'He lodges with us. He was in his room. He came running.'

'Where was everyone else?'

Richard looked to his wife for some sort of answer. She shook her head, saying only, 'Mother Davies and I were in the kitchen, starting dinner. It was Sonia's bath time and . . .' She hesitated, as if saying her daughter's name made more real what she could not bear to think about.

'And you don't know where everyone else was?'

Richard Davies spoke. 'Dad and I were in his sitting room. We were watching that . . . God, that infernal, stupid football game. We were actually watching *football* while Sosy was drowning upstairs.'

It seemed the diminutive form of their daughter's name was what broke Eugenie. She finally began to weep in earnest.

Richard Davies, caught up in his own grief and despair, didn't take his wife into his arms as Webberly would have had him do. He merely said her name, telling her uselessly that it was all right, that the baby was with God who loved her as much as they did. And Eugenie herself above all people knew that, didn't she, she whose faith in God and God's goodness was absolute?

Cold comfort, that, Webberly thought. He said, 'I'll want to talk to everyone else, Mr and Mrs Davies.' And then to Richard Davies alone, 'She might need a doctor,' in reference to his wife.

'Better phone him.'

The drawing room door opened as he spoke and DS Leach entered. He nodded to indicate he'd completed his list and sealed the bathroom off, and Webberly told him to set up the drawing room to conduct interviews with the residents of the house.

'Thank you for helping us, Inspector,' Eugenie said.

Thank you for helping us. Webberly thought about those words now as he lumbered to his feet. How curious it was that five simple words spoken in such a wretched voice had actually managed to transform his life: from detective to knight errant in the space of a single second.

It was because of the kind of mother she was, he told himself now as he called to Alfie. The kind of mother that Frances—God forgive her—could never have hoped to be. How could anyone help admiring that? How could any man help wanting to be of service to such a mother?

'Alfie, come!' he shouted as the Alsatian loped after a terrier with a Frisbee in his mouth. 'Home. Come. We won't use the lead.'

As if the dog actually understood this last promise, he dashed back to Webberly. He'd had an excellent run this morning, if his heaving sides and his dangling tongue were any indication. Webberly nodded towards the gate and the dog walked to it and sat obediently, eyes on Webberly's pockets for a treat to reward him for such a display of good manners.

'You'll have to wait till we get home,' Webberly told him and afterwards considered his own words.

Indeed, that's the way life played out, didn't it? At the end of the day and for too many years, everything that mattered in Webberly's sorry little world had found itself put off till he got home.

*   *   *

Lynley noted that Helen hadn't taken more than a mouthful of tea. She'd changed her position in bed, however, and she was observing him make a mess of his tie while he was watching her in the mirror.

'So she's someone Malcolm Webberly knew?' Helen asked. 'How dreadful for him, Tommy. And on his anniversary night.'

'I wouldn't go so far as to say he knew her,' Lynley replied. 'She was one of the principals in the first case he ran as a DI over in Kensington.'

'That would have been years ago, then. It must have made an enormous impression on him.'

'I dare say it did.' Lynley didn't want to tell her why. Indeed, he didn't want to tell her anything else about that long ago death that Webberly had investigated. The drowning of a child was horrific enough to contemplate under any circumstances, but under these newly changed circumstances in their lives, it seemed to Lynley that a certain amount of discretion and delicacy was going to be in order now that his wife was carrying a child of her own.

A child of *our* own, he corrected his thinking, a child to whom no harm would ever come. So elaborating on the harm that had befallen another child seemed like tempting fate. At least that was what Lynley told himself as he went about the rituals of dressing.

In bed, Helen turned on her side, away from him, her knees drawn up and an extra pillow bunched into her stomach. 'Oh Lord,' she moaned.

Lynley went to her, sat on the edge of the bed, and smoothed her chestnut hair. 'You've not touched much of your tea,' he said. 'Would you like something different this morning?'

'I'd like to stop feeling so wretched.'

'What does the doctor say?'

'She's a fount of wisdom on that front: "I spent the first four months of every pregnancy embracing the bowl of the loo. It'll pass, Mrs Lynley. It always does."'

'Till then?'

'Think positive thoughts, I suppose. Just don't make them of food.'

Lynley studied her fondly: the curve of her cheek and the way her ear lay like a perfect shell against her head. There was a greenish cast to her skin, though, and the way she was clutching onto the pillow suggested another round of sickness was fast on its way. He said, 'I wish I could do this for you, Helen.'

She laughed weakly. 'That's just the sort of thing men say out of guilt when they know very well that the last thing on earth they would *ever* choose to do is to have a baby for anyone.' She reached for his hand. 'I do appreciate the thought, though. Are you off, then? You will have breakfast, won't you, Tommy?'

He assured her that he would have a meal. Indeed, he knew there was no escape from it. If Helen wasn't insisting upon his eating, then Charlie Denton—manservant, housekeeper, cook, valet, aspiring thespian, unrepentant Don Juan, or whatever else he was choosing to call himself on a given day—would bar the door until Lynley had downed a plate of something.

'What about you?' he asked his wife. 'What d'you have on? Are you working today?'

'Frankly, I wish not, because I'd like to remain immobile for the next thirty-two weeks.'

'Shall I phone Simon, then?'

'No. He's got that acrylamide business to sort out. They need it in two days.'

'Yes, I see. But does he need you?' Simon Allcourt-St James was a forensic scientist, an expert witness whose specialities took him into the witness box regularly to confirm the Crown Prosecution's evidence or to bolster the position of the defence. In this particular instance, he was working on a civil case in which the litigation involved determining how much acrylamide— absorbed through the skin—constituted a toxic dose.

'I like to think so,' she replied. 'And anyway . . .' She gazed at him, a smile curving her mouth. 'I'd like to tell him our news. I told Barbara last night, by the way.'

'Ah.'

'*Ah?* Tommy, what's that supposed to mean?'

Lynley rose from the bed. He went to the wardrobe where the mirrored door illustrated the disaster he'd created with his tie. He unknotted it and began again. 'You did tell Barbara that no one else knows, didn't you, Helen?'

Across from him, she struggled to sit up. The movement cost her, however, and she quickly sank back. 'I told her that, yes. But now that she knows, I think we may as well tell—'

'I'd rather not just yet.' The tie looked worse than the first time round. Lynley gave up on the

130

effort, blamed it on the material, and fetched another. He was aware that Helen was watching him, and he knew she expected some very sound reasoning behind his decision. He said, 'Superstition, darling. If we keep it to ourselves, there's less chance something might go wrong. It's silly, I know. But there you have it. I hadn't thought to tell anyone till . . . well, I guess till it took.'

'Till it took.' She repeated the phrase thoughtfully. 'Are you worried, then?'

'Yes. Worried. Terrified. Nervous. Apprehensive. Preoccupied. And frequently incoherent. That's about it.'

She smiled gently. 'I love you, darling.'

And that smile asked for a further admission. He owed her that much. 'There's also Deborah to consider,' Lynley said. 'Simon'll be able to cope with the news, but it's going to hurt Deborah like the devil when you tell her you're pregnant.'

Deborah was Simon's wife, a young woman with so many miscarriages to her name that it seemed like a deliberate act of cruelty to mention a successful pregnancy in her hearing. Not that she wouldn't feign joy for the couple. Not that she wouldn't *feel* that joy at some level. But at a deeper level where her own hopes lay, she would feel the hot brand of failure scorch the skin of dreams, and that skin had been scorched enough times already.

'Tommy,' Helen said kindly, 'Deborah's going to find out eventually. How much more hurtful is it going to be if she suddenly realises I've switched to maternity clothes without mentioning the fact that we're having a baby? She'll know *why* we haven't told her at that point. Don't you think that will hurt her even more?'

'I'm not suggesting we let it go that long,' Lynley said. 'Just for a while, Helen. For luck, actually, more than for Deborah. Will you do this for me?'

Helen studied him as he'd studied her. He felt himself chafing under her scrutiny, but he didn't turn from it, waiting for her answer. She said, 'Are you happy about this baby, darling? Are you truly happy?'

'Helen, I'm delighted.'

But even as he spoke, Lynley wondered why he did not feel that way. He wondered why what he actually felt was a duty he'd long left undone.

CHAPTER FOUR

Jill Foster was grunting through the final series of pelvic tilts with her antenatal trainer counting them when Richard came into the flat. He looked more haggard than she'd expected, and she didn't like the way this made her feel. He'd been divorced from Eugenie for sixteen years. As far as she could see, the identification of his former wife's body should merely be an inconvenient exercise undertaken as a helpful member of society doing his duty to assist the police.

Gladys, the antenatal trainer whom Jill had come to think of as a cross between an Olympic athlete and a fitness Nazi, said, 'Ten more, Jill. Come along, now. You'll thank me when you're in labour, luv.'

Jill grunted, 'Can't.'

'Nonsense. Take your mind off exhaustion. Think of that dress instead. You'll thank me at the end of the day. Do ten more.'

The dress in question was a wedding gown, a Knightsbridge creation that had cost a small fortune and that hung from the sitting room door, where Jill had placed it to give her inspiration when the hungries came upon her and when the fitness Nazi was taking her through her sweating, miserable, and embarrassing paces. 'I'm sending you Gladys Smiley, darling,' Jill's mother had announced upon being told of the grandchild to come. 'She's the best antenatal specialist in the south and that's including London, mind you. She's generally booked up, but she'll fit you in for me. Exercise is crucial. Exercise and diet, of course.'

Jill had cooperated with her mother, not because Dora Foster *was* her mother but because she'd delivered five hundred babies at five hundred successful home births. So she knew what she was talking about.

Gladys counted down from ten. Jill was sweating like a race horse and feeling like a sow, but she managed a glowing smile for Richard. He'd argued against what he'd called 'the unique absurdity' of Gladys Smiley from the first, and he was still standing firm against the idea of Dora Foster delivering her first granddaughter at the family home in Wiltshire. But since Jill had compromised on the wedding—agreeing to the more modern approach of postnatal connubiality rather than what she would have preferred: engagement, marriage, and childbirth in that order—she knew that Richard was ultimately going to have to give in to her desires. *She* was the one giving birth, after all. And if she wanted her mother to deliver her— her mother with thirty years of experience doing

133

just that—then that's the way it was going to be. 'You're not my husband yet, darling,' Jill informed him pleasantly each time he protested. 'I haven't yet said a word in front of anyone about loving, honouring, and obeying you.'

She had him there, and she knew it. So did he. Which was why she was going to have her way in the end.

'Four . . . three . . . two . . . one . . . Yes!' Gladys cried. 'Excellent work. You keep this up and that little one'll slide right out of you. See if she doesn't.' She handed Jill a towel and nodded at Richard, where he stood in the doorway, looking grey round the mouth. 'Settled on a name, then, have you?'

'Catherine Ann,' Jill said firmly as Richard said just as firmly, 'Cara Ann.'

Gladys looked from one to the other, saying, 'Yes. Well. Keep up the good work, Jilly. I'll see you day after tomorrow, yes? Same time?'

'Hmm.' Jill remained on the floor as Richard saw Gladys out of the flat. She was still there— feeling like a beached whale—when he came back into the sitting room. She said, 'Darling, there is no way on earth that I'm naming a child Cara. I'd be the laughing stock of every one of my friends. Cara indeed. Honestly, Richard. She's a child, not a character in a romance novel.'

In the normal course of events, he'd have argued. He'd have said, 'Catherine is far too ordinary, so if it's not to be Cara, then it's not to be Catherine, and we'll have to compromise on something else.'

Which was what they'd been doing since the day that they'd met when she'd found herself going

134

head to head with the man during a documentary the BBC had been filming about his son. 'You may speak to Gideon about his music,' Richard Davies had informed her during the contract negotiations. 'You may question him about the violin. But my son does not discuss his personal life or his history with the media, and I insist upon making that perfectly clear.'

Because he doesn't *have* a personal life, Jill thought now. And what went for his history could have been summed up in four syllables: the violin. Gideon was music and music was Gideon. So it had been and always would be.

Richard, on the other hand, was electricity itself. She'd liked matching wits and battling wills with him. She'd found that appealing and sexy, despite the enormous gap in their ages. Arguing with a man was such an aphrodisiac. And so few men in Jill's life were actually *willing* to argue. Especially English men, who generally decomposed into passive-aggression at the first sign of a row.

Arguing, however, was not what Richard had in mind at the moment: arguing about the name of their daughter, the location of the freehold they had yet to purchase, the choice of wallpaper once that freehold was theirs, or the size and the date of their future wedding. All those had been subjects of past rows between them, but she could see he hadn't the heart for a heated discussion now.

His colourless face was an advertisement for what he'd undergone in the past few hours, and despite the fact that his clinging to the idea of Cara was rather more maddening than she'd anticipated it might be when he first suggested the name five months ago, Jill wanted to appear sympathetic to

135

his recent experiences. No matter that she felt like saying, 'What on *earth's* wrong? For God's sake, Richard, the beastly woman walked out on you nearly twenty years ago.' She knew the wisdom of saying instead, 'Was it bad, darling? Are you quite all right?' in the gentlest of tones.

Richard went to the sofa and sat, his scoliosis looking worse for the dejection that drooped his shoulders. He said, 'I couldn't tell them.'

She frowned. Couldn't tell them . . .? 'What, darling?'

'Eugenie. I couldn't tell them if the woman was actually Eugenie.'

'Oh.' In a small voice. Then, 'She'd changed that much? Well, I suppose it's not that odd, is it, Richard? So long since you've seen her. And perhaps she's had a rough time . . .'

He shook his head. He dug two fingers into his eyebrows and rubbed. 'It isn't that, although I couldn't have told them even if it was.'

'Then what?'

'She was hit quite badly. They wouldn't say exactly what happened, even if they knew. But she looked as if a lorry had run over her. She was . . . she was mangled, Jill.'

'My God.' Jill struggled into a sitting position. She put a supportive hand on his knee. This *was* something to go all grey in the face about. 'Richard, I'm so terribly sorry. What an ordeal for you.'

'They showed me a Polaroid first, which was good of them. But when I couldn't identify her from that, they showed me her body. They asked if there were distinguishing marks somewhere on her that might identify her. But I couldn't remember.'

136

His voice was dull, like an old copper coin. 'All I could tell them was the name of her dentist twenty years ago and think of that, Jill. I could remember the name of her dentist but not if she had a birthmark somewhere that might tell the police that she is—that she was—Eugenie, my wife.'

Former wife, Jill wanted to add. Deserting wife. Wife who selfishly left behind a child whom you raised to adulthood alone. *Alone*, Richard. Let's not forget that.

'But I could remember the name of her bloody dentist,' he was saying. 'And only because he's mine as well.'

'What will they do?'

'Use the x-rays to make sure it's Eugenie.'

'What do you think?'

He looked up. He seemed so tired. With an unaccustomed sense of guilt, Jill thought of how little sleep he was managing to get on her sofa and how kind and solicitous it was of him to stay the nights with her now when her time was drawing near. Since Richard had already had two children—although only one of them was actually still alive—Jill hadn't honestly expected him to be as lovingly concerned for her welfare as he'd been during most of the pregnancy. But from the moment her stomach had started to swell and her breasts had begun to grow heavier, he'd treated her with a tenderness she'd found rather poignant. It served to open her heart to him and to bind them more closely together. This unit they were forming was something she warmed to. It's what she'd longed for and dreamed of having and despaired of finding among men her own age.

'What I think,' Richard said in answer to her

137

question, 'is that the likelihood of Eugenie's having had the same dentist since our marriage ended—'

Since she deserted you, Jill corrected him silently.

'—is fairly remote.'

'I still don't understand how they connected you with her. And how they tracked you down.'

Richard stirred on the sofa. In front of him on the large plump ottoman that served as a coffee table, he fingered the latest copy of *Radio Times.* Its cover featured a toothy American actress who'd agreed to simulate what would undoubtably be a wildly imperfect English accent so she could play the part of Jane Eyre in yet another resurrection of that eponymous and utterly implausible Victorian melodrama. Jane Eyre indeed, Jill thought with a scoff, she who fostered within the soft brains of more than one hundred years of mentally pliable female readers the nonsensical belief that a man with a past as dark as licorice could be elevated by the love of a decent woman. What utter nonsense.

Richard wasn't answering. Jill said, 'Richard, I don't understand. How did they connect you with Eugenie? I realise she must have kept your surname, but Davies isn't so uncommon that one would make the leap that you and she had once been married.'

'One of the police on the scene,' Richard said. 'He knew who she was. Because of the case . . .' He aimlessly shifted the copy of *Radio Times* so that the one beneath it was on top. This one pictured Jill herself in modern garb among the costumed cast of her triumphant production of *Desperate Remedies,* filmed within weeks of Jill's final breakup with Jonathon Stewart, whose passionate vows to leave his wife 'once our Steph has finished up at Oxford, darling' had proved to be just about as steadfast as his performance in bed had been reliable. Two weeks after 'our Steph' had her diploma in her grubby little grasp, Jonathon was making another excuse which involved settling the wretched girl 'in her new digs up in Lancaster, darling'. Three days later Jill had pulled the plug on their relationship and buried herself in *Desperate Remedies,* whose title couldn't have been more appropriate to her emotional state at the time.

Jill said, 'The case?' and a moment later realised what case he was speaking about. *The* case, of course, the only one that mattered. The case that had broken his heart, destroyed his marriage, and coloured the last two decades of his life. She said, 'Yes, I suppose the police might remember.'

'He was involved. One of the detectives. So when he saw her name on her driving licence, he tracked me down.'

'Yes. I see.' She half-rolled into a kneeling position from which she was able to touch his curved shoulder. 'Let me make you something. Tea, coffee.'

'I could do with a brandy.'

She lifted an eyebrow although since he was looking at the magazine cover and not at her, he didn't see the action. She wanted to say, At this hour? Surely not, darling. But she heaved herself to her feet and went to the kitchen where she took a bottle of Courvoisier from one of the sleek cupboards and poured him an exact two tablespoons, which seemed an adequate amount to restore him.

He joined her in the kitchen and took the glass without comment. He drank a sip and swirled the remaining liquid in the glass. He said, 'I can't get the sight of her out of my mind.'

This seemed too much to Jill. All right, the woman was dead. And yes, she'd died in a dreadful way, with much to be pitied. Indeed, it was a grim affair, having to look upon her broken body. But Richard hadn't had a single word from his former wife in nearly two decades, so why would he be so distraught at her death? Unless he was still carrying a torch for her . . . Unless, perhaps, he'd not been quite truthful about the death of their marriage and what he'd done with the corpse.

Jill said with care and placing a loving hand on his forearm, 'I know this must be a terrible time for you. But you've not actually . . . seen her in all these years, have you?'

A flicker in his eyes. Of their own accord, her fingers tightened. Don't make this into a Jonathon situation, she told him silently. Lie to me now, and I will end this, Richard. I will not live in a fantasy again.

He said, 'No, I've not seen her. But I've spoken to her recently. A number of times in the last month or so.' He seemed to feel the shield she put up to protect her heart from damage at this piece of news because he went on quickly. 'She phoned me because of Gideon. She'd read about what happened at Wigmore Hall. When he didn't recover from that . . . situation . . . quickly, she phoned to ask me about him. I haven't told you because . . . I don't actually know *why* I haven't told you. It didn't seem very important at the time. And beyond that, I didn't want anything to upset you in these final weeks . . . the baby. It hardly seemed fair to you.'

'That's completely outrageous.' Jill felt a swelling of righteous anger.

Richard said, 'I'm sorry. We spoke for only five minutes . . . ten minutes at the most each time she phoned. I didn't consider—'

'I don't mean that,' Jill interrupted. 'I don't mean it's outrageous that you didn't tell me. But that she phoned you at all. That she had the audacity to phone you, Richard. That she could walk out of your life—out of *Gideon's* life, for God's sake—and then phone up when she reads about him because she's curious that he's had a bit of trouble at a performance. My *God,* what cheek.'

Richard said nothing in reply to this. He merely swirled the brandy round in his glass and observed the thin patina it left on the sides. There was something more here, Jill concluded. She said, 'Richard? What is it? There's something you're not telling me, isn't there?' And she felt once again a basic shutting down when confronted with the idea that a man with whom she was so intimately involved might not be as forthcoming as she required of him. Odd, she thought, how one humiliating and disastrous relationship had the potential to affect every involvement that followed it. 'Richard? Tell me. Is there something more?'

'Gideon,' Richard said. 'I didn't tell him that she'd been phoning me about him. I didn't know *what* to tell him, Jill. It's not as if she was asking to see him because she wasn't asking to see him at all. So what would have been the point? But now she's dead and he's got to be told about that and I'm terrified that hearing it is going to make him take a

141

turn for the worse.'

'Yes. I can see how it could.'

' "Is he well?" she wanted to know, Jill. "Why isn't he playing, Richard?" she asked. "How many concert engagements has he actually broken? And why? Why?" '

'What was she after?'

'She must have phoned me a dozen times in the last two weeks alone,' Richard said. 'There she was, this voice from the past which I thought I'd *bloody* well recovered from and—' He stopped himself.

Jill felt the chill. It started from her ankles and swept up quickly to close round her heart. She said carefully, 'Thought you'd recovered?' and tried to stop herself from thinking what she couldn't bear to think but the words ricocheted round her head anyway: He still loves her. She walked out on him. She disappeared from his life. But he continued to love her. He climbed into my bed. He joined his body to mine. But all the time he was loving Eugenie.

No wonder he'd never remarried. The only question was: Why was he remarrying now?

The damn man read her mind. Or perhaps her face. Or maybe he felt the chill as well since he said, 'Because it took me that much time to find you, Jill. Because I love you. Because at my age, I never expected to love again. And every morning when I awake, even on that miserable sofa of yours, I thank God for the miracle that you love me. Eugenie is a distant part of my past. Let's not make her part of our future.'

And the truth of it was, as Jill knew well, that they both had pasts. They were not adolescents, so neither of them could expect the other to come into their new life unburdened. The future was what was important, at the end of the day. Their future and the future of the baby. Catherine Anne.

*   *   *

Henley-on-Thames was easily accessible from London, especially when the morning commute along the M40 created tailbacks that extended in the opposite direction only. So DI Thomas Lynley and DC Barbara Havers were rolling south in the direction of Henley from Marlow just under an hour after having left Eric Leach's incident room in Hampstead.

DCI Leach, fighting off either a head cold or flu, had introduced them to a squad of detectives who, while slightly leery of the presence of New Scotland Yard among them, also seemed willing to accept their participation in a work load that currently included a series of rapes on Hampstead Heath and an arson in the Grade II listed cottage of an ageing actress of both title and considerable reputation.

Leach detailed the preliminary findings from the post mortem examination first, pending blood, tissue, and organ analysis, and they amounted to a multitude of injuries on a body that had ultimately been identified through dental records as belonging to one Eugenie Davies, aged sixty-two. First came the fractures she had sustained: the fourth and fifth cervical vertebrae, the left femur, ulna, and radius, the right clavicle, and the fifth and sixth ribs. Then came the internal ruptures: liver, spleen, and kidneys. The cause of death had been determined as massive internal haemorrhaging and shock, and the time had been set between ten o'clock and midnight. An evaluation of trace evidence on the body would be forthcoming.

'She was thrown about fifty feet,' Leach told the detectives assembled in the incident room as they stood among the computers, the china boards, the filing cabinets, the copy machines, and the photographs. 'According to forensic she was then driven over at least twice, possibly three times, as indicated by contusions on the body and markings left on her mac.'

A general murmur greeted this remark. Someone said, 'Nice neighbourhood, that' with heavy irony.

Leach corrected the DC's misapprehension. 'We're assuming a single car, not three, did the damage, McKnight. We'll maintain that position till we hear otherwise from Lambeth. One hit from the vehicle put her flat out on the pavement. Then once over her, once in reverse, and back again.'

Leach indicated several pictures on the china board before he went on. They depicted the street as it had been in the aftermath of the hit and run. He gestured to one in particular showing a section of tarmac photographed between two orange traffic cones with a line of cars along the pavement in the background. 'The point of impact appeared to be here,' he said. 'And the body landed here, square in the centre of the road.' Another set of traffic cones, plus a large rectangle of the street taped off. 'The rain took care of some of the blood that would have been where the body landed. But it wasn't raining hard enough to carry away all the blood from the site or the tissue and bone fragments either. However, the body's not where the tissue and bone are. Instead, it's over here next to this Vauxhall at the kerb. And notice how she's tucked a bit under it? We reckon that our driver, having knocked her down and having done his bit of back and forthing over her body, then got out of his car, dragged the woman to one side, and drove off.'

'She couldn't have been dragged beneath a set of wheels? Lorry, perhaps?' The question came from a DC who was noisily eating from a cup of instant noodles. 'Why rule that out?'

'Nature of what few tyre marks we've got,' Leach informed him, reaching for his coffee, which he'd left on a nearby desk heaped with files and computer print-outs. He was more loosely strung than Lynley had expected upon their first introduction not forty minutes earlier in his office. Lynley took this as a good sign of what it was going to be like working with the DCI.

'But why not three cars, sir?' one of the other DCs asked. 'The first knocks her down, drives off in a panic. She's wearing black so the next two don't even see her lying in the road and run over her before they know what's happened.'

Leach took a gulp of coffee and shook his head. 'You won't find anyone giving you good odds on our having three conscienceless citizens all in the same neighbourhood on the same night running over the same body and not one of them reporting it. And nothing in your scenario explains how the hell she ended up part way under that Vauxhall. Only one explanation does that, Potashnik, and it's why we're the ones looking at the situation.'

There was a murmur of agreement at this.

'I'd put good money on the bloke who reported

145

it being the driver we're looking for,' someone from the back of the room called out.

'Pitchley pulled in a brief and put in the plug straightaway,' Leach acknowledged, 'and that bears the stench of manure, you're right. But I don't think we've heard the last from him, and that car of his is going to be what unseals his lips, make no mistake.'

'Pinch a bloke's Boxster and he'll sing "God Save the Queen" on demand,' a DC at the front pointed out.

'That's what I'm relying on,' Leach agreed. 'I'm not saying he's the driver who did her in in the first place, and I'm not saying he's not. But no matter which way the wind's blowing, he won't be getting that Porsche off us till we know why the dead woman had his address on her. If it takes holding the Porsche to shake the information from him, then holding the Porsche and going over it six times with granny's Hoover is exactly what's going to happen. Now . . .'

Leach went on to make the action assignments, most of which put his team into the street where the hit and run had occurred. It was lined with houses—some conversions and some individual homes—and the DCs were to get a statement from everyone in the area about what had been seen, heard, smelled, or dreamed about on the previous night. His directions allocated other DCs to dog the forensic lab: some of them monitoring the progress made on the examination of Eugenie Davies' car, others given the responsibility for pulling together all the information regarding trace evidence on the woman's body, still others matching the trace evidence from the body to the

Boxster that the police had impounded. This same group would be evaluating all tyre prints left in the West Hampstead street and on Eugenie Davies' body and her clothes. A final group of constables— the largest—was assigned to search for a car with damage to its front end. 'Body shops, car parks, car hire firms, streets, mewses, and lay-bys on the motorway,' Leach informed them. 'You don't run down a woman in the street and drive away with no damage.'

'That does put the Boxster out of the running,' a female DC noted.

'Possession of the Boxster's how we prise information from our man,' Leach said. 'But there's no telling if—and where—this bloke Pitchley might have himself another car stowed away. And we'd be wise not to forget that.'

The meeting concluded, Leach met with Lynley and Havers privately in his office. As their superior officer of record, he gave Lynley and Havers instructions in a manner that suggested more than mere homicide—if that were not already enough— was involved in the case. But what that more was, he didn't mention. He merely handed over Eugenie Davies' address in Henley-on-Thames, telling them that the house was their starting point. He assumed, he told them pointedly, that they had enough experience between them to know what to do with what they found there.

'What the hell was that supposed to mean?' Barbara asked now as they swung into Bell Street in Henley-on-Thames where school children were taking their morning exercise in a local playground. 'And why've we been given the house while the rest of that lot are beating the pavement from West

147

Hampstead to the river? I don't get it.'

'Webberly wants us involved. Hillier's given his blessing.'

'And *that's* reason enough to do some serious tip-toeing, if you ask me.'

Lynley didn't disagree. Hillier had no love for either of them. And Webberly's state of mind on the previous evening had suggested a few things but declared nothing. 'I expect we'll sort things out soon enough, Havers. What's the address again?'

'Sixty-five Friday Street,' she said and with a glance at their street map, 'Take a left here, sir.'

Sixty-five turned out to be a dwelling seven buildings up from the River Thames on a pleasant street that mixed residences with a veterinarian's surgery, a book shop, a dental clinic, and the Royal Marine Reserve. It was the smallest house that Lynley had ever seen—bar his own companion constable's tiny dwelling in London that often struck him as fit for Bilbo Baggins and no one else. It was painted pink and it consisted of two floors and a possible attic if the microscopic dormer window on the roof was any indication. It bore an enamel plaque which named it, appropriately, Doll Cottage.

Lynley parked a short distance away from it, across the street from the book shop. He fished the dead woman's set of keys from his pocket while Havers took the opportunity to light up and fortify her bloodstream with nicotine. 'When are you going to drop that loathsome habit?' he asked her as he checked the front of the house for an alarm system and put the key in the lock.

Havers inhaled deeply and offered him her most maddening smile of tobacco-induced pleasure.

148

'Listen to him,' she said to the sky. 'There may be something more obnoxious than a reformed smoker, but I don't know what it is. Child pornographer come to Jesus on the day of his arrest? Tory with a social conscience perhaps? Hmm. No. They don't quite match up.'

Lynley chuckled. 'Put it out in the street, Constable.'

'I wouldn't even dwell on another option.' She flicked the cigarette over her shoulder, after taking another three hits.

Lynley opened the door, which admitted them into a sitting room. This looked about as large as a shopping trolley, and it was furnished with near monastic simplicity and with a taste that veered towards Oxfam rejects.

'And I thought *I'd* achieved drab-with-a-vengeance,' Havers remarked.

It wasn't an inappropriate description, Lynley thought. The furniture was of post war vintage, crafted at a period when rebuilding a capital devastated by bombing had taken precedence over interior design. A threadbare grey sofa accompanied by a matching armchair of an equally disenchanting hue sat against one wall. They formed a little seating area round a blond-wood coffee table spread with magazines and two similar end tables, both of which someone had attempted unsuccessfully to refinish. Three lamps in the room all sported tassled shades, two of them askew and the third bearing a large burn that could have been turned to the wall but wasn't. Nothing save a single print above the sofa, featuring an unattractive Victorian-era child with her arms round a rabbit, decorated the walls. On either side of a mouse hole

149

fireplace, fitted shelves held books, but they were spottily placed here and there, and it seemed as if something had stood among them but had been removed.

'Bloody poverty-stricken,' Havers said in assessment. She was, Lynley saw, fingering through the magazines on the coffee table, her hands—latex gloved—fanning the publications out so even Lynley could see from his place by the bookshelves that they all bore pictorial covers that placed them years out of date.

Havers moved into the kitchen that lay just beyond the sitting room as Lynley turned to look at the bookshelves. She called out, 'One mod con in here. She's got an answer machine, Inspector. Light's blinking.'

'Play it,' Lynley said.

The first disembodied voice floated from the kitchen as Lynley took his reading spectacles from his jacket pocket in order to examine more closely the few volumes on the fitted bookshelves.

A man's deep and sonorous voice said, 'Eugenie. Ian,' as Lynley picked up a book called *The Little Flower* and opened it to see it was a biography of a Catholic saint called Therese: French, from a family of daughters, a cloistered nun, suffered an early death from whatever one would contract living in a cell with no heating in France in midwinter. 'I'm sorry about the row,' the voice continued from the kitchen. 'Phone me, will you? Please? I've got the mobile with me,' and he followed this declaration with a number that began with a recognisable prefix.

'Got it,' Havers called out from the kitchen.

'It's a Cellnet number,' Lynley said and picked

up the next book as the next voice—this one a woman's—left her message, saying, 'Eugenie, it's Lynn. Dearest, thank you so much for the call. I was out for a walk when you rang. It was so very kind of you. I hardly expected . . . Well. Yes. There it is. I'm just about coping. Thanks for asking. If you ring me back, I'll give you an update. But I expect you know what I'm going through.'

Lynley saw he was holding another biography, this one of a saint called Clare, an early follower of St Francis of Assisi: gave away all she owned, founded an order of nuns, lived a life of chastity and died in poverty. He picked up a third book.

'Eugenie,' another man's voice from the kitchen, but this one distraught and obviously familiar to the dead woman since he spoke without attribution, saying, 'I need to speak to you. I had to ring again. I know you're there, so will you pick up the phone? . . . Eugenie, pick up the God damn phone.' A sigh. 'Look. Did you actually expect me to be happy about this turn of events? How could I be? . . . Pick up the phone, Eugenie.' A silence was followed by another sigh. 'All right. Fine. If that's how you're going to play it. Flush history down the lavatory and get on with things. I'll do the same.' The phone banged down.

'That sounds like a decent field to plough,' Barbara called.

'Hit one-four-seven-one at the end of the messages and pray for good luck.' The third book, Lynley saw, detailed the life of St Teresa of Avila, and a quick examination of its jacket was enough to inform him that thematic unity was being achieved on the bookshelves: the convent, poverty, an unpleasant death. Lynley read this and frowned

151

thoughtfully.

Another man's voice, again without attribution, came from the answer machine in the kitchen. He said, 'Hullo, darling. Still asleep or are you out already? I'm just ringing about tonight. The time? I've a bottle of claret that I'll bring along if that suits. Just let me know. I'm . . . I'm very keen to see you, Eugenie.'

'That's it,' Havers said. 'Fingers crossed, Inspector?'

'Metaphorically,' he replied as in the kitchen Havers punched in 1471 to trace whoever had made the most recent call to Eugenie Davies' home. As she did so, Lynley saw that the rest of the books on the shelves were also biographies of Catholic saints, all of them female. None of them were recently published, most of them were at least thirty years old, and some of them had been printed prior to World War II. Eleven of them had the name *Eugenie Victoria Staines* inscribed on their fly leaves in a youthful hand; four of them were stamped *Convent of the Immaculate Conception,* and five others bore the inscription *To Eugenie, with fondest regards from Cecilia.* Out of one of this last group—the life of someone called Saint Rita— a small envelope fell. It bore no postmark or address, but the single sheet of paper had been dated nineteen years earlier in a beautifully schooled hand that had also written:

Dearest Eugenie,
   You must try not to give in to despair. We can none of us understand God's ways. We can only live through the trials He chooses for us to endure, knowing that there is a purpose behind

152

them which we may not be able to understand at the time. But we will understand eventually, dear friend. You must believe that.

We deeply miss you at morning Mass and all of us hope that you will return to us soon.

With Christ's love and my own, Eugenie, Cecilia

Lynley returned the paper to its envelope and snapped the book closed. He called out, 'Convent of the Immaculate Conception, Havers.'

'Are you recommending a lifestyle change for me, sir?'

'Only if it suits you. In the meantime, make a note to track down the convent. We want someone called Cecilia if she's still alive, and I've a feeling that's where we might find her.'

'Right.'

Lynley joined her in the kitchen. The simplicity of the sitting room was repeated there. The kitchen hadn't been updated in several generations, by the look of it, and the only appliance that could be said to be remotely modern was the refrigerator although even it appeared to be at least fifteen years old.

The answer machine was sitting on a narrow wooden worktop. Next to it stood a *papier mâché* holder containing several envelopes. Lynley picked these up as Havers went over to a small table and two chairs that abutted one of the walls. Lynley glanced over to see that the table was set not for a meal but for an exhibition: Three neat lines of four framed photographs apiece stood upon it as if for inspection. Envelopes in hand, Lynley went to Havers' side as she said, 'Her kids, d'you think,

Inspector?'

Every photograph indeed depicted the same subjects: two children who advanced in age in each picture. They began with a small boy—perhaps five years old—holding an infant who, in later pictures, turned out to be a little girl. From first to last, the boy looked desperately eager to please, wide-eyed and smiling so broadly and anxiously that every tooth in his mouth was on display. The little girl, on the other hand, seemed mostly unaware that a camera was focused on her at all. She looked right, she looked left, she looked up, she looked down. Only once—with her brother's hand on her cheek—had anyone managed to get her to look into the camera.

Havers said in her usual blunt fashion, 'Sir, doesn't it look like there's something wrong with this kid? And she's the one that died, right? The one the superintendent told you about? This is her, right?'

'We'll need someone to confirm it,' Lynley replied. 'She could be someone else. A niece. A grandchild.'

'But what d'you *think*?'

'I think yes,' Lynley said. 'I think she's the child who died.' Drowned, he thought, drowned in what could have gone down as an accident but instead turned into something far more.

The photo must have been taken not long before she died. Webberly had told him that the girl had died at two, and Lynley saw that she couldn't have been much less than that at the time of this final picture. But Webberly hadn't told him everything, he realised as he studied the photo.

He felt his guard go up and his suspicions

154

heighten.

And he didn't much like either one of those sensations.

CHAPTER FIVE

Major Ted Wiley didn't think in terms of the police when the silver Bentley pulled to the kerb across the street from his book shop. He was in the middle of ringing up a purchase at the till for a youthful housewife with a sleeping toddler in a push chair, and rather than concentrate on the presence of a luxury vehicle in Friday Street during non-Regatta season, he instead engaged the youthful housewife in conversation. She'd bought four books by Dahl, which clearly were not intended for herself, so it appeared she was one of the few modern young parents who understood the importance of introducing a child to reading. Along with the insidious dangers of cigarette smoking, this was one of Ted's favourite topics. He and his wife had read to all three of their girls—not that there had been a surfeit of other nighttime activities for children to engage in in Rhodesia all those years ago—and he liked to think that the early start which he and Connie had given to them resulted in everything from respect for the written word to a determination to attend first class universities.

So seeing a young mother in possession of a stack of children's books delighted Ted. Had she herself been read to as a child? he wanted to know. What were the little one's favourites? Wasn't it astonishing how quickly children attached themselves to a story they'd been read, demanding it over and over again?

Thus, Ted saw the silver Bentley only out of the corner of his eye. He gave it little thought other than, Fine motor, that. It was only when the car's occupants got out and approached Eugenie's house that he bade a friendly farewell to his customer and moved closer to the window to watch them.

They were an odd pair. The man was tall, athletically built, blond and admirably dressed in the sort of well-made suit that ages over time like a fine wine. His companion wore red trainers, black trousers, and an overlarge navy donkey jacket that hung to her knees. The woman lit up a fag before she had the car door closed, which made Ted's lip curl in distaste—the world's tobacco manufacturers were surely going to burn for eternity in a section of hell designed just for them—but the man walked straight to Eugenie's door.

Ted waited for him to knock, but he didn't. As his companion sucked at her cigarette like someone with a death wish, the man examined an object in his hand, which turned out to be a key to Eugenie's front door, because he inserted this key in the lock and after making a remark to his companion, they both went inside.

At this sight, Ted went numb from his feet to his earlobes. First that unfamiliar man at one in the morning, then last night's encounter between Eugenie and that same individual in the car park, and now these two strangers in possession of a key to the cottage . . . Ted knew he had to get over there at once.

He glanced round the shop to see if any more

156

customers were considering purchases. There were two others. Old Mr Horsham—Ted liked to call him Old Mr Horsham because it was such a relief to find someone out and about who was older than himself—had taken a volume about Egypt off the shelf and appeared to be weighing it rather than inspecting it. And Mrs Dilday was, as usual, reading another chapter from a book she had no intention of purchasing. Part of her daily ritual was to select a bestseller, carry it casually to the back of the shop where the arm chairs were, read a chapter or two, mark her place with a grocery receipt, and hide the book among second hand volumes of Salman Rushdie where—considering the tastes of the average citizen in Henley—it would not be noticed.

For nearly twenty minutes Ted waited for these two customers to remove themselves from the premises so that he could invent a reason to go across the road. When old Horsham finally bought Egypt for a gratifying sum, saying 'Saw action there in the war,' as he handed over two twenty-pound notes which he extricated from a wallet that looked old enough to have seen action with its owner, Ted then turned his hopes towards Mrs Dilday. But this, he saw, was going to be fruitless. She was firmly ensconced in her favourite overstuffed armchair, and she'd brought a Thermos of tea with her as well. She was pouring, sipping, and reading quite happily, just as if she were in her own home.

Public libraries exist for a reason, Ted wanted to tell her. But instead he alternated between watching her, sending her mental messages about leaving at once, and peering out of the window for any kind of indication of who the people were in

Eugenie's house.

In the midst of his mental imaging of Mrs Dilday actually purchasing her novel and trotting off to read it, the telephone rang. His eyes still on Eugenie's house, Ted felt behind him for the receiver and picked it up on the fifth double ring.

He said, 'Wiley's Books,' and a woman asked, 'Who's this speaking, please?'

He said, 'Major Ted Wiley. Retired. Who's this?'

'Are you the only person who uses this line, sir?'

'What . . . ? Is this BT? Is there a problem?'

'Your phone number registers on one-four-seven-one as the last to have called this number that I'm speaking from, sir. It belongs to a woman called Eugenie Davies.'

'Right. I phoned her this morning,' Ted informed his caller, trying to keep his voice as steady as he could. 'We've a dinner engagement.' And then because he had to ask it although he already knew the answer, 'Is something wrong? Has something happened? Who are you?'

The receiver at the other end was covered for a moment as the woman spoke to someone else in the room. She said, 'Metropolitan police, sir.'

Metropolitan . . . that meant London. And suddenly Ted could see it again: Eugenie driving into London last night with the rain beating down against the roof of the Polo and the spray from the tyres arcing out into the road. 'London police?' he asked nonetheless.

'That's right,' the woman told him. 'Where are you, exactly, sir?'

'Across from Eugenie's house. I've a book shop . . .'

Another consultation. Then, 'Would you mind

stepping over here, sir? We've one or two questions we'd like to ask you.'

'Has something . . .' Ted could barely force himself to say the words, but they had to be said. If nothing else, the police would expect to hear them. 'Has something happened to Eugenie?'

'We can come to you if that's more convenient.'

'No. No. I'll be there at once. I must close up first, but I'll—'

'Fine, Major Wiley. We'll be here for quite some time.'

Ted walked to the back of the shop where he told Mrs Dilday that an emergency required him to shut up shop for a time. She said, 'Dear me. I hope it's not your mum?' because that was indeed the most rational emergency: his mother's death, although at eighty-nine it was only the stroke that was preventing her from taking up kick-boxing in her declining years.

He said, 'No, no. Just . . . There's something I need to take care of.'

She peered at him intently but accepted the vague excuse. In a welter of nerves, Ted waited as she drank down the rest of her tea, donned her wool coat, thrust her hands into her gloves, and— without the least attempt to disguise her actions— put the novel she was reading behind a copy of *The Satanic Verses*.

Once she was gone, Ted hurried up the stairs to his flat. He found that his heart was alternately fluttering then pounding, and he was becoming rather light-headed. With the lightness came voices, so real that he swung round without thinking, anticipating a presence that was not there.

159

First the woman's voice again: 'Metropolitan police. We've one or two questions we'd like to ask . . .'

Then Eugenie's: 'We'll talk. There's so much to say.'

And then, unaccountably, his own Connie's murmur coming to him from the grave itself, Connie who'd known him as no one else had: 'You're a match for any man alive, Ted Wiley.'

Why now? he wondered. Why Connie now?

But there was no answer, only the question. And there was also what had to be faced and dealt with across the street.

*   *   *

As Lynley began going through the letters he'd pulled from the *papier mâché* holder, Barbara Havers went up the narrowest staircase she'd ever seen to the first floor of the tiny house. There, two very small bedrooms and an antiquated bathroom opened off a landing that wasn't much larger than a drawing pin's head. Both bedrooms continued the theme of monastic simplicity bordering on shabbiness that began in the sitting room below. The first room contained three pieces of furniture: a single bed covered by a plain counterpane, a chest of drawers, and a bedside table on which stood yet another tassled lamp. The second bedroom had been turned into a sewing room and contained, aside from the answer machine, the only remotely modern appliance in the entire building: an advanced sewing machine next to which lay a considerable pile of tiny garments. Barbara fingered through these and saw that they were

160

dolls' clothes, elaborately designed and more elaborately fashioned with everything from beadwork to *faux* fur. There were no dolls anywhere in the sewing room nor were there any in the bedroom next door.

There Barbara went first to a chest of drawers where she found a humble paucity of clothing, even by her own indifferent standards of dress: threadbare knickers, equally worn brassieres, a few jumpers, a limp collection of tights. There was neither a fitted clothes cupboard nor a wardrobe in the room, so the few skirts, trousers, and dresses that the woman had owned were folded carefully into the chest of drawers as well.

Among the trousers and the skirts, at the back of the drawer, Barbara saw that a bundle of letters had been tucked. She fished these out, removed the rubber band that held them together, laid them out across the single bed, and saw that they had all been written in the same hand. She blinked at this hand. She took a moment to assimilate the fact that she recognised the black, decisive scrawl.

The envelopes bore postmarks as old as seventeen years. The most recent, she saw, had been sent just over one decade ago. She reached for this one and slid the contents out.

He called her 'Eugenie my darling.' He wrote that he didn't know where to begin. He said those things that men always say when they claim to have reached the decision that they no doubt intended to reach all along: She must never doubt that he loved her more than life itself; she must know, remember, and hold to her heart the fact that the hours they had spent together had made him feel alive—truly and wonderfully alive, my darling—for

161

the first time in years; indeed, the feeling of her skin beneath his fingers had been like liquid silk shot through with lightning . . .

Barbara rolled her eyes at the purple phrasing. She lowered the letter and gave herself a moment to react to it and, more important, to what it implied. Read more or not, Barb? she asked herself. Read more and she felt unclean. Not and she felt unprofessional.

She went back to the letter. He'd gone home, she read, intending to tell his wife everything. He'd screwed his courage to the sticking place—Barbara winced at the pilfering from Shakespeare—and held the image of Eugenie in his mind to give him the strength to deal a mortal blow to a perfectly good and decent woman. But he'd found her unwell, Eugenie darling, unwell in a manner that he couldn't explain in a mere letter, but that he *would* explain, would lay before her in all its desperate detail, when next they met. This *didn't* mean they would not be together at the end of the day, darling Eugenie. This didn't mean they had no future. Above all, this didn't mean everything that had passed between them counted for nothing, because that was not the case.

He'd concluded with, 'Wait for me. I beg you. I'm coming to you, darling.' And he'd signed it with the scrawl that Barbara had seen on notes, on Christmas cards, on departmental letters, and on memos for years.

At least she now knew what had seemed off at the Webberly party, she thought as she stuffed the letter back into its envelope. All that jolly-good-fellowing to celebrate twenty-five years of sham.

'Havers?' Lynley was in the doorway, spectacles

162

sliding down his nose and a greeting card in his hand. 'Here's something that fits in with one of the phone messages. What've you found?'

'Swap,' she said and handed over her envelope in exchange for what he was carrying.

This card was from someone called Lynn, with an envelope that bore a London postmark but no sender's address. Its message was simple:

Thank you so much for the floral tribute, dearest Eugenie, and for your presence which meant so much to me. Life will go on. I know that. But, of course, it will never be the same.
Fondly,
Lynn.

Barbara examined the date: a week ago. She agreed with Lynley. Thematically, it sounded like the same woman who'd left the message on the answer machine.

'Damn.' This was Lynley's reaction to the letter Barbara had handed to him. He gestured to the other letters that lay across Eugenie Davies' bed. 'What about those?'

'All from him, Inspector, if the writing on the envelopes is anything to go by.'

Barbara watched the play of reactions as they crossed Lynley's face. She knew that her superior officer and she had to be thinking along the same lines: Had Webberly known these letters—so embarrassing and potentially damaging to him— would be in Eugenie Davies' possession? Had he merely suspected or feared that they might be? And in either case, had he arranged to have Lynley—and by extension Havers as well—work

163

the case in order to run interference no matter which circumstance arose?

'D'you think Leach knows about them?' Barbara asked.

'He phoned Webberly when he had a potential i.d. on the body. At one in the morning, Havers. What does that suggest to you?'

'And guess who he asked to go to Henley this morning.' Barbara took the letter that Lynley handed back to her. 'What's to do, then, sir?'

Lynley walked to the window. She watched as he gazed down at the street. She expected the regulation reply from him. Asking the question in the first place had been merely rote.

'We'll take them with us,' he said.

She got to her feet. 'You've got evidence bags in the boot, haven't you? I'll fetch—'

'Not like that,' Lynley said.

Barbara said, 'What? But you just said take—'

'Yes. We'll take them with us.' He turned back to her from the window.

Barbara stared at him. She didn't want to think what he was implying. *We'll take them with us.* Not, We'll bag them and log them as evidence, Havers. Not, Be careful with them, Barbara. Not, We'll have forensic check them for fingerprints, for the prints of someone other than the recipient who might have found them, might have read them, might have become consumed with jealousy because of them and despite their age, someone who might have looked for vengeance because of them . . .

She said, 'Hang on, Inspector. You can't mean—'

But she wasn't able to complete her protest.

Below them, someone knocked on the door.

*   *   *

Lynley answered it to find an elderly gentleman in a waxed jacket and peaked cap standing on the pavement, his hands sunk into his pockets. His ruddy face was mapped with the markings of broken capillaries, and his nose was just that shade of rose that would grow purple over time. But it was his eyes that Lynley took note of most closely. They were blue, intense, and wary.

He introduced himself as Major Ted Wiley, army, retired. 'Someone from the police . . . You must be one of them. I had a call . . . ?'

Lynley asked the man to step inside. He introduced himself and then introduced Havers who descended the stairs as Wiley moved tentatively into the room. The old gentleman looked round him, glanced at the stairs, then lifted his eyes to the ceiling as if he were trying to determine what Barbara Havers had been looking for or had found on the floor above.

'What's happened?' Wiley removed neither his hat nor his jacket.

'You're a friend of Mrs Davies?' Lynley asked him.

The man didn't respond at once. It was as if he were trying to decide what the word *friend* actually meant in reference to his relationship with Eugenie Davies. He finally said, looking from Lynley to Havers and back again to Lynley, 'Something's happened to her. You wouldn't be here otherwise.'

'That was you on the phone, that last message on her machine? A man talking about plans for tonight?' Havers asked this. She remained by the

165

stairs.

'We were . . .' Wiley seemed to hear the past tense and made the adjustment. 'We're supposed to have dinner. Tonight. She said . . . You're from the Met and she went to London last night. So something's happened to her. Please tell me what.'

'Sit down, Major Wiley,' Lynley said. The old man didn't seem frail, but there was no telling the condition of his heart or his blood pressure from just one look at him, and Lynley didn't like to take risks with someone when he had bad news to pass on.

'It was raining hard last night,' Wiley said, more to himself than to either Lynley or Havers. 'I talked to her about driving in the rain. And the dark. Dark's bad enough but rain makes it worse.'

Havers crossed the few feet to Wiley and took him by the arm. 'Have a seat, Major,' she said.

'It's bad,' he responded.

'I'm afraid so,' Lynley said.

'The motorway? She said she'd be careful. She said not to worry. She said we'd talk. Tonight. We'd talk. She wanted to talk.' He was speaking not so much to them but to the coffee table in front of the sofa on which Havers had deposited him. She sat next to him, perched on the edge.

Lynley took the armchair. He said gently, 'I'm afraid Eugenie Davies was killed last night.'

Wiley turned his head to Lynley in a what looked like slow motion. 'The motorway,' he said. 'The rain. I didn't want her to go.'

For the moment, Lynley didn't disabuse him of the notion that there had been a motorway crash. The BBC early morning news had carried the story of the hit and run, but no mention had been made

166

of Eugenie Davies' name at that time since her body had yet to be identified and her family had yet to be tracked down. He said, 'She left after dark, then? What time was this?'

Wiley said numbly, 'Half past nine, I think? Ten? We were walking back from St Mary the Virgin—'

'Evensong?' Havers had taken out her notebook and was jotting down the information.

'No, no,' Wiley said. 'There was no service. She'd gone in . . . to pray? I don't actually know because . . .' He removed his cap then, as if he were in church himself. He held it with both hands. 'I didn't go in with her. I had my dog. My golden. PB? That's her name. We waited in the churchyard.'

'This was in the rain?' Lynley asked.

Wiley twisted the cap. 'Dogs don't mind rain. And it was time for her last walk of the evening. PB's last walk.'

Lynley said, 'Can you tell us why she was going to London?'

Wiley gave the cap another twist. 'She said she had an appointment there.'

'With whom? Where?'

'I don't know. She said we'd talk tonight.'

'About the appointment?'

'I don't know. God. I don't *know*.' His voice fractured but Ted Wiley wasn't a retired Army man for nothing. He regained control within a second. Then he said, 'How did it happen? Where? Did she skid? Hit a lorry?'

Lynley gave the facts to him, offering just enough details to tell Wiley where and how she had died. He didn't use the word *murder* in his explanation. And Wiley didn't interrupt to ask why

167

the Metropolitan police were trolling through the belongings of a woman who, to all intents and purposes, was the victim of a simple hit and run.

But a moment after Lynley had finished his explanation, Wiley made the leap. He seemed to take measure of the fact that Havers had descended the stairs upon his arrival, wearing latex gloves. He put this together with the police punching one-four-seven-one on Eugenie's phone. He added to this what they had said about Eugenie's answer machine. And he said, 'This can't have been an accident. Because why would you . . . the two of you coming out here from London . . .' His eyes focused on something else, perhaps someone else, a vision in the distance that seemed to prompt him to say, 'That bloke in the car park last night. This isn't an accident, is it?' And he rose.

Havers rose as well and urged him back down. He cooperated, but now he was changed, as if an unnamed purpose had begun to consume him. From twisting his cap, he went to slapping it against his palm. He said, quite as if he were giving an order to a subordinate, 'Tell me what happened to Eugenie.'

There seemed little risk that he would have a heart attack or stroke, so Lynley told him that he and Havers were part of a murder squad, leaving him to fill in the rest of the blanks. He went on to say, 'Tell us about the man in the car park,' which Wiley did without hesitation.

He'd walked up to the Sixty Plus Club where Eugenie worked. He went with PB to walk Eugenie home in the rain. When he got there, he observed her in an altercation with a man. Not a local man, Wiley said. This was someone from Brighton.

168

'She told you that?' Lynley asked.

Wiley shook his head. He'd got a glimpse of the number plate as the car sped off. He couldn't get it all, but he saw the letters: ADY. 'I was worried about her. She'd been acting a little peculiar for several days, so I looked the letters up in the registration mark guide. I saw ADY is Brighton. The car was an Audi. Navy or black. I couldn't tell in the dark.'

'You keep a copy handy?' Havers asked. 'The registration mark guide? Is this a hobby or something?'

'It's in the book shop. Travel section. I sell a copy now and then. People who want to give their kids something to do in the car. That sort of thing.'

'Ah.'

Lynley knew Havers' *ah*. She was watching Wiley curiously. He said, 'You didn't intercede in the altercation between Mrs Davies and this man, Major Wiley?'

'I came into the car park only at the end of it. I heard a few shouted words—on his part, this was. He got into the car. Took off before I was close enough to say anything. That was it.'

'Who did Mrs Davies say this man was?'

'I didn't ask her.'

Lynley and Havers exchanged a look. Havers was the one to ask, 'Why not?'

'As I said. She'd been acting peculiar, different from usual, for several days. I assumed there was something on her mind and . . .' Wiley shifted his eyes to his cap, and seemed surprised to find it still in his hands. He stuffed it into his pocket. 'See here. I'm not the sort who pries. I decided to wait for her to tell me whatever she wanted to tell me.'

169

'Had you ever seen this man before?'

Wiley said no, no, he didn't know the man. He hadn't seen him before that moment, but he'd got a good look at him if the detectives wanted a description. When they said that they did, he provided it: the approximate age, the height, the iron grey hair, the dominant hawk-like nose. 'He called her Eugenie,' Wiley concluded. 'They knew each other.' This, he said, he'd assumed from what he'd seen in the car park: Eugenie had touched the man's face, but he'd pulled away.

'But you still didn't ask her who he was?' Lynley said. 'Why was that, Major Wiley?'

'It seemed . . . too personal, somehow. I thought she'd tell me when she was ready. If he was important.'

'And she did say she had something she wanted to talk to you about,' Havers noted.

Wiley nodded and let out a slow breath. 'She did say that. She talked about confessing her sins.'

'Sins,' Havers said.

Lynley leaned forward, avoiding Havers' meaningful look in his direction. He said, 'May we assume from all this that you and Mrs Davies had a close relationship, Major Wiley? Were you friends? Lovers? Engaged?'

The question seemed to discomfit Wiley. He altered his position on the sofa. 'It'd been three years. I wanted to be respectful with her, not like one of these randy modern blokes with nothing more on his mind. I was willing to wait. She finally said that she was ready, but she wanted to have a talk first.'

'Which was what was supposed to happen tonight,' Havers concluded. 'That's why you phoned her.'

It was.

Lynley asked the old gentleman to come into the kitchen with them, then. He said that there were other voices on Eugenie Davies' answer machine, and Major Ted Wiley—three years into a relationship with the dead woman, no matter what the relationship was—might be able to identify them.

In the kitchen, Wiley stood by the table and looked at the photographs of the two children. He reached for one of them, but he stopped himself when he finally seemed to take in the fact that Lynley and Havers were wearing gloves for a reason. As Havers readied the answer machine to play its messages again, Lynley said, 'Are these Mrs Davies' children, Major Wiley?'

'Her son and daughter,' Wiley said. 'Yes. They're her children. Sonia died a number of years ago. And the boy . . . They were estranged, Eugenie and the boy. Been estranged for I don't know how long. They had some sort of falling out ages back. She never spoke of him to me except to say they no longer saw each other.'

'And Sonia? Did Mrs Davies ever speak to you about Sonia?'

'Just that she died young. But,' Wiley cleared his throat and stepped away from the table as if wishing to distance himself from what he was about to say, 'Well, look at her. One can't be surprised that she died young. They . . . they often do.'

Lynley frowned, wondering that Wiley seemed unaware of a case that certainly must have dominated the newspapers at the time. He said, 'Were you in the country twenty years ago, Major

Wiley?'

No, he'd been . . . Wiley seemed to do a backward progression in his head, cataloguing the years he'd spent on active duty in the Army. He said he'd been in the Falklands, then. But that was long ago and he might have been in Rhodesia at the time . . . or what was left of Rhodesia. Why?

'Mrs Davies never told you that Sonia was murdered?'

Dumbly, Wiley returned his gaze to the photographs. He said, 'She didn't tell me . . . She didn't say . . . No, never once. Good God.' He dug into his back pocket and brought out a handkerchief, but he didn't use it. Instead he said only, 'This lot don't belong here, on the table, you know. Did you move them?' in apparent reference to the photographs.

'This is where we found them,' Lynley told him.

'They should be scattered round the house. The sitting room. Upstairs. In here. That's how they always were.' He pulled out one of the two chairs beneath the table and lowered himself into it heavily. He looked fairly spent at this point, but he nodded at Havers where she stood by the answer machine.

Lynley studied the major as he listened to the messages. He tried to read Wiley's reaction when he heard the voices of two other men on the machine. From their words and their tone, it was obvious that they were both involved with Eugenie Davies in some way. But if Wiley reached that conclusion himself and if that conclusion distressed him, he gave no indication other than colour in a face already so rubicund as to make measuring further redness impossible.

At the end of the messages, Lynley asked, 'Do you recognise anyone?'

'Lynn,' he said. 'Eugenie did tell me that. The child of an old friend called Lynn passed away suddenly, and Eugenie went to the funeral. She told me that when she'd heard that the child had died, she knew how Lynn felt and she wanted to commiserate.'

'Heard that she'd died?' Havers asked. 'Heard from who?'

Wiley didn't know. He hadn't thought to ask. 'I assumed the woman must have rung her up. This Lynn person,' he said, 'whoever she is.'

'Do you know where the funeral was?'

He shook his head. 'She went off for the day.'

'When was this?'

'Last Tuesday. I asked her if she wanted me to go as well. Funerals being what they are, I thought she might welcome the company. But she said she and Lynn had some talking to do. "I need to see her," she said. That was all.'

'Need to see her?' Lynley asked. 'That's what she said?'

'Yes.'

Need, Lynley thought. Not want, but need. He considered the word and everything it implied. What follows need, he knew, is usually action.

But was that the case here in this kitchen in Henley, where it appeared several needs were colliding? There was Eugenie Davies' need to confess sin to Major Wiley. There was an unidentified man's need to talk to Eugenie, declared on her answer machine. And there was Ted Wiley's need . . . for what?

Lynley asked Havers to play the messages one

173

more time, and he wondered if Wiley's slight change of posture—drawing his arms closer to his body—was an indication of steeling himself. He kept his gaze fixed on the major as once again the two men on the machine declared their need to speak to Eugenie.

I had to ring again, the one voice declared. *Eugenie, I need to speak to you.*

And there it was again: that word *need.* What would a man do with a desperate need?

*   *   *

How wd u do it 2 me if u cd?

TongueMan read the question from LadyFire without his usual surge of gratification. They'd been dancing round this moment for weeks, despite an initial—and inaccurate—assessment of her on his part which had suggested he'd have her ready well in advance of CreamPants. It just went to show that you couldn't judge the outcome by someone's ability to engage in suggestive cyberchat, didn't it? LadyFire had come on strong at first in the descriptive arena, but she'd faded quickly when the talk shifted from fantasy fucks between celebrities (she'd been astonishing in her ability to convey a hot encounter between a purple-haired rock star and their nation's monarch) to fantasy fucks in which she herself was one of the partners. Indeed, TongueMan had thought for a time that he'd lost her altogether by pushing too soon and revealing too much. He'd even considered moving on to the next possibility—EatMe—and he was about to do so when LadyFire reappeared on the cyberscene. She'd needed some time to think, evidently. But

174

now she knew what she wanted. So *How wd u do it 2 me if u cd?*

TongueMan studied the question and took note of the fact that his mind didn't kick into high gear at the thought of another supercharged semi-anonymous encounter with another cyberlover so soon after his last. He was doing his best to forget his last anyway, and especially to forget everything that had followed: the flashing lights, the barriers blocking off both ends of his street, the eyes of suspicion coming to rest on him, the Boxster—damn them—being hauled off for police inspection. But he'd handled it all well enough, he decided. Yes. He'd handled it like a pro.

The Met certainly weren't prepared for someone who was wise to their ways, TongueMan thought. They expected one to lie down, belly up, the moment they started to ask their questions. They reckoned that Joseph Q. Average Citizen—eager to prove he had nothing to hide—would jump onto the cooperation wagon and ride it to whatever destination the cops were hoping to take. So when the police said, 'We have a few questions, if you wouldn't mind coming down to the station for a chat,' most people sauntered right along without a second thought, assuming they had some sort of immunity from a legal system that anyone with a grain of sense knew could ride roughshod over the uninitiated in about five minutes.

TongueMan, however, was anything but a member of the uninitiated. He knew what could happen when one cooperated, blithely believing that doing one's civic duty was synonymous with demonstrating one's guilelessness. Bollocks, that. So when the cops said that his address had been in the possession of that woman in the street and could they ask him a few questions please, Tongueman knew which way the wagon ride was heading, and in short order he had his solicitor on the phone.

Not that Jake Azoff had liked being torn from his bed at midnight. Not that he didn't whine privately about 'duty solicitors and what they are being paid by the government to do'. But there was no way on earth that TongueMan was going to place his future—not to mention his present—into the hands of a duty solicitor. True, the representation wouldn't have cost him a penny, but a duty solicitor had no vested interest in TongueMan's future whereas Azoff—with whom he enjoyed a rather complicated relationship involving shares, bonds, mutual funds, and the like—actually did. Besides, what was he paying Azoff for, if not to be ready when legal advice of any sort was needed?

But TongueMan was worried. Obviously. He could lie to himself about it. He could attempt to distract himself by phoning in sick from work and logging onto the Net for a few hours of pornographic fantasising with utter strangers. But his body couldn't prevaricate when it came to unacknowledged anxiety. And the fact that he was enjoying no physical reaction whatsoever to *How wd u do it 2 me if u cd?* said it all.

He typed *U wdnt 4get it soon.*

She typed *R u shy 2day? Cm on. Tell how.*

How? he wondered. Yes, that was it. How? He tried to be loose. Just let the mind roam. He was good at this. He was a master. And she was certainly what all the others had been: older and

176

looking for a sign that she still had what it took.

He typed *Whr do u want my tong?* in an attempt to get her to do the work.

She typed *No fair. R U jst all tlk?*

He wasn't even talk today, TongueMan thought, which she'd discover soon enough if they carried on much longer in this vein. It was time to get huffy with LadyFire. A break was called for till he sorted himself out.

He typed *If thts wt u thnk, bby* and logged off. Let her stew in that juice for a day or two.

He checked how the market was doing before he pushed back from the keyboard. He swung his chair round and left the study, descending to the kitchen where the glass carafe on the coffee maker offered him a final cup. He poured and savoured the flavour of coffee the way he liked it: strong, black, and bitter. Rather like life itself, he decided.

He gave a brief laugh devoid of amusement. There was a real irony to the last twelve hours, and he was sure if he thought about it long enough, he'd discover what that irony was. But thinking about it was the last thing he wanted to do at the moment. With a Hampstead murder squad breathing down his neck, he knew he had to maintain his composure. That was the secret of life, composure: in the face of adversity, in the face of triumph, in the face of—

Something flicked against the kitchen window. Roused, TongueMan looked out to see two roughly dressed, unshaven men standing in the middle of his back garden. They'd come in from the park that ran the length of nearly all the Crediton Hill back gardens on the east side of the street. Since he had no fence between his property and the park, his visitors hadn't encountered much of an obstacle in gaining access. He was going to have to do something about that.

The two men saw him and nudged each other simultaneously. One of them called out, 'Open up, Jay. Long time, no see,' and the other added, 'We're giving you a break, coming in the back way' with a maddening smirk.

TongueMan cursed. First a body in the street, then the Boxster towed away, then himself under the eyes of the cops. And now this. Always guard against thinking a day couldn't possibly get worse, he told himself as he went to the dining room and opened the french windows.

'Robbie, Brent,' he said to the men in greeting, every bit as if he'd seen them only last week. It was cold outside, and they were hunched against it, stamping their feet and blowing steam like two bulls waiting for the matador. 'What're you doing here?'

'Ask us in?' Robbie said. 'Not a very pleasant day for the garden, this.'

TongueMan sighed. It seemed as if every time he took a step forward, something came along to drag him two steps back. He said, 'What's this about, then?' But what he meant was, How did you find me this time?

Brent grinned, saying, 'The usual, Jay,' but at least he had the decency to look uncomfortable and to shift his feet.

Robbie, on the other hand, was the one to watch out for. Always had been and always would be. He'd throw Granny under a bus if he thought he stood to gain by it, and TongueMan knew the last thing he could hope for was consideration, respect, or sympathy from the bloke.

'Street's blocked off.' Robbie cocked his head in the general direction of the bottom of the road. 'Something happen?'

'A woman was hit by a car last night.'

'Ah.' But the way Robbie said the word declared that he wasn't learning anything new. 'And that's why you're not at work today?'

'I work from home sometimes. I've told you that.'

'Might've, yeah. But it's been a while, ha'n't it?' He didn't go on to mention what hung unspoken between them: the time it had been since he'd last come calling and what he'd gone through to track down this address. Instead, he said, 'But your office tol' me you had to cancel a meeting today and you phoned in with flu. Or was it a cold? You remember, Brent?'

'You *talked* to my—' TongueMan stopped himself. This, after all, was the reaction Robbie sought. He said, 'I thought we'd got that straight. I asked you not to speak to anyone but me when you phone me at work. You've got the private line. There's never any need to talk to my secretary.'

'You ask for a lot,' Robbie said. ' 'N't that so, Brent?' This last was obviously meant to remind the other man—possessing the lesser intelligence—which side he was supposed to be on.

Brent said, 'Right. You asking us in, or what, Jay? Cold out here.'

Robbie added, as if superfluously, 'There's three tabloid blokes down the end of the street. You know that, Jay? Wha's going on?'

TongueMan cursed in silence and stepped back from the door. The two men outside laughed,

179

knocked hands in a clumsy high five, crossed the flagstones, and came up the steps. 'There's a boot scraper. Use it,' TongueMan told them. Last night's rain had made a swamp of the ground beneath the trees that formed the boundary between the houses and the park. Robbie and Brent had tramped right through it like farmers raising pigs. 'I've a decent carpet in here.'

'Take the daisies off, Brent,' Robbie said cooperatively. 'How's that, Jay? We leave our mucky boots on the step. We know how to be proper guests, me and Brent.'

'Proper guests wait for invitations.'

'Wouldn't want to stand on that sort of ceremony now, would we?'

Both men were inside, and they seemed to fill the room. They were enormous, and while they'd never used their size to intimidate him, he knew they wouldn't hesitate to use anything within their power to bend his will to theirs.

'Why's those tabloid blokes hanging about?' Robbie asked. 'Far's I know, the only way tabloids get their stuff's if someone rings them up with something hot.'

'Yeah,' Brent said, bending to peer into the china cabinet, which he used as a mirror to inspect his hair. 'Something hot, Jay.' He jiggled the cabinet door.

'That's antique. Be careful, all right?'

'It looked dodgy, those blokes hanging round the barriers at the bottom of the road,' Robbie said. 'So we had a word with them, me and Brent did, didn't we?'

'Yeah. A word.' Brent opened the door and took out one of the china cups inside. 'Nice, this. Old, is

180

it, Jay?'

'Come on, Brent.'

'He asked a question, Jay.'

'Fine. It's old. It's early nineteenth century. If you're going to break it, just get it over with and spare me the suspense, all right?'

Robbie chuckled. Brent grinned and replaced the cup. He shut the cabinet with the care a neurosurgeon might give to repositioning a section of skull.

Robbie said, 'One of the tabloid blokes said the cops're interested in someone on this street. Said a snout at the station tol' him the dead bird was carrying an address with her last night. Wouldn't give us the address, though, me and Brent, if he knew it. Thought we might be competition.'

Small chance of that, TongueMan thought. But he anticipated the direction they were about to take, and he did what he could to brace himself for the inevitable course of the conversation.

'Tabloids,' Robbie said. 'Amazing what they c'n dig up 'less someone tries to head them off.'

'Yeah. Amazing,' Brent agreed. And then as if he'd merely been playing the other man's stooge instead of living the rôle, he said, 'Rolling Suds, Jay. It needs some bolstering.'

'I "bolstered" it not six months ago.'

'Right. But that was then, in spring. Season's slow now. And there's this matter of . . . well, you know.' Brent glanced at Robbie.

Which was when the pieces clicked into place. 'You've borrowed against the business, haven't you?' TongueMan said. 'What is it this time? Horses? Dogs? Cards? I'm not *about* to—'

'Hey, you listen.' Robbie took a step forward as

181

if to demonstrate the considerable difference in their sizes. 'You owe us, mate. Who stood by you? Who gave aggro to every Tom and Willie who even thought 'bout whispering behind your back? Brent got his *arm* broke because of you, and I—'

'I know the story, Rob.'

'Good. So hear the ending, okay? We need some oscar, we need it today, and if that's a problem, then you best speak up.'

TongueMan looked from one man to the other and saw the future unrolling before him like an endless carpet with a repetitive design. He would sell up again, move house again, establish himself, change his job if necessary . . . and they would still find him. And when they found him, they would trot out the same manoeuvre they'd used with so much success for so many years. This was the way it was going to be. They believed he owed them. And they never forgot.

'What do you need?' he asked them wearily.

Robbie named his price. Brent blinked and grinned.

TongueMan fetched his chequebook and scrawled the amount. Then he saw them out the way they had come: through the dining room door and into the back garden. He watched till they ducked beneath the bare branches of the plane trees at the edge of the park. Then he went to the phone.

When he had Jake Azoff on the line, he took a breath that felt like a stab in the heart. 'Rob and Brent found me,' he informed his solicitor. 'Tell the police I'll talk.'

Gideon

10 SEPTEMBER

I don't understand why you won't prescribe something for me. You're a medical doctor, aren't you? Or will the act of writing out a prescription for migraines reveal you as a charlatan? And please don't produce that tedious commentary about psychotropic medication again. We're not talking about antidepressants, Dr Rose. About antipsychotics, tranquillisers, sedatives, or amphetamines. We are talking about a simple pain killer. Because what I have in my head is simple pain.

Libby's trying to help. She was here earlier and she found me where I'd been all morning: in my bedroom with the curtains drawn and a bottle of Harvey's Bristol Cream tucked into the crook of my arm like a Paddington bear. She sat on the edge of the bed and loosened my grip on the bottle, saying, 'If you're planning on getting blitzed on this, you'll be hurling chunks in an hour.'

I groaned. Her style of language, so bizarre and so graphic, was the last thing I needed to hear. I said, 'My head.'

She said, 'The pits. But booze's going to make it worse. Let's see if I can help.'

She put her hands on my head. The tips of her fingers, resting lightly on my temples, were cool and they traced small circles, circles that diminished the pounding in my veins. I felt my body relax beneath her touch, and it seemed to me that I could easily fall asleep with her sitting there so quietly.

She moved and lay next to me and placed her

183

hand on my cheek. The same gentle touch of the same cool flesh. She said, 'You're burning.'

I murmured, 'It's the headache.'

She turned her hand so my cheek felt the backs of her fingers, then. Cool, they were so wonderfully cool.

I said, 'Feels good. Thanks, Libby.' I took her hand, kissed her fingers, and placed them back against my cheek.

She said, 'Gideon . . . ?'

I said, 'Hmm?'

'Oh, never mind.' And then when I did just that, she sighed and went on. 'D'you ever think about . . . us? I mean, like, where we're headed and all?'

I made no reply. It seems to me that it always comes down to this with women. That plural pronoun and the quest for validation: thinking about us confirms that there is an us in the first place.

She said, 'D'you realise how much time we've spent together?'

'A great deal of time.'

'Geez, we've even, like, slept together.'

Women, I have also noted, have a marvellous ability to state the obvious.

'So d'you think we should go on? Dyou think we're ready for the next level in all this? I mean, I've got to say I feel totally ready. Really ready for what comes next. What about you?' And as she spoke, she lifted her leg to rest her thigh against mine, crossed my chest with her arm, and tilted her hips—just the ghost of a tilt, this was—to press her pubis against me.

And suddenly I am back with Beth, back at that point in a relationship when something more is supposed to happen between the man and the woman and when nothing does. At least, not for me. With Beth the next level was permanent commitment. We

184

were lovers, after all, and had been lovers for eleven months.

She is the liaison between East London Conservatory and the schools from which the conservatory draws its students. A former music instructor, she is also a cellist. She is perfect for the conservatory in that she speaks the language of the instruments, the language of the music and, most importantly, the language of the children themselves.

I am not aware of her at first. Not until we must deal with a parent whose child has run away from home, seeking a shelter that the conservatory cannot provide. The child, we learn, has been prevented from practising by the mother's boyfriend who, we also learn, has other activities in mind for her. She has become little more than a servant in their squalid home. But that little more is defined by sexual favours she has been told to perform on both of them.

Beth is Nemesis to this pathetic excuse for a human couple. She is pure Fury. She waits for neither police nor Social Services to deal with the situation because she trusts neither police nor Social Services. She deals with it herself with a private detective and with a meeting between herself and the couple during which she makes it clear what will happen to them both should this child come to any harm. And to make sure that they understand, she defines harm for them in the explicit street terms that they are accustomed to.

I am not there for any of this, but I hear of it from more than one of the other instructors. And the ferocity of her devotion to this student touches something deep within me. A longing, perhaps. Or perhaps a chord of recognition.

At any rate, I seek her out. We fall into together *in*

185

the most natural fashion I can imagine. For a year all is well.

But then as tends to happen, she talks of having more. It's logical, I know. Pondering the next step is rational for a man and a woman, although perhaps more for a woman who has her basic biology to consider.

When the subject of next *comes up between us, I know I should want what follows those professions of love we've made for each other. I realise that nothing stays the same forever and to expect that she and I will be forever content to be fellow musicians and ardent lovers is a form of delusion. But, still, when she broaches the idea of marriage and children, I feel myself grow cool. I avoid the topic at first and when it can no longer be shunted to one side with the excuse of rehearsals, practices, recording sessions, and personal appearances, I find that the coolness within me has increased and now has iced over the idea of not only a future with Beth but also a present as well. I can't be with her as I was before. I feel no passion, and I have no desire. I attempt to go through the motions at first but it's just not there for me any longer. Whatever* it *was: desire, fervour, attachment, devotion.*

We grind against each other, then, which is probably the way it happens when a man and a woman are trying to preserve a connection that's already been severed. And in that grinding, we wear each other away until what we had is so distant a memory that we can no longer sift through the discord of our present to locate the harmony that defined our past. And it ends. We end. She goes on to find another man whom she marries twenty-seven months and one week later. I remain as I am.

So when Libby spoke of next levels, I felt my spirit shudder. And yet I knew it would always come down to this same conversation between me and a woman, as long as I allowed any woman into my life.

The shouldn'ts *began their bows in my mind. I shouldn't have shown her the basement flat. I shouldn't have agreed to let it to her. I shouldn't have taken her out for coffee. I shouldn't have bought her a meal, played that first concerto on her stereo, flown kites from Primrose Hill with her, eaten at her table, fallen asleep with her spooned into my body and her night shirt accidentally hiked up so that I could feel her naked arse warm and soft resting against my flaccid penis.*

That should have told her the tale: that flaccidity. That unchanging, indifferent, laodicean flaccidity. But it did not. Or if it did, she did not wish to draw the conclusion implied by that lifeless piece of flesh.

I said, 'It feels good, having you here like this.'

She said, 'It could feel better. We could have more.' And she moved her hips three times in that way women have, that unconsciously mimes the rotation against which a normal man wants to thrust.

But I, as we know, am not a normal man.

I knew that I was supposed to desire at least the act if not the woman herself. But I did not. Nothing stirred in me except, perhaps, the ice. And what came over me was stillness and shadow and that disembodied feeling of being outside myself, above myself, looking down on this pitiful excuse for a man and wondering what the hell it was going to take, for God's sake, to move the bastard.

Libby said, her cool hand on my hot cheek again, 'What's wrong, Gideon?' And she became quite still on the bed next to me. She didn't move away,

187

however, and the fear that a precipitate movement on my part might give her an idea I did not wish her to have prompted me to remain immobile as well.

I said, 'I've been to the doctor. I've had all the tests. There's nothing to account for them, Libby. It happens.'

'I'm not talking about the migraines, Gid.'

'Then what?'

'Why aren't you playing? You always play. You're like a clock. Three hours every morning, three hours every afternoon. I've seen Rafe's car in the square every day, so I know he's been here, but I haven't heard either of you guys playing.'

Rafe. She has that American tendency to give everyone a nickname. Raphael became Rafe the first time she met him. Nothing could suit him less, if you ask me, but he doesn't appear to mind the sobriquet.

And he has been here every day, as she pointed out. Sometimes for an hour, sometimes for two or three. He mostly paces while I sit in the window seat and write. He sweats, he mops his forehead and his neck with a handkerchief, he casts apprehensive looks in my direction, and he no doubt projects us into a future in which my anxiety state prematurely terminates an otherwise brilliant career and in which his reputation as my musical Rasputin is summarily ruined. He pictures himself as a footnote in history, one written in typescript so infinitesimal as to require a magnifying glass to be read.

I have been his hope for immortality-by-proxy. There he has been for fifty-whatever years, a man incapable of rising even to the level of first violin despite his talent and his every best effort, condemned by a reservoir of stage fright that has unloosed its floodgates in a deluge of terror whenever he's had a

188

chance to audition. The man's a brilliant musician in a family of equally brilliant musicians. But unlike the rest of them—all playing in one orchestra or another, right down to his sister who for twenty-some years has played electric guitar in a hippie band called Plated Starfire—Raphael has excelled only at passing his artistry on to others. Public performance has defeated him.

And I have been his claim to fame and the means by which he's attracted, like a benevolent Pied Piper, a following of hopeful prodigies and their parents for more than two decades. But that's all set to be sacrificed if I don't get a grip on what's gone wrong in my head. Never mind that Raphael has never once bothered to get a grip on what's wrong in his head—it can't be normal for one man to sweat through three shirts and one suit jacket every day of his life, can it?—I am to devote all my waking hours to getting a grip on what's wrong in mine.

Raphael, as I've said, is the person who tracked you down initially, Dr Rose. Or at least, he tracked your father down once the neurologists decided that there was nothing physically wrong with me. So he has a dual vested interest in my recovery: Not only has he been significant in bringing me into your care, which might well put me into his debt in a very large way should you and I overcome my problem, but also my continued career as a violinist will mean his continued career as my muse. So Raphael would very much like to see me get well.

You're thinking this is cynicism, aren't you, Dr Rose? A new wrinkle in the blanket of my character. But remember that I have experienced Raphael Robson for years, so I know how he thinks and what he intends, probably better than he knows himself.

189

For example, I know that he dislikes my father. And I know that Dad would have sacked him a dozen times throughout the years had Raphael's style of instruction—allowing the student to develop his own method rather than imposing a preformed method upon him—not been exactly what I needed to thrive.

Why does Raphael dislike your father? you ask me curiously, unsure if this animosity between them is what's at the root of my present difficulty.

I don't have an answer to that question, Dr Rose, at least not an answer that's both lucid and complete. But I expect it has to do with my mother.

Raphael Robson and your mother? you clarify, and you look at me so intently that I wonder what nugget I've offered you.

So I dig into my mind. I try to see what is there. And I make a logical connection from examining everything I've been able to dredge out thus far because those words placed all in a row just now— Raphael Robson and my mother—have stirred something within me, Dr Rose. I can feel an uneasiness creeping outward from my gut. I've chewed and swallowed something rotten, and I feel *the consequences roiling round in me.*

What have I inadvertently unearthed? Raphael Robson has disliked my father for twenty-plus years because of my mother. Yes. I feel something like truth in this. But why?

You suggest that I take myself back in time to a moment when they are together, perhaps. Raphael and my mother. But the canvas is there, that damned black canvas and if they are on it, the paint has long ago been obscured.

And yet you've placed their names together,

Raphael's and your mother's, you point out to me. For their names to be linked, other links must exist, even if only within the subconscious mind. You're thinking of them together, you tell me. Do you see them together as well?

See *them? Together? The idea is preposterous.*

Which part? you ask. The seeing part or the together part, Gideon.

And I know where you're heading with both those alternatives. Don't think I don't. I'm to choose between Oedipal conflicts and the primal scene. That's where we're going, isn't it, Dr Rose? Little Gideon can't abide the fact that his music instructor a le béguin pour sa mère. *Or, what's worse, little Gideon walked in on* sa mère et l'amoureux de sa mère *in flagrante delicto, with* l'amoureux de sa mère *being Raphael Robson.*

Why the coy switch to French? you ask me. What does using English do to the facts? How does using English feel, Gideon?

Absurd. Ridiculous. Outrageous. Raphael Robson and my mother as lovers? What a ludicrous notion. How could she cope with his sweat? Even twenty years ago he sweats enough to water the garden.

12 SEPTEMBER
The garden. Flowers. God. I've remembered those flowers, Dr Rose. Raphael Robson coming to the house with an enormous spray of flowers. They're for my mother, and she's there in the house so it's either night time or she hasn't gone into work that day.

Is she ill? you ask me.

I don't know. But I see the flowers. Dozens of them. All different kinds, so many different kinds that

191

I can't even name them. It's the largest bouquet I've ever seen and yes, yes, she must be ill because Raphael takes the flowers to the kitchen and arranges them himself in a number of vases that Gran digs out for him. But Gran can't stay to help him with the flowers because Granddad must be watched for some reason. For days and days we've had to keep an eye on Granddad, and I don't know why.

An episode? you ask me. Is he having a psychotic episode, Gideon?

I don't know. Just that everyone *is out of sorts. Mother is ill. Granddad is being confined upstairs with music playing all the time to calm him. Sarah-Jane Beckett keeps huddling in corners with James the Lodger and if I get too close to them, she tightens her mouth and tells me to get back to my prep when I haven't actually been given any prep in the first place. I've caught Gran weeping on the stairs. I've heard Dad shouting somewhere: behind a closed door, I think. Sister Cecilia has called in, and I've seen her talking to Raphael in the upstairs corridor. And then there are all those flowers. Raphael and flowers. Scores of flowers that I can't even name.*

He takes them to the kitchen and I'm required to wait in the sitting room where he has provided an exercise for me to master. And I remember that exercise even today. It is scales. Scales, *which I loathe and which I feel are far beneath me. So I refuse to do them. I kick over my music stand. I shout that I'm bored, bored,* bored *with this* stupid *music and I won't play it a minute more. I demand the telly. I demand biscuits and milk. I demand.*

And Sarah-Jane is there in a flash. She says—and I do remember exactly what she says, Dr Rose, because it is so foreign to my ears, 'You're not *the* centre of the world any longer. Behave yourself.'

Not the centre of the world any longer? *you muse. So this must be after Sonia was born.*

It must be, Dr Rose.

Can you make any connections, then?

What sort of connections?

Raphael Robson, the flowers, your grandmother weeping, Sarah-Jane Beckett and the lodger gossiping—

I didn't say that they are gossiping. They're just talking together, their heads together, sharing a secret perhaps? I wonder. Are they lovers?

Yes, yes, Dr Rose. I see how I return to the theme of lovers. No need to point it out to me. And I know where you're heading, in an inexorable process that takes us towards my mother and Raphael. I see where that process is going to end if we examine the clues with rational calm. The clues are these: Raphael with those flowers, Gran crying and Dad shouting, Sister Cecilia in attendance, Sarah-Jane and the lodger tittering in a corner . . . I see where this takes us, Dr Rose.

What stops you from saying it, then? you ask, with those sombre sad sincere eyes on mine.

Nothing *stops me, except uncertainty.*

If you say it, you'll be able to test how it feels, to see if it fits.

All right, then. All right. Raphael Robson has impregnated my mother and together they have produced this child, Sonia. My father realises he's been cuckolded—God, where did that word come from? I feel like I'm taking part in a Jacobean melodrama—and the shouting that ensues behind closed doors is his reaction. Granddad hears this, puts together the pieces and is sent round the bend

193

and on his way to another episode. Gran reacts to the chaos between Mother and Dad as well as to the potential of another episode. Sarah-Jane and the lodger are all agog with the excitement. Sister Cecilia is brought in to attempt to mediate the dispute, but Dad can't bear to live in the same house with a constant reminder of Mother's infidelity, and he demands that the baby be sent away somewhere, adopted or something. Mother can't bear the thought of this and she weeps in her room.

And Raphael? you ask.

He's the proud father, isn't he? Bearing flowers like every proud father before him.

How does that feel? you want to know.

It makes me want to have a shower. And not because of the thought of my mother 'in the rank sweat of an unseaméd bed—' if you'll pardon the obvious allusion—but because of him. *Because of Raphael. Yes, I do see that he may have loved my mother and hated my father for possessing what he himself wanted. But that my mother would have returned his love . . . would have thought of taking that sweaty and perpetually sun-incinerated body into her bed or wherever else they might have accomplished the act . . . this thought is too incredible to be embraced.*

But children, you point out to me, always find the contemplation of their parents' sexuality abhorrent, Gideon. This is why the actual sight of intercourse—

I did not witness intercourse, Dr Rose. Not between my mother and Raphael, not between Sarah-Jane Beckett and the lodger, not between my grandparents, not between my father and anyone. Anyone.

Your father and anyone? you are quickly upon it. Who is anyone? *Where does* anyone *come from?*

194

Oh God. I don't know. I don't know.

15 SEPTEMBER
I went to see him this afternoon, Dr Rose. Ever since unearthing Sonia and then having the recollection of Raphael and those obscene flowers and the chaos in the house in Kensington Square, I've felt that I needed to talk to my father. So I went down to South Kensington and found him in the garden next to Braemar Mansions, which is where he's lived for the past few years. He was in the little greenhouse that he's commandeered from the rest of the residents of the building, and he was doing what he usually does with his free time. He was hovering over his infant hybrid camellias, examining their leaves with a magnifying glass, looking for either entomological intruders or incipient buds. I could not tell which. It's his dream to create a bloom worthy of the Chelsea Flower Show. Worthy of a prize at the show, I should say. Anything less would be a waste of his time.

From the street, I saw him inside the greenhouse, but as I don't have a key to the garden gate, I entered through the building. Dad has the first floor flat at the top of the stairs, and because I could see that the door was ajar up there, I headed up with the thought of securing it. But I found Jill inside at Dad's dining table, working on her lap top with her feet propped up on a hassock she'd brought in from the sitting room.

We exchanged pleasantries—what exactly does one say to one's father's young, pregnant mistress?—and she told me what I already knew, specifically that Dad was in the garden. She said, 'He's nurturing the rest of his children,' with one of those long-suffering rolls of the eyes that are intended to convey fond exasperation. But that phrase the rest of his children *seemed heavily laden with meaning today, and I couldn't put it from my mind as I left her.*

I realised that I'd failed to notice something before that was obvious to me as I made my way back through the flat. Walls, chest tops, table tops, and bookshelves announced a single bald fact that had never once touched upon my consciousness, and that fact was what I first dealt with when I entered the greenhouse, because it seemed to me that if I could wrest a truthful answer from my father, I would be one step closer to understanding.

Wrest? *You seize upon that word, don't you, Dr Rose? You seize upon it and everything it implies. Is your father less than truthful, then? you ask me.*

I'd never thought him so. But now I wonder.

And what will you understand? you want to know. Wresting the truth from your father will take you one step closer to understanding what?

To understanding what has happened to me.

It's connected to your father?

I don't want to think so.

When I walked into the greenhouse, he didn't look up, and I thought about how his body has begun to suit him for this current employment, bending over small plants. His scoliosis seems to have worsened over the past few years, and although he's just sixty-two years old, he seems older to me because of his growing curvature. Looking at him, I wondered how Jill Foster—nearly thirty years his junior—had come to see him as a sexual object. What draws human beings together is a puzzle to me.

I said, 'Why are there no pictures of Sonia in your flat, Dad?' An unexpected frontal assault seemed most likely to garner results. 'You've got me from every

196

angle at every age, with violin and without; but you haven't got Sonia. Why?'

He did look up then, but I think he was buying time because he took a handkerchief from the back pocket of his jeans and he used it to polish the magnifying glass. He refolded the handkerchief, stowed the lens in a chamois sack, and took the sack to a shelf at the end of the greenhouse where he keeps his gardening tools.

'Good afternoon to you as well,' he said. 'You had more of a greeting for Jill, I hope. Is she still on the computer?'

'In the kitchen.'

'Ah. The screenplay proceeds apace. She's doing The Beautiful and Damned. *Have I mentioned that? Ambitious to offer another Fitzgerald to the BBC, but she's determined to prove that an American novel about Americans in America can be made palatable for the British viewing public. We shall see. And how is your own American these days?'*

That's what he's taken to calling Libby. She has no name other than 'your American' although sometimes she becomes 'your little American' or 'your charming American'. She's particularly my charming American when she commits a social solecism of some kind, as she does with what seems like religious fervour. Libby does not stand on ceremony, and Dad has not forgiven her for referring to him by his Christian name when I first introduced them. Nor has he forgotten her immediate reaction to Jill's pregnancy: 'Holy shit. You knocked up a thirty-year-old? *Great going, Richard.' Jill's older than thirty, of course, but that was a small matter next to the effrontery of Libby's mentioning the great gap in their ages.*

197

'She's fine,' I said.

'Still riding her motorcycle round London, then?'

She's still working for the courier service, if that's what you mean.'

And how is she liking her Tartini these days? Shaken or stirred?' He removed his glasses, crossed his arms, and studied me in that way he always does, the way that says, 'Steady on or I'll sort you out.'

That look has managed to derail me on more than one occasion and in combination with his comments about Libby, it probably should have derailed me then. But having a sister pop into my mind where there had been no sister before was enough to bolster me to face whatever attempt at obfuscation he might make. I said, 'I'd forgotten Sonia. Not just how she died, but that she'd ever existed in the first place. I'd completely forgotten I ever had a sister. It's like someone took a rubber to my mind and erased her, Dad.'

'Is that why you've come, then? To ask about photographs?'

'To ask about her. Why don't you have any photographs of her?'

'You're looking for something sinister in the omission.'

'You have photos of me. You have an entire exhibit of Granddad. You have Jill. You even have Raphael.'

'Posing with Szeryng. Raphael was secondary.'

'Yes. All right. But that begs the question. Why is there nothing of Sonia?'

He observed me for a good five seconds before he moved. And then he merely turned and began cleaning off the potting bench where he'd earlier been working. He picked up a brush and used it to sweep loose leaves and the remains of soil into a bucket, which he took from the floor. This done, he sealed the soil bag, capped a bottle of fertiliser, and returned his gardening tools to their respective cubby holes. He cleaned each tool as he put it away. Finally, he removed the heavy green apron he wore when working with his camellias, and he led the way out of the greenhouse and into the garden.

There's a bench at one side, and he made his way over to it. It sits beneath a chestnut tree, long the bane of my father's existence. 'Too much God damn shade,' he always grumbles. 'What the hell is supposed to grow in shadow?'

Today he seemed to welcome the shade, though. He sat and winced a little, as if he had a pain in his back, which he might well have had because of his spine. But I didn't want to ask about that. He'd avoided my question for long enough.

I said, 'Dad, why is there—'

He said, 'This comes of that doctor, doesn't it? That woman . . . what's her name?'

'You know it. Dr Rose.'

He muttered, 'Shite,' and pushed himself off the bench. I thought he was going to return to the house in a temper rather than talk about a subject that he clearly didn't want to address, but he eased himself to his knees and began pulling at weeds in the flower bed that lay before us. He said, 'If I had my way, residents who don't take proper care of their plots would have their plots confiscated. Just look at this muck.'

It was hardly that. True, too much water had produced mould and moss on the border stones, and weeds tangled with an enormous fuchsia that appeared to need trimming. But there was something appealing about the natural look of the plot, with its central birdbath overgrown with ivy and its stepping

199

stones sunk deeply into greenery. 'I rather like it,' I said.

Dad gave a derisive snort. He continued pulling weeds, tossing them over his shoulder and onto the gravel path. 'Have you touched the Guarnerius yet?' he asked. He objectifies the violin that way, always has done. I prefer to call it by its maker's name, but Dad has melded the maker into the instrument, as if Guarneri himself had no other life.

'No. I haven't.'

He leaned back on his heels. 'That's brilliant, then. That's bloody brilliant. That's the great plan come to nothing, isn't it? Tell me, what's this gaining us? What exact advantage are you being blessed with as you and the good doctor take your shovels to the past? It's the present where our problem is, Gideon. I wouldn't think you'd need reminding of that.'

'She's calling it psychogenic amnesia. She says that—'

'Bollocks. You had a case of nerves. You still have a case of nerves. It happens. Ask anyone. Good God. How many years did Rubenstein not play? Ten? Twelve? And d'you think he spent that time scribbling in a notebook? I expect not.'

'He didn't lose the playing,' I explained to my father. 'He feared the playing.'

'You don't know that you've lost it, do you? If you haven't picked up the Guarnerius yet, you don't know what you've lost and what you're just afraid that you've lost. Anyone with an ounce of common sense would tell you that what you're experiencing is cowardice: plain and simple. And the fact that this doctor hasn't brought herself round to mentioning the word . . .' He went back to his weeding. 'Bollocks.'

'You wanted me to see her,' I reminded him. 'When

200

Raphael suggested it, you seconded the idea.'

'I thought you'd be learning to cope with your fear. I thought that's what she'd be giving you. And if, by the way, I'd known it was going to be a flaming she in that doctor's chair, I would have thought twice about carting you round there to weep on her shoulder in the first place.'

'I'm not—'

'This is what comes of that girl, that bloody blasted God damn girl.' And on the last word, he tugged a particularly entangled weed from the plot and uprooted one of the dormant lilies in the process. He swore and began to pound the earth round the plant in an attempt to undo the damage. 'This is how Americans think, Gideon, and I hope you see that,' he informed me. 'This is what comes of coddling an entire generation of layabouts who've had everything handed to them on a platter. They know nothing but leisure so they use that leisure to blame their anomie on their parents. She's encouraged this fault-finding in you, boy. Next, she'll be promoting chat shows as a venue for airing what ails you.'

'That's not fair on Libby. She's nothing to do with this.'

'You were bloody all right till she came along.'

'Nothing's happened between us to cause this problem.'

'Sleeping with her, are you?'

'Dad—'

'Shagging her properly?' He looked over his shoulder as he asked this last question, and he must have seen what I preferred to keep hidden. Seeing it, he said ironically, 'Ah. Yes. But she is not the root of your problem. I see. So tell me, exactly what does Dr Rose consider the appropriate moment for you to pick

201

up the violin again?'

'We haven't talked about that.'

He shoved himself to his feet. 'That's bloody rich. You've seen her . . . what? . . . three times a week for how many weeks? Three? Four? But you haven't yet got round to talking about the problem? See anything singular in that state of affairs?'

'The violin—the playing—'

'You mean the not playing.'

'All right. Yes. Not playing the violin. It's a symptom, Dad. It's not the disease.'

'Tell that to Paris, Munich, and Rome.'

'I'll make the concerts.'

'Not the way you're going at it now.'

'I thought you wanted me to see her. You asked Raphael—'

'I asked Raphael for help. Help to get you back on your feet. Help to put the violin in your hands. Help to get you back in the concert hall. Tell me—just tell me, swear to it, reassure me, anything—that that's what you're getting from this doctor. Because I'm on your side in this, son. I am on your side.'

'I can't swear to it,' I said and I know that my voice reflected all the defeat I felt. 'I don't know what I'm getting from her, Dad.'

He wiped his hands on the sides of his jeans. I heard him curse in a low tone that seemed tinctured with anguish. He said, 'Come with me.'

I followed him. We went back into the building, up the stairs, and into his flat. Jill had made tea and she raised her cup to us, saying, 'Want one, Gideon? Darling?' as we passed the kitchen. I thanked her and demurred, but Dad made no response. Jill's face clouded in that way I've seen when Dad ignores her: not as if she's hurt but as if she's comparing his

202

behaviour with some unmentioned catalogue of appropriate behaviours she's developed in her head.

Dad strode on, oblivious of this. He went to what I call the Granddad Room, where he keeps a bizarre but nonetheless revealing collection of memorabilia: everything from silver-encased childhood locks of Granddad's hair to letters from the 'great man's' wartime commanding officer commending him upon his comportment while imprisoned in Burma. It sometimes seems to me that Dad has spent the better part of his life trying to pretend his father was either a normal or a supernormal man, rather than what he actually was, a broken mind who spent more than forty years balancing on the brink of insanity for reasons no one would ever mention.

He shut the door behind us, and at first I thought he'd taken me into the room in order to recite some sort of panegyric to Granddad. I felt myself getting irritated at what I saw as yet another attempt on his part to deflect a proper conversation.

He's done this before? you want to know, don't you? It's the logical question.

And I would have to say Yes, he's done this before. I hadn't much considered that fact until recently. I hadn't actually had to consider it because my music was central to our relationship and that's always what we talked about. Practice sessions with Raphael, work at the East London Conservatory, recording sessions, personal appearances, concerts, tours . . . There was always my music to occupy us. And because I was so engaged with my music, any question I asked or subject I wanted to pursue could easily be avoided by directing my thoughts to the violin. How's the Stravinski coming along? What about the Bach? Is The Archduke still giving you trouble? God. The

Archduke. *It always gave me trouble. It's my Nemesis, that piece. It's my Waterloo. It is, in fact, what I was scheduled to play at Wigmore Hall. First time in public to master the bastard and I couldn't do it.*

Ah. You see how easily I become distracted by the thought of my music, Dr Rose. Even then I did it to myself, so you can imagine how skilfully Dad could manage to divert our conversations.

But this afternoon, I couldn't be distracted, and Dad must have realised this because he didn't attempt either to regale me with a story of Granddad's feats of ostensible bravery during his imprisonment or to move me with a review of his gallant battle against a monstrous mental condition that had its tendrils buried deep in his brain. Instead, he shut the door behind us, and I realised he'd done so to gain us some privacy.

He said, 'You're looking for something nasty, aren't you? Isn't that what psychiatrists are always after?'

'I'm trying to remember,' I told him. 'That's what this is about.'

'How is remembering Sonia supposed to gain you ground with your instrument? Has your Dr Rose explained that to you?'

You haven't, have you, Dr Rose? All you've said is that we'll begin with what I can remember. I'll write about everything I have in my memory, but you don't explain how doing this exercise will manage to dislodge whatever it is that's blocking my ability to play.

And what has Sonia to do with my playing? She must have been a baby when she died. Because surely I would remember an older sibling, one who walked and talked, who played in the sitting room, who created mud puddles in the back garden with me. I would remember that.

I said, 'Dr Rose calls this psychogenic amnesia.'

'Psycho . . . what?'

I explained it to him as you explained it to me. I ended with, 'Because there's no physical cause for the memory loss—and you know the neurologists have cleared the screen on that—the cause has to come from somewhere else. From the psyche, Dad, and not from the brain.'

'That's a load of rubbish,' he said but I could tell that the words were a form of bravado. He sat in an armchair and stared at nothing.

'All right.' I sat as well, in front of the old roll top desk that belonged to Gran. I did what I'd never considered doing before because I'd never felt it necessary. I called his bluff. 'All right, Dad. Accepted. It's rubbish. What should I do then? Because if all I'm feeling is nerves and fear, I'd be able to play my music alone, wouldn't I? With no one there? With even Libby out of the house so that I could be certain I had no eavesdroppers anywhere? I could play then, couldn't I? And if I couldn't manage so much as a simple arpeggio, who'd be the wiser? Isn't that the case?'

He looked at me. 'Have you tried, Gideon?'

'Don't you see? I haven't had to try. I don't need to try when I already know.'

He moved his head, then, away from me. He seemed to go inward and while he did so, I was aware of the silence in the flat and the silence outside, no breeze even blowing to sussurate the tree leaves. When he finally spoke, it was to say, 'No one knows the pain of having a child before the child is born. It seems as if it'll be so simple, but it never is.'

I made no reply. Was he speaking of me? Of Sonia? Or the other, that longer ago child of a distant marriage, the one called Virginia, who had never been spoken of?

He went on. 'You give them life and you know you'd do anything to protect them, Gideon. That's how it is.'

I nodded, but he still wasn't looking at me so I said, 'Yes.' Affirmation of what, I couldn't tell you. But I had to say something, and that was what I said.

It seemed enough. Dad said, 'Sometimes you fail. You don't intend to. You don't even contemplate failure. But it happens. It comes out of nowhere and it takes you by surprise and before you have a chance to stop—even to react in some useless way—it's on you. Failure.' He met my eyes, then, and the look he gave me was so filled with suffering that I wanted to retreat and to spare him whatever was causing him such pain. Hadn't it been bad enough that his childhood, adolescence, and adulthood had been filled with the sorrow of having a father whose infirmities tried his patience and depleted his reserves of devotion? Was he now supposed to be saddled with a son who appeared to be heading in the same direction? I wanted to retreat. I wanted to spare him. But I wanted my music more. So I said nothing. I let the silence lie like a gauntlet between us. And when my father could bear the unseen sight of that gauntlet no longer, he picked it up.

He stood and came towards me and for a moment I thought he intended to touch me. But instead he rolled back the top of my grandmother's desk. From his key ring, he inserted a small key in the central interior drawer. From the drawer, he took a neat stack of papers, and carried them back to his chair.

We'd arrived somewhere, and I was aware of the drama and significance of the moment, as if we'd crossed a boundary that neither of us had recognised as even existing before. I felt a churning in my gut as he fingered through the papers. I saw the sparkling crescent in the field of my vision that always heralds the pounding in my head.

He said, 'I have no pictures of Sonia for the simplest of reasons. Had you thought it through—and had you been less distressed you probably would have—I'm certain you would have worked it out for yourself. Your mother took the pictures when she left us, Gideon. She took every one of them. Except for this.'

He took a single snapshot from a soiled envelope. He passed it to me. And for a moment, I found that I didn't want to take it from him, so fraught with meaning had Sonia suddenly become.

He read my hesitation. He said, 'Take it, Gideon. It's all I have left of her.'

So I took it, hardly daring to wonder what I might see, but somehow fearing what I would see all the same. I swallowed and steeled myself. I looked.

What was in the picture was this: a baby cradled in the arms of a woman I did not recognise. They were seated in the back garden of the Kensington Square house, on a striped deck chair in the sun. The woman's shadow fell across Sonia's face, but her own was fully exposed to the light. She was young and blonde, very blonde. She was aquiline featured. She was very pretty.

'I don't . . . Who is this?' I asked my father.

'That's Katja,' he said. 'That's Katja Wolff.'

Gideon

<u>20 SEPTEMBER</u>
This is what I've been wondering ever since Dad showed me that photograph: If Mother took with her every photograph of Sonia that was in the house, why did she leave that one photo behind? Was it because Sonia's face was so much in shadow that she might have been any baby and consequently not memorable to my mother, not something she could cling to in her grief . . . if grief was indeed what took her from us? Or was it because Katja Wolff was in it? Or was it because Mother didn't know about the photo in the first place? Because, you see, the one thing I cannot tell from the photo—which I have now with me and which I will show you when next we meet—is who took it.

And why did Dad have this particular photo, this photo in which the focal figure is not his daughter, his very own daughter who died, but a young and smiling and golden woman who is not his wife was never his wife never became his wife and was certainly not the mother of that child.

I asked Dad about Katja Wolff because asking was the natural thing to do. He told me that she was Sonia's nanny. She was a German girl, he said, with very limited English. She'd made a dramatic and foolhardy escape from East to West Berlin in a hot air balloon that she and her boyfriend had manufactured in secret, and she'd gained some notoriety from that.

Do you already know this story, Dr Rose? Perhaps not. You would have been less than ten years old at that time, I expect, and living . . . where? In America at that point?

Living here in England so much closer to where it all happened, I don't remember it myself. But it was, as Dad told me, quite a story then because Katja and her boyfriend didn't attempt their crossing from somewhere in the countryside where it would have been at least marginally safer to go from east into west but instead they sailed from East Berlin itself. The boy didn't make it all the way. The border guards got him. But Katja did make it. She earned her fifteen minutes that way and became a standard bearer for freedom. Television news, front page headlines, magazine stories, radio interviews. She ended up being invited to England.

I listened carefully as Dad told me all this, and I watched him closely. I looked for signs and for inner meanings, and I tried to make inferences, leaps, and deductions. Because even now in the situation in which I find myself—sitting here in the music room in Chalcot Square with the Guarneri fifteen feet away, taken from its case at least and surely that's progress God tell me that's progress, Dr Rose, although I can't bring myself to lift the violin to the height of my shoulder—there are questions I'm afraid to ask my father.

What sort of questions? you want to know.

Questions like these, questions that rise to my mind without effort: Who took that picture of Sonia and Katja? Why did my mother leave only that single photo behind? Did she even know about it? Did she actually take the other pictures or did he destroy them? And why, above all, did my father never speak of them before now: never speak to me of Sonia, of Katja, of my mother?

Obviously, he hadn't forgotten they existed. After

209

all, once I brought Sonia up, he produced her picture and from its condition I'd swear before God that it was something he's held and contemplated hundreds of times. So why the silence?

People sometimes avoid, you tell me. They dodge subjects too painful for them to face.

So what is too painful for my father to face? Sonia herself? Her death? My mother? Her leaving? The pictures?

Katja Wolff perhaps?

But why would Katja Wolff be a painful subject to Dad? Except for the most obvious reason.

Which is?

You want me to say it, don't you, Dr Rose? You want me to write it. You want me to stare at it sitting on this page, and thus to weigh its truth or its falsehood. But where the hell is that going to get me? She's holding my sister, she's cradling her just beneath her breast, her eyes look kind and her face is serene. One of her shoulders is bare because she's wearing a dress or a top with straps too loose and it's brightly coloured, bizarrely coloured, that dress or top, so much yellow and orange and green and blue. And that bare shoulder is smooth and round and yes all right it's an invitation and I'd have to be blind not to see it so if a man is taking that picture of Katja and if that man is my father—but it could be Raphael it could be James the Lodger it could be Granddad or the gardener or the postman or any man because she is splendid beautiful seductive and even I a cocked up mess of a paltry excuse of a healthy laughable male can see who she is and what she is and how she's offering what she's offering—then that man has an alliance with her and I've a fairly good idea what sort it is.

210

So write about her, you instruct me. Write about Katja. Fill a page with her name alone if that's what it takes and see where filling that page takes you, Gideon. Ask your father if there are other pictures he can show you: family pictures, casual pictures, snapshots of holidays, fêtes, parties, gatherings, dinners, anything at all. Look at them closely. See who's in them. Read their expressions.

Look for Katja? I ask.

Look for what's there.

21 SEPTEMBER

Dad says I was six when was Sonia was born. I was just short of eight when she died. I phoned and asked him those two questions outright. Aren't you pleased, Dr Rose? The horns were there and I actually grabbed them.

When I asked him how Sonia died, Dad said, 'She drowned, son.' The answer seemed to cost him much, and his voice seemed to come from a place that was distant. I felt a tightness inside me, having asked him anything at all, but that did not stop me going on. I asked him her age when she died: two years. And the strain in his voice told me that she had been quite old enough not only to have established a permanent place in his heart but also to have made an indelible mark on his spirit.

The sound of that strain and the comprehension that accompanied it explained so much to me about my father: his focus on me throughout my childhood, his determination that I should have and see and be and experience the very best, his single-minded protection of me when I began my public career, his wariness of anyone who came too close and might do

211

me harm. Having lost one child—no, my God, having lost two because Virginia his oldest had died young as well—he was not about to lose another.

So I finally understand why he's stayed so close, been so involved, finessed so much of my life and career. Early on I said aloud what I wanted—the violin, my music—and he did what it took to see to it that his remaining child was given just that, as if by providing me the means to my dream he would somehow assure my longevity. So he had two jobs; he sent Mother out to work as well; he employed Raphael; he arranged that I should be educated at home.

Except all this was before *Sonia, wasn't it? It couldn't have been the result of Sonia's death. Because if, as he said, she was born when I was six years old, Raphael Robson and Sarah-Jane Beckett would already have been in place in the house. And James the Lodger would have been there as well. And into this already* established *group Katja Wolff would have come as Sonia's nanny. So that's what must have happened, isn't it: An established group was forced to accept an interloper in their midst. An intruder, if you will. A foreigner as well. And not just any, but a German foreigner. Briefly famous, yes. But German all the same: our wartime enemy and Granddad forever a prisoner of that war.*

So Sarah-Jane Beckett and James the Lodger are whispering about her *in that corner in the kitchen, not about my mother, not about Raphael, and not about those flowers. They are whispering about* her *because Sarah-Jane is like that,* was *like that from the first, a whisperer. Her whispering grows out of jealousy because Katja is lithe and pretty and seductive and Sarah-Jane Beckett—with her short red*

212

*hair like a pudding bowl sprouting from her scalp and
her body not much different to mine—sees how the
men in the household look at Katja, especially James
the Lodger who helps Katja with her English and
laughs when she says with a shiver 'Mein Gott, my
corpse is not yet used to such rain in this country'
instead of* my body, *which is what she means. She's
asked if she would like a cup of tea, and she says, 'Oh
yes. Most voluntarily and with many gratitudes,' and
they laugh the men laugh but it's laughter that's
charmed. My father, Raphael James the Lodger, even
Granddad.*

And I remember that. Dr Rose, I remember.

22SEPTEMBER

*So where has she been all these years, Katja Wolff?
Buried with Sonia? Buried because of Sonia perhaps?*

Because *of Sonia? You pounce upon the word,
don't you? Why* because, *Gideon?*

*Because of her death. If Katja was Sonia's nanny
and Sonia died when she was two years old, Katja
would have left us then, wouldn't she? I would have
had no need for a nanny with Raphael and Sarah-
Jane attending to me. So Katja would have left us
after two years—perhaps even less—and that would
be why I'd forgotten her. I was, after all, only eight at
the time, and she wasn't my nanny but Sonia's, so I
would have had little to do with her. I was consumed
with my music and when the violin wasn't devouring
my time, my school lessons were. I'd already had my
first public performances, and the fallout from them
was an offer to study at Juilliard for a year. Imagine
that. Juilliard. What age could I have been: seven?
eight?*

213

'A virtuoso in the making,' I was called.
But I didn't want making. *I wanted* made.

23 SEPTEMBER
I don't go to Juilliard as things turn out, despite the honour and what it can mean to my development as an international musician. Because of the history of the place, scores of people three times my age would have done anything to have the same opportunity, to experience the endless possibilities that could come from having this extraordinary transcendent invaluable experience . . . But there is no money and even if there were, I am far too young to go that distance by myself, let alone to live there. And since my family cannot move there en masse, *the opportunity passes me by.*

En masse. *Yes. I somehow know that* en masse *is the only way Juilliard will happen to me, money or not. So I say Please* please *let me go, Dad, I must go, I want to go to New York because even then I know what it means in my present and can mean to my future. Dad says Gideon, you know we can't go. You can't be there alone, and we can't go as a group. Naturally, I demand to know why. Why why why can't I have what I want when until this moment I have always had it. He says—and yes, I remember this well—Gideon, the world will come to you. I promise you that, I swear it, son.*

But it's clear that we can't go to New York.

For some reason I know *this even as I ask again and again and again, even as I bargain, beg, behave as badly as I've ever done, as I kick the music stand, fling myself into my grandmother's treasured demi-lune table and crack two of its legs . . . even then I*

214

know *there will be no Juilliard no matter what I do. Alone, with my family, with one of my parents, accompanied only by Raphael, or with Sarah-Jane dogging my heels as my shadow or protector, I will not be going to that Mecca of music.*

Know, *you point out to me. Know before you ask, know as you ask, know despite everything you do to change . . . what, Gideon? What are you trying to change?*

Reality, obviously. And yes, Dr Rose, I know that's an answer that takes us nowhere. What's the reality that I already understand as a seven or eight-year-old?

It appears to be this: We are not a rich family. Oh yes, we live in an area that not only indicates but also requires money, but the family's owned that house for generations and the only reason the family still owns it is due to the lodgers, to Dad's two jobs, to Mother's going to work, and to Granddad's pension. But money is not something we ever discuss. Talk of money is like speaking of bodily functions at the dinner table. Yet I know I won't go to Juilliard and I feel a tightening inside me as I know this. It starts in my arms. It moves to my stomach. It rises upwards into my throat till I shout oh I shout and I remember what I shout, 'It's because she can't go!' And that's when I kick and pound and fling. That's when, Dr Rose.

She can't go?

She. Of course. It must be Katja.

<u>*26 SEPTEMBER 5:00 P.M.*</u>
Dad was here again. He came for two hours and was replaced by Raphael. They wanted to make it look as

if they weren't taking it in shifts at a death watch, so I had at least five minutes alone between the time Dad left and Raphael arrived. But what they don't know is that I saw them from the window. Raphael came walking into Chalcot Square from the direction of Chalcot Road, and Dad intercepted him in the middle of the garden. They stood on either side of one of the benches and they talked. At least, Dad talked. Raphael listened. He nodded and did what he always does: ran his fingers left to right on his scalp to arrange the fretwork that's left of his hair. Dad was passionate. I could tell that much from the way he gestured, one hand up at the level of his chest and closed into a fist like a punch withheld. The rest I didn't need to interpret because I knew what he was passionate about.

He'd come in peace. No mention of anything regarding my music. 'Had to get away from her for a while,' he sighed. 'I've come to believe that women the world over in the last months of pregnancy are all the same.'

Jill's moved in, then?' I asked him.

'Why tempt fate?'

Which was his way of saying that they're sticking to their original plan: have the baby first, combine their households second, and marry when the dust settles on the first two events. It's the fashion these days to go at relationships in that way, and Jill is nothing if not fashionable. But I sometimes wonder how Dad feels about an arrangement so foreign to his other marriages. He's a traditionalist at heart, I believe, with nothing so important as his family and with only one way in mind to make a family. Once he learned Jill was pregnant, I can't see him doing anything but dropping hastily to one knee in order to claim her.

216

Indeed, that's what he did with his first wife although he doesn't know that I learned that from Granddad. He met her while he was on leave from the Army—his intended career, by the way—he got her pregnant, and he married her. That he's not gone the same route with Jill tells me it's Jill's agenda being followed.

'She sleeps when she can now,' he told me. 'It's always like that in the last six weeks or so. They're so blasted uncomfortable and if the baby's decided to be awake from midnight till five a.m . . .' He brushed his hand through the air dismissively. 'Then you've got what you've been waiting for for years: a nightly chance to read War and Peace.*'*

'Are you staying with her now?'

'I'm doing time on the sofa.'

'Not good for your back, Dad.'

'Don't remind me.'

'Have you settled on the name?'

'I still want Cara.'

'She still wants—' and the import dawned upon me so suddenly that I scarcely said it but I forced myself to go on. 'She's holding fast for Catherine?'

He and I locked eyes, and she was there between us, as if she were corporeal, immediate, and eternally that captivating girl in the picture. And I said, even though my palms were damp and my gut was beginning to feel the first spark of a fire to come, 'But that would remind you of Katja, wouldn't it? If you called the baby Catherine?'

His response was to get up and make coffee, and he took his time with the activity. He commented upon my choice of ready ground beans and what they did to destroy freshness. He went from there to an expatiation of what the presence of yet another Starbucks—this one on Gloucester Road not far from

217

Braemar Mansions—has done to the atmosphere of his neighbourhood.

As he did all this, the pain in my gut began to move slowly down where it planned, as always, to wreak havoc with my bowels. I listened to him make the leap from Starbucks to the Americanisation of global culture, and I pressed my arm hard against the lowest part of my intestines, willing the pain to stop and the urgency to ease because if that did not happen, Dad would have won.

I let him exhaust the subject of America: international conglomerates dominating business, Hollywood megalomaniacs determining cinematic art forms, astronomical and singularly obscene salaries and share options becoming the measure of a capitalist's success. When he reached the peroration of his speech—evidenced by the fact that the great gulps he was taking from his coffee cup were becoming more frequent—I repeated my question, except this time I didn't ask it as a question. 'Katja,' I said. 'Catherine would remind you.'

He poured what remained of his coffee down the drain. He strode into the music room. As he moved, he said, 'God damn it. Show me, Gideon.' And then, 'Ah. This is what's going for progress, is it?'

He'd seen the Guarneri back in its case and although the case was open, he somehow knew that I hadn't yet attempted to play it. He took it from the case and the absence of the reverence with which he'd touched that violin in the past told me just how angry—or agitated, irritated, infuriated, frightened, worried, I do not know which—he actually was. He held the instrument out to me, fingers round its neck with that brilliant scroll emerging from his fist like hope coiled round an unspoken promise. He said,

218

'Here. Take it. Show me where we are. Show me exactly where weeks of excavating through the dreck of the past has taken you, Gideon. A note will do. A scale. An arpeggio. Or, miraculously because something tells me it would be miraculous at this point, a movement from the concerto of your choice. Any concerto. Too tough? Then what about a little encore piece?'

And the fire was in me but it was changed to a single coal. White hot, silver hot, incandescent, and it moved like acid down through my body.

And yes, yes, I see what my father has done, Dr Rose. You don't need to point it out. I see what he's done. But in that moment I could only say, 'I can't. Don't make me. I can't,' like a nine-year-old who's been asked to play a piece that he cannot master.

Dad used that next, saying, 'Perhaps that's beneath you. Too easy for you, Gideon. An insult to your talent. So let's start with The Archduke, shall we?'

Let's start with The Archduke. The acid ate through me and what's left when the pain has knotted my viscera and rendered me useless is blame. I am at fault. I placed myself into this position. Beth set the programme for the Wigmore Hall benefit and she said 'What about The Archduke, Gideon?' in absolute innocence. And because it was Beth who made the suggestion, Beth who'd already experienced my other more personal brand of failure, I couldn't bring myself to say, 'Forget it. That piece is a jinx.'

Artists believe in jinxes. The word Macbeth spoken inside a theatre has its counterpart in every field of art. So if I'd called The Archduke what I needed to call it—my personal jinx—Beth would have understood, despite the way she and I ended. And Sherill wouldn't have cared as much as a sprat what

219

we played. He would have said, in that Do-I-actually-give-a-shit American fashion of his that he uses to hide a monstrous talent, 'Just point me to the keyboard, boys and girls,' and that would have been that. So it was all down to me and I let it happen. I am to blame.

Dad found me where I'd taken myself off to when I could not face the challenge he was issuing: in the shed in the garden where I sketch the designs and make my kites. That's what I was doing then—sketching—and he joined me, the Guarneri replaced in its case and the case itself left inside the house.

He said, 'You are the music, Gideon. That's what I want you for. That's all that I want.'

I said, 'That's what we're trying to get to.'

He said, 'It's bollocks, going at it this way, scratching in notebooks and having a snooze on the trick cyclist's sofa every three days.'

'I don't lie on a sofa.'

'You know what I mean.' He placed his hand across the sketch I was working on, the better to force me to pay attention. He said, 'We can hold people at bay only so long for you, Gideon. We're doing it—Joanne is doing a bloody brilliant job, in fact—but there's going to come a point when even a publicist like Joanne, loyal as she is, is going to start asking exactly what the term exhaustion means. When that happens, I'm either going to have to tell her the truth or I'm going to have to invent a fiction for her to offer people that might damn well make the situation worse.'

'Dad,' I said, 'it's mad to think the tabloid-reading public gives a toss about—'

'I'm not talking about tabloids. Right. A rock star disappears from view and the journalists are digging

220

through his rubbish every morning, looking for something that will tell them why. That's not the case here and that's not what concerns me. What concerns me is the world that we live in with a schedule of concerts set up through the next twenty-five months, Gideon, as you well know, and with phone calls— almost daily, mind you—from musical directors enquiring about the state of your health. Which is, as you also know, a euphemism for your playing. "Is he recovering from exhaustion?" means "Do we tear up the contract or keep the programme in place?"' As he said all this, Dad slowly eased my drawing towards him and although his fingers had begun to smear the lines that sketched out the two bottom spreaders, I didn't point this out to him and I didn't stop him. So he went on. 'Now, what I'm asking you to do is simple: Walk inside that house, go up to the music room, and pick up that violin. Don't do it for me because this isn't about me and it never was. Do it for yourself.'

'I can't.'

'I'll be with you. I'll be next to you, holding you upright or whatever you want. But you've got to do it.'

We stared at each other, Dr Rose. I could feel him willing me out of that shed where I make my kites, out of the garden, and into the house.

He said, 'You won't know if you've made progress with her, Gideon, unless you pick up the instrument and try.'

By that, he meant you, Dr Rose. He meant progress with you. He meant these hours of writing I've been doing. He meant this sifting through the past we've engaged in which, it appeared, he was willing to assist me in . . . if I only gave him a demonstration that at the very least I could pick up the violin and scrape the

221

bow across the strings.

So I said nothing, but I left the shed and went back to the house. In the music room, I walked not to the window seat where I've done most of this notebook writing, but to the violin case instead. The Guarneri lay there, its top and its purfling gleaming, the repository of two hundred and fifty years of music-making shimmering from its F holes, its sides, and its pegs.

I can do this. Twenty-five years do not vanish in an instant. Everything I've learned, everything I know, every natural talent I ever possessed may be obscured, may be buried under a landslide I cannot yet identify, but all of it is there.

Dad stood next to me at the violin case. He put his hand on my elbow as I reached for the Guarneri. He murmured, 'I won't leave you, son. It's all right. I'm here.'

And just at that moment, the phone began to ring.

Dad's fingers tightened on my elbow like a reflex. He said, 'Leave it,' in reference to the phone. And since that's what I'd been doing for weeks, I had no trouble accommodating him.

But it was Jill's voice that spoke into the answer machine. When she said, 'Gideon? Is Richard still there? I must speak to Richard. Has he left? Please pick up,' Dad and I reacted identically. We both said, 'The baby,' and he strode to the phone.

He said, 'I'm still here. Are you all right, darling?' And then he listened.

There was no simple yes or no in her reply. As she made it, Dad turned from me, and said, 'What sort of phone call?' He listened to another lengthy response and he finally said, 'Jill . . . Jill . . . Enough. Why on earth did you answer it?'

She responded at length again. At the end of her reply, Dad said, 'Wait. Hang on. Don't be silly. You're working yourself into a real state . . . I can hardly be responsible for an unsolicited call when—' His face darkened suddenly as she apparently interrupted him. 'God damn it, Jill. Listen to yourself. You're being completely irrational.' And the tone in which he spoke those final words was one I'd heard him use before to dismiss a subject he didn't wish to pursue. Glacial, it was. Dismissive, superior, and in control.

But Jill was not one to release a topic so lightly. She went on again. He listened again. His back was to me, but I could see him stiffening. It was nearly a minute before he spoke.

'I'm coming home,' he told her brusquely. 'We're not having this discussion over the phone.'

He rang off then, and it sounded to me as if she was in midsentence when he did so. He turned round, and said with a glance at the Guarneri, 'You've had a reprieve.'

'Everything all right at home?' I asked him.

'Nothing's right anywhere,' was his curt reply.

26 SEPTEMBER 11:30 P.M.

The fact that I'd failed to play for him was undoubtedly what Dad shared with Raphael in the square when he left me because when Raphael joined me not three minutes after he and Dad parted, I could see the information incised on his face. His glance went to the Guarneri.

'I can't,' I said.

'He says you won't.' Raphael touched the instrument gently. It was a caress that he might have given to a woman had any woman ever found him an

223

object of sexual attraction. But no woman had done, as far as I knew. Indeed, it seemed to me as I watched him that I alone—and my violin—had prevented Raphael from leading a completely solitary life.

As if to confirm my thoughts, Raphael said, 'This can't go on forever, Gideon.'

'If it does?' I asked him.

'It won't. It can't.'

'Do you take his side, then? Did he ask you out there—'here I nodded at the window—'to demand that I play for you?'

Raphael looked out at the square, at the trees whose leaves were beginning to change now, dressing themselves in the colours of autumn. 'No,' he said. 'He didn't ask that I force you to play. Not today. I dare say his mind was on other things.'

I wasn't sure I believed him, considering the passion I'd witnessed in my father as he'd spoken to Raphael in the square. But I seized on the idea of 'other things' and I used that to turn the conversation. 'Why did my mother leave us?' I asked. 'Was it because of Katja Wolff?'

Raphael said, 'This isn't a subject for you and me.'

'I've remembered Sonia,' I told him.

He reached for the latch on the window, and I thought he meant to open it, either to let in the cool air or to climb outside onto the narrow balcony. But he did neither. He merely fumbled with the mechanism uselessly, and it came to me, watching him, how that simple gesture said so much about the lack in every interaction he and I had had that did not involve the violin.

I said, 'I've remembered her, Raphael. I've remembered Sonia. Katja Wolff as well. Why has no one ever spoken of them?'

He looked pained, and I thought he meant to avoid answering me. But just as I was ready to challenge his silence, he said, 'Because of what happened to Sonia.'

'What? What happened to Sonia?'

His voice contained wonder when he replied. 'You really don't remember, do you? I always thought you never spoke of it because the rest of us didn't. But you don't remember.'

I shook my head, and the shame of that admission swept through me. She was my sister *and I could not remember a single thing about her, Dr Rose. Until you and I began this process, I'd completely forgotten she'd ever existed. Can you begin to imagine how that feels?*

Raphael went on, using great kindness to excuse the obsessive self-interest that had erased my younger sister from my mind. He said, 'But you weren't even eight years old then, were you? And we never spoke of it once the trial was over. We barely spoke of it during the trial, and we agreed not to speak of it afterwards. Even your mother agreed, although she was broken by everything that happened. Yes. I can see how you might have wiped it all from your mind.'

I said although my mouth was dry, 'Dad told me that she drowned, that Sonia drowned. *Why was there a trial? Who was tried? For what?'*

'Your father didn't tell you more?'

'He didn't say anything other than Sonia drowned. He seemed so . . . He looked like he was paying a price just to tell me how she died. I didn't want to ask him for more. But now . . . a trial? That must mean . . . a trial?'

Raphael nodded, and all the possibilities implied by what I've recalled so far swarmed into my mind at

225

once before he went on: Virginia died young, Granddad had episodes, Mother is weeping and weeping in her room, someone has taken a picture in the garden, Sister Cecilia is in the hall, Dad is shouting, and I'm in the sitting room kicking at the legs of the sofa, upending my music stand, hotly and defiantly declaring that I will not play those infantile scales.

'Katja Wolff killed your sister, Gideon,' Raphael told me. 'She drowned her in her bath.'

28 SEPTEMBER

He wouldn't say more. He simply shut off, shut down or whatever it is that people do when they've reached the limit of what they can force themselves to speak of. When I said, 'Drowned? Deliberately? When? Why?' *and felt the apprehension that attended those words streak cold fingers down my spine, he said,* 'I can't say more. Ask your father.'

My father. He sits on the edge of my bed and he watches me and I am afraid.

Of what? you ask me. How old are you, Gideon?

I must be young because he seems so big, like a giant when actually he's much the same size as I am now. He puts his hand on my forehead—

Are you comforted by the touch?

No. No, I shrink away.

Does he speak?

Not at first. He just sits with me. But after a moment he moves to place his hands on my shoulders as if he expects me to rise and wishes to hold me still where I lie so I might listen to him. So that's what I do. I lie there and we gaze at each other and then finally he starts to speak.

226

He says, 'You're safe, Gideon. You are safe.'

What's he talking about? you ask. Have you had a bad dream? Is that why he's there? Or is it something more? Katja Wolff, perhaps? Are you safe from her? Or is this something from further back, Gideon, from the time before Katja lived at your house?

There've been people at the house. I remember that. I've been sent to my room in the company of Sarah-Jane Beckett, and she's talking talking talking to herself in a voice that I'm not meant to hear. She's pacing, talking, and pulling at her fingernails as if she wants to tear them off. She's saying, 'I knew it. I could see this coming.' She's saying, 'Bloody little whore,' and I know those are bad words, and I'm surprised and frightened because Sarah-Jane Beckett doesn't use bad words. 'Thought we wouldn't know,' she says. 'Thought we wouldn't notice.'

Notice what?

I don't know.

Outside my bedroom, there are footsteps and someone is crying, 'Here! In here!' I recognise the voice as barely my father's because it is tinged with so much panic. Above his cries, I hear my mother, and she's saying, 'Richard! Oh my God, Richard! Richard!' Granddad is raving, Gran is keening, and someone is calling for everyone to 'clear the room, clear the room'. This last is a voice I don't recognise and when Sarah-Jane hears it, she stops pacing and murmuring and she waits with her head bent, standing next to the door.

And there are other voices—more strangers' voices—that I hear. One asks a series of sharp questions beginning with how.

And there are more footsteps, constant movement, metal toolboxes hitting the floor, orders being barked

227

by a man, other tense male voices responding, and through it all, someone is crying out, 'No! I do not leave her alone!'

That must be Katja because she says do *instead of* did, *which might be what someone unfamiliar with English would say in a moment of panic. And when she says this, weeping as she says it, Sarah-Jane Beckett puts her hand on the doorknob and says, 'Little bitch.'*

I think she means to go into the corridor where all the noise is, but she doesn't do that. Instead, she looks towards the bed where I'm watching her, and she says, 'I won't be leaving now, I expect.'

Leaving, Gideon? Had she been going somewhere? Was it time for her annual holiday?

No. I don't think that's what she's talking about. Somehow I think this leaving was to be permanent.

Perhaps she's been sacked as your home teacher?

That doesn't seem reasonable. If she's been sacked for incompetence, dishonesty, or some sort of malfeasance, what does Sonia's death have to do with keeping her on as my teacher? Which is what happens, Dr Rose: Sarah-Jane Beckett remains my teacher until I'm sixteen, when she marries and moves to Cheltenham. So she was planning to leave for another reason, but that reason is cancelled with Sonia's death.

Does that make Sonia the reason that Sarah-Jane Beckett was leaving?

It seems so, doesn't it? But I can't think why.

CHAPTER SIX

Doll Cottage possessed an attic, which was the last stop DC Barbara Havers and her superior officer made in Eugenie Davies' house. It was a tiny garret tucked into the eaves. They gained access to it through a hatch in the ceiling just outside the bathroom. Once inside, they were reduced to crawling across an expanse of flooring whose dust-free condition suggested that someone made regular visits, either to clean or to look through the small room's contents.

'So what d'you think?' Barbara asked as Lynley pulled on a cord affixed to a light bulb in the ceiling. A cone of yellow illumination shone down on him, casting shadows from his forehead that hid his eyes. 'Wiley *says* she wanted to talk to him, but all he would really have to do is play a little fast and loose with the time line he's given us, and Bob would definitely be your et cetera.'

'Is that your colourful way of indicating Major Wiley has a motive?' Lynley asked her. 'There are no cobwebs in here, Havers.'

'Already noted. No dust either.'

Lynley ran his hand over a wooden sea chest that stood next to several large cardboard boxes. It had a hasp as a fastener, but there was no lock, so he lifted the top and peered inside as Barbara crawled to the first of the boxes. He said, 'Three years of patient effort, establishing a relationship that he hoped would be more than what she had on offer. She informs him, reluctantly, that there can never be more between them than there is because—'

'Because of some bloke driving a navy—or black—Audi with whom she has a row in a car park?'

'Possibly. In frustration he follows her to London—Major Wiley, this is—and runs her down. Yes. I suppose it could have happened that way.'

'But you don't think so?'

'I think it's early days yet. What've you got there?'

Barbara examined the contents of the box she'd opened. 'Clothes.'

'Hers?'

Barbara lifted the first garment out and held it up: a small child's pair of corduroy dungarees, pink, embroidered with yellow flowers. 'The daughter's, I expect.' She rustled downwards and scooped out an entire pile of clothing: dresses, jumpers, pyjamas, shorts, tee shirts, Babygros, shoes, and socks. All of it was thematically identical: The colours and the decorations indicated it had been used to dress the child who'd been murdered. Barbara packed it back into the box that had held it and turned to the next box as Lynley lifted out the contents of the wooden sea chest.

The second box contained what appeared to be the linens and the other objects that had been used on a baby's cot. Peter Rabbit sheets lay folded neatly inside, and what accompanied them were a musical mobile, a well worn Jemima Puddleduck, six other stuffed animals in a condition that suggested they'd been less favoured than Jemima, and the padding that was used round the sides of a cot to prevent a small child from banging her head.

The third box held bathing accoutrements:

everything from rubber ducks to a miniature dressing gown. Barbara was about to comment on the macabre nature of having kept this particular set of items—considering the end that the child had met—when Lynley said:

'This is interesting, Havers.'

She looked up to see that he'd put on his glasses and was holding a stack of newspaper articles, the first of which he'd opened to peruse. Next to him on the floor he'd piled the rest of the sea chest's contents, which comprised a collection of magazines and newspapers and five leather albums suitable for photographs or scrapbooks. 'What?' she asked him.

'She's kept a virtual library on Gideon.'

'From newspapers? For what?'

'For playing his violin.' Lynley lowered the magazine article he was looking at and said, 'Gideon Davies, Havers.'

Barbara rested back on her heels, a washing mitt shaped like a cat in her hand. 'Should I be swooning at this bit of news?'

'You don't know . . .? Never mind,' Lynley said. 'I forget myself. Classical music isn't your forte. Were he the lead guitarist for Rotting Teeth—'

'Do I sense scorn for my musical preference?'

'—or some other group, no doubt you'd have leapt upon his name.'

'Right,' Barbara said. 'So who is this bloke when he's at home in the shower?'

Lynley explained: a virtuoso violinist, a former child prodigy, the possessor of a worldwide reputation who'd made his professional debut before he was ten years old. 'It appears that his mother kept everything associated with his career.'

231

'In spite of her estrangement from him?' Havers said. 'That suggests he was the one who wanted it. Or the dad, perhaps.'

'Doesn't it, though,' Lynley agreed, sifting through the material. 'She's got a treasure trove here. Everything from his latest appearance especially, tabloids included.'

'Well, if he's famous . . .' Barbara pulled out a smaller box from among the bathing items. She opened it to discover a collection of prescription medicines, all made out to the same person: Sonia Davies.

'No. This was something of a fiasco,' Lynley told her. 'A piece of music for a trio. At Wigmore Hall, this was. He refused to play. He left the platform at the start of the piece, and he hasn't played in public since.'

'Got his knickers in a twist about something?'

'Perhaps.'

'Stage fright?'

'Also possible.' Lynley held up the newspapers: tabloids and broadsheets. 'She appears to have collected every article that made mention of it, no matter how small.'

'Well, she *was* his mum. What's in the albums?'

Lynley opened the first of these as Barbara moved to look over his shoulder. More newspaper articles had been preserved inside the leather volumes. These were accompanied by concert programmes, publicity pictures and brochures for an organization called East London Conservatory.

'I wonder exactly why they were estranged,' Barbara asked, seeing all of this.

'That's certainly the question,' Lynley replied.

They sorted through the rest of the contents of

232

the boxes and the chest and found everything inside was associated with either Gideon or Sonia Davies. It was as if, Barbara thought, Eugenie Davies had herself not existed before her children had. It was as if she had ceased to exist when she'd lost them. Except, of course, she'd actually lost only one of them.

'I expect we're going to have to track down Gideon,' Barbara noted.

'He's on the list,' Lynley agreed.

They replaced everything and lowered themselves back into the cottage proper. Lynley pulled the hatch's cover into position. He said, 'Fetch those letters from the bedroom, Havers. Let's go up to the Sixty Plus Club. We might be able to fill in some gaps there.'

Outside, they headed up Friday Street, away from the river, passing opposite Wiley's Books where, Barbara noted, Major Ted Wiley made no effort to hide the fact that he was watching them through the front window, standing just behind a display of picture books. He raised a handkerchief to his face as they moved along the pavement. Crying? Pretending to cry? Or just honking his nose? Barbara couldn't help wondering. Three years was a long time to wait for a commitment, only to be foiled at the end.

Friday Street was a mixed bag of businesses and residences. It gave way to Duke Street, where Henley Piano Galleries featured a display of violins and violas—along with a guitar, a mandolin and a banjo—in the window. Lynley said, 'Hang on a moment, Barbara,' and sauntered over to study them. Barbara took the opportunity to light a fag, and she gazed at the instruments in collegial cooperation, wondering what she and Lynley were supposed to be seeing.

She finally said, 'What? *What?*' to Lynley when he continued gazing, his fingers pulling meditatively at his chin.

He said, 'He's like Menuhin. There are all sorts of similarities in their early careers. But one wonders if the family is similar. Menuhin had his parents' complete devotion from the first. If Gideon hadn't—'

'Menu-who?'

Lynley glanced her way. 'Another prodigy, Havers.' He folded his arms and shifted his weight, preparatory—it seemed—to settling in for a lecture on the topic. 'It's something to think about: what happens to the parents' lives when they discover they've produced a genius. A set of responsibilities falls upon them entirely different to those faced by the parents of average children. Now take that set of responsibilities and to them add the responsibilities faced by the parents of a different sort of child.'

'A child like Sonia,' Havers said.

'Those responsibilities are equally challenging, equally demanding, and equally difficult but in an entirely different way.'

'But are they equally rewarding to the parents? And if they aren't, how do the parents cope? And what does the daily act of coping do to their marriage?'

Lynley nodded, looking to the violins again. Considering his words, Barbara wondered how far into his own future he was gazing as he studied the instruments. She hadn't yet mentioned to him the conversation she'd had with his wife on the previous evening. Now didn't seem like the time to do it. But on the other hand, he'd given her an entrée that was tough to ignore. And wouldn't it benefit him to have a friendly ear he could speak his potential concerns into during the months of Helen's pregnancy? He would hardly want to do so with his wife.

She said, 'Bit worried, sir?' and dragged on her Player with marginal apprehension because, although she'd worked in partnership with Lynley for three years, they rarely ventured into the realm of their personal lives in conversation.

'Worried, Havers?'

She blew smoke from the side of her mouth, the better to avoid hitting him in the face with it when he turned back to her. She said, 'Helen told me last night about . . . you know. I expect there're worries connected with that. Everyone now and again would have them. You know. I mean . . .' She rustled her hair and fastened the top button of her donkey jacket, which she immediately then unfastened when it felt like a noose.

Lynley said, 'Ah. The baby. Yes.'

'Scary moments connected with that, I expect.'

'Moments indeed,' he replied evenly. Then he said, 'Let's move on,' and headed round the corner from the piano gallery, the conversation between them dismissed.

Odd answer, Barbara thought. Odd reaction. And she realised how stereotypical she'd expected to find his response to impending fatherhood. The man had a distinguished family tree. He had a title and a family estate that he'd inherited in his early twenties. Wasn't he supposed to produce an heir to all that in fairly short order after marrying? And shouldn't he be delighted at the prospect of a duty fulfilled within a few months of having taken the marital plunge?

She frowned then tossed the dog end of her fag into the street where it landed in a puddle at the kerb. The volumes one didn't know about men, she thought.

The Sixty Plus Club was a modest building that sat on one side of a car park in Albert Road, and when they entered, Barbara and Lynley were immediately greeted by a large-toothed woman with red hair who was dressed in a diaphanous flowery affair more suitable for a sunny garden party than for the grey November day outside. She displayed her fearsome oral pearls at them and introduced herself as Georgia Ramsbottom, club secretary, 'by unanimous vote for the fifth consecutive year.' Could she assist them? With a parent, perhaps, who might be reluctant to inquire about the club's amenities? A mother recently widowed? A father trying to come to terms with the passing of a beloved spouse? 'Sometimes our pensioners'—one of whom she obviously did not consider herself to be, despite the shiny and taut facial flesh that spoke of her efforts to retard the ageing process—'drag their feet a bit when it comes to making life changes, don't they?'

'Not only pensioners,' Lynley said pleasantly as he produced his warrant card and introduced himself and Barbara.

'Oh. Goodness me. Sorry. I naturally assumed . . .' Georgia Ramsbottom lowered her voice. 'Police? I don't know that I can assist you. I'm only *elected* you see.'

'Five consecutive years,' Barbara noted

236

helpfully. 'Cheers.'

'Is there something . . .? But then, you'll want to talk to our director, won't you. She's not in yet today—I can't think why except to say Eugenie often has pressing business to attend to elsewhere—but I can ring her at home if you wouldn't mind waiting in the games room?'

She indicated the door through which she herself had come to greet them. Beyond it at small tables foursomes sat playing cards, twosomes sat playing chess or draughts, and a onesome played Patience with very little of it, if his muttered, '*Bugger* it' was anything to go by. She herself took a step towards a closed office on whose door the word *Director* was stencilled on a translucent window. She said, 'I'll just pop in her office and phone her.'

Lynley said, 'You're speaking about Mrs Davies, I take it?'

'Eugenie Davies. Yes, of course. She's generally here save for the periods she spends at one of her nursing homes. Very *good*, is our Eugenie. Very generous. A perfect example of . . .' She seemed at a loss to complete her metaphor, so she changed gears with, 'But if you're looking for her, then you already know . . .? I mean about her reputation for good works? Because otherwise . . .'

'I'm afraid she's dead,' Lynley said.

'Dead,' Georgia Ramsbottom repeated after a moment during which she stared at them in incomprehension. 'Eugenie? Eugenie Davies? Dead?'

'Yes. Last night. In London.'

'London? Was she . . .? What on earth happened? Oh my *God*, does Teddy know?'

237

Georgia's eyes flicked to the doorway through which Lynley and Barbara had come. Her face said that she was inclined to dash out to bear the bad tidings to Major Wiley post haste. 'He and Eugenie,' she said rapidly and in a low voice as if the card players in the nearby room might attend to something other than their games. 'They were . . . Well, of course, neither of them ever came out and *said* directly but that was Eugenie all over, wasn't it? Very discreet. She wasn't one to divulge the intimate details of her life to just anyone. But one could see when they were together that Ted was besotted with her. And I, for one, was thrilled for them both because although Ted and I were an item ourselves when he first came to Henley, I'd concluded that he wasn't *quite* right for me and when I passed him on to Eugenie, I couldn't have been happier that they just seemed to click. Chemistry. That certain something between them that he and I just never had. You know how it is.' She showed her teeth again. 'Poor darling Ted. Poor dear man. Such a pleasure, he is. Such a favourite here in the club.'

'He knows about Mrs Davies,' Lynley said. 'We've spoken to him.'

'Poor man. First his wife. Now this. My God.' She sighed. 'Goodness. I shall have to let everyone know.'

Barbara wondered fleetingly exactly how much the woman was going to enjoy the employment.

'If we may have access to her office . . .' Lynley indicated the room with a nod.

Georgia Ramsbottom said, 'Oh, yes. Oh, of course. It shouldn't be locked. It isn't usually. The phone's in there and if Eugenie's not here and it rings, someone must answer. Naturally. Because some of our members have spouses in nursing homes and a ringing phone could easily mean . . .' Her voice trailed off meaningfully. She turned the knob and swung the door open, waving Barbara and Lynley inside. She said, 'If you wouldn't mind my asking . . .

Lynley hesitated just inside the door. He turned to the woman as Barbara passed by, going to the single desk in the room and lowering herself into the chair. On the desk top was a daily diary, which she slid towards her as Lynley said, 'Yes?'

'Was Ted . . . Is he . . .' She seemed to strive for a funereal tone. 'Is Ted terribly distraught, Inspector? We're such *friends,* and one wonders if one should phone immediately? Or perhaps drop by to offer a word of comfort?'

Good grief, Barbara thought. The corpse wasn't cold yet. But, obviously, when a man came up for grabs, there was no time to waste. As Lynley made all the right well-bred noises about only a friend having the ability to judge the suitability of a phone call or a visit and as Georgia Ramsbottom took herself off to the nether world to chew this over, Barbara gave her attention to Eugenie Davies' diary, where she saw that the director of the social club kept herself busy with committee meetings that were associated with club events, visits to places called Quiet Pines, River View, and The Willows which seemed to be nursing homes, engagements with Major Wiley that were indicated by *Ted* written across a time, and a set of appointments designated by what seemed to be the names of pubs and hotels. These last appeared regularly throughout the year. They were

239

inconsistent as to day and week, but they marked each month of the year at least once. Interestingly, the entries occurred not only in the previous months of the year, not only in the current month, but clear through to the end of the diary, which included the first six months of the coming year as well. Barbara pointed these out to Lynley as he ventured through a personal telephone directory that he'd pulled from the top right hand drawer of the desk.

'Standing appointment,' he said.

'As a pub crawler?' Barbara asked. 'A hotel critic? I don't think so. Listen: Catherine Wheel, King's Head, Fox and Glove, Claridges . . . Now that's something different. What does that suggest to you? It suggests an assignation to me.'

'One hotel?'

'No, there are others. Here's the Astoria. And Lords of the Manor. Le Meridien as well. In town, out of town. She was seeing someone, Inspector, and I'll bet it wasn't Wiley.'

'Phone the hotels. See if she booked a room.'

'Grunt work.'

'One of the job's chief glories.'

As she placed the calls, Barbara went through the rest of Eugenie Davies' desk. The other drawers contained office supplies: business cards, envelopes and stationery, Sellotape and staples, rubber bands, scissors, pencils, and pens. Filing folders held contracts with suppliers of food products, furniture, computers, and copying equipment. By the time she'd learned from the first of the hotels that there was no record of a Eugenie Davies staying with them, Barbara had also concluded that there was nothing of a personal

240

nature inside her desk.

She turned her attention to the top of the desk as Lynley bent over a computer that was set in sleep mode. She delved into the dead woman's **In** tray. Lynley sank into her cyberworld.

Like the hotels, the **In** tray, Barbara found, wasn't exactly a fountain of riveting information. It held three applications for membership to the Sixty Plus Club—all from recent widows in their seventies—as well as what appeared to be drafts of announcements for upcoming activities. Barbara whistled softly when she saw what the club had on offer for its members. With the approaching holiday season, the pensioners were scheduling themselves into an admirable round of events: Everything from a coach trip to Bath for dinner and the panto to a New Year's Eve Gala was available. There were cocktail parties, dinners, dances, Boxing Day outings, and midnight church services advertised for the over sixties crowd who certainly weren't taking their golden years in anything resembling a supine position.

Behind her, Barbara heard the whir and beep of Eugenie Davies' computer coming out of sleep. She got up and went to the single filing cabinet as Lynley took her place at the desk and swung the chair round to face the computer behind it. The filing cabinet had a lock, but it wasn't fastened, so Barbara pulled open the first drawer and began leafing through the files. These appeared to be largely devoted to correspondence with other pensioners' organisations in the UK. However, there were also documents that dealt with the National Health, with a travel and study programme called Elder Hostel, with geriatric issues from Alzheimer's to osteoporosis, and with legal issues surrounding wills, trusts, and investments. A manila folder was devoted to correspondence from the children of adult members of the Sixty Plus Club. Most of these were letters of gratitude and appreciation for what the club was doing to bring Mum or Dad out of his or her shell. A few questioned the devotion Mum or Dad had apparently developed for an organisation unrelated to the immediate family. Barbara pulled this last group out and set them on the desk. No telling if a pensioner's relative had got a bit worried over Mum's or Dad's affection for the director of the club, not to mention where that affection might have led. She checked to make sure none of the letters were signed *Wiley*. None were, but that didn't mean that the major had no married daughter who'd written to Eugenie.

One of the files was particularly interesting as it was filled with photographs of the club during a variety of events. As Barbara flipped through these, she noted that Major Wiley was a frequent subject of the pictures and that he was generally in the company of a woman who hung on his arm, draped herself over his shoulder, or sat on his lap. Georgia Ramsbottom. *Dear Teddy.* Ah yes, Barbara thought. She said, 'Inspector,' at the same moment as Lynley said, 'Here's something, Havers.'

Photographs in hand, she went to the computer. She saw that he had accessed the internet and that he'd brought Eugenie Davies' e-mail onto the screen. 'She didn't have a password?' Barbara asked as she handed him the prints.

'She had,' Lynley said. 'But it was easy enough to suss out, all things considered.'

'One of the kids' names?' Barbara asked.

'*Sonia*,' he said, and then a moment later, 'Damn.'

'What?'

'There's nothing here.'

'No convenient message threatening her life? No arrangement for a trip to Hampstead? What about an invitation to Le Meridien?'

'Nothing at all.' Lynley peered at the screen. 'How do you trace someone's e-mail, Havers? Might she have old messages hidden somewhere?'

'You're asking me? I've only just got used to mobile phones.'

'We need to find them. If they're here.'

'We'll need to take it, then,' Barbara said. 'The computer, sir. There's going to be someone in London who'll be able to sort it out.'

'There is indeed,' Lynley replied. He sifted through the pictures she'd handed to him, but he didn't appear to give them much attention.

'Georgia Ramsbottom,' Barbara prompted him. 'She and dear Teddy appear to have been quite an item at one time.'

'Sixty-year-old women running each other down in the road?' Lynley queried.

'It's a thought,' Barbara said. 'I wonder if her car's bashed up.'

'Somehow I doubt it,' Lynley replied.

'But we should have a look. I don't think we can—'

'Yes, yes. We'll have a look. It's bound to be in the car park.' But he sounded dismissive, and Barbara didn't much like it when he set the photographs down summarily and returned to the computer, his mind made up. He logged off

243

Eugenie Davies' e-mail, shut down the machine and began to unplug it. 'Let's trace where Mrs Davies has been on the internet,' he said. 'No one goes online without leaving a trail of breadcrumbs.'

*　　　*　　　*

'CreamPants.' DCI Eric Leach kept his face impassive. He'd been a cop for twenty-six years, and he'd long ago realised that in his line of work only a numbskull optimistically concluded he'd heard everything there was to hear from fellow members of the human race. But this one was clearly something for the record books. 'You did say CreamPants, Mr Pitchley?'

They were in an interview room at the police station: J.W. Pitchley, his solicitor—a diminutive man called Jacob Azoff with nostril hairs like feather dusters and a large coffee stain decorating his tie—a police constable called Stanwood, and Leach himself, who was doing the questioning as he tossed back Lemsip like cider and wondered sourly how long it was going to take his immune system to catch up with the single life he was back to leading. One night pub crawling and he became a breeding ground for every virus known to man.

Pitchley's solicitor had rung not two hours prior to this meeting. His client wanted to make a statement to the police, Azoff had informed Leach briefly. And he wanted to be assured that this statement would be confidential, just between us boys, treated with kid gloves, and blessed with holy water. In other words, Pitchley didn't want the press to get hold of his name, and if there was a ghost of a chance that the press were going to be

244

given his name . . . et cetera, et cetera, et cetera. Yawn.

'He's been down that road before,' Azoff had said in a tone that was portentous. 'So if we can reach a preliminary agreement about the confidentiality of this conversation, Detective Chief Inspector Leach, I believe we have on our hands a man who deeply wishes to assist you with your enquiries.'

So Pitchley and his brief had shown up, had been ushered through the back door of the station like covert operatives, had been given the refreshment they requested—fresh orange juice and sparkling mineral water with ice and lime not lemon, thank you—and had ensconced themselves at the interview table where Leach had pressed the tape recorder's play button, reciting the day, the time, and the names of all individuals present.

Pitchley's story had so far not altered from what he'd told them on the previous night although he'd become more detailed as to arrangements and places and relatively more specific as to names. Unfortunately, aside from the sobriquets adopted by his partners in amorous encounters at the Comfort Inn, he was unable to come up with the *actual* name of anyone who could confirm his story.

Thus, Leach asked reasonably, 'Mr Pitchley, how is it that you expect us to track down this woman? If she wasn't willing to give her name to the bloke who was poking her—'

'We don't use that term,' Pitchley said with some offence.

'—then how do you expect her to be forthcoming when the coppers want to track her down? Doesn't the withholding of her name

245

suggest something to you?'

'We always—'

'Doesn't it suggest she might not *wish* to be tracked down in ways other than through the internet?'

'It's merely part of the game that we—'

'And if she doesn't wish to be tracked down doesn't *that* suggest she's got someone hanging round—like a husband—who might not look kindly on a bloke—who's had a naked romp with his wife—showing up on the front steps with flowers and chocolates and the hope that she'll confirm his alibi?'

Pitchley's colour was growing high. But then, so was Leach's level of disbelief. With much hemming and hawing, the man had confessed to being an online Casanova who regularly seduced women of advancing years, none of whom gave him their names or ever knew his. Pitchley claimed that he couldn't remember the number of women he'd had assignations with since the birth of e-mail and chat rooms, and he certainly couldn't remember all their cybernames, but he could swear on a stack of eighty-five religious books of DCI Leach's choice that he observed the same procedure with all of them once an agreement to meet had been reached: drinks and dinner in the Valley of Kings in South Kensington followed by several hours of athletically creative sexual intercourse at the Comfort Inn on Cromwell Road.

'So you'll be remembered at either the restaurant or the hotel?' Leach asked the man.

That might be, Pitchley was sad to admit, a bit of a problem. The waiters at the Valley of Kings were foreigners, weren't they? The night receptionist at the Comfort Inn was a foreigner as well. And foreigners often had a spot of difficulty remembering an English face, didn't they? Because foreigners—

'Two-thirds of bloody *London* are foreigners,' Leach cut in. 'If you can't come up with something more solid than what you've come up with so far, Mr Pitchley, we're wasting our time.'

'Might I remind you, DCI Leach, that Mr Pitchley's visit to the station is voluntary,' Jake Azoff pointed out at this juncture. His had been the orange juice, and Leach noticed that a particle of pulp clung to his moustache like a punk-dyed bird dropping. 'Perhaps a more marked degree of civility would serve to encourage a deeper recollection on his part.'

'I assume that Mr Pitchley came to the station because he had something more to tell me than he told me last night,' Leach retorted. 'So far, we're getting a variation on a theme here, and all it's doing is producing more quicksand in which your boy is already up to his chest.'

'I don't see how that conclusion is at all accurate,' Azoff said, affronted.

'Don't you, now? Let me enlighten you. Unless I've been dreaming, Mr Pitchley has just informed us that his hobby is to use the internet to root out women over fifty to chat up and coax into bed. He's just informed us that he's enjoyed a rather marked degree of success in this arena. So much so that he can't even recall how many women have been on the receiving end of his erotic talents. Am I correct, Mr Pitchley?'

Pitchley shifted position and took a sip of water. His skin was still flushed, and his hair—dust

247

coloured with a central parting that created wings which flopped into his face—swept downwards when he nodded. He kept his head lowered. From embarrassment or regret, as a means of obfuscation . . . Who the hell could tell?

'Fine. Let's continue. Now, we have an older woman who's run down by a vehicle on Mr Pitchley's street, a few doors from his own home. This woman just happens to be in possession of Mr Pitchley's address. What does that suggest to you?'

'I wouldn't draw any conclusion myself,' Azoff said.

'Naturally. But it's my job to draw conclusions. And the conclusion I draw is that this lady was on her way to see Mr Pitchley.'

'We've made no admission that Mr Pitchley was expecting or knew the woman in question.'

'And if she *was* on her way to see him, we have from Mr Pitchley's own lips one hell of an excellent reason why.' Leach pressed his point by leaning forward, the better to see beneath Pitchley's protection of hair. 'She was just round the age you like them, Pitchley. Sixty-two. Nice shape to her body—what was left of it after the car did its work with her, that is. She was divorced. No remarriage. No children at home. I wonder if she'd got herself a computer? Something to use to while away the nights when she was feeling lonely out there in Henley?'

'That's just not possible,' Pitchley said. 'They never know where I live. They never know how to find me after we've . . . once we've . . . well, after we've left Cromwell Road.'

'You just fuck 'em and flee,' Leach said. 'That's rich, that is. But what if one of them decided she

248

didn't like that arrangement? What if one of them followed you home? Not last night, of course, but on another night. Followed you, saw where you live, and bided her time when you never contacted her again.'

'She didn't. She *can't* have done.'

'Why not?'

'Because I don't ever go straight home. I drive round for at least thirty minutes—sometimes an hour—once we leave the hotel to make certain . . .' He paused and managed to look relatively miserable about the admission he was making, 'I drive round to make certain she's . . . well, not on my tail.'

'Very wise,' Leach said with irony.

'I know how it sounds. I know it makes me look a perfect shit. And if that's what I am, then that's what I am. But what I'm not is a man who'd run down a woman in the street and you damn well know it if you've examined my car and not used the opportunity to joyride it round London. So I'd like the Boxster returned, Inspector Leach.'

'Would you, now?'

'I would. You wanted information, and I've given you information. I've told you where I was last night, I've told you why, and I've told you with whom.'

'With CreamPants.'

'All right. I'll go online again. I'll get her to come forward if that's what you want.'

'You can and will,' Leach agreed. 'But by your own admission, I don't see how that's going to help much in the larger picture.'

'Why? I can't have been in two places at once.'

'True enough. But even if Miss CreamPants, or

perhaps it's Mrs CreamPants—' Leach couldn't hide his smirk and he didn't bother to try— 'confirms your story, there's part of it she can't help you with, isn't there? She can't tell us where you drove for an hour or thirty minutes after you finished with her. And if you're about to argue that she may have followed you, then you're on thin ice again. Because if she followed you, there's a very good chance that Eugenie Davies, after a similar romp on the Cromwell Road, once did the same.'

Abruptly, Pitchley pushed back from the table, and with so much force that his chair shrieked like a siren against the floor. 'Who?' His voice was hoarse, as if it were sandpaper trying to speak. 'Who did you say?'

'Eugenie Davies. The dead woman.' Even as he spoke, DCI Leach read the new reality on the other man's face. 'You know her. And by that name. You *know* her, Mr Pitchley?'

'Oh God. Oh hell.' Pitchley moaned.

Azoff said to his client in a flash, 'Need five minutes?'

No answer was required of the suspect because a quick tap sounded on the door of the interview room, and a female PC popped her head inside. She said to Leach, 'DI Lynley on the phone, sir. Now or later?'

'Five minutes,' Leach said curtly to Pitchley and Azoff. He picked up his paperwork and left them alone.

*   *   *

Life wasn't a continuum of events, although it wore the guise of exactly that. Instead, it was actually a

250

carousel. In infancy, one mounted a galloping pony and started out on a journey during which one assumed that circumstances would change as the expedition continued. But the truth of life was that it was an endless repetition of what one had already experienced . . . round and round and up and down on that pony. And unless one dealt with whatever challenges one was meant to deal with along the route, those challenges appeared again and again in one form or another till the end of one's days. If he hadn't subscribed to that notion before, J.W. Pitchley was a believer now.

He stood on the steps of the Hampstead police station with his solicitor and listened to the peroration of Jake Azoff's harangue. This consisted of a soliloquy on the topic of trust-and-veracity between a client and his lawyer. He was ending with, 'Do you think I would have bloody well walked in there if I'd bloody well known what you were bloody well *hiding*, you arsehole? You made me look like a fool and what the *hell* do you think that does for my credibility with the cops?'

Pitchley wanted to say that the current situation wasn't *about* Azoff, but he didn't bother. He didn't say anything, which encouraged the solicitor to demand, 'So what would you like me to call you, sir?' The *sir* was no indication of anything other than contempt, which coloured it appreciably. 'Is it to be Pitchley or Pitchford for what remains of our legal relationship?'

'Pitchley's perfectly legal,' J.W. Pitchley replied. 'There's nothing dodgy in how I changed my name, Jake.'

'In that, perhaps,' Azoff retorted. 'But I want the whys, the wherefores, and the hows in writing on my desk, by fax, messenger, e-mail or carrier pigeon, before six o'clock. And then we'll look at what happens next in our professional relationship.'

J.W. Pitchley, AKA James Pitchford, AKA TongueMan to his cyber-acquaintances, nodded cooperatively even though he knew Jake Azoff was blowing hot air. Azoff's track record of managing his money was so appalling that he wouldn't be able to exist for a month without someone at the helm of his investments, and Pitchley-Pitchford-TongueMan had been handling them for so many years and with such a degree of expertise in the financial legerdemain department that to give control over to a lesser fiscal guru would be to put Azoff within striking distance of the Inland Revenue, which the solicitor was understandably loath to have happen. But he needed to let off steam, did Azoff, and J.W. Pitchley—formerly James Pitchford and currently AKA TongueMan—couldn't really blame him. So he said, 'Will do, Jake. Sorry about the surprise,' and he watched as Azoff huffed, raised the collar of his overcoat against a chill wind, and set off down the street.

For his part, Pitchley, with no access to his car and no invitation from Azoff to drive him back to Crediton Hill, set off disconsolately for the railway station near Hampstead Heath and prepared to submit himself to its insalubrious embrace. At least it wasn't the underground, he told himself. *And* there hadn't been a smash-up between competing railway lines vying for the Excellence in Ineptitude Award in at least a week.

He walked up Downshire Hill and pondered the death of Eugenie Davies in Crediton Hill, Eugenie

Davies, who had been carrying *his* address.

When he first knew Eugenie, he'd been James Pitchford, twenty-five years old, three years graduated from university and one year graduated from a bedsit in Hammersmith the approximate size of a fingernail. A year in those lodgings had offered him access to the language school he needed where, for an exorbitant sum that took ages to recoup, he'd purchased individual instruction in his native language, suitable for business dealings, for academic purposes, for social gatherings, and for cowing doormen at fine hotels.

From there, he'd snagged his first job in the City from whose perspective a central London address had sounded so abso*lute*ly right. And since he never invited office mates home for drinks, dinner, or anything else, there was no way for them to know that the letters, documents, and thick party invitations sent to a lofty address in Kensington were actually delivered to the fourth floor bedroom he occupied, which was even smaller than the bedsit he'd begun with in Hammersmith.

Cramped accommodation had been a small price to pay all those years ago, not only for the address but also for the companionship the address had afforded. In the time since those days in Kensington Square, J.W. Pitchley had schooled himself not to think of that companionship. But James Pitchford, who had revelled in it and had deemed himself an unmitigated success in self-reinvention because of it, had scarcely lived a single moment without experiencing some passing thought about one member of the household or another. Especially Katja.

'You can help my talking English, please?' she

253

had asked him. 'I am here one year. I learn not as good as I wish. I will be so grateful.' All those charming v's in place of w's when she spoke were her own variation of the abhorrent missing aitch he'd worked so hard upon.

He agreed to help her because she was so earnest in supplicating him. He agreed to help her because—although she couldn't know it and he would die before telling her—they were two of a kind. Her escape from East Germany, while far more dramatic and awe-inspiring, mirrored an earlier flight of his own. And although their motivations werc different, the core of them was identical.

They already spoke the same language, he and Katja. If he could help her better herself through something as simple as grammar and pronunciation, he was glad to do so.

They met in her free time, when Sonia was asleep or with her family. They used his room or hers, where they each had a table that was just large enough for the books from which Katja did her grammar exercises and for the tape recorder into which she spoke. She was earnest in her efforts at diction, enunciation, and pronunciation. She was courageous in her willingness to experiment in a language that was as foreign to her as Yorkshire pudding. Indeed, it was for her courage that James Pitchford had first learned to admire Katja Wolff. The sheer audacity that had carried her over the old Berlin Wall was the stuff of a heroism he could only hope to emulate.

I will make myself worthy of you, he told her silently as they sat together and worked on the mystery of irregular verbs. And while the table light

254

shone on her soft blonde hair, he visualised himself touching it, running his fingers through it, feeling it caress his naked chest as she lifted herself from their shared embrace.

On her chest of drawers across the room, the intercom broke into James Pitchford's reveries just about as often as he allowed himself to dream them. From two floors below, the child would whimper and Katja's head would rise from her nightly lesson.

'It's nothing,' he'd say because if it was something, their shared time that was so precious to him and already too brief would be over for the evening. For if Sonia Davies' whimper escalated to a cry, the possibilities were endless as to what the trouble might be.

'The little one. I must go,' Katja said.

'Wait a moment.' He used the opportunity to cover her hand with his own.

'I cannot, James. If she weeps and Mrs Davies hears and finds me not with her . . . You know how she is. And this is my job.'

Job? he thought. It was more like indentured servitude. The hours were long, and the duties were endless. Caring for a child so constantly ill required the efforts of more than one young woman with virtually no experience.

Even at twenty-five, James Pitchford could see this. Sonia Davies needed a professional nurse. Why she didn't have one was one of the mysteries of Kensington Square. He wasn't in a position to delve into this mystery, however. He needed to keep his head down and his profile obscure.

Still, when Katja hurried off to the child in the midst of an English lesson, when he heard her leap out of her bed in the middle of the night and rush down the stairs to come to the aid of the little girl, when he returned from work and found Katja feeding her, bathing her, occupying her with one stimulation or another, he thought, The poor creature *has* a family, hasn't she? What are *they* doing to care for her?

And it seemed to him that the answer was nothing. Sonia Davies was left in Katja's charge while the rest of the crew hovered round Gideon.

Could he blame them? Pitchford wondered. And even if he could, had they any choice? The Davieses had embarked upon Gideon's fashioning long before Sonia's birth, hadn't they? They were already committed to a course of action, as evidenced by the presence of Raphael Robson and Sarah-Jane Beckett in their world.

Thinking of Robson and Beckett, Pitchley-Pitchford entered the station and dropped the required coins into a ticket machine. As he wandered out onto the platform, he reflected upon the astounding fact that he hadn't thought of either Robson or Beckett for years. Robson, of course, he might well have forgotten since the violin instructor had not lived among them. But it was strange that he hadn't given a passing consideration to Sarah-Jane Beckett in all this time. She had been, after all, so very much a presence.

'I find my position here more than suitable,' she told him early in her employ, in that peculiar pre-Victorian manner of speaking she used when she was in full Governess Mode. 'Whilst difficult at times, Gideon is a remarkable pupil, and I feel most privileged to have been chosen from nineteen candidates to be his instructor.' She'd just joined

256

the household and her room would be up with his among the eaves on the house's top floor. They would have to share a bathroom the size of a pin head. No bath, just a shower in which an average size man could barely turn around. She'd seen this on the day she moved in, looked at it disapprovingly, but finally sighed with martyred acceptance.

'I don't do washing in the bathroom,' she informed him, 'and I prefer that you refrain from doing so as well. If we have consideration for each other in this small way, I dare say we shall manage quite well together. Where are you from, James? I can't quite place you. Normally, I'm very good at accents. Mrs Davies, for instance, grew up in Hampshire. Can you tell? I quite like her. Mr Davies as well. But the grandfather? He does seem a bit . . . Well. One doesn't like to speak ill, *but* . . .' She tapped a finger to her temple and lifted her eyes in the direction of the ceiling.

Barmy was the word James would have chosen at another time in his life. But instead he said, 'Yes. He's queer fish, isn't he? But if you give him a wide berth, you'll find he's harmless enough.'

So for just over a year, they'd lived in harmony and with the spirit of cooperation. Daily, James left for his job in the City as Richard and Eugenie Davies took themselves to their own places of employment. The elder Davieses remained at home, where Granddad occupied himself in the garden and Gran kept house. Raphael Robson took Gideon through his sessions on the violin. Sarah-Jane Beckett gave the boy lessons in everything from literature to geology.

She spent time with him when she wasn't with

257

Gideon. She asked him out to the cinema or for a drink at the Greyhound, 'just as friends'. But often on those just-as-friends evenings, her leg pressed against his in the darkness as the celluloid flickered its images on the screen, or she took his arm as they entered the pub and she slid her hand from his biceps to his elbow to his wrist so that when their fingers touched it was only natural that they clasp and remain clasped once they were seated.

'Tell me about your family, James,' she said. 'Do tell me. I want every detail.'

So he manufactured tales for her because telling tales had long ago become his stock in trade. He was flattered by the attention that she—an educated girl from the Home Counties—was willing to show him. He had held his own counsel and kept his head down for so many years that Sarah-Jane Beckett's interest in him stirred an appetite for companionship that he'd kept suppressed for most of his life.

She wasn't the companion he was seeking, however. And while he couldn't have said exactly who that companion would be in his evenings with Sarah-Jane, he felt no heaving of the earth when her leg touched his and no pleasurable longing for the pressure of something more than her palm against his own when she took his hand.

Then Katja Wolff arrived, and with Katja the situation was different. But then, Katja Wolff had been as different from Sarah-Jane Beckett as was humanly possible to be.

CHAPTER SEVEN

'She might have been meeting with the ex,' DCI Leach said in reference to the man Ted Wiley had seen in the car park of the Sixty Plus Club. 'Divorce doesn't mean goodbye forever, take it from me. He's called Richard Davies. Track him down.'

'He could be the third male voice on her answer machine as well,' Lynley acknowledged.

'What did that voice say again?'

Barbara Havers read the message from her notes. 'Sounded angry,' she added and tapped her biro meditatively against the paper. 'You know, I wonder if our Eugenie played men off against each other.'

'You're thinking of this other bloke . . . Wiley?' Leach said.

'Could be something there,' Havers noted. 'We've got three separate men on her answer machine. We've got her—this is according to Wiley—arguing with a bloke in the car park. We've got her wanting to talk to Wiley, having something to tell him, something he apparently feels was important . . .' Havers hesitated and glanced at Lynley.

He knew what she was thinking and what she wanted to say: We've also got love letters from a married man and a computer with access to the internet. She was clearly waiting for him to give her the go-ahead to say this, but he held his tongue, so she finished lamely with, 'We've got reason to look closely at every bloke who knew her, 'f you ask me.'

Leach nodded. 'Go after Richard Davies, then.

259

Get what you can.'

They were in the incident room, where detective constables were reporting in on the activities to which they'd been assigned. Following Lynley's phone call to the DCI on the way back into town, Leach had allocated further manpower to the PNC in order to trace all navy and black Audis with number plates ending in ADY. He'd put a constable on to BT for a list of the incoming and outgoing phone calls from Doll Cottage in Henley, and another constable was getting on to Cellnet to track down the mobile phone whose owner had left a message on Eugenie Davies' answer machine.

Of the activities reported as being completed so far that day, only the DC with the responsibility for gathering information from forensic had offered a useful detail: A number of minute paint particles had been found on the dead woman's clothing when it was examined. Further particles had also been found on her body, specifically upon her mangled legs.

'They're putting the paint under analysis,' Leach said. 'Broken down, it might well give us the make of the car that hit her. But that'll take time. You know the routine.'

'Have you got a colour on the paint?' Lynley asked.

'Black.'

'What colour is the Boxster you're holding?'

Leach told his team to get on with their work and he led the way back to his office, saying, 'Car's silver. And it's clean. Not that I'd expect some bloke—no matter how much he's rolling in it—to run down a woman in a motor that cost more than my mum's house. We're still holding it, though. It's proving useful.'

He paused at a coffee machine and plugged in a few coins. A viscous liquid drizzled pathetically into a plastic cup. Leach said, 'You?' and held the cup up in offer. Havers accepted, although she looked as if she regretted the decision once she tasted the brew; Lynley chose the course of wisdom and demurred. Leach purchased another cup for himself and took them into his office, where he used his elbow to shoot the door home. His phone was ringing, and he barked 'Leach,' into it as he set down his coffee and sank into his desk chair, nodding Lynley and Havers to chairs of their own. 'Hello, love,' he said to his caller, his face brightening. 'Nope . . . Nope . . . She's what?' with a glance at the other detectives, 'Esmé, I can't actually talk at the moment. But let me say this: *No one* has said anything at all about getting remarried, okay? . . . Yes. Right. We'll speak later, love.' He dropped the receiver back into place, saying, 'Kids. Divorce. It's a real nightmare.'

Lynley and Havers made noises of sympathy. Leach slurped coffee and dismissed the phone call. He said, 'Our bloke Pitchley came by for a little chat this morning, solicitor in tow,' and he brought them up to date on what the man from Crediton Hill had revealed: that he not only had recognised the name of the hit-and-run victim, that he not only had once known the hit-and-run victim, but that he'd also lived in the very same house with the hit-and-run victim at the time of the murder of said victim's daughter. 'He's changed his name from Pitchford to Pitchley for reasons he's not talking about,' Leach concluded. 'I like to think I would have twigged his identity eventually, but it's been twenty years since I last saw the bloke and a hell of a lot of fish have swum under the bridge in the meantime.'

'Not surprising,' Lynley said.

'Now that I know who he is, though, I've got to tell you he smells sweet to me for this business, Boxster or not. He's got something the size of a T-Rex marching through his conscience. I can feel it.'

'Was he a suspect in the child's death?' Lynley asked. Havers, he noted, had flipped over a new page in her notebook and was jotting the information down on a sheet that looked stained with brown sauce.

'No one was a suspect at first. Until all the reports came in, it looked like a case of negligence. You know what I mean: A flaming idiot goes to take a phone call while the toddler's in the bath. The kid tries to reach for a rubber ducky. She slips, knocks herself on the head, and the rest is academic. Unfortunate and tragic, but it happens.' Leach slurped more coffee and picked up a document from his desk, which he used to gesture with. 'But when the reports came in on the child's body, there were bruises and fractures no one could explain, so everyone became a suspect. It all came down to the nanny dead quick. And she was a real piece of work, she was. I might've forgotten Pitchford's face, but as to that German cow . . . There's not a chance in hell I'd ever forget her. Cold as a cod, that woman was. Gave us one interview—*one* interview, mind you, about a toddler that died in her care—and she never said another word. Not to CID, not to her solicitor, not to her barrister. Not to anyone. Took her right to silence straight to Holloway. Never shed a tear either. But then, what else could you expect from a Kraut? Family were mad to engage her in the first place.'

From the corner of his eye, Lynley saw Havers tap her biro against the paper she was writing on. He glanced her way to see her eyes had narrowed at Leach. She wasn't a woman who put up with bigotry in any of its forms—from xenophobia to misogyny—and he could tell she was about to make a comment that wouldn't endear her to the detective chief inspector. He interceded, saying, 'The German girl's origins worked against her, then.'

'Her flaming Kraut personality worked against her.'

' "We will fight them on the beaches," ' Havers murmured.

Lynley shot her a look. She shot him one back.

Leach either didn't hear or chose to ignore Havers, for which Lynley was grateful. The last thing they needed was a division among them, with lines being drawn on the issue of political correctness.

The DCI leaned back in his chair and said, 'The diary and phone messages are all you came up with?'

'So far,' Lynley answered. 'There was also a card from a woman called Lynn, but that doesn't appear to be germane at the moment. Her child died and Mrs Davies went to the funeral, apparently.'

'There was no other correspondence?' Leach asked. 'Letters, bills, the like?'

Lynley said, 'No. There was no other correspondence,' and he didn't look Havers' way.

'She had a sea chest filled with materials relating to her son, though. Newspapers, magazines, concert programmes. Major Wiley said that Gideon and Mrs Davies were estranged, but from the look of her collection, I'd guess it wasn't Mrs Davies who wanted the estrangement.'

'The son?' Leach asked.

'Or the father.'

'We're back to the argument in the car park, then.'

'We could be. Yes.'

Leach swallowed the rest of his drink and crushed the plastic cup. He said, 'But it's odd, don't you think, to have found so little information about her in the woman's own home?'

'It was a fairly monastic environment, sir.'

Leach studied Lynley. Lynley studied Leach. Barbara Havers scribbled furiously into her notebook. A moment passed during which no one admitted to anything. Lynley waited for the DCI to give him the information he wanted. Leach didn't do it. He merely said, 'Go for Davies then. He shouldn't be tough to track down.'

So the plans were set and the assignments made, and Lynley and Havers were soon back in the street and heading for their respective cars. Havers lit a cigarette and said, 'What're you going to do with those letters, Inspector?'

Lynley didn't pretend to need clarification. 'I'm giving them back to Webberly,' he said, 'eventually.'

'*Giving* them . . .' Havers drew in on her cigarette and blew the smoke out in a burst of frustration. 'If word gets out that you've taken them from the scene and not turned them in . . . That *we've* taken them from the scene and not turned them in . . .

264

Bloody hell, do you know where that puts us, Inspector? And on top of it, there's that computer. Why didn't you tell Leach about that computer?'

'I'll tell him, Havers,' Lynley said. 'Once I know exactly what's on it.'

'Jesus in a basket!' Havers cried. 'That's suppressing—'

'Listen, Barbara. There's only one way it would come to light right now that we've got the computer and those letters, and we both know what that one way is.' He looked at her evenly and waited for her to connect the dots.

Her expression altered. She said, 'Hey. I don't grass, Inspector,' and he could see the affront she'd taken.

He said, 'That's why I work with you, Barbara,' and he disarmed the Bentley's security system. He opened the door before he spoke to her again, over the car's roof. 'If I've been brought in on this case to keep Webberly protected, I'd like to know that and I'd like it said to my face. Wouldn't you?'

'I'd like to keep my nose clean is what I'd like,' Havers replied. 'One of us got demoted two months ago, Inspector, and if memory serves me right, it wasn't you.' She was white faced, watching Lynley with an expression that was completely unlike the belligerent officer he'd worked with for the past several years. She'd taken a professional and psychological beating in the last five months, and Lynley realised that he owed her the opportunity to avoid another one. He said, 'Havers, would you prefer to be out of this? That's not a problem. One phone call and—'

'I don't want to be out.'

'But it could get dicey. It's *already* dicey. I more

265

than understand how you might—'

'Don't talk rubbish. I'm in, Inspector. I'd just like us to have a little care with what we're doing.'

'I'm taking care,' Lynley assured her. 'Those letters from Webberly are not an issue in this case.'

'You'd better hope that's true,' Havers replied. She pushed away from the Bentley. 'Let's get on with it, then. What's next?'

Lynley accepted her words and dwelt for a moment on how best to approach the next phase of their job. 'You've the look of a woman in need of spiritual guidance,' he said. 'Track down the Convent of the Immaculate Conception.'

'What about you?'

'I'll follow our DCI's suggestion. Richard Davies. If he's seen or talked to his former wife recently, he might know what she wanted to confess to Wiley.'

'He might *be* what she wanted to confess to Wiley,' Havers pointed out.

'There's that as well,' Lynley said.

*   *   *

Jill Foster had never run into a serious snag while she was ticking off accomplishments from the Master List that she'd first compiled as a fifteen-year-old schoolgirl. Reading all of Shakespeare (done by age twenty), hitch-hiking the length of Ireland (done by twenty-one), taking a double first at Cambridge (by age twenty-two), travelling alone in India (by twenty-three), exploring the Amazon River (twenty-six), kayaking the Nile (twenty-seven), writing a definitive study of Proust (still in progress), adapting the novels of F. Scott Fitzgerald for television (also in the works) . . . From athleticism to intellectualism, Jill Foster hadn't experienced even a hiccup on her progress through life.

In the personal realm, however, she'd had more difficulty. She'd placed the achievement of marriage and children before her thirty-fifth birthday, but she'd found it more challenging than she'd anticipated to attain a goal that involved the enthusiastic cooperation of another person. And it was marriage and children that she'd wanted: in that order. Yes, it was trendy to be 'partners' with someone. Every third pop singer, film star, or professional athlete was living proof of that, congratulated in the tabloids on a daily basis for their mindless ability to reproduce, as if the act of reproduction itself took some sort of talent that only they possessed. But Jill was not a woman easily swayed by what bore the appearance of a trend, particularly when it came to her Master List of Accomplishments. One did not achieve one's goals by taking shortcuts that were nothing but passing vogues.

The aftermath of her affair with Jonathon had for a time seriously undermined her confidence in her ability to reach her marital and maternal objective. But then Richard had come into her life, and she'd quickly seen that an accomplishment that had so far eluded her was finally within her reach. In the world of her grandparents—even of her parents—to have become lovers with Richard before a formal commitment had been made between them would have been both foolhardy and ruinous. Indeed, even today there were probably a dozen agony aunts whose advice—considering Jill's

267

ultimate objective—would have been to wait for the ring, the church bells, and the confetti before embarking on any kind of intimacy with one's intended bridegroom, or at least to have used what were euphemistically called 'precautions' until such a time as the deal was signed, sealed, and registered in the customary way. But Richard's earnest pursuit of her in the aftermath of Jonathon's failure to leave his wife constituted a phase in Jill's life that was both flattering and essential. His desire *for* her had aroused an equal desire *in* her, and she was deeply gratified to feel it since, after Jonathon, she'd begun to wonder if she would ever feel that hot aching hunger—unlike any other hunger—for a man again.

And that hunger, Jill had found, was firmly tied to impregnation. It might have been due to a dawning knowledge of how few years she actually had left for childbirth, but every time she and Richard made love in those first months, her body had strained to take him into her more deeply, as if the sole act of surging towards him would ensure that their contact produced a child.

So she'd gone at marriage backwards, but what did it matter? They were happy with each other, and Richard was devotion itself.

Still, she had the occasional flicker of doubt, a memento left her by Jonathon's promises and Jonathon's lies. And while, when doubts surfaced, she reminded herself that the two men were absolutely nothing alike, there were times when a shadow cast on Richard's face or a silence in the midst of a discussion between them triggered a set of worries within her that she tried to tell herself were unnecessary and unreal.

Even if Richard and I don't marry, she would lecture herself in her worst moments, Catherine and I shall be perfectly all right. I've a career to fall back on, for heaven's sake. And the age of unmarried mothers being social pariahs has long since passed.

But that wasn't really the point, was it, her long-range planning self would argue. The point was marriage and husband as well. And the larger point was family, which she chose to define as father-mother-child.

So now she said pleasantly to Richard with that ultimate goal in mind, 'Darling, if you'd only see it, I know you'd agree.' They were in Richard's car on the way to South Kensington from Shepherd's Bush in order to keep an engagement with an estate agent who was going to determine a selling price for Richard's flat. This was progress in the right direction to Jill's way of thinking, since they obviously couldn't live *en famille* in Braemar Mansions once the baby was born. There was far too little room.

She was privately grateful for this additional indication of Richard's positive marital intentions, but she hadn't yet been able to understand why they couldn't take the next step and have a look at a suitable detached house—completely renovated—that she'd managed to locate in Harrow. Looking at the house didn't mean they were going to have to *buy* it, for heaven's sake. And since she hadn't yet put her own flat up for sale—'Let's not both be homeless at once,' Richard had advised when she'd suggested doing so—there was little chance that having a simple look at a building on offer would result in their owning it on this very day. 'It would give you a sense of what I have in mind for us,' she told him. 'And if you don't like what I have mind once you see it, at least we'll know straightaway and I can change course.' Not that she would, naturally. She would merely expend more careful and subtle effort to bring him round to her way of thinking.

'I don't need to see it to know what you have in mind, darling,' Richard replied as they trundled along in moderately bearable traffic, considering the time of day. 'Modern conveniences, double glazing, fitted carpet, and large gardens in both front and back.' He looked over at her and smiled affectionately. 'Tell me I've got it wrong and I'll buy you dinner.'

'You'll buy me dinner either way,' she told him. 'If I'm on my feet long enough to cook you a meal, I'll swell up like a ham.'

'But tell me I've got it wrong about the house.'

'Oh, you know you haven't got it wrong,' she laughed. And she touched him fondly, smoothing her fingers against his temple where his hair was grey. 'And don't begin a lecture, if you're thinking of one, all right? I didn't go anywhere on my own to find it. The estate agent drove me up to Harrow.'

'Which is as it should be,' Richard said. His hand moved to her stomach, monstrously huge, the skin stretched taut like a kettle drum. 'Are you awake, Cara Ann?' he inquired of their child.

Catherine Ann, Jill corrected him patiently. But she didn't make the correction aloud. He'd somewhat recovered from the distress in which he'd arrived in Shepherd's Bush earlier that day. There was no point to upsetting him all over again.

While an argument concerning the name of their child was hardly going to cause an emotional upheaval, she did believe that what Richard had been through deserved her sympathy.

He didn't still love the woman, she assured herself. After all, they'd been divorced for years. It was merely the shock of everything that had made him so ill, having to gaze upon the bloodied corpse of someone who had once shared his life. That was something to make anyone ill, wasn't it? Asked to look upon the broken body of Jonathon Stewart, wouldn't she have reacted likewise?

With this in mind, she decided she could compromise on the house in Harrow. She was confident that her willingness to do so would prompt an important compromise on his part. She led into this compromise by saying, 'All right, then. We won't go up to Harrow today. But the modern bit, Richard. Are you quite happy with that?'

'Decent plumbing and double glazing?' he asked. 'Fitted carpet, dishwasher, and all the rest? I dare say I can live with it. As long as you're there. Both of you, that is.' He smiled at her, but still she sensed something deeper in his eyes, looking like regret for what might have been.

But he *doesn't* still love Eugenie, she thought insistently. He doesn't and he can't, because even if he does, she's dead. She's dead.

'Richard,' she said, 'I've been thinking about the flats. Mine and yours. And which of them we *should* sell first, actually.'

He braked for a light near Notting Hill station, where an unappealing crowd dressed in London black were clogging the pavements and distributing into the street their share of London rubbish. 'I thought we'd decided all that,' he said.

'We had, yes. But I've been thinking . . .

'And?' He looked wary.

'Well, it seems to me that my flat would go faster, that's all. It's been done up. It's completely modernised. The building's smart. The neighbourhood's lovely. And it's freehold. I expect it would fetch quite enough for us to put money down on a house and not have to wait to sell both flats before we have a place for all of us.'

'But we've already made the decision,' Richard pointed out. 'We've an estate agent coming—'

'We can put him off surely. We can say we've changed our minds. Darling, let's face it. Your flat's hopelessly old-fashioned. It's as ancient as Methuselah. And it's got less than fifty years left on the lease. It's in a good enough building—if the owners would ever get round to fixing it up—but it's going to be *months* before it sells. Whereas mine . . . You must see how different things could be.'

The light changed and they continued through the traffic. Richard didn't speak till he made the turn into the antiques shop heaven that was Kensington Church Street. He said, 'Months. Yes. Right. It could take months to sell my flat. But is that really a problem? You can't want to move house for at least six months anyway.'

'But—'

'It would be impossible in your condition, Jill. Worse, it would be nothing short of torture, and it might be dangerous.' He swung them past the Carmelite Church and onwards down towards Palace Gate and South Kensington, weaving his way through buses and taxis. Another stretch of

272

road, and he made the turn into Cornwall Gardens, going on to say, 'Are you nervous, darling? You haven't said much about actually *having* the baby. And I've been preoccupied—first Gideon, now this . . . this other business—so I haven't done as right by you as I should have. Listen, I do know that.'

'Richard, I quite understand how concerned you've been with Gideon unwell. I don't mean you to think—'

'I think nothing but that I adore you, you're having our child, and we've a life to establish together. And if you'd like me to be in Shepherd's Bush with you more frequently now that you're nearly due, I'm happy to do that.'

'You're there every night already. I can hardly ask for more than that, can I?'

He reversed into a parking space some thirty yards distant from Braemar Mansions, after which he switched off the engine and turned to her. 'You can ask me for anything, Jill. And if it pleases you to offer your flat for sale before mine, then it pleases me. But I won't have any part of your moving house till you've had the baby and recovered from that, and I seriously doubt your mother would disagree with me.'

Jill herself couldn't disagree. She knew her mother would have a heart attack at the thought of her packing up her belongings and trekking *anywhere* other than from kitchen to loo in less than three months after giving birth. 'Childbirth puts the female body through a trauma, darling,' Dora Foster would have said. 'Coddle yourself. It may be your only chance to do so.'

'Well?' Richard said, smiling at her fondly. 'What's your reply?'

273

'You are so wretchedly logical and reasonable. How can I argue? What you've said makes such sense.'

He leaned towards her and kissed her. 'You're ever gracious in defeat. And if I'm not mistaken—' He nodded towards the old Edwardian building as he came round her side of the car and eased her up and onto the pavement—'our estate agent is right on time. Which bodes well, I think.'

Jill hoped that was the case. A tall blond man was mounting the front steps of Braemar Mansions, and as Jill and Richard approached, he studied the line of bells and pushed what appeared to be Richard's.

'You're looking for us, I believe,' Richard called out.

The man turned, saying, 'Mr Davies?'

'Yes.'

'Thomas Lynley,' he said. 'New Scotland Yard.'

*   *   *

Lynley always made it a habit to gauge reactions when he introduced himself to people who weren't expecting him, and he did so now as the man and woman on the pavement paused before mounting the front steps to what was a considerably down-at-heel building at the west end of Cornwall Gardens.

The woman looked as if she'd normally be quite small although at the moment she was swollen in every conceivable way from pregnancy. Her ankles in particular were the size of tennis balls, giving undue emphasis to her feet, which were themselves large and out of proportion to her height. She walked with the rolling gait of someone trying to

274

keep her balance.

Davies himself walked with a stoop that promised to worsen as he grew older. He had hair that was faded from its original colour—ginger or blond, it was difficult to tell—and he wore it swept straight back from his forehead with no effort made to disguise its thinness.

Both Davies and the woman appeared surprised when Lynley introduced himself, the woman perhaps more so because she looked at Davies and said 'Richard? Scotland Yard?' as if she either needed his protection or wondered why the police were coming to call.

Davies said, 'Is this about . . .?' but changed course, perhaps with the realisation that a conversation on the front steps wasn't what he wanted to engage in with a police officer. He said, 'Come in. We were expecting an estate agent. You've given us a surprise. This is my fiancée, by the way.'

He went on to say that she was called Jill Foster. She looked to be somewhere in her thirties—plain but with very good skin and hair the colour of currants, cut simply just beneath her ears—and Lynley had assumed upon seeing her that she was another of Richard Davies' children or perhaps a niece. He nodded to her, taking note of the tightness with which she clutched Davies' arm.

Davies let them into the building, where he led up the stairs to his first floor flat. It had a sitting room that overlooked the street, a dim rectangle broken by a window that was at the moment covered by shutters. Davies went to fold these back, saying to his fiancée, 'Sit down, darling. Put your feet up,' and to Lynley, 'May I offer you something? Tea? Coffee? We're expecting an estate agent—as I said—and we haven't a great deal of time before he gets here.'

Lynley assured them that the visit wouldn't take long, and he accepted a cup of tea to buy time to have a look round the sitting room at its clutter of belongings. These took the form of amateur photographs of outdoor scenes, countless pictures of Davies' virtuoso son, and a collection of hand-carved walking sticks that formed a circular decoration over the fireplace in the fashion of weaponry found in Scottish castles. There was also a surfeit of prewar furniture, stacks of newspapers and magazines, and a display of other memorabilia related to his son's career as a violinist.

'Richard's a bit of a pack rat,' Jill Foster told Lynley as she lowered herself with some care into a chair whose need for re-stuffing and re-upholstering was evidenced by the tufts of what looked like yellowish cotton wool pushing upwards like springtime's new growth. 'You should see the other rooms.'

Lynley picked up a photograph of the violinist in childhood. He was standing attentively, his instrument in his hand, gazing up at Lord Menuhin who was in turn gazing down at him, instrument also in hand, smiling beneficently. 'Gideon,' Lynley said.

'The one, the only,' Jill Foster replied.

Lynley glanced at her. She smiled, perhaps to take the sting from her words. 'Richard's joy and the centre of his life,' she said. 'It's understandable but sometimes it is a bit wearing.'

'I expect it is. How long have you known Mr Davies?'

276

With a grunt and a heave, she said, 'Bother. This won't do,' and moved from the armchair she'd chosen to lower herself to the sofa, where she raised her legs and put a cushion into position beneath her feet. She said, 'God. Two more weeks. I begin to understand why they call it "being delivered".' She rested her back against a second cushion. Both were as threadbare as the furniture. 'Three years now.'

'He's looking forward to new fatherhood?'

'When most men his age are looking forward to grandfatherhood,' Jill replied. 'But even at his age, yes. He's looking forward.'

Lynley smiled. 'My own wife's pregnant.'

Jill's face altered brightly, the connection between them made. 'Is she? Is this your first, Inspector?'

Lynley nodded. 'I can take a leaf out of Mr Davies' book. He seems devoted.'

She smiled and rolled her eyes in good humour. 'He's like a mother hen. Don't walk down the stairs too quickly, Jill. Don't take public transport. Don't drive in traffic. No. Don't drive at all, my dear. Don't go for a walk without a companion. Don't drink anything that contains caffeine. Carry your mobile everywhere you go. Avoid crowds, cigarette smoke, and preservatives. The list is endless.'

'He's anxious for you.'

'It's rather touching when it doesn't make me want to lock him in a cupboard.'

'Did you have a chance to compare notes with his former wife? About her own pregnancies?'

'Eugenie? No. We never met. Previous wives and current wives. Or in my case wives-to-be. Sometimes it's in the interest of wisdom to keep

277

them apart, isn't it?'

Richard Davies returned to them then, bearing a plastic tray on which sat a single cup and saucer accompanied by a small jug of milk and a bowl of sugar cubes. He said to his fiancée, 'Darling, you weren't wanting tea as well, were you?'

Jill said that she wasn't, and Richard settled in next to her, raising her painfully swollen feet to his lap after placing Lynley's tea on the side table next to the chair in which Jill had first been sitting.

'How can we help you, Inspector?' he asked.

Lynley took a notebook from his jacket pocket. He thought it an interesting question. Indeed, he thought all of Davies' behaviour interesting. He couldn't remember the last time he'd turned up on someone's doorstep unexpected, offered his identification, and been given a cup of tea in welcome. The general responses to an unanticipated visit from the police were suspicion, alarm, and anxiety, no matter how hidden the recipient of the visit attempted to keep them.

Davies said, as if in expectation of just this reaction on Lynley's part, 'I expect you've come about Eugenie. I wasn't much help to your Hampstead colleagues when I was asked to look . . . well, to look at her, actually. I hadn't seen Eugenie in years, and the injuries . . .' He raised his hands from his fiancée's feet, a hopeless gesture.

Lynley said, 'I've come about Mrs Davies. Yes.'

At which point Richard Davies looked at his fiancée, saying, 'Would you prefer to have a lie down, Jill? I can let you know when the estate agent arrives.'

'I'm fine,' she said. 'I share your life, Richard.'

He squeezed her leg, saying to Lynley, 'If you're

278

here, then it must have been Eugenie. It would have been too much to hope for that someone other than Eugenie would have been carrying her identification.'

'It was Mrs Davies,' Lynley said. 'I'm sorry.'

Davies nodded, but he didn't look mournful. He said, 'It's been nearly twenty years since I last saw her. I feel sorry she had such an accident as she had, but my loss of her—our divorce—was long ago. I've had years to recover from her death, if you see what I mean.'

Lynley could see. Permanent mourning on Davies' part would have suggested either a devotion to match Victoria's or an unhealthy obsession, which was fairly much the same. However, Davies had a misconception that needed correcting. Lynley said, 'I'm afraid it wasn't an accident. Your former wife was murdered, Mr Davies.'

Jill Foster raised herself from the cushion supporting her back 'But wasn't she . . . ? Richard, didn't you say . . . ?'

For his part, Richard Davies looked at Lynley steadily, his pupils growing larger. 'I was told a hit and run,' he said.

Lynley explained. Given information was always scant until they had the first of their reports from forensic. An initial inspection of the dead woman's body—not to mention where she'd been found— had certainly called for the conclusion that she'd been hit by someone who then fled the scene. But a closer examination had revealed that she'd been hit more than once, her body had been moved, and what tyre tracks they had found on her clothing and her corpse indicated the damage had been done by a single vehicle. So their hit-and-run motorist was a murderer, and the death was no accident but a homicide.

'Good God.' Jill held out a hand to Richard Davies, but he didn't take it. Instead, he seemed to go into himself, stunned, to a dark place from which she couldn't draw him.

Davies said, 'But they gave me absolutely no indication . . .' He stared into nothing, murmuring, 'God. How can things possibly get worse?' Then he looked at Lynley. 'I shall have to tell Gideon. You will allow me to be the one to tell my son? He's been unwell for several months. He's been unable to play. This could push him . . . You *will* allow me to be the one? It won't be in the papers yet, will it? In the *Evening Standard*? Not before Gideon's been told?'

'That's in the hands of the press office,' Lynley said. 'But they'll hold back till the family's been notified. And you can help us with that. Aside from Gideon, are there other family members?'

'Her brothers, but God only knows where they are. Her parents were still alive twenty years ago, but they may well be dead by now. Frank and Lesley Staines. Frank was an Anglican priest, so you might start there—through the Church—to find him.'

'And the brothers?'

'One younger, one older. Douglas and Ian. Again, I can't say if they're living or dead. When I first met Eugenie, she hadn't seen any of her family in years and she never saw them the entire time we were married.'

'We'll try to find them.' Lynley took up his cup in which a Typhoo tea bag drooped soggily against

280

the side. He removed it and added a splash of milk before he said, 'And you, Mr Davies? When exactly did you last see your former wife?'

'When we were divorced. Perhaps . . . sixteen years ago? There were papers to sign in the course of the proceedings, and that was when I saw her.'

'Since then?'

'Nothing. I'd spoken to her recently, though.'

Lynley set his cup down. 'When was this?'

'She'd been phoning regularly to ask about Gideon. She'd learned he wasn't well. This would have been . . .' He turned to his fiancée. 'When was that awful concert, darling?'

Jill Foster met his gaze so steadily that the fact that he knew exactly when the concert had been was more than apparent. She said, 'The thirtieth of July, wasn't it?'

'That sounds right, yes.' And to Lynley, 'Eugenie phoned shortly afterwards. I can't recall exactly when. Perhaps round the fifteenth of August. She'd kept in touch since then.'

'The last time you spoke to her?'

'Sometime last week? I don't know exactly. I didn't think to make note of it. She phoned here and left a message. I phoned her back. There wasn't much to tell her, so the conversation was brief. Gideon—and I'd very much appreciate this bit staying confidential, Inspector—is suffering from acute stage fright. We've given out that it's exhaustion, but that's a bit of a euphemism. Eugenie wasn't taken in by it, and I doubt the public's going to accept it much longer.'

'But she didn't visit your son? Did she contact him?'

'If she did, Gideon's said nothing to me about it.

Which in itself would be a surprise. My son and I are quite close, Inspector.'

Davies' fiancée lowered her eyes. Lynley made a mental tick next to the possibility of filial-paternal devotion's being a one way street with only Richard Davies travelling down it. He said, 'Your wife was on her way to see a man in Hampstead, evidently. She had his address with her. He's called J.W. Pitchley but you may know him by his previous name, James Pitchford.'

Davies' hands stopped caressing Jill Foster's feet. He became as still as a life size Rodin.

'You remember him?' Lynley asked.

'Yes. I remember him. But . . .' Again, to his fiancée, 'Darling, are you certain you don't want a lie down?'

Her expression said volumes about her intentions: There was no way on earth that Jill Foster was going to toddle off to the bedroom now.

Davies said, 'I'd be unlikely to forget anyone from that period of time, Inspector. Nor would you had you lived through it. James lodged with us for a number of years before Sonia, our daughter . . .' He left off the rest of the sentence, using that gesture with his fingers lifted briefly to express the rest.

'Have you any idea if your former wife kept in touch with this man? He's been interviewed and he himself says no. But in your phone conversations, did your wife ever mention him?'

Davies shook his head. 'We never entertained any subject at all other than Gideon and Gideon's health.'

'She made no mention of her family, then, of her life in Henley-on-Thames, of friends she may have made there, of lovers?'

282

'Nothing at all like that, Inspector. Eugenie and I didn't part under the best circumstances. She walked out one day and that was the end of it. No explanation, no argument, no excuse. One day she was there; the next day she was gone, and four years later I heard from her solicitors. So the blood between us wasn't exactly flowing with the milk of human kindness. I'll admit that I wasn't particularly pleased to hear from her when I finally did.'

'Could she have been involved with another man at the time she left you? This would be someone who may have recently re-entered her life.'

'This . . . you said Pitches?'

'Pitchley,' Lynley said. 'Yes. Could she have been involved with Pitchley when he was James Pitchford?'

Davies considered this. 'He was a good deal younger than Eugenie—fifteen years, perhaps? Ten? But Eugenie was an attractive woman, so I suppose it's possible there was something between them. Let me top up your tea, Inspector.'

Lynley acquiesced in this idea. Davies eased himself from beneath Jill Foster's legs and took himself into the kitchen where running water indicated a minute or two in which he'd be waiting for the kettle to boil. Lynley wondered about the time that this gained the man: why he wanted it, why he needed it. Surprise was piling upon shock, it was true, and Davies was of the generation for whom a display of emotion was tantamount to baring one's backside in Piccadilly Circus. And his fiancée was taking much careful notice of his every reaction, so he had good reason to want some moments to pull himself together. But still . . .

Richard Davies returned to them then, this time

carrying a glass of orange juice as well, which he pressed upon his fiancée, saying, 'You need the vitamins Jill.'

Lynley took his tea cup with thanks and said, 'Your wife was involved with a man in Henley-on-Thames, a man called Wiley. Did she mention him to you in any of your conversations?'

'No,' Davies said. 'Really, Inspector, we confined ourselves to Gideon.'

'Major Wiley tells us they were estranged, Gideon and his mother.'

'Does he?' Richard asked. 'I wouldn't choose that word myself. Eugenie left one day and never returned. If you want to call it estrangement, I suppose you can. I prefer abandonment.'

'Her sin?' Lynley asked.

'What?'

'She told Major Wiley she had something she wished to confess to him. Perhaps abandoning her child and her husband was it. She never was able to confess, by the way. Or so Major Wiley tells us.'

'You think that Wiley . . . ?'

'We're just gathering information at this point, Mr Davies. Is there anything you can add to what you've already told me? Is there anything your former wife might have said in passing that you didn't think of at the time as having significance, but that now—'

'Cresswell-White.' Davies said it almost like a meditation, but when he repeated the name, he did so with more conviction. 'Yes. There's Cresswell-White. I had a letter from him, so Eugenie must have done as well.'

'And Cresswell-White is . . . ?'

'She *would* have had a letter from him, certainly,

284

because when killers are released, the families are informed as a matter of course. At least, that's what my letter said.'

'Killers?' Lynley said. 'Have you had word about your daughter's killer?'

In answer Richard Davies left the room and walked down a short corridor where he entered another room. The sound of drawers and cupboards opening and shutting ensued. When he returned, he bore a legal size envelope, which he handed over to Lynley. It contained a letter from one Bertram Cresswell-White, Esq., Queen's Counsel and all the window dressing, and it had been sent from Number Five Paper Buildings, Temple, London. It informed Mr Richard Davies that HM Prison Holloway would be releasing Miss Katja Wolff on parole on the date given below. Should Miss Katja Wolff harass, threaten, or even contact Mr Davies in any way, Mr Davies was to inform Mr Cresswell-White, Q.C., immediately.

Lynley read the message and examined the date: twelve weeks to the day that Eugenie Davies had died. He said to Richard Davies, 'Has she made contact with you?'

'No,' Davies said. 'Had she done so, believe me, I swear to God I would have . . .' His bravado receded, the stuff of the younger man he no longer was. He said, 'Might she have located Eugenie?'

'Mrs Davies didn't mention her?'

'No.'

'Would she have mentioned her had she seen her?'

Davies shook his head, not so much in denial as in confusion. 'I don't know. At one time, yes. Of course she would have said something to me. But after all this time . . . I just don't know, Inspector.'

'May I keep this letter?'

'Of course. Will you look for her, Inspector?'

'I'll have a man track her down.' Lynley went through the rest of his questions, from which he learned only the identity of the Cecilia who'd written the note to Eugenie Davies: Sister Cecilia Mahoney, she was called, Eugenie Davies' close friend at the Convent of the Immaculate Conception. The convent itself was in Kensington Square where the Davies family had long ago lived. 'Eugenie was a convert to Catholicism,' Richard Davies said. 'She hated her father—he was a raging maniac when he wasn't holier than thou from the pulpit—and it seemed the best way to get vengeance on him for a hellish childhood. At least that's what she told me.'

'Were your children baptised Catholics, then?' Lynley asked.

'Only if she and Cecilia did it in secret. My own dad would have had a seizure otherwise.' Davies smiled with fondness. 'He was quite a tyrannical paterfamilias in his own way.'

And have you taken a page from that book, Lynley wondered, despite your air of helpfulness now? But that was something he'd have to learn from Gideon.

Gideon

1 OCTOBER
Where is this taking us, Dr Rose? You ask me to consider my dreams now as well as my memories,

286

and I wonder if you know what you're doing. You ask me to write my random thoughts, to free myself from worrying about how they connect or where they might lead or how they might produce the key that will fit into the lock of my mind, and my patience is wearing thin.

Dad informs me that your previous work in New York was primarily with eating disorders. He's been doing his prep where you're concerned—a few phone calls to the States was all it took—because as he sees no progress, he's begun to question how much more time I want to devote to dredging up the past instead of dealing with the present. 'For God's sake, she doesn't work with musicians,' he said when I spoke to him today. 'She doesn't even work with other artists. So you can continue to line her coffers with money and get nothing in return—which is all that's been happening so far, Gideon—or you can try something else.'

'What?' I asked him.

'If you're so insistent upon psychiatry as the answer, then at least try someone who'll address the problem. And the problem is the violin, Gideon. The problem is not what you do or do not remember about the past.'

I said, 'Raphael told me.'

'What?'

'That Katja Wolff drowned Sonia.'

There was silence at this and as we were on the phone and not having the conversation in person, I could only guess at Dad's expression. His face would have hardened as the muscles tightened, and his eyes would have gone opaque. In telling me even as little as he did, Raphael had broken an agreement of twenty years' standing. Dad would not like that.

287

'What happened?' I asked.

'I won't discuss this.'

'It's why Mother left us, isn't it?'

'I've told you—'

'Nothing. You've told me nothing. If you're so intent on helping me, why won't you help me with this?'

'Because this has sod all to do with your problem. But digging it all up, dissecting every nuance, and dwelling on them ad infinitum are brilliant ways to sidestep the real issues, Gideon.'

'I'm going at this the only way I can.'

'Bollocks. You're dancing to her tune like a nancy boy.'

'That's bloody unfair.'

'I'll tell you what's unfair. Unfair is being asked to stand to one side and watch your son throw his life away. Unfair is having lived solely for that son's benefit for a quarter of a century so that he can become the musician he wishes to be, only to have him fall to pieces the first time he has a setback. Unfair is crafting a relationship with that son unlike any I could ever have had with my own father and then watching the love and trust that I've had with him for years get transferred to a thirty-year-old psychiatrist with nothing more to recommend her than having managed to hike up to Machu Picchu without having to be carried there.'

'Jesus. How much nosing round have you done?'

'Enough to know how much time you're wasting. God damn it, Gideon—' but his voice wasn't hard when he said those words—'have you even tried?'

To play, naturally. That was what he wanted to know. It was as if, to him, I'd ceased to be anything other than a music-making machine.

288

When I didn't reply, he said not unreasonably, 'Don't you see, then, that this could be nothing more than a momentary blackout? A loose connection in your brain. But because you've never had the smallest blip in your career, you've panicked. Pick up the violin, for God's sake. Do it for yourself before it's too late.'

'Too late for what?'

'To overcome the fear. Don't let it drag you down. Don't dwell on it.'

By the end, his words didn't seem illogical. Instead, they seemed to indicate an action that was reasonable and sound. Perhaps I was making a mountain out of a dust speck, using a manufactured 'illness of spirit' as a cover for a wound to my professional pride.

So I picked up the Guarneri, Dr Rose. In the cause of optimism, I put the shoulder rest in place. I gave myself the break of sheet music—alleviating the pressure of having to produce a measure from memory by choosing the Mendelssohn that I'd played a thousand times before—and I found my body, as Miss Orr would have told me. I could even hear her: 'Body up, shoulders down. Upbow with whole arm. Only the tops of the fingers move.'

I heard it all, but I could do none of it. The bow skittered across the strings, and my fingers flailed the gut with as much delicacy as a butcher dressing a pig.

Nerves, I thought. This is all about nerves.

So I tried a second time, and the sound was worse. And that's all it was that I produced: sound, Dr Rose. I didn't come close to approaching music. As for actually playing the Mendelssohn . . . I might have been attempting a moon landing from the music room, so impossible was the task I'd undertaken.

How did it feel to make the attempt? you want to

289

know.

How did it feel to close the coffin on Tim Freeman? I reply. Husband, companion, cancer victim, and everything else that he was to you, Dr Rose. How did it feel when he died? Because this is a death to me and if there's going to be a resurrection, what I need to know is how it's going to be effected by sifting through the past and writing down my dreams? Tell me that, please. For God's sake, tell me.

2 OCTOBER

I didn't tell Dad.

Why? you ask.

I couldn't face it.

Face what?

His disappointment, I suppose. He's fashioned his entire life round mine, and my entire life has been fashioned round my playing. Both of us are hurtling towards oblivion right now, and it seems an act of kindness if only one of us knows it.

When I set the Guarneri back into its case, I made my decision. I left the house.

On the front steps I met Libby, however. She was leaning next to the wrought iron railing with a bag of marshmallows open on her lap. She didn't appear to be eating them, although she did look as if she were contemplating doing so.

I wondered how long she'd been sitting there, and when she spoke, I had my answer.

'I heard.' She got to her feet, looked down at the bag, then stuffed it into the capacious front of her dungarees. 'That's what's been wrong, isn't it, Gid? That's why you haven't been playing. Why didn't you tell me? I mean, I thought we were friends.'

'We are.'

'No way.'

'Way,' I said.

She didn't smile. 'Friends help each other out.'

'You can't help with this. I don't even know what's wrong with me, Libby.'

She looked off bleakly into the square. She said, 'Shit. What are we doing, Gid? Why're we flying your kites? Why the hell are we sleeping together? I mean, if you can't even talk to me—'

The conversation was a reenactment of a hundred discussions with Beth, with a slight change in subject. With her, it had been, 'Gideon, if we can't even make love any longer . . .'

With Libby things hadn't gone far enough to make that a subject, for which I was grateful. I heard her out but had nothing to say. When she had finished talking and realised there would be no reply, she followed me to my car, saying, 'Hey! Wait a minute. I'm talking to you. Wait a minute. Wait.' She grabbed my arm.

'I've got to go,' I told her.

'Where?'

'Victoria.'

'Why?'

'Libby . . .'

'Fine.' And when I'd unlocked the car, she climbed inside. 'Then I'm coming with you,' she said.

To rid myself of her, I would have had to remove her bodily from the car. And there was a set to her jaw and a steeliness in her eyes that told me she wouldn't be removed without putting up a monumental fight. I didn't have the energy or the heart for that, so I started the car and we drove to Victoria.

The Press Association has its offices just round the

291

corner from *Victoria Station* in *Vauxhall Bridge Road*, and that's where I took us. On the way, Libby brought out the marshmallows, which she started to consume.

I said, 'Aren't you on the "no-white-diet"?'

'These are coloured pink and green, in case you didn't notice.'

'You once said a white that's coloured artificially counts as white,' I reminded her.

'I say lots of things.' She slapped the plastic bag against her lap and appeared to reach a decision because she said, 'I want to know how long. And you'd better be totally straight with me.'

'How long what?'

'How long not playing. Or playing like that. Just then. Like that. How long?' And then, in a switch that wasn't atypical of her, she said, 'Never mind. I ought to have noticed before now. It's because of that bastard Rock.'

'We can hardly blame your husband—'

'Ex. Please.'

'Not yet.'

'Close enough.'

'Fine. But we can't blame him—'

'Loathsome as he is.'

'—if I'm having a rough time just now.'

'That's *so not* what I was talking about,' she said, irritation in her voice. 'There's more people on earth than you, Gideon. I was talking about myself. I would've noticed what's been happening with you if I hadn't been so strung out about Rock.'

But I hardly heard what she said about her husband because I was struck by her words: more people on earth than you, Gideon *and how they echoed almost exactly Sarah-Jane Beckett's sentiments all those years ago.* You're not the centre

292

of the universe any longer. *And I couldn't see Libby in the car with me because all I could see was Sarah-Jane Beckett. I can see her still, I can see her eyes peering at me, her face bending over me. It's pinched, that face, with eyes that are narrowed to a band of stubby lashes.*

What's she talking about when she says that? you ask me.

Yes. That's the question, all right.

I've been naughty while she was responsible for me. It's been left to her to determine my punishment, which has been a thorough wigging, Sarah-Jane style. There's a wooden box in Granddad's wardrobe and I've got into it. It's filled with old boot black, shoe polish, and rags, and I've used all this as paints. All along the first floor corridor I've smeared brown polish and boot black on the walls. Bored, bored, bored, *I've thought as I ruined the wallpaper and wiped my hands on the curtains. But I'm not bored, really, and Sarah-Jane knows it. That's not why I've done it.*

Do you know why you did it? you ask me.

I'm not sure now. But I think I'm angry, and I feel afraid. Quite distinctly and very much afraid.

I see the spark of interest in your face when I tell you this, Dr Rose. Now we're getting somewhere. Angry and afraid. Emotion. Passion. Something, by God, that you can work with.

But I have little to add to that. Only this: When Libby said more people on earth than you, Gideon, *what I felt distinctly was fear. It was a fear quite apart from the fear of never being able to play my instrument again, however. It was a fear that seemed entirely unrelated to the conversation that she and I were having. Yet I felt it in such a sudden paroxysm that I heard myself cry, 'Don't!' at Libby, and all the while it wasn't Libby I was talking to at all.*

And what is it you were afraid of? you inquire.

That, I would have thought, is obvious.

<u>*3 OCTOBER 3:30 P.M.*</u>

We were directed up to the news library, a storage room where rack after rack of news cuttings are filed in manila folders and catalogued by subject along scores of rolling shelves. Do you know this place? Readers spend their days there, poring through every major paper, clipping and identifying stories which then become part of the library's collection. Nearby, a single table and a photocopier serve members of the public who want to do research.

I told a poorly dressed, long-haired boy what I was looking for. He said, 'You should've rung first. It'll take twenty minutes or so. That stuff's not kept up here.'

I said that we'd wait, but I found that my nerves were tangled so excessively that I couldn't remain in the library once the young man had gone off on his search. I couldn't breathe, and I shortly found myself sweating as much as Raphael. I said to Libby that I needed some air. She followed me out onto Vauxhall Bridge Road. But I couldn't breathe there either.

It's the traffic,' I said to Libby, 'the fumes,' and I found myself gasping like a winded runner. And then my viscera went into action: stomach clenching and bowels loosening, threatening a humiliating explosion right there on the pavement.

Libby said, 'You look like hell, Gid.'

I said, 'No. No. I'm all right.'

She said, 'You're all right like I'm the Virgin Mary.

294

C'mere. Get out of the middle of the sidewalk.'

She led me round the corner to a coffee bar and sat me at a table. She said, 'Don't move unless you're, like, going to faint, okay? In which case, put your head . . . somewhere. Where is it you're supposed to put your head? Between your knees?' Then she went to the counter, and came back with some orange juice. 'When was the last time you ate?' she asked.

And I—sinner and soft-spined poltroon—let her believe her own explanation. I said, 'Can't remember exactly,' and I downed the orange juice as if it were an elixir that could return to me everything that I have so far lost.

Lost? you say, ever vigilant for triggers.

Yes. What I've lost: my music, Beth, my mother, a childhood, memories that other people take for granted.

Sonia? you ask. Sonia as well? Would you have her back if you could, Gideon?

Yes, of course, is my reply. But a different Sonia.

And that answer stops me. Because contained within it is a reservoir of remorse for what I'd forgotten about my sister.

3 OCTOBER 6:00 P.M.

When I was able to breathe normally, Libby and I returned to the news library. There, five bulging manila envelopes folders awaited us, crammed with newspaper cuttings from over twenty years ago. They were roughly clipped from papers and dog-eared; they were musty smelling and discoloured with age.

While Libby searched out a second chair so that she could join me at the table, I reached for the first envelope and opened it.

KILLER NANNY CONVICTED leaped out at me, with the unspoken reassurance that newspaper headlines have changed little in the last two decades. The words were accompanied by a picture, and there she was before me, my sister's killer. The photograph looked as if it had been taken very early on in the legal process since Katja Wolff had been caught by the lens not at the Old Bailey or in prison somewhere but in the Earl's Court Road as she came out of the Kensington police station in the company of a stubby man in an ill-fitting suit. Just behind him, partially obscured by the doorway, was a figure I would not have been able to make out had I not known the shape of him and the size of him and the general look of him from nearly twenty-five years of daily sessions on the violin: Raphael Robson. I registered the presence of these two men—assuming the former to be Katja Wolff's solicitor—but what I focused on was Katja herself.

Much had changed for her since the day of the sunny picture that had been taken in the back garden. Of course, that photograph had been posed while this one hd obviously been snapped in that frantic rush that exists between the time a newsworthy figure leaves a building and the time she enters a vehicle which whisks her away. What was evident in the picture was that public notoriety—at least of this sort—hadn't suited Katja Wolff. She looked thin and ill. And whereas the back garden shot had depicted her smiling up at the camera openly and happily, this shot had captured her trying to hide her face. The photographer must have got in quite close, because the picture wasn't grainy as one would expect from a telephoto shot. Indeed, every detail of Katja Wolff's face seemed harshly highlighted by the camera's proximity.

Her mouth was pressed shut so her lips were thin. Dark skin formed half moon bruises beneath her eyes. Her aquiline features had sharpened unappealingly from loss in weight. Her arms were sticklike and where her blouse formed a V, her collar bone looked like the edge of a plank. Beyond Raphael's presence behind her and the badly suited man with Katja's skeletal elbow in his hand that's what I noticed about my sister's killer.

I read the copy to find that Mr Justice St John Wilkes had passed the mandatory life sentence for murder upon Katja Wolff, with an unusual recommendation made to the Home Office that she serve no less than twenty years. According to the correspondent, who evidently had been present in the courtroom, the defendant had leapt to her feet upon hearing the sentence pronounced and demanded to speak. 'Let me tell what happened,' she was reported as saying. But her offer to speak now—after having maintained her right to silence not only through the trial but throughout the investigation as well— smacked of panic and deal-making, and it came too late.

'We know what happened,' Bertram Cresswell-White, senior Treasury Counsel, declared later to the press. 'We heard it from the police, we heard it from the family, we heard it from the forensic laboratory and from Miss Wolff's own friends. Placed in circumstances which she found increasingly difficult, seeking to vent her anger in a situation in which she felt she was being unfairly disciplined, and given the opportunity to rid the world of a child who was imperfect anyway, she wilfully and with malice towards the Davies family shoved Sonia Davies

297

beneath the water in her own bathtub and held her there—despite the child's pathetic struggles—until she drowned. At which point, Miss Wolff raised the alarm. This is what happened. This is what was proved. And it is for this that Mr Justice Wilkes handed down the sentence required by law.'

'She'll serve twenty years, Dad.' Yes. Yes. That's what he says to Granddad when my father comes into the room where we are waiting for word: Granddad, Gran and I. I remember. We are in the drawing room, lined up on the sofa, myself in the middle. My mother is there as well, and she's crying. As she always is, it seems to me, not just after Sonia's death but after Sonia's birth as well.

Birth is supposed to be a joyful time, but Sonia's birth could not have been. I finally realised that as I flipped the first news cutting over and looked at the second one—a continuation of the front page story— that lay beneath it. For there I discovered a photograph of the victim, and to my shame I saw what I had forgotten or deliberately erased from my mind for more than two decades about my younger sister.

What I'd forgotten was the first thing that Libby noticed and mentioned when she rejoined me with a second chair, towing it along behind her as she came into the news library again. Of course, she didn't know it was my sister's picture since I hadn't told her why we'd come to the Press Association office in the first place. She'd heard me ask for cuttings on the Katja Wolff trial, but that was the extent of it.

Libby scooted herself to the table, half-turned towards me, and she reached for the picture, saying, 'What've you got?' And then when she saw, she said, 'Oh. She's Down's Syndrome, right? Who is she?'

298

'My sister.'

'Really? But you've never said . . .' She looked from the picture to me. She went on carefully, either choosing her words or choosing how far she wished to go with their implications, 'Were you, like . . . ashamed of her or something? I mean . . . Gosh. It's no big deal. Down's Syndrome, I mean.'

'Or something,' I said. 'I was or something. Something contemptible. Something bad.'

'What, then?'

'I couldn't remember her. Or any of this.' I gestured to the files. 'I couldn't remember any of this. I was eight years old, someone drowned my sister—'

'Drowned your—'

I clutched her arm to stop the rest. I had no need for the staff of the news library to know who I was. Believe me, my shame was great enough without having my identity attached to it openly.

'Look,' I told Libby tersely. 'Look for yourself. And I couldn't remember her, Libby. I couldn't remember the first thing about her.'

'Why?' she asked.

Because I didn't want to.

3 OCTOBER 10:30 P.M.

I expect you to leap upon that admission with a warrior's triumph, Dr Rose, but you say nothing. You merely watch me and while you have schooled your features to betray nothing, you have little power over the light that comes to your eyes, dark though they might be. I see it there for just an instant—that spark again—and it tells me you wish me to hear what I myself have just said.

I couldn't remember my sister because I didn't

299

want *to remember her. That must be the case. We don't want to remember, so we choose to forget. Except isn't the truth that sometimes we simply don't need to remember. And other times we are* told *to forget.*

Here's what I can't understand, though. My grandfather's episodes were the Great Unspoken in Kensington Square, and yet I remember them clearly. So why do I remember them—and him—but not my sister?

He figures larger in your life than your sister, you tell me, because of your music. To repress him as you've apparently repressed the memory of Sonia—

Repressed? Why repressed? *Are you agreeing that I haven't* wanted *to remember my sister, Dr Rose?*

Repression isn't a conscious choice, you tell me, and your voice is quiet, compassionate, calm. It's associated with an emotional, psychological, or physical state too overwhelming for someone to handle, Gideon. For example, if as children we witness something terrifying or incomprehensible to us—sexual intercourse between our parents is a good illustration—we shove it out of our conscious awareness because at that age we have no tools to deal with what we've seen, to assimilate it in a fashion that makes sense to us. Even as adults, people who suffer horrific accidents generally have no memory of the catastrophe simply because it is horrific. We don't actively make the choice to shove an image from our mind. We simply do it. Repression is how we protect ourselves. It's how our mind protects itself from something it isn't yet prepared to face.

Then what—what—can I not face about my sister, Dr Rose? Although I did remember Sonia, didn't I? When I was writing about Mother, I remembered her.

300

I'd blocked just one detail about her. Until I saw the picture, I didn't know she was Down's.

So the fact that she was Down's *figures in all this, doesn't it? It must because it's the one detail that had to be revealed to me. I couldn't dredge it up. Nothing led me to it.*

You weren't able to dredge up Katja Wolff either, you point out to me.

So Down's and Katja Wolff are connected, aren't they, Dr Rose? They must be.

5 OCTOBER

I couldn't remain in the news library once I saw that picture of my sister and heard Libby voice what I myself could not say. I wanted to remain there. I had five envelopes of information in front of me, all detailing what had happened to my family twenty years ago. No doubt I would also have discovered within those envelopes every significant name of every person who had been involved in the investigation and the legal proceedings that followed it. But I found that I couldn't read any further once I saw that picture of Sonia. Because seeing that picture allowed me to visualise my sister under the water: with her so-round head turning side to side and her eyes—those eyes which even in a newspaper photograph show that she was born anomalous—looking looking always looking because they cannot keep themselves from looking upon her killer. This is someone she trusts, loves, depends upon, and needs who is holding her down beneath the water, and she doesn't understand. She is only two years old and even if she had been a normal child, she would not have understood what was happening. But she isn't normal. She wasn't born

301

normal. And nothing in the two years that comprise her short life has ever been normal.

Abnormality. Abnormality leading to crisis. That's it, Dr Rose. We have lurched from crisis to crisis with my sister. Mother weeps at Mass in the morning, and Sister Cecilia knows that she needs help. Not only does she need help to cope with the fact that she has given birth to a child who is different, imperfect, unusual, outstanding or whatever else you want to call her, but she also needs practical help in caring for her. Because despite the presence of one child a prodigy and the other child handicapped by a defect of birth, life must continue, which means Gran must still be in attendance on Granddad, Dad must have two jobs as before, and if I'm to continue with the violin, Mother must work as well.

The logical expense to cut is the violin and everything associated with it: release Raphael Robson from his duties, sack Sarah-Jane Beckett and send me to day school. With the enormous amount of money saved from these simple and expedient economies, Mother can stay at home with Sonia, see to her growing needs, and nurse her through the health traumas that come up continually.

But making this change is unthinkable to everyone because at six and a half years old, I have already made my public debut, and to deny the world the gift of my music seems an act of egregious pettiness. Doing this, however, has certainly been mooted among my parents and grandparents. Yes. I remember now. Mother and Dad are having a discussion in the drawing room and Granddad enters into it vociferously. 'Boy's a genius, a goddamn genius,' he bellows at them. And Gran is there, because I hear her anxious. Jack, Jack,' and I picture her scurrying to

302

the stereo and throwing on a Paganini for the savage breast residing directly beneath Granddad's flannel shirt. 'He's already giving concerts, goddamn it,' Granddad rages. 'You'll cut him off from that over my dead body. So for once in your life—just for flaming once, Dick—will you please make the right decision?'

Neither Raphael nor Sarah-Jane is involved in this debate. Their futures hang in the balance along with my own, but they have as much say in what will happen as I do, which is none at all. The dispute goes on for hours and days during my mother's convalescence from her pregnancy, and both the dispute and the difficulties of my mother's recovery are exacerbated by the health crises that Sonia experiences.

The baby's been taken to the doctor . . . to hospital . . . to casualty. There is all round us a pervasive sense of tension, urgency, and fear that has never been in the house before. People are stretched to breaking point with anxiety. Always the question hangs in the air, What will happen next?

Crises. People are gone a great deal of the time. There are gaps in which no one seems at home at all. Just Raphael and I. Or Sarah-Jane and I. While everyone else is with Sonia.

Why? you ask. What sort of crises did Sonia have?

I can only remember He says he'll meet us at the hospital. Gideon, go to your room, and the sound of Sonia's weak crying, and I can hear that crying as it fades away when they carry her downstairs and out into the night.

I go to her room, which is next to mine. This is the nursery. A light has been left on, and there's some sort of machine next to her cot and straps that keep her hooked onto it while she sleeps. There is a chest of *drawers with a carousel lamp on it, the same carousel lamp that I can remember watching turn round and round as I lay in my own cot, this very same cot. And I see the marks where I bit the railing, and I see the Noah's ark transfers that I used to stare at. And I climb into the cot though I am six and a half years old and I curl up there and wait for what will happen.*

What does happen?

In time, they return as they always do, with medicine, with the name of a doctor they're to see in the morning, with a behavioural prescription or a cutting edge diet that they're to adhere to. Sometimes they have Sonia with them. Sometimes she's being kept in hospital.

Which is why my mother weeps at Mass. And yes, this is what she and Sister Cecilia must be talking about when we go with her into the convent that day that I overturn the bookshelf and break the statue of the Virgin. She murmurs mostly, this nun, and I assume it's to comfort my mother, who must feel . . . what? Guilt because she's given birth to a child who's suffering one illness after the next, anxiety because the what can happen next *is always loitering outside her front door, anger at the inequities of life, and sheer exhaustion from trying to cope.*

Out of all this fertile turbulent soil must grow the idea of hiring a nanny. A nanny could be the solution for everyone. So Katja Wolff comes to us. As things turn out, she isn't a trained nanny, however. She hasn't been to a specialised course or a college to earn a certificate in childcare. But she is educated and she is helpful, affectionate, grateful and—it must be said—affordable. She loves children, and she needs the job. And the Davies family need help.

6 OCTOBER

I went to see Dad that same evening. If anyone holds the anamnestic key I'm trying to find, it's going to be my father.

I found him at Jill's flat in Shepherd's Bush, on the front steps of the building, in fact. The two of them were in the midst of one of those polite but tense arguments that loving couples have when they each have reasonable desires that have come into conflict. This one apparently involved whether Jill—as she approached her due date—was still going to drive herself round London.

Dad was saying, 'That's dangerous and irresponsible. It's a wreck, that car. For God's sake, I'll send a taxi round for you. I'll drive you myself.'

And Jill was saying, 'Would you stop treating me like a piece of Lalique? I can't even breathe when you're like this.'

She began to go inside the building, but he took her by the arm. He said, 'Darling. Please,' and I could tell how afraid for her he was.

I understood. My father hadn't been blessed with luck in his children. Virginia, dead. Sonia, dead. Two out of three were not the sort of odds to give a man peace of mind.

To her credit, Jill seemed to recognise this as well. She said, more quietly, 'You're being silly,' but I think there was a part of her that appreciated the degree to which Dad was solicitous for her well-being. And then she saw me standing on the pavement, hesitating between skulking off and striding forward with a hearty hello that attempted to demonstrate a level of bonhomie that I did not feel. She said, 'Hullo. Here's Gideon, darling,' and Dad swung round, releasing her arm, which freed her to unlock the front door and usher both of us up to her flat.

Jill's flat is supremely modern in a period building that was gutted several years ago by a clever developer who completely updated it within. It's all fitted carpets, copper pans hanging from the kitchen ceiling, gleaming mod cons that actually work, and paintings that look as if they intend to slide off their canvases and do something questionable on the floor. It is, in short, perfectly Jill. I wonder how my father is going to cope with her decorating preferences when at last they begin to cohabit. Not that they're not already as good as cohabiting. My father's hovering over Jill is becoming somewhat obsessive.

With his paranoia about the new baby rising daily, I wondered if I should broach the subject of Sonia with him. My body told me not: I found that my head had begun a vague aching, and my stomach burned, but it burned in a way that told me I could not attribute it to anything other than nerves.

Jill said, 'I've got some work to do, so I'll leave you two to your own devices. I don't expect you've come to visit me, have you?'

I supposed I should have considered dropping in to see Jill now and again, especially as she was to be my step-mother, odd though the proposition seemed. But I could tell by the way she asked that she was merely sorting out information and not implying anything the way so many women do.

I said, 'There are one or two things . . .'

She said, I expect there are. I'll be in the study,' and she went in that direction.

When Dad and I were alone, we repaired to the kitchen. Dad moved Jill's impressive coffee maker into the centre of the worktop and fetched some

306

espresso beans, which he poured inside. The coffee maker—like the flat itself—is quintessentially Jill. It's an amazing machine with a capability of producing one fresh cup of anything in less than a minute: coffee, cappuccino, espresso, latte. It steams milk and boils water and I expect it would doing the washing up, the laundry, and the hoovering if you programmed it thus. Dad used to scoff at the appliance, but I noticed that he was using it like a pro.

He took out two demitasse cups and their saucers. From a bowl near the sink, he found a lemon. He was searching for the proper knife with which to carve us each a curl of the peel when I spoke.

'Dad, I've seen a picture of Sonia. I mean a better picture than the one you showed me. A newspaper picture from the time of the trial.'

He turned a dial on the coffee machine, replaced its single spout with a double one that he took from a drawer, and put the two small cups in position. He pushed a button. A gentle whirring ensued. He gave his attention to the lemon again, making a curving sliver that would have done credit to a chef at the Savoy. 'I see,' was all he said. He began a second slice.

'Why did no one tell me about it?' I asked.

'About what?'

'You know. The trial. How Sonia died. Everything. Why didn't we talk about it?'

He shook his head. He had finished with the second lemon peel curl—as perfectly carved as was the first—and when the espresso was done, be plopped a curl in each cup, and handed me mine. He said, 'Out here?' and cocked his head in the direction of the sitting room off which a terrace overlooked

307

other similar period buildings nearby.

On a grey day such as this, the terrace didn't promise much comfort. But it did offer the benefit of privacy, which I wanted with Dad, so I followed him out.

As I suspected, we were completely alone. Jill's outdoor furniture was already covered, but Dad removed the plastic sheeting from two of the chairs and we sat. He set his espresso on his knee and zipped his parka. He said, 'I didn't keep the newspapers. I didn't look at them. What I wanted more than anything was to forget. I realise that's probably anathema to current thinking. Aren't we all supposed to wallow in recollection till we reek of the stench? But I don't come from an age when that was fashionable, Gideon. I lived through it—the days and weeks and months of it—and when it was over, I wanted nothing more than to forget it had ever happened.'

'Is that how Mother felt as well?'

He lifted his cup. He drank, but he observed me as he did so. 'I don't know how your mother felt. We couldn't talk about it. None of us could talk about it. To talk about it meant to relive it and living through it once was horror enough.'

'I need to talk about it now.'

'More of your Doctor Rose's sterling recommendations? Sonia loved the violin, if that's of interest to you. She loved you and the violin, more precisely. She spoke very little—language comes late to a Down's child—but she could say your name.'

That was like the precise administering of a wound, a delicate but perfectly accurate incision into my heart. I said, 'Dad—'

He cut in. 'Never mind. That was low of me.'

308

'Why did no one speak of her afterwards?' I asked the question but the answer was obvious: We never spoke of anything unpleasant. Granddad raged like a maniac periodically; he was carted off and did not return for weeks, and we did not mention the fact at any time. Mother vanished one day, taking with her not only every possession she owned but also every reminder that she had ever been part of the family, and we did not discuss where she might have gone or why. And there I sat on my father's lover's terrace, wondering why we never spoke of Sonia's life or her death when we were and had always been a group of people who spoke of nothing: nothing painful, nothing heartbreaking, nothing horrifying, nothing grievous.

'We wanted to forget it had happened.'

'Forget Mother had happened? Forget Sonia herself had happened?'

He observed me and I saw that opaqueness in his eyes, that expression that had always succeeded so well in defining a territory whose landscape was ice, bitter wind, and endless smoke-coloured sky. 'That's unworthy of you,' he said. 'I think you know what I'm talking about.'

'But never to say her name. All those years. To me. Never say even the words your sister . . .'

'Do you think you would have gained something had Sonia's murder become part of the daily fabric of our lives? Is that your conclusion?'

'I just don't understand—'

He drank down the rest of his espresso and put the cup on the terrace, next to the leg of his chair. He leaned forward. His face was as grey as his hair which swept back from his forehead as my own hair does, with that very same widow's peak in the centre, with *those same indentations like fjords on either side. He said, 'Your sister was drowned in her bath. She was drowned by a German girl we'd taken into our home.'*

'I know—'

'Nothing. That's what you know. You know what the papers might have told you but you don't know what it was to be there. You don't know that Sonia was murdered because she was growing progressively more difficult to care for and because the German girl—'

Katja Wolff, I thought. Why won't he say her name?

'—was pregnant.'

Pregnant. The word was a snap of the fingers in front of my face. The word brought me back to my father's world and what he had lived through and what the present circumstances were asking him to live through again. I thought back to the picture of Katja Wolff smiling dreamily up at the camera in the Kensington Square garden with Sonia in her arms. I thought of the picture of her leaving the police station, stick thin and ill-looking with features sharpened by excessive weight loss. Pregnant.

I murmured, 'She didn't look pregnant in the photo,' and I looked away from Dad to one of the other terraces where, I noticed, an Old English sheep dog was watching us curiously. As he saw me take note of him, he rose on his hind legs, front paws on the iron rail that surrounded the terrace. He began to bark. I shivered at the sound. He'd had his vocal cords removed and what remained was a hopeful but pathetic yelp that was air and muscle and mostly cruelty. It made me feel sick.

Dad said, 'What photo?' And then he must have realised because he said, 'It wouldn't have shown.

310

She was deadly ill at the start of her pregnancy, so she didn't put on weight, she lost it. We noticed first that she'd gone off food, that she didn't look well, and we thought it was a lover's tiff of some kind. She and the lodger—'

'That would've been James.'

'Yes. James. They were close. Obviously, a hell of a lot closer than we originally assumed. He liked to help her with her English when she had free time. We had no objection to that. Until she became pregnant.'

'Then what?'

'We told her she'd have to go. We weren't running a home for unmarried mothers, and we needed someone whose attention would stay on Sonia, not on herself: her illness, her difficulty, her condition, whatever you want to call it. We didn't throw her out on the street or even tell her she had to leave at once. But as soon as she was able to find another . . . situation, job, she would have to go. That would have taken her away from James, though, and she snapped.'

'Snapped?'

'Tears, anger, hysteria. She couldn't cope. Not with pregnancy, unremitting illness, looming homelessness, and your sister as well. Sonia was just out of hospital at the time. She needed constant care. The German girl snapped.'

'I remember.'

'What?' I could hear the reluctance behind the question, that conflict between Dad's desire to put an end to a reminiscence that was painful for him and his wish to liberate from a prison of mind the son he loved.

'Crises. Sonia being carried to the doctor, to hospital, to . . . I don't know where else.'

311

He sank back in his chair and, like me, looked over at the dog who so wanted our attention. He said, 'No place for a creature with complicated needs,' and I couldn't tell if he was referring to the animal, to himself, to me, or to my sister. 'At first it was her heart. An atrioseptal defect, it was called. It wasn't long—just after her birth—when we knew from her colour and her pulse that there was trouble. So they performed an operation on her and we thought, Right. That's taken care of the problem. But then it was her stomach: duodenal stenosis. Very common among Down's children, we were told. As if her being Down's in the first place was as minor an issue as the poor creature having a wandering eye. More surgery then. After that, imperforate anus. Hmm, we were told, this particular little one appears to be at the farthest extreme of the syndrome. So many problems. Let's see if we can cut her open again. And again. And again. And then give her hearing aids. And bottles of medicine. And of course, we can only hope she'll be happy to have her body invaded and probed and rearranged on a regular basis till we get her sorted out.'

'Dad . . .' I wanted to prevent the rest. He'd said enough. He'd gone through enough: not only to have lived through her suffering but also to have lived through her death. And before that death, to have borne his own grief, my mother's, and no doubt his parents' . . .

Before I could finish what I'd wanted to say to him, I heard my grandfather all at once again. I felt the breath leave me as if I'd taken a punch to the gut, but I had to ask. I said, 'Dad, how did Granddad cope with all this?'

'Cope? He wouldn't attend the trial. He—'

312

'I don't mean the trial. I mean Sonia. How she . . . how she was.'

And I can hear him, Dr Rose. I can hear him howling as he always howled—Lear like—although the storm that raged round him was not of the moors but of his own mind. *Freaks!* he's shouting. *You're capable of giving me nothing but freaks!* There's spittle at the corners of his mouth and although my grandmother takes his arm and murmurs his name, he hears and is aware of nothing but the wind and the rain and the thunder in his head.

Dad said, 'Your grandfather was a troubled man, Gideon. But a great and good man. His demons were fierce, but so was his battle against them.'

'Did he love her?' I asked. 'Did he hold her? Did he play with her? Did he think of her as his grandchild?'

'Sonia was ill for a great part of the time she was with us. She was fragile. She went through one trauma after another.'

'So he didn't, did he?' I asked my father. 'He didn't . . . anything.'

Dad made no reply. Instead, he rose and walked to the railing. The Old English sheep dog yelped in near soundlessness, pawing at his own rails with an eagerness that was as obvious as it was pathetic. 'Why do they do that to animals?'Dad said. 'For the love of God, it's so bloody unnatural. If people want a pet, they should accommodate the pet. If they don't, they should damn well get rid of it.'

'You aren't going to tell me, are you?' I asked him. 'About Granddad and Sonia. You aren't going to tell me.'

'Your grandfather was who your grandfather was,' my father replied. And that was the end of it.

313

CHAPTER EIGHT

Liberty Neale knew that if she'd only had the luck to meet Rock Peters somewhere in Mexico and to marry him there, she wouldn't have been in her current position because she could have divorced the creep in a micro flash and that would have been the end of it. But no, she hadn't met him in Mexico. She hadn't even *gone* to Mexico. She'd come to England because she'd been such a total zero in foreign language in high school that England was the closest place to California that resembled a foreign country, where people spoke a language that Libby understood. Canada hardly counted.

She would have preferred France—she had a major thing for croissants, although the less said about *that* the better—but a few days in London had provided her with a wider range of eating experiences than she'd anticipated, so she'd managed to settle in happily, out of the reach of her parents and, more importantly, thousands of miles away from that living example of human perfection, her older sister. Equality Neale was tall, thin, intelligent, articulate, and disgustingly successful at everything she did. *And* she'd been elected homecoming queen at Los Altos High School which was enough to make anyone blow major chunks into the next time zone. So getting away from Ali had been priority numero uno, and London had made that possible.

But in London, Libby had met Rock Peters. In London, she had married the creep. And in London—where she hadn't yet got around to scoring anything closely resembling a work permit or a permanent resident's card despite her marriage—she was at Rock's mercy, whereas in Mexico, it would have been 'kiss my ass, Jack', and money or not, she could have gotten away from him. She still wouldn't have had the bucks to do it, but that wouldn't have mattered because the thumb spoke a universal language and she wasn't afraid to put herself out on the road and use it. Which was something she couldn't do from England since hitching a ride across the Atlantic to get away from Rock wasn't exactly possible.

Rock had her . . . well, he had her by the balls, figuratively speaking. She wanted to stay in England because she didn't want to go home and admit defeat when *every* letter she got from California was filled to the brim with Ali's latest success. But to stay in England, she needed money. And to get money, she needed Rock. True, she could have made some bucks even more illegally than she was already making them, but getting caught would have meant getting deported which would have meant back to Los Altos Hills, back to Mom and Dad, and back to 'Why don't you go to work for Ali for a time, Lib? In public relations, you could—' blah blah blah. No way in hell, Libby told herself, was she going to put herself anywhere *near* her sister. She'd smashed up Ali's BMW just before she left for England. It had felt oh so good at the time—just what Ali needed to get her attention—but the sisters had parted on the worst of terms.

So she was stuck here with Rock, and she was basically his slave. Which was why she was back to screwing the shithead two or three times a week

315

upon demand. She'd try to avoid it, usually by pointing out that there was a delivery needing to be made and since she was the most reliable of his couriers, shouldn't she make it? But that usually didn't work because when Rock wanted sex, Rock wanted sex, and it never took him much time to ride the train to the station anyway.

That was what had happened this day, back in the Bermondsey hovel above the grocery store where, if she concentrated on the traffic noises below, she'd always been able to avoid hearing Rock grunting in her ear like a constipated pig. As always, she'd been so pissed off after screwing him that she wanted to amputate his cock with a saw. That not being possible, she'd gone to her tap dancing lesson instead.

She'd tapped herself into the sweat of the century, shuffling, chugging, flapping, and spanking till she was dripping wet. The instructor kept yelling, 'Libby, what are you *doing* over there?' above the strains of 'On the Sunny Side of the Street', but Libby had ignored her. It hadn't mattered whether she was in step, out of step, in line, out of line, or even in the same hemisphere as her fellow tappers. What mattered was doing something hard, something fast, something that was demanding and physical in order to put Rock Peters from her mind. If she didn't do that, she'd end up in front of the closest refrigerator, and approximately six billion calories later, she'd find herself recovered from Rock's brand of blackmail.

'Think of it this way, Lib,' he'd say when it was over and she lay beneath him defeated again, 'It's tit for tat, pardon the pun' and he'd offer that grin she'd first thought so cool and later learned to

316

recognise for the sign of contempt it actually was. 'You scratch my itch and I scratch yours. 'Sides, you're not getting any from the fiddler, are you? I know when a bird's been rogered proper and you've the look of someone who hasn't had a decent shagging in more'n a year.'

'That's right, I haven't, you total dickhead,' she'd snap. '*Think* about it, Rock. And he's not a fiddler. He plays the violin.'

'Ooooh. Pardon my French,' he'd say. And it mattered exactly zero to the former Rocco Petrocelli that she'd put down his ability as a lover. To him, success in bed meant getting his rocks off. What happened to his partner was left to self-stimulation or total coincidence.

Libby departed the dance studio in a better frame of mind, her leotard and tap shoes stuffed into her backpack and that outfit replaced by the leathers which she wore when she made her courier stops. Helmet under her arm, she strode to the Suzuki and she used the kick starter instead of the electric ignition, the better to think about tromping on Rock's face.

The streets were clogged—like, when *weren't* they clogged?—but she'd spent enough time on the bike to know not only which side streets to take but also how to squeeze between cars and delivery trucks when traffic had come to a standstill. She had a Walkman that she usually wore on deliveries, the recorder tucked into an inner pocket of her leathers and the helmet holding the earphones in place. She liked bubble gum music, she liked it loud, and she generally sang along because the combination of music blasting against her ear drums and her own voice singing at maximum

317

volume pretty much took care of whatever was left in her head that she didn't want to think about.

But she didn't use the Walkman today. The tap dancing had wiped the image of Rock's hairy body mashed on top of her and his salami red cock shoving between her legs. And as for the rest of what was in her head: That was something she *wanted* to think about.

Rock was right: She still hadn't gotten Gideon Davies to bed—as in *really* to bed—and she couldn't figure out why. He seemed to like being with her, and he seemed normal in every way other than what wasn't happening between them in the sack. Yet in all the time she'd been living below him and hanging out with him, they'd never progressed beyond the point where they'd been that first night when they fell asleep on her bed while listening to a CD. That was it with a capital *I* as far as the sex part went.

At first she'd thought the dude was gay and her radar had gone totally down for the count after being with Rock for so long. But he didn't *act* gay or do the gay scene in London or even have younger guys, older guys, or obviously twisted guys up to his place in private. All he had was his dad—who hated her guts and was all Mr Major Attitude whenever she and he were actually breathing the same air for five seconds—and Rafe Robson who hung around Gideon day and night like a case of the hives. All of this had long ago made Libby conclude that there was nothing strictly *wrong* with Gideon that a decent relationship couldn't straighten out . . . if she could just get him away from his keepers for a while.

Having left the South Bank where her tap lesson

was, having woven her way through the City and upwards to Pentonville Road, she opted to shoot through the by-ways of Camden Town rather than take on the crush of cars, taxis, buses, and trucks that were always making a mess of every street within spitting distance of King's Cross Station. Her route to Chalcot Square wasn't a direct one as a result, but that was cool as far as Libby was concerned. She didn't mind having more time to plan an approach that might work as a breakthrough with Gideon. To her way of thinking, Gideon Davies had to be more than simply a man who'd been playing the violin since he was just out of diapers. Yeah, it was cool that he was a major big deal as a musician, but he was also a *person*. And that person was more than just the music he made. That person could exist whether he played the violin or not.

When Libby finally arrived in Chalcot Square, the first thing she saw was that Gideon wasn't alone. Raphael Robson's ancient Renault stood at the south edge of the square, parked with one wheel on the sidewalk like he'd been in a hurry. Through the lit window to Gideon's music room, Libby noted that the unmistakable shape of Rafe— handkerchief, as always, mopping up the sweat on his face—was moving about, and he was talking. Preaching, more likely. And Libby knew about what.

'Shit,' she muttered as she gunned up to the house. She revved the engine a few times in the cause of letting off steam and she pulled the Suzuki onto its kick stand. Rafe Robson didn't usually turn up in Chalcot Square at this time of day, and to have him here now was a real bummer that, in combination with what she'd already been through, having to screw Rock Peters, really ticked her off.

She shoved through the gate in the wrought iron railing and didn't stop it from clanging against the concrete that defined the upper steps to the house. She flung herself downwards, banged her way into the basement flat, and without a second thought dived straight for the refrigerator.

She'd been trying to stay on the No White Diet, but now—tap dancing be damned—she was definitely craving something pale. Vanilla ice cream, popcorn, rice, potatoes, cheese. She thought she might freak if she didn't have it.

Months ago, however, she'd prepared the refrigerator door for a moment just like this. Before she could open the appliance, she was forced to look at a picture of herself at sixteen years of age, a tubbo in a one piece bathing suit standing next to her size five sister in a butt floss bikini . . . *and* with a perfect tan, of course. Libby had put a sticker over Ali's face: a spider wearing a cowboy hat. But now she peeled the sticker off, gazing long and hard upon her sister, and just for good measure she read the message that she'd penned for herself across the refrigerator door. *IN THROUGH THE LIPS AND ONTO THE HIPS.* She took her inspiration where she could.

She sighed and backed off, which was when she heard it: the violin music floating down from above. She thought for a moment, 'Omigod! He's cracked it,' and she felt a surge of pleasure at the realisation that Gideon's problems might be over, that his most recent plan for solving his problem had actualy done the job.

This was very cool. This would make him happy.

And it had to be Gideon who was playing upstairs. It wouldn't, after all, be Rafe Robson who couldn't possibly be so uncool as to torture Gid by playing the violin in front of him while Gid was having such trouble playing himself.

But just as she was celebrating the fact of Gideon Davies' return to his music, the rest of the orchestra started grinding away. A CD, Libby thought despairingly. It was Rafe's little pep talk for Gideon's ears: See how you once played the music, Gideon? You did it then. You can do it now.

Why, Libby wondered, wouldn't they leave him the hell alone? Did they think he'd start playing if they bugged him enough? Because they sure as hell were beginning to bug her. 'He's more than this stupid *music*,' she snarled at the ceiling above her.

She left the kitchen and marched to her own small CD player. There, she selected a disk that was guaranteed to drive Raphael Robson right up the wall. It was bubble gum squared, and she played it loud. Just for good measure, she opened her windows. Banging on the floor above ensued in short order. She turned the volume up to full blast. Time for a nice long bath, she thought. Bubble gum music was, like, *so* perfect for soaking, soaping, and singing along.

Thirty minutes later, bathed and dressed, Libby turned off the CD player and listened for any more sounds from above. Silence. She'd made her point.

She left the flat and popped her head above the level of the street to see if Rafe's car was still in the square. The Renault was gone, which meant Gideon might be free from his keepers and ready for a visit from someone who cared more about him as a person than as a musician. She trotted up the stairs from her flat to his front door where she gave a hardy knock.

No answer prompted her to turn back to the square, taking a look for Gideon's Mitsubishi and seeing the GPS five cars along. Libby frowned, gave another knock, and called out, 'Gideon? You still in there? It's me.'

This roused him. The dead bolt was released from the other side of the door. The door swung open.

Libby said, 'Hey, sorry about the music. I sort of lost control and—' She cut her own words off. He looked like hell. True, he hadn't looked good in weeks, but now he was positively bird-do on a cracker. Libby's first thought was that Rafe Robson had worked Gideon over by making him listen to his own recordings. Bastard, she thought.

She said, 'Where's good ol' Rafe? Gone to make his report to your dad?'

Gideon merely stepped back from the door and let her in. He went up the stairs, and she followed him. His destination was where he'd obviously been when she'd knocked on his door: the bedroom. The imprint of his head on the pillow and his body on the bed looked pretty recent.

A dim light was burning on the bedside table and the shadows not dispelled by its glow fell on Gideon's face and made him look cadaverous. He'd been surrounded by an aura of anxiety and defeat since the Wigmore debacle, but Libby saw that there was something more edging that aura now, something that looked . . . what? Excruciating, she realised. So she said, 'Gideon, what's wrong?'

He said simply, 'My mother's been murdered.'

She blinked. Her jaw dropped. She snapped it

closed. 'Your *mom*? Your *mother?* Oh *no*. When? How? Holy *shit*. Sit down.' She urged him over to his bed and he sat, his hands hanging limply between his knees. 'What happened?'

Gideon told her what little there was to know. He concluded with, 'Dad was asked to identify her body. The police've been to see him since. A detective, Dad said. He rang a while ago.' Gideon clutched his arms around himself, bent forward, and rocked like a child. He said, 'That's it, then.'

'What?' Libby asked.

'There's no hope after this.'

'Don't say that, Gideon.'

'I might as well be dead, too.'

'Geez. Hey. Don't *say* that.'

'It's the truth.' He shivered as he said this and glanced round the room as if looking for something while he continued to rock.

Libby thought about what it meant that his mother was dead. She said, 'Gideon, you're going to get through all this. You're going to get past it,' and she tried to sound like she really meant those words, like whether he played his music or not was as important to her as it was to him.

She noticed that his shivering had turned to trembling. At the foot of his bed was a knitted blanket, and she grabbed this and dropped it around his thin shoulders. 'You want to talk about it?' she asked him. 'About your mom? About . . . I don't know . . . anything?' She sat beside him and put her arm around him. She used her other hand to close the blanket at his throat till he grasped it as well and clutched it.

He said, 'She was on her way to see James the Lodger.'

'Who?'

'James Pitchford. He lived with us when my sister was . . . when she died. And it's odd because I'd been thinking of him recently, although before that he hadn't crossed my mind in years.' Gideon grimaced then, and Libby noticed that the hand not clutching the blanket was pressed into his stomach as if something inside were burning his guts. 'Someone ran her down in James Pitchford's street,' he said. 'More than once, Libby. And because she was on her way to see James, Dad thinks the police are going to want to track down everyone who was involved . . . back then.'

'Why?'

'Because of the kind of questions they asked him, I dare say.'

'I don't mean why does he think the cops want to track down everyone. I mean why would they *want* to track down everyone. Is there a connection between then and now? I mean, obviously if your mom was going to see James Pitchford, there's some sort of connection. But if someone from twenty years ago killed her, why wait till now to do it?'

Gideon bent forward farther, his face contorted with pain. He said, 'God. It feels like a coal's burning right through me.'

'Here, then.' Libby lowered him to bed. He curled on his side, his legs drawn up to his chest. She removed his shoes. His feet were sockless and as pale as milk, and he rubbed them together spasmodically, as if the friction could take his mind from the pain.

Libby lowered herself next to him, spooning her body into his beneath the blanket. She insinuated her hand beneath his arm and laid her palm on his stomach. She could feel his spine curved into her, every knob of it like a marble. He'd become so thin that she wondered how he kept his bones from poking through his papery skin.

She said, 'I bet you've had a brain lock on this stuff, huh? Well, forget about it. Not for always. Just for now. Lay here with me and just forget.'

'I can't,' he said, and he gave a bitter laugh. 'Remembering everything is my assignment.' His feet rubbed. He curled into himself further still. Libby held him closer. He finally said, 'She's out of gaol, Libby. Dad knew, but he didn't tell me. That's why the police want to look at twenty years ago. She's out of gaol.'

'Who is? You mean . . . ?'

'Katja Wolff.'

'Do they think she might have run down your mom?'

'I don't know.'

'Why would she? It makes more sense that your mom would want to run down her.'

'In the normal way of things,' Gideon said. 'Except nothing about my life has been normal, so there's no reason why my mother's death should be normal either.'

'Your mom must have testified against her,' Libby said. 'And she could have spent her time locked up planning to get everyone who put her there. But if she did, how'd she find your mom, Gideon? I mean, you didn't even know where she was. How could this Wolff chick have tracked her down? And if she *did* track her down, and if she did kill her, why'd she kill her on this Pitchford guy's street?' Libby thought about her question and then

325

answered them herself. 'To give Pitchford a message?'

'Or to give someone else one.'

* * *

A phone call relayed to Barbara Havers what Lynley had learned from Richard Davies, including the name she needed to gain access to the Convent of the Immaculate Conception. There, he told her, she should find someone who could give her the whereabouts of a Sister Cecilia Mahoney.

The convent sat on a piece of land that was probably worth a king's ransom, tucked among a host of listed properties dating from the 1690s. This would have been where the movers and shakers had built their rural retreats during the time that William and Mary had built their own little humble country cottage in Kensington Gardens. Now the movers and shakers in the square were the employees of several business establishments that had shoe-horned themselves into the historic buildings, denizens of a second convent—where the bloody hell did *nuns* get the lolly to have digs round here? Barbara wondered— and inhabitants of a number of homes that had probably been handed down through families for more than three hundred years. Unlike some of the city squares that had suffered bomb damage or the ravages of greed from consecutive Tory governments with big business, vast profits, and the privatisation of everything in mind, Kensington Square stood largely untouched, with four sides of distinguished buildings overlooking a central garden where the fallen autumn leaves made an

326

umber skirt on the lawn beneath each tree.

Parking was impossible, so Barbara pulled her Mini onto the pavement at the northwest edge of the square where a strategically placed bollard prevented the traffic from the distant high street from creating a short cut and disturbing the quiet of the neighbourhood. She shoved her police identification onto what went for the Mini's dashboard. She clambered out and shortly found herself in the company of Sister Cecilia Mahoney who was still a resident of the convent and who was, when Barbara called, at work in the chapel next door.

Barbara's first thought upon encountering the nun was that she didn't look much like one. Nuns were supposed to be women two or three decades past their prime who wore heavy black robes, clanking rosary beads, and veils and wimples from the Middle Ages.

Cecilia Mahoney didn't fit this picture. In fact when Barbara was directed to the chapel to find her, her first assumption when she saw the figure up on a small step ladder with a can of marble polish in her hand was that she was a tartan-skirted cleaning woman since cleaning an altar that featured a statue of Jesus pointing to His own exposed, anatomically incorrect, and partially gilded heart was what she was doing. Barbara told this woman that, pardon me but she was looking for Sister Cecilia Mahoney, whereupon the woman turned and said with a smile, 'Then it's me you're looking for,' in a brogue that sounded as if she'd just landed from Killarney.

Barbara identified herself, and the nun took some care in climbing down from the steps. She

327

said, 'Police, is it? Why, you haven't the look of a policeman at all. Is there some sort of trouble, Constable?'

The chapel was dimly lit, but down from the steps Sister Cecilia put herself into a pool of rose light created by a single votive candle that burned on the altar she was polishing. It did much to flatter her, smoothing away the lines on her middle-aged face and casting highlights into hair that was short but whose curls—as black and as shiny as obsidian—couldn't be disciplined even by the slides she used to manage them. She had violet eyes, darkly lashed, and they looked upon Barbara kindly.

Barbara said, 'Is there somewhere we can go to have a word?'

The nun said, 'Sad to say, Constable, it's unlikely that we'll be disturbed in here if it's privacy you're wanting. Time was that would have been out of the question. But these days . . . even the students who live in our dormitory only frequent the chapel when they've got an exam and are hoping for God's intervention in the matter. Come. Let's go up here and you can tell me what it is that you're wanting to know.' She smiled, revealing perfect white teeth, and went on to say, as if in explanation of her smile, 'Or is it that you're wanting to join us in the convent, Constable Havers?'

'It might give me the fashion make-over I need,' Barbara admitted.

Sister Cecilia laughed. 'Come this way. It'll be a bit warmer by the main altar. I've an electric fire there for the Monsignor when he says Mass in the morning. He's become a bit arthritic, poor man.'

Taking her cleaning supplies in hand, she led

328

Barbara up the single centre aisle in the chapel, beneath a deep blue ceiling punctuated by gilded stars. Barbara saw that it was a church of women: Apart from the statue of Jesus and a stained glass window dedicated to St Michael, all other windows and statues were female: St Theresa of Lisieux, St Clare, St Catherine, St Margaret. And atop the ornamental pillars on either side of each of the windows were carvings of even more women.

'Here we are.' Sister Cecilia went to one side of the altar and switched on a large electric fire. As it began to heat, the nun explained that she'd continue her work right here in the sanctuary if the constable didn't mind. There was this altar to be seen to as well: the candlesticks and the marble to be polished, a reredos to be dusted, and altar cloths to be replaced. 'But you might wish to sit by the fire, my dear. The cold seeps in.'

As Sister Cecilia set to her cleaning, Barbara told her that she'd brought what might be bad news for the nun. Her name had been found inside several books on the lives of saints—

'Not a surprise, I hope, considering my calling,' Sister Cecilia murmured as she removed the brass candlesticks from the altar and set them carefully on the floor next to Barbara. She went on to the altar cloths, folding and placing them over an ornate altar rail. She then fished in her bucket and brought out a jar and some rags, which she took with her to work upon the altar.

Barbara told her that the books in question had been among a collection kept by a woman who'd died the previous evening. There had been a note penned to that woman as well, a note written by Sister Cecilia herself. 'She was called Eugenie

Davies,' Barbara said.

Sister Cecilia hesitated. She'd just scooped up a palmful of marble polish and she held it motionless as she said, 'Eugenie? Oh, I'm sorry to hear that, I am. It's been years since I last saw the poor woman. Was it sudden, her passing?'

'She was murdered,' Barbara said. 'In West Hampstead. On her way to see a bloke called J.W. Pitchley, who was once James Pitchford.'

Sister Cecilia moved to the altar slowly, like an underwater diver in a strong, cold current. She smoothed some polish onto the marble, using small round strokes, as her lips worked their way round a thought or a prayer.

'We've learned,' Barbara said, 'that the killer of the daughter—a woman called Katja Wolff—has recently got out of prison as well.'

The nun turned from the altar at this, saying, 'You can't be thinking poor Katja had anything to do with this.'

Poor Katja. Barbara said, 'Did you know the girl?'

'Of course I knew her. She lodged here at the convent before she went to work for the Davies family. They lived at that time just along the square.'

Katja had been a refugee from the former East Germany, Sister Cecilia explained, and she went on to relate the facts of the girl's immigration to England.

She had dreamed as all girls dream. She had been born in Dresden of parents who believed in the system of economy and government under which they had lived. A teenager during the second world war, her father had seen the worst that could

330

happen when nations engage in conflict and he embraced the lifestyle of equality for the masses, believing that only communism and socialism held out the promise that global destruction would not occur. As good party workers with no members of the intelligentsia in their past for whose sins they would have had to pay, the family prospered under this system. From Dresden they moved to East Berlin.

'But Katja wasn't like the rest of them,' Sister Cecilia said. 'Indeed, Constable, God love the girl, but wasn't Katja Wolff living proof that children are born with their personalities intact.'

Unlike her parents and her four siblings, Katja hated the atmosphere of socialism and the omnipresence of the State. She hated the fact that their lives were 'described, prescribed, and circumscribed' from birth. And in East Berlin—so close to the West by the presence of that other half of the city just a few hundred yards across No Man's Land—she got her first taste of what could be if she only could escape the land of her birth. For from East Berlin for the first time she could see western television and from westerners who travelled to the East on business, she could learn what life was like in what she came to call The World of Bright Colours.

'She was expected to go to university, to study in one field of science or another, to marry, and to have babies who would be looked after by the State,' Sister Cecilia explained. 'This is what her sisters were doing and this is what her parents intended her to do as well. But she wanted to be a fashion designer.' Sister Cecilia turned from the altar with a smile. 'And can you not imagine,

331

Constable Havers, how that idea was greeted by members of the Party with other plans for the girl?'

So she escaped and in escaping *as* she'd escaped, she gained a degree of celebrity that had brought her to the attention of the convent, where there existed a programme for political refugees: one year at the convent to have shelter and food, to learn the language, and to assimilate into the culture if they could. 'She came to us with not a word of English and only the clothes on her back, Constable. She was with us that full year before she went to the Davies family to help out with the new baby.'

'Is that when you got to know them?'

Sister Cecilia shook her head. 'It was years and years that I'd known Eugenie. She attended Mass here, so she was familiar to all of us, she was. We spoke now and again and I lent her a book or two—which is what you must have seen amongst her collection—but it was only after Sonia's birth that I came to know her better.'

'I saw a picture of the little girl.'

'Ah, yes.' Sister Cecilia rubbed polish along the front of the altar, tucking her cloth into its ornate carving. 'Eugenie was devastated when that baby was born. And I suppose any mother would feel the same. A period of adjustment is necessary—isn't it—when a child is born who isn't what we expect her to be. And indeed, it must have been worse for Eugenie and her husband than it might have been for other parents, because their first child was so gifted, you see.'

'The violin player. Right. We know about him.'

'Yes. Young Gideon. An astonishing lad.' Sister Cecilia lowered herself to her knees and saw to the elaborate barley sugar column at the end of the altar. She said, 'Eugenie didn't talk about little Sonia at first. All of us knew she was pregnant, of course, and we knew when she'd delivered the child. But the first we knew anything was wrong was when she returned to Mass one or two weeks later.'

'She told you then?'

'Ah no. Poor thing. She just wept. Wept her eyes out every morning for three or four days, there at the back of the chapel with that poor frightened little boy at her side, stroking her arm and watching her with those big eyes of his and trying to comfort her. As for us at the Immaculate Conception, none of us had actually seen the infant, you understand. I'd gone to the house. But Eugenie was never "available for visitors".' Sister Cecilia clucked and went back to her bucket of cleaning items from which she took another rag and set about buffing. 'When I finally spoke to Eugenie and learned the truth from her, I understood her sorrow. But not the depth of it, Constable. That, I must tell you, I never understood. Now perhaps it's because I'm not a mother, and have no idea what it's like to give birth to a child who isn't perfect as the world deems perfection, but it seemed to me then—and it seems to me now—that God gives us what we're *meant* to have. We may not understand His reason for giving us what He gives us at the moment we're given it, but there is a plan for us which time allows us to comprehend.' She rested on her heels and looked over her shoulder at Barbara, softening what she seemed to feel might be harsh words by adding, 'But then, that's an easy thing for one such as myself to say, isn't it, Constable? Here I

333

am—' she extended her arms—'surrounded by God's love manifesting itself in a thousand different ways every day. Who am I to judge another's ability—or lack of such—to accept the will of God when I myself have been blessed with so much? Will you see to the candlesticks for me, dear? There's a tin of polish in the bucket there.'

Barbara said, 'Oh. Right. Sorry.' She rooted through the bucket for the appropriate tin and a rag whose black spots suggested it was the correct one to use on the candlesticks. Housewifely chores were not exactly her line, but she reckoned she could do a job on the brass without destroying it permanently. 'When was the last time you talked to Mrs Davies?'

'That would have been soon after Sonia's death. There was a service for the child.' Sister Cecilia looked down at her polishing rag. 'Eugenie wouldn't hear of a Catholic funeral because she'd stopped attending Mass herself. Her faith was gone: that God would have given her such an afflicted child in the first place and taken the child in such a way . . . Eugenie and I never spoke again. I tried to see her. I wrote to her as well. But she would have none of me, none of my faith, none of the Church. In the end I had to leave her to God and I only pray the dear woman found peace at last.'

Barbara frowned, candlestick in one hand and polish tin in the other. There was a vital part of the story that was missing and it was named Katja Wolff. She said, 'How exactly did the German girl end up working in the Davies household?'

'That was my doing.' Sister Cecilia got to her feet with a little grunt. She genuflected in front of the tabernacle at the centre of the altar and then began to attack its marble sides. 'Katja needed employment at the end of her year here at the convent. A position with the Davies family, which included her room and board, would have allowed her to save for design college. It seemed a solution fabricated by God because Eugenie so needed someone to help her.'

'And then the baby was killed.'

Sister Cecilia looked over at her, one hand on the tabernacle. She said nothing but her face, muscles loosening so that expression was drained from it entirely, spoke the inference that she herself did not make.

Barbara said, 'Have you stayed in contact with anyone else from that time, Sister Cecilia?'

'It's Katja you're asking about, is it, Constable?'

Barbara prised the lid from the brass polish and said, 'If you like.'

'I went once a month for two years to see her. First while she was on remand in Holloway, then when she was imprisoned. She spoke to me only once, in the beginning, when she was arrested. Then not again.'

'What did she say?'

'That she did not kill Sonia.'

'Did you believe her?'

'I did.'

But then, she would have had to do so, Barbara thought, because believing that Katja Wolff had murdered a child would have been a monstrous burden to carry through the rest of her life, especially for the woman—devoted or not to an omnipotent and sagacious God—who had facilitated the German girl's placement in that

335

family. She said, 'Have you heard from Katja Wolff since she got out of prison, Sister Cecilia?'

'Indeed, I have not.'

'Would there be any reason, aside from a need to declare her innocence, that she might have contacted Eugenie Davies once she was released?'

'None at all,' Sister Cecilia said firmly.

'You're certain of that?'

'I am. If Katja were to contact anyone at all from that terrible time, it would be no one from the Davies family. It would be myself. But I've not heard from her.'

She sounded so positive, Barbara thought. She sounded so firm. Indeed, she sounded as if there were no wiggle room whatever in what she had to say in the matter. Barbara asked her why.

'Because of the baby,' Sister Cecilia said.

'Sonia?'

'No. Katja's own child, the child she had in prison. When he was born, she asked me to place him with a family. So if she's out of prison and dwelling on her past, I think it's safe to say that what she wants is to know what happened to her son.'

CHAPTER NINE

Yasmin Edwards locked up her shop for the evening the way she always did: with maximum care. Most of the businesses on Manor Place had been boarded up for ages, and they were suffering the way derelict buildings usually suffered south of the river. They had become the urban outdoor canvases for graffiti artists, and where they had front windows and not sheets of either steel or plywood, those windows were broken. Yasmin Edwards' shop was one of the few new or resurrected businesses in the Kennington neighbourhood, apart from two pubs which had long survived the urban rot that had invaded the street. But then when did pubs *not* survive and when wouldn't they survive as long as there was drink to be served and blokes like Roger Edwards to guzzle it?

She tested the padlock that she'd put through the hasp, and she made certain that the grillwork was fixed properly in place. That done, she scooped up the four carrier bags which she'd filled inside the shop, and she walked in the direction of home.

Home was in the Doddington Grove Estate, a short distance away. She lived in Arnold House—had lived there for the last five years since her release from Holloway and from the hoop-jumping she'd had to do in open conditions—and she was lucky to have a flat that overlooked the horticultural centre across the street. It wasn't a park, a common, or a garden square, true. But it was green and it was a bit of nature and that's what she wanted for Daniel. He was only eleven and he'd spent most of her prison term in care—thanks to her younger brother who 'couldn't cope with a kid, Yas, look I'm sorry but it's just a fac', innit?'—and she was determined to make it up to her son in every possible way that she could.

He was waiting for her just outside the lift, across the strip of tarmac that did for the Arnold House car park. But he wasn't alone, and when Yasmin saw who was chatting to her son, she doubled her pace. The neighbourhood wasn't a bad one—could have been a lot worse and wasn't *that* the truth?—but candymen and chicken hawks could turn up anywhere, and if one of them so much suggested to her son that there was a life to be had outside of school, homework and study, she would kill the flaming bastard.

This bloke looked just like a candyman with his expensive togs and the glitter of a gold watch in the lights from the car park. And he had the patter as well. Because as Yasmin approached, calling, 'Dan, what you *do*ing out here this time of day?' she could see that the man had her son in thrall.

Both of them turned. Daniel called out, 'Hi, Mum. Sorry. Forgot my key.' The man said nothing.

Yasmin said, 'Why'd you not come by the shop, then, tell me?' with all her suspicions on top alert.

Daniel dropped his head like he always did when he was embarrassed about something. He said, examining his trainer-shod feet—Nikes that had cost her a fortune—'Went over to the Army Centre, Mum. A bloke was inspecting them and they were all lined up outside and they let me watch and after they let me stay for tea.'

Charity, Yasmin thought. Sodding *charity*. 'They not think you had a home to go to?' she demanded.

'They know me, Mum. They know you. One said, "Isn't your mummy the lady got the beads in her hair? Right pretty, she is."'

Yasmin harrumphed. She'd been studiously ignoring her son's companion. She handed over two of the carrier bags to her son, said, 'Mind how you go with these. You've some washing to do,' and punched in the code to call the lift.

That was when the man spoke, saying in a voice that was south of the river like hers, but more deeply influenced by West Indian roots, 'Missus Edwards, that right?'

'I already had too much of what you're selling,' she replied, but she spoke to the lift door and not to him. She said, 'Daniel?' and he came to stand in front of her to wait for the lift. She put a protective hand on his shoulder. Daniel peered round at the man. She straightened him back to face the lift.

'Winston Nkata,' the man then said. 'New Scotland Yard.'

That got her attention. He extended an identity card which she looked at before she looked at him. A copper, she thought. A brother *and* a copper. There was only one thing worse than a brother who was a raasclat and that was a brother who joined the Bill.

She dismissed the identification with a toss of her head, and the beads at the end of her multitude of plaits offered him the music of her contempt. He was looking at her the way men always looked at her and she knew what he saw and what he was thinking. What he saw: the body, all six feet of her; the face coloured walnut, a face that could have been like a model's face with a model's bones and a model's skin except that her lip—her upper lip, this was—was split permanently and scarred like an exploding purple rose where that bastard Roger Edwards had broken a vase against it when she wouldn't give him her Sainsbury wages or go on the game to support his habit; the eyes, coloured coffee and angry, angry but wary as well; and if she took her coat off in the cold evening air, he'd see the rest of her but especially the summertime cropped top she wore because her stomach was flat and her skin there was smooth and if she wanted to show off a smooth, tight stomach then she was going to, no matter the weather. That's what he saw. And what he thought? What they all thought, what they always thought: Wouldn't mind doing her long as she wears a bag on her head.

He said, 'C'n I have a word, Missus Edwards?' and he sounded the way they always sounded, like they'd lay in front of a bus for their mummies.

The lift arrived and the door slid open slowly, like there was melted cheese on its track. It slid like it was saying if you were so stupid as to get in and ride it to the third floor where you had your flat, you might not get out because the door might decide not to open again.

She tapped Daniel's shoulder to move him inside. The cop said, 'Missus Edwards? C'n I have a word with you?'

She said, 'Like I've a choice?' and punched the button marked three.

The cop said, 'Cheers,' and got inside.

He was big. That was what she noticed first in the harsh overhead light inside the lift. He was taller than she was by a good four inches. And he had a scar on his face as well. It ran like a chalk mark from the corner of his eye right down his cheek and she knew what it was—a razor slash— but not how he'd got it. So she said, 'What's that, then?' with a nod at his face.

He glanced at Daniel, who was looking up at him the way he always looked at black men: with that face so shiny so open so wanting, that face that revealed what'd gone missing in his life since the night his mum had taken on Roger Edwards one last time. The cop said, 'A reminder, this is.'

'Of what?'

'How stupid one bloke can be when he thinks he's cool.'

The lift jerked to a stop. She made no comment. The cop was closest to the door, so he got out first when it groaned open. But he made a point of holding the door back—like it was going to slide shut and smack either Yasmin or her son . . . fat lot he knew about the flaming lift. He stepped to one side, and she swept past him, saying, 'Mind those bags, Dan. Don't drop the wigs, you'll never get the filth out.'

She admitted them into the flat and switched on one of the lamps in what passed for the sitting room. She said to her son, 'Mind you fill the tub. Be easier with the shampoo this time round.'

'Right, Mum,' Daniel said. He shot a shy look at the cop—a look that so clearly said *This is our gaff, what you think of it, man?* that Yasmin ached for him, physically ached, and that ache made her angry because it told her once again just what she and Daniel had lost.

She said, 'Get on with it then,' to her son and to the cop, 'What you want, man? Who'd you say you were?'

Dan said, 'Winston Nkata, Mum.'

She said, 'Told you what to do, d'n't I, Dan?'

He grinned, with those big white teeth—the teeth already of the man he'd become far sooner than she wanted him to—shining in a face that was lighter than her own, a mixture of the colours of her skin and Roger's. He disappeared into the bathroom, where he turned the bath taps on, setting the water to roaring in a way that

341

announced he was doing his job smartly, just like Mum'd told him to do.

Winston Nkata stayed near to the door, and Yasmin found that this irritated her more than if he'd sauntered through the rooms of the flat—four rooms only so it wouldn't have taken him more than a minute even if he was studying what he saw in every one of those rooms—inspecting every piece of her property. She said, 'What's this about, then?'

He said, 'Mind 'f I look round?'

'Why? I'm not holding nothing. You got a warrant? And I checked in like I always check in with Sharon Todd last week. If she's told you different—if that bitch's told prison service *anything* different . . .' Yasmin could feel the scare creeping up her arms as she realised yet again the amount of power her parole officer had over what went for her freedom. She said, 'She'd gone to see her GP. Least, that's what I was told, wasn't I? Had some sort of attack in the office, she did, and they told her to have it checked out straightaway. So when I got there . . .' She drew a breath to slow herself down. And she was angry—*angry*—at the fear that she felt and the fact that this man with his razor-scarred face had brought fear with him into her house. This copper held every card in the deck, and both of them knew it. She said with a shrug, 'Look round, then. Whatever you want, you'll not find it here.'

He engaged her eyes for a long clear time, and she refused to look away because to look away would tell him he'd squashed her beneath his thumb like a flea. So she stood where she was by the passage to the kitchen while the water roared in the bathroom and Daniel saw to the wigs that needed washing.

The cop said, 'Cheers,' with a nod that she was meant to believe was shy and polite. He went first to her bedroom and flipped on the light. She could see him move to the paint-chipped clothes cupboard, and he opened it, but he didn't empty the pockets of any of the garments inside, although he fingered several pairs of trousers. He didn't pull out the drawers in the chest, either. But he studied the top of it—particularly one hair brush and the blond hairs caught up in its bristles, particularly the dish of beads that she used when she wanted a change on the ends of her plaits. He took the most time with the photograph of Roger, twin to the one that she had in the sitting room, triplet to the one that stood in the other bedroom on the table next to Daniel's small bed, quadruplet to the one that hung on the kitchen wall above the table. Roger Edwards, aged twenty-seven when the snap had been taken, one month arrived from New South Wales, and two days fresh from Yasmin's bed.

The cop came out of her bedroom, nodded at her politely, and went into Daniel's where the music was the same: clothes cupboard, top of the chest, photo of Roger. He went from there to the bathroom, where Daniel started chatting to him straightaway, saying, 'This is my reg'lar job, these wigs. Mum p'rvides them for ladies what have cancer, see? When they take their med'cine, their hair falls out mostly. Mum gives them hair. She does their faces as well.'

'Gives them beards, does she?' the cop asked.

Daniel laughed. 'Not with hair, man! She does them with make-up. Dead good she is at it, Mum is.

I c'n show you a—'

'Dan!' Yasmin barked. 'Mind you've a job to do.' She saw her son duck back to the bath tub.

The cop came out of the bathroom, gave her another nod, and went into the kitchen. There a door led onto a tiny balcony where she dried their clothes, and he opened this door, peered outside, then closed it carefully and ran his hand—a large hand, large like the rest of him—along the jamb like someone looking for splinters. He opened no cupboards or drawers. He did nothing else, in fact, except stand at the table and look, at that same photograph that he'd been looking at in every room.

He said, 'Who's this bloke, then?'

'Dan's dad. My husband. He's dead.'

'Sorry.'

'No need to be sorry,' she said. 'I killed him. But I 'spect you know that already. I 'spect that's why you're here, right? Some Aussie with a habit for henry got found dead with a knife in his neck and you lot ran the specifics through your computers and Yasmin Edwards' name popped up like toast.'

'I didn't know that,' Winston Nkata said. 'Sorry all the same.'

He sounded . . . what? She couldn't put a name to it, just as she couldn't put the name she wanted to put to the expression in his eyes. And she felt the bubbling of rage grow in her, which was something that she couldn't think through and she could never explain. It was the rage she'd learned to feel young and always—*always*—at the hands of a man: blokes she met and thought well of for a day or a week or a month till who they were showed through what they pretended to be.

344

She snapped, 'What you want, then? Why're you messing with me? Why're you outside chatting to my son like you were in'erested in something he got to tell you? 'F you think I done something, then you speak proper and you speak now or you get your bum *out* 'f here. Hear me? Because if you don't—'

He said, 'Katja Wolff,' and that stopped her. What the hell did he want with Katja? He said, 'Probation service list this as her address. That right?'

'We got approval,' Yasmin said. 'I'm out five years. 'S no mark against me. We got approval.'

'They got her working at a laundry up Kennington High Street,' Winston Nkata said. 'Stopped there first to have a word with her, but she'd not been in all day. Called in ill, they said. 'Flu. So I came here.'

Alarms rang in Yasmin's head, but she made sure the sound of them didn't play on her face. She said, 'So she's gone off to the doctor.'

'All day?'

'NHS,' she replied, with a shrug.

He said as politely as he'd so far said everything else to her, 'Fourth time she's phoned in, they tell me at the laundry, Missus Edwards. Fourth time in twelve weeks. Not happy, that lot in Kennington High Street. They spoke to her probation officer today.'

Alarm bells were changing to full blown sirens. The frights were charging up Yasmin's spine. But she knew how coppers lied to you when they wanted to rattle you into saying something they could twist like a rag, and harshly she reminded herself of that fact, saying inwardly, Bitch, don't

345

you lose it now.

She said, 'I don't know nothing about any of that. Katja lives here, right, but she goes her own way. I got 'nough on my mind with Daniel, don't I?'

He looked in the direction of her bedroom, where the full-size bed and the hairbrush on the chest and the clothes in the cupboard told a different story. And she wanted to scream, Yeah! And wha' about it, Charlie? You ever *been* inside? You ever known for five minutes what's it like to think that f'r a stretch of time that feels like forever you'll have exactly *no one* in your life? Not a friend, not a mate, not a lover, not a partner? You know what that's like?

But she said nothing. She merely met his eyes with defiance. And for five long seconds that felt like fifty, the only sound in the flat came from the bathroom where Dan started singing some pop song as he scrubbed the wigs.

Then that sound was interrupted by another. A key scraped into the lock. The door swung open.

And Katja was with them.

*   *   *

Lynley made Chelsea his final stop of the day. After leaving Richard Davies with his card and with instructions to phone should he hear from Katja Wolff or have any further information to impart, he negotiated the congestion round South Kensington station and cruised down Sloane Street where the street lamps glowed on an upmarket neighbourhood of restaurants, shops, and houses and the autumn leaves patterned the pavements in bronze. As he drove, he thought about connections

346

and coincidence and whether the presence of the former obviated the possibility of the latter. It seemed very likely. People were often in the wrong place at the wrong time, but rarely were they at the wrong place, at the wrong time, and with the intention of calling on someone who figured in a violent crime from their past. That sort of coincidence bore diligent scrutiny.

He grabbed the first parking space he found in the relative vicinity of the St James house, a tall umber brick building on the corner of Lordship Place and Cheyne Row. From the Bentley's boot, he took the computer he'd removed from Eugenie Davies' office.

He heard a dog's immediate barking when he rang the bell. It came from the left—that would be from St James's study, where Lynley could see through a window that a light was burning—and it approached the door with the enthusiasm of a canine doing the job properly. A woman's voice said, 'Good grief, that's *enough*, Peach,' to the dog who, in best dachshund fashion, completely ignored her. A bolt slid back, the outside light above the door flicked on, and the door itself swung open.

'Tommy! Hullo. What a treat!' It was Deborah St James who'd answered the bell, and she stood with the long-haired dachshund in her arms, a squirming barking bunch of brandy coloured fur who wanted nothing better than to sniff Lynley's leg, hands, or face to see if he met with her canine approval. 'Peach!' Deborah remonstrated. 'You know very well who this is. Stop it.' She stepped back from the door, saying, 'Come in, Tommy. Helen's already gone home, I'm afraid. She was

347

tired, she said. Round four, this was. Simon accused her of keeping late nights to avoid compiling data on whatever it is they're doing—I can never keep it straight—but she swore it was because you'd had her up till dawn listening to all four parts of *The Ring*. Except I can't remember if there *are* four parts. Never mind. What have you brought us?'

Once the door was closed behind them, she put the dog on the floor. Peach gained a good whiff of Lynley's trousers, registered his scent, took a step backwards, and wagged her tail in greeting. 'Thank you,' he told the dachshund solemnly. She trotted into the study where a gas fire burned and a lamp was lit on St James's desk. There, a number of printed pages were scattered, some of them bearing black and white photographs and some of them bearing only script.

Deborah led Lynley into the room, saying, 'Do put that thing down somewhere, Tommy. It looks heavy.'

Lynley chose a coffee table that stood in front of a sofa facing the fireplace. Peach came to investigate the computer before returning to a basket that exposed her to the best warmth of the fire. There, she curled herself into a ball, sighed happily, and watched the proceedings in a dignified head-on-paws position from which she blinked drowsily from time to time.

'You must be wanting Simon,' Deborah said. 'He's just upstairs. Let me fetch him for you.'

'In a moment.' Lynley said the words without thinking, and so quickly on the heels of her own that Deborah brought herself up short, smiled at him quizzically, and shoved a portion of her heavy hair behind one ear.

She said, 'All right,' and walked to an old drinks trolley by the window. She was a tallish woman, lightly freckled across the bridge of her nose, not thin like a model, not stout, but well-shaped and completely female. She wore black jeans and a sweater that was the colour of green olives and made an attractive contrast with her coppery hair.

He saw that the room was stacked along the walls and the bookshelves at floor level with dozens of mounted and framed photographs. Some of them were dressed in bubble wrap, which reminded him of Deborah's upcoming show in a gallery in Great Newport Street.

She said, 'Sherry? Whisky? We've got a new bottle of Lagavulin that Simon's telling me is nothing short of potable heaven.'

'Simon's not given to hyperbole.'

'Like the fine man of science that he is.'

'It must be good then. I'll have the whisky. You're working on the show?'

'It's nearly ready. I'm at the catalogue stage.' Handing over the whisky, she nodded to her husband's desk and said, 'I've been going over the proofs. The pictures they've selected are fine, but they've edited out some of my timeless prose—' She grinned; her nose wrinkled as it always did, making her look much younger than her twenty-six years—'and I'm finding that I don't like that much. Look at me. My fifteen minutes arrive and straightaway I become the great *artiste*.'

He smiled. 'That's unlikely.'

'Which part?'

'The part about fifteen minutes.'

'You're very quick this evening.'

'I speak only the truth.'

She smiled at him fondly, then turned and poured herself a glass of sherry. She took it up, held it out, and said, 'Here's to . . . Hmm . . . I don't know. What shall we drink to?'

Which was how Lynley knew that Helen had been as good as her word, not telling Deborah about the coming baby. He was relieved at this. At the same time he was ill-at-ease. Deborah would have to know sometime, and he knew that he had to be the person to tell her. He wanted to do so now, but he couldn't think of a place to begin, apart from saying outright, Let's drink to Helen. Let's drink to the baby my wife and I have made. Which was, of course, completely impossible.

He said instead, 'Let's drink to the sale of every one of your pictures next month. On opening night, to members of the royal family who will summarily demonstrate they've a taste for something beyond horses and blood sports.'

'You never did get over your first fox hunt, did you?'

' "The unspeakable in pursuit." '

'Such a traitor to your class.'

'I like to think it's what makes me interesting.'

Deborah laughed, said, 'Cheers, then,' and took a sip of sherry.

For his part, Lynley took a deep gulp of the Lagavulin and considered everything that was going unsaid between them. What a thing it was to come face to face with one's cowardice and indecision, he thought.

He said, 'What will you do after the show is mounted? Have you another project in mind?'

Deborah looked round at the photographs piled

350

in their serried ranks and considered the question, head cocked and eyes thoughtful. 'Bit frightening, that is,' she admitted frankly. 'I've been working on this since January. Eleven months now. And I suppose what I'd *like* to do if the gods allow it . . .' Her head tilted upwards to indicate not only the heavens but her husband who'd probably be given his say in the matter. 'I'd like to do something foreign, I think. Portraits still, I do love portraits. But foreign faces this time. Not foreign-in-London faces because obviously I could find hundreds of thousands of those but they've been Britished, haven't they, even if they don't think so themselves. So what I'd like is something quite different. Africa? India? Turkey? Russia? I don't quite know.'

'But portraits all the same?'

'People don't hide from the camera when the picture's not for their own use. That's what I like about it: the openness, the candour with which they gaze at the lens. It's rather addictive, looking at all those faces being real for once.' She took another swallow of sherry and said, 'But you can't have come to talk about my pictures.'

He took the opportunity for escape, even as he loathed himself for doing so. He said, 'Is Simon in the lab?'

'Shall I fetch him for you?'

'I'll just go up, if that's all right.'

She said that it was, of course it was, he knew the way. And she crossed back to the desk where she'd been working, set down her glass and came back to him. He finished his whisky, thinking she meant to take his own glass, but she squeezed his arm and kissed him on the cheek. 'Lovely to see you. D'you

351

need help with that computer?'

'I can manage,' he said. And he did just that, not feeling particularly proud of himself for accepting the escape route she offered, but telling himself that there was work to be done and work came first, which was certainly a fact that Deborah St James understood.

Her husband was on the fourth floor of the house, where he had a work room that had long been called his laboratory, and Deborah had a darkroom adjacent to it. Lynley climbed to this floor, pausing at the top of the stairs to say, 'Simon? Are you in the middle of something?' before he walked across the landing to the open door.

Simon St James was at his own computer, where he appeared to be studying a complicated structure that resembled a three dimensional graph. When he tapped a few keys, the graphic altered. When he tapped a few more, it revolved on its side. He murmured, 'That's damn curious,' and then turned to the door. 'Tommy. I thought I heard someone come in a few minutes ago.'

'Deb offered me a glass of your Lagavulin. She was seeking confirmation as to its quality.'

'And?'

'Pretty damn good. May I . . . ?' He nodded down at the computer.

St James said, 'Sorry. Here. Let me move . . . Well, something can be moved, I think.'

He rolled his chair back from his computer table and hit the side of his leg brace at the knee with a metal ruler when it didn't adjust properly as he rose. He said, 'I've been having the most *blasted* trouble with this thing. It's worse than arthritis. As soon as the rain starts, the knee hinge doesn't want to work properly. It's time for an overhaul. That or a visit to Oz.' He spoke with an utter lack of concern that Lynley knew he felt but could not feel himself. Whenever St James had taken a step in Lynley's line of vision in the last thirteen years, it had required every ounce of control he had not to avert his eyes in abject shame for having wreaked such physical devastation on his friend.

St James cleared a space on the worktable nearest to the door by stacking up papers and manila folders and moving several scientific journals to one side. He said casually, 'Is Helen all right? She was looking rather pale when she left this afternoon. All day, in fact, now that I think of it.'

'She was fine this morning,' Lynley said, and he told himself that the statement comprised the approximate if not the literal truth. She was fine. Morning sickness did not constitute illness in the usual sense. 'Bit tired, I expect. We were out late at Web—' But that wasn't, he recalled, the story his wife had told Deborah and Simon earlier, was it? Blast Helen, he thought, for being so creative when it came to spinning tales. 'No. Sorry. That was the other night, wasn't it. Christ. I can't keep anything straight. Anyway, she's fine. I expect it was a late night catching up with her.'

'Right. Well. Yes,' St James said, but his examination of Lynley was rather too lengthy for Lynley's comfort. In the small silence that ensued, rain began to fall outside. It hit the window like timpani in miniature, and it was accompanied by a sudden gust of wind that rattled the casement like an unspoken accusation. St James said, 'What've

353

you brought me?' with a nod at the computer.

'Some detective work.'

'That's your bailiwick, isn't it?'

'This requires a more delicate touch.'

St James hadn't known Lynley for more than twenty years to find himself suddenly incapable of reading between the lines. He said, 'Are we on thin ice, Tommy?'

Lynley said honestly, 'A singular pronoun is all that's required. You're clean. If you'll help me, that is.'

'That's remarkably reassuring,' St James said dryly. 'Why do I picture myself in an unpleasant future scenario, sitting in the dock or standing in the witness box, but in either case sweating like a fat man in Miami?'

'That's your natural sense of fair play among men, a quality I deeply admire in you, by the way, if I've not mentioned the fact before now. It's also, however, one of the first things that gets tossed out of the window after a few years dealing with the criminal element.'

'This is from a case, then?' St James said.

'You didn't hear that from me.'

St James fingered his upper lip thoughtfully as he gazed at the computer. He would know what Lynley ought to be doing with the piece of machinery. But as to why he wasn't doing it . . . That was something he'd be better off not asking. He finally drew a breath and let it out, giving a shake of his head that indicated it was against his better judgement to say, 'What do you need?'

'All internet activity. Her use of e-mail particularly.'

'Her?'

'Yes. Her. She may have received mail in the past from an internet Lothario, who calls himself TongueMan—'

'Good God.'

'—but there was nothing on the machine from him when we logged onto it in her office.' Lynley went on to tell St James Eugenie Davies' password, which the other man jotted down on a piece of yellow legal paper that he ripped from a pad on the worktable.

'Am I looking for anything besides TongueMan?'

'You're looking for all activity, Simon. E-mail in, e-mail out. Surfing the net. Whatever she's done once she's logged on. That's possible, isn't it?'

'Most of the time, yes. But I don't have to tell you how much more quickly an expert from the Yard could manage this for you, not to mention an order from some legal authority should you need to strong-arm the internet provider.'

'Right. I know that.'

'Which leads me to conclude that you suspect there's something here—' He placed his hand on the machine—'that puts someone in a difficult position, someone you'd rather not see get into a difficult position. Is that right?'

Lynley said steadily, 'Yes. That's right.'

'It's not you, I hope.'

'Great Scot. No.'

St James nodded. 'I'm glad of that, then.' He looked momentarily uncomfortable and tried to hide the discomfort by lowering his head and rubbing the back of his neck. 'So things are well with you and Helen, then,' he settled on saying.

Lynley saw his line of reasoning. A mysterious *her,* a computer in Lynley's possession, an unnamed someone getting into difficulty should his e-mail address show up on Eugenie Davies' computer . . . It added up to an illicit something, and St James's longstanding relationship with Lynley's wife—after all, he'd known Helen since she was eighteen—would make him more protective of her than one would necessarily expect of someone's employer.

Lynley hastened to say, 'Simon, it's nothing to do with Helen. Nor with me. You have my word on that. So will you do this for me?'

'You're going to owe me, Tommy.'

'In spades. But I'm so far in debt to you at this point that I might as well sign over the land in Cornwall and have done with it.'

'That's a tempting offer,' St James smiled. 'I've always fancied myself a country squire.'

'You'll do it, then?'

'I expect I will. But without the land. God knows we don't want to set your ancestors spinning in their graves.'

*   *   *

DC Winston Nkata knew the woman was Katja Wolff before she opened her mouth, but put to the rack he wouldn't have been able to tell anyone exactly how he knew. She had a key to the flat, true, so there was that to identify her since this flat in the Doddington Grove Estate had been listed as her address when he'd tracked down her probation officer at DI Lynley's request a short time earlier. But it was more than the key unlocking the door that told him whom he was looking at. There was the way she carried herself, like someone wary of every potential encounter, and there was also her expression, a perfect blank, the sort of expression a lag wore inside so as not to draw attention to herself.

She stopped right inside the door and her glance went from Yasmin Edwards to Nkata and back to Yasmin Edwards, where it remained. She said, 'Am I interrupting you, Yas?' in a husky voice that bore less of the German accent than Nkata had expected. But, she'd been more than twenty years in the country at this point. And she hadn't been surrounded by her fellow Germans.

Yasmin said, 'This is the Bill, this is. Detective Constable. He's called Nkata,' and Katja Wolff's body went on the alert: a subtle, tensing awareness that someone not born into the land of gang activity like Winston Nkata might not have noticed.

Katja removed her coat—cherry red—and the close-fitting grey hat with its matching band of the coat's bright colour. Beneath, she had on a sky blue pullover, looking like cashmere but worn to a paperlike thinness at the elbows, and pale grey trousers of a slick material threaded through with silver when she moved in the light.

She said to Yasmin, 'Where's Dan?'

Yasmin indicated the bathroom with her head. 'Doing wigs.'

'And this bloke?' She tilted her chin at Nkata.

He took the reins while he had the chance, saying, 'You're Katja Wolff?'

She didn't reply. Instead she walked over to the bathroom and said hello to Yasmin's son, who appeared to be up to his elbows in bubbles. The boy looked over his shoulder at her, then into the sitting room, where he managed to lock eyes with Nkata for a moment. But he said nothing. Katja

357

closed the bathroom door on him and strode to the old three piece suite that constituted the sitting room furniture. She sat on the sofa, opened a packet of Dunhills that lay on the table next to it, and took out a cigarette, which she lit. She picked up the television remote and was about to punch the set on when Yasmin said her name: not in supplication but in warning, it sounded to Nkata.

At that, Winston found that he wanted to study Yasmin Edwards because he wanted to understand: her, the situation here in Kennington, her son, the relationship between the two women. He'd got beyond the fact that she was beautiful. He was still sorting through her anger, though, as well as through the fears she was doing her best to hide. He wanted to say, 'You're all *right* here, girl,' but he recognised the foolishness of doing so.

He said to Katja Wolff, 'Laundry up on Kennington High Street says you didn't show up to work today.'

She said, 'I was ill this morning, all day in fact. I've just been to the chemist. There is no law broken in that, I believe,' and she drew in on the cigarette and examined him.

Nkata saw Yasmin glance between them. She clasped her hands in front of her, just at the level of her sex as if she wished to hide it. He said, 'Go to the chemist by motor, then?'

'Yes. What about it?'

'Got your own motor, have you?'

Katja said, 'Why? Have you come to request that I drive you somewhere?' Her English was nearly perfect, remarkable really, as impressive as the woman herself.

'Got a car, Miss Wolff?' he repeated patiently.

'No. They don't generally provide parolees with modes of transport when they release them. It's a pity, I think. Especially for those who serve time for armed robbery. How bleak their future must look to them, knowing they'll have to escape from the scenes of their future crimes on foot. While for someone like me . . .?' She tapped her cigarette against a ceramic ashtray that was shaped, seasonally, like a pumpkin. 'A car is quite inessential for working in a laundry. One only needs a high tolerance for both endless boredom and insufferable heat.'

'So it's not your car, then?'

Yasmin crossed the room as Nkata completed the question. She joined Katja on the sofa and neatly rearranged a few magazines and tabloids on the iron-legged coffee table in front of it. Having done this, she placed a hand on Katja's knee. She looked at Nkata across the line she'd drawn as clearly as if she'd wielded chalk on the carpet squares.

She said, 'What'd you want with us, man? Time to spit it out or time to leave.'

'Got a car yourself?' Nkata asked her.

' 'f I do?'

'Like to see it, I would.'

Katja said, 'Why? Who is it you've come to speak to, Constable?'

'We'll get to that soon enough, I expect,' Nkata said. 'Where's the car?'

The two women were motionless for a moment during which a resumption of water roaring into the bathtub told everyone that Daniel was taking his mother's wigs through a manual rinse cycle. Katja was the one to break the silence, and she did it with the confidence of a woman who'd spent two decades educating herself as to her rights with regard to the police. 'Have you a warrant? For anything, by the way?'

'Didn't think I'd need one, conversation being what's on my mind.'

'Conversation about Yasmin's car?'

'Missus Edwards' car. Ah. Right. Where is it?' Nkata tried not to look smug. The German woman flushed anyway, perhaps realising that her own dislike and distrust of Nkata had caused her to trip.

'What's this *about*, man?' Yasmin snapped, but her voice was higher now and anxiety was tightening her hold on Katja's knee. 'You're wanting a warrant if you mean to go through my car, hear me?'

Nkata said, 'I don't need to go through it, do I, Missus Edwards. But I'll have a look at it all the same.'

The women exchanged a glance after which Katja rose and went into the kitchen. There, cupboards opened and closed, a kettle clanged onto the cooker, and a burner hissed. For her part, Yasmin waited for a moment as if for a sign from the kitchen of something other than tea being made. When she didn't receive one, she got to her feet and snatched a key from a hook to the right of the flat's front door. She said, 'Come on, then,' to Nkata and, coatless despite the weather, she led him outside. Katja Wolff remained behind.

Yasmin took lengthy strides towards the lift, as if she didn't care one way or another if the detective was following her. When she moved, her plaits—so long that they reached her shoulder blades—made a music that was both hypnotic and soothing, and

Nkata realised that he couldn't account for the effect that that music had on him. He felt the reaction in his throat first, then behind his eyes, then in his chest. He shook it away and looked down at the car park, then over at what appeared to be allotments across the street, then in the direction of Manor Place, where he could glimpse the first of a row of derelict buildings that expressed what years of government indifference and urban decay had done to the neighbourhood.

In the lift, he said, ' 'D you grow up round here?'

Yasmin stared him down in silence so he finally moved his gaze to the words *eat me till I scream* that someone had painted in nail varnish on the lift wall in line with Yasmin's right shoulder. The graffiti brought his mother immediately to Nkata's mind: a female vigilante who would no more allow graffiti to foul her landscape than would she permit a profanity uttered within her hearing. Alice Nkata would have been so quickly inside that lift with the varnish remover that the imperative wouldn't have had a chance even to dry before she had obliterated it. Thinking of this and his dignified mother and how she'd managed to maintain her dignity in a society that saw a black woman first and the woman herself only second and if she was lucky that day, Nkata smiled fondly.

Yasmin said, 'Like to have women under your thumb, do you, man? That why you joined the Bill, was it?'

He wanted to tell her that she shouldn't sneer, not because the expression distorted her face and stretched the scar on her lip so that it seemed to bloom, but because when she sneered, she looked frightened. And fear was a woman's enemy on the streets.

He said, 'Sorry. Thinking of my mum.'

'Your mum.' She rolled her eyes. 'You telling me next I remind you 'f her, yeah?'

Nkata laughed outright at the thought of the comparison. He said, 'Not at all, girl.' And he chuckled more.

Her eyes narrowed. The lift door creaked open. She stalked outside.

Across a strip of dying lawn, the car park held a small array of cars that spoke of the general economic status of the people in the Doddington Grove estate. Yasmin Edwards took Nkata to a Fiesta with a rear bumper that clung to the vehicle like an inebriate to a lamppost. The car had once been red but the colour had long ago oxidized so it was mostly rust. Nkata walked round it carefully. The front right headlamp had a jagged crack in it but apart from the rear bumper, that was the extent of the damage.

He squatted at the front of the Fiesta and peered beneath it, using a pocket torch to shed some light on its undercarriage. He did the same thing at the back of the vehicle, taking his time. Yasmin Edwards stood by in silence, her arms wrapped round her against the chill, her summertime top meagre protection against the wind that was blowing and the rain that had begun to fall.

Nkata straightened, his inspection finished. He said, 'When'd that headlamp get smashed?'

'What headlamp?' She went to the front of the car and examined it herself. 'I don't know,' she said, and for the first time since learning who and what Nkata was, she did not sound combative as

362

she ran her fingers across the uneven crack in the glass. 'Lights still work proper, so I didn't notice.' She was shivering now, but it seemed more likely with the cold than with concern. Nkata removed his overcoat, saying, 'Here,' and handing it over. She took it.

Nkata waited till she had slid her arms into his coat, till she had snugly wrapped it round her, till he saw what she looked like with the collar raised and expressing a curve against her dark skin. Then he said, 'You both drive this car, Missus Edwards? Right that, isn't it? Both 'f you drive it? You and Katja Wolff?'

And the coat was off and thrust back at him instantly, almost before he finished the question. If there had been a moment of anything more than hostility between them, he'd just managed to shatter it. Yasmin looked up to the flat where Katja Wolff was making tea. She returned her glance to Nkata and said evenly, arms encircling her body once more, 'That all you want with us, man?'

He said, 'No. Where were you last night, Missus Edwards?'

She said, 'Here. Where else would I be? I got a boy needs his mum, I expect you noticed.'

'Miss Wolff here as well?'

She said, 'Yeah. Tha's right. Katja was here.' But there was an undercurrent in the way she made the statement that suggested the facts might prove otherwise.

Something always alters in a person when he lies. Nkata had been told that a hundred times. Listen to the timbre of the voice, he'd been lectured. Watch for changes in the pupils of the eyes. Look for the head's movement, the shoulders either relaxing or tensing, the muscles of the throat constricting. Look for something—anything—that wasn't there before, and that something will tell you exactly where the speaker stands in relation to the truth.

He said, 'I'll need another word,' and he nodded upwards.

'I've given you words.'

'Yeah. I know.' He headed back to the lift and they went through the exercise they'd gone through before. But the silence between them felt charged to Nkata, and charged with something more than a man to woman charge, more than copper to suspect, more than former lag to potential screw.

'She was here,' Yasmin Edwards said. 'But you don't believe me 'cause you can't believe me. 'Cause if you sussed where Katja was living then you sussed the rest and you know I did time and lags and liars are one 'n the same when it comes to the filth. I'n't that right, man?'

He'd reached the door to her flat. She slid in front of it, blocking his way. She said, 'You ask her what she did last night. You ask her where she was. She tell you she was here. An' just to make sure I can't mess with your process, I'll keep myself out here while you ask her.'

Nkata said, 'Suit yourself, but put this round you if you mean to stay outside,' and he himself put the coat round her shoulders this time, drawing the collar up to protect her neck from the wind. She flinched. He wanted to say, 'How'd you get this way, woman,' but instead he ducked back inside the flat to have his confrontation with Katja Wolff.

CHAPTER TEN

'There were letters, Helen.' Lynley was standing at the cheval mirror in their bedroom, gloomily attempting to make a choice among three ties that dangled limply from his fingers. 'Barbara found them in a chest of drawers, just like love letters, all of them together with envelopes included. Everything was in place except the traditional blue ribbon tying them up.'

'Perhaps there's an innocent explanation.'

'What the hell was the man even thinking?' Lynley went on as if his wife hadn't spoken. 'The mother of a murdered child. The victim of a crime. You don't find anyone more vulnerable than that, and when you do, you put distance between yourself and her. You don't seduce her.'

'If that's what happened, Tommy.' Lynley's wife watched him from the bed.

'What else could it have been? "Wait for me, Eugenie. I'm coming for you." That doesn't sound to me like your average bread-and-butter letter straight out of Mrs Beeton.'

'I don't think Mrs Beeton advised housewives on their letter writing, darling.'

'You know what I mean.'

Helen rolled onto her side, took his pillow, and cradled it to her stomach. She said, 'Lord,' in a hollow tone that he couldn't ignore.

'Bad this morning?' he asked.

'Awful. I've never felt like this in my life. When will it progress to the rosy glow of a woman fulfilled? And why are pregnant women in novels

365

always described as *glowing* when in reality they'd have faces like paste and stomachs at war with the rest of their bodies?'

'Hmm.' Lynley considered her question. 'I don't actually know. Is it a conspiracy to keep the species propagating? I wish I could bear this for you, darling.'

She laughed weakly. 'You've always been such a terrible liar.'

There was truth in that and because of it, he held up the three ties for her inspection. 'I was thinking about the dark blue with the ducks. What do you say?'

'Very appropriate for fostering in suspects the false belief that you'll be gentle with them.'

'Just what I thought.' He returned to the mirror, draping the other two ties round one of the bed posts on his way.

She said, 'Did you tell DCI Leach about the letters?'

'No.'

'What did you do with them?' Their glances met in the mirror and she read his reply on his face. 'You *took* them? Tommy . . .'

'I know. But consider the alternative: to hand them over as evidence or to leave them there for someone else who might track down Webberly at the worst possible time and return them. To his home, for instance. With Frances standing there, just waiting for someone to deal her a death blow. Or even to the Yard, where it wouldn't do much for his career to have it made public that he'd involved himself with the victim of a crime. Or how about to a tabloid or two? They've such a profound love for the Met, after all.'

'Is that the only reason you took them? To protect Frances and Malcolm?'

'What other reason is there?'

'Perhaps the crime itself They could be evidence.'

'You aren't suggesting Webberly was involved in some way, are you? He was in our presence the whole evening. As was Frances, who'd have far more reason to want to be rid of Eugenie Davies than would Webberly if it came down to it. Beyond that, the last of the letters was written over a decade ago. Eugenie Davies has been a closed book for Webberly for years. It was mad for him to have involved himself with her in the first place, but at least it ended before lives were shattered.'

Helen read him, as usual. 'But you're not sure of that, are you, Tommy?'

'I'm sure enough. So I don't see the letters' relevance to the present, to today.'

'Unless there's been recent contact between them.'

Which was, in part, why he'd taken Eugenie Davies' computer. Lynley was relying on gut instinct with regard to that, instinct which told him that his superior officer was a decent man who had a difficult life, a man who never sought to harm another human being, but who had submitted to temptation in a moment of weakness that he no doubt regretted to this day.

'He's a good man,' Lynley said into the mirror, more to himself than to his wife.

She responded all the same. 'As are you. And that might explain why he asked DCI Leach to allow you in on the case. You believe in his decency, so you'll protect him, without his having

367

to ask you to do so.'

And that's the way it was playing out, Lynley thought morosely. Perhaps Barbara had been right. Hand the letters over as potential evidence; leave Malcolm Webberly to his fate.

Across the room, Helen suddenly threw back the covers and dashed to the bathroom. The retching began, just beyond the open door. Lynley looked at himself in the mirror and tried to close his ears to the sound.

Funny how one could talk oneself into believing just about anything if one was desperate enough. In a twist of thinking, Helen's morning sickness could become the result of a bad bit of chicken eaten yesterday on a lunchtime salad. Another twist, and she had 'flu, which was going round now anyway. Or perhaps it was a case of nerves. She was facing a challenge later in the day, and this was the way her body reacted to anxiety. Or pushed to an extreme of rationalisation, he could say that she was simply afraid. They hadn't been together long, had they, and she wasn't as easy being with him as he was being with her. There were, after all, differences between them: of experience, of education, and of age. And all that counted for something, didn't it, no matter how they tried to talk themselves into believing otherwise?

The retching continued. He forced himself to deal with it in some reasonable way. He turned from the mirror and strode across to the bathroom. He flipped on the light, which in her haste Helen had not switched on. He found her draped round the toilet, her back heaving mightily as she gulped in air.

He said, 'Helen?' But he found he could not

move from the doorway.

Selfish *bastard,* he told himself as a prod to action. This is the woman you love. Go to her. Touch her hair. Wipe her face with a cool damp flannel. *Do something.*

But he couldn't. He was frozen to one spot as if he'd inadvertently looked upon Medusa, fixed on the sight of his beautiful wife reduced to vomiting into the toilet bowl, her now daily ritual that celebrated the fact of their union.

He said, 'Helen?' and he waited for her to tell him that she was all right, that she needed nothing. He waited hopefully for her to send him on his way.

She turned her face to him. He could see its damp sheen. And he knew that she was waiting for him to make some move in her direction that would underscore the love and concern that he felt for her.

He made do with a question. 'Can I get you something, Helen?'

Her eyes held his. He saw the subtle change come over her as her dawning realisation that he would not go to her metamorphosed into hurt.

She shook her head and turned away. Her fingers gripped the edges of the toilet. 'I'm fine,' she murmured.

And he was happy to accept the lie.

*   *   *

In Stamford Brook, the sound of a cup rattling in its saucer awakened Malcolm Webberly. He cracked open his eyes to see his wife setting a cup of morning tea on the scarred surface of the bedside table.

The room was claustrophobically hot, the result of a poorly designed central heating system and Frances's refusal to have any windows open at night. She couldn't bear the sensation of night air on her face. She also couldn't sleep for thinking that someone might break into their house should so much as an inch's gap exist between a window and its sill.

Webberly lifted his head from the pillow, then sank back down with a groan. It had been a rough night. He ached in every joint in his body, which was secondary to the ache in his heart.

'I've brought you some nice Earl Grey,' Frances said. 'Milk and sugar. It's piping hot.' She went to the window and opened the curtains. The limp light of late autumn filtered into the room. 'All grey and nasty today, I'm afraid,' she went on. 'It looks like rain. There's to be a wind coming from the west later on. Well, November. What else can one expect?'

Webberly elbowed his way upwards through the covers, becoming aware of the fact that he'd sweated through another set of pyjamas during the night. He took up the cup and saucer and looked down at the steaming liquid, its colour telling him that Frances hadn't let it steep, that it would taste like milky water. He hadn't been a morning tea drinker for years. Coffee was his beverage of choice. But tea was what Frances herself drank and it was easier to plug in the kettle and pour the boiling water over the teabags than it was to go through the scooping, measuring, and pouring that resulted in a decent cup of what he preferred.

It's all the same at the end of the day, he told himself. Getting caffeine into the body is the main point, boy. So drink up now and have at the morning.

'I've made out the shopping list,' Frances said. 'It's by the door.'

He grunted an acknowledgment.

She seemed to take this sound as a protest, saying anxiously, 'Really, there's not much to get. Just the odd thing. Tissues, kitchen rolls, that sort of thing. We've still got all that food from the party. It shouldn't take long.'

'Fine, Fran,' he said. 'No problem. I'll stop on my way home from work.'

'If something comes up, you needn't—'

'I'll stop on my way home.'

'Well, only if it's not too much trouble, dear.'

Not too much trouble? Webberly thought and he hated himself for the disloyalty he was showing even as he allowed himself to experience a momentary swelling of resentment towards his wife. Not too much trouble to see to everything and anything that involved an excursion into the world, Fran? Not too much trouble to shop for groceries, to drop by the chemist, to collect the dry cleaning, to have the car serviced, to see to the garden, to walk the dog, to . . . Webberly forced himself to stop. He reminded himself that his wife wouldn't have chosen this illness, that she wasn't attempting to make his life a misery, that she was doing her best to cope and so was he, and coping with what was dished onto your plate was what life was all about.

'It's no trouble, Fran,' he told her as he sipped the tasteless drink. 'Thanks for the tea.'

'I hope it's all right. Something special this morning. Something a bit different.'

'Good of you,' he said.

He knew why she'd done it. She'd brought him tea for the same reason that she would go downstairs as soon as he was out of bed and begin to cook him a sumptuous breakfast. It was the only way she could apologise to him for not managing to do what she'd claimed she would do a brief twenty-four hours earlier. Her plan to work in the garden had come to nothing. Even protected behind the walls that marked the boundaries of their property, she hadn't felt safe so she hadn't left the house. Perhaps she had tried: placing one hand on the doorknob—*I can manage this*—cracking the door open—*yes, I can do this as well*—feeling the fresh air wash against her cheeks—*there's nothing to fear*—and even curling the fingers of one hand round the door jamb before panic claimed her. But that's as far as she'd got and he knew it because—God forgive him for his own insanity—he'd inspected her Wellingtons, the tines of the rake, the gardening gloves, and even the rubbish bags for evidence that she'd gone outside, done something, picked up a single leaf, made an inroad into her irrational fears.

He swung out of bed, swilling down the rest of the tea. He could smell the sweat on his pyjamas and the feel of them was clammy against his skin. He felt weak, oddly off balance, as if he'd come through a long period of fever and was only now recovering from it.

Frances said, 'I'm going to make you a proper breakfast, Malcolm Webberly. None of this corn flakes nonsense today.'

'I need a shower,' he said in reply.

'Brilliant. That'll give me just enough time.' She

372

headed to the door.

He said, 'Fran,' to stop her. And when she paused, 'There's no need for all that.'

'No need?' Her head tilted to one side. She'd combed her red hair—dyed with the colour that she sent him to Boots once a month to fetch so that it would match their daughter's hair, which it never did—and she wore her pink dressing gown precisely belted, with a perfect bow.

'It's all right,' he said. 'You don't need to . . .' To what? Saying the words would take them somewhere neither of them wanted to go. Webberly settled on, 'You don't need to coddle me. I can manage with corn flakes.'

She smiled. 'Of course, you can *manage* with them, darling. But every once in a while, it's lovely to have a proper breakfast. You've got time, haven't you?'

'There's the dog to walk.'

I'll walk him, Malcolm. But that was an announcement she could not make. Not after yesterday's proclamation about gardening. Two defeats in a row would be an injury that she wouldn't want to risk inflicting on herself. Webberly understood that. The hell of it was, he'd always understood it. So he was unsurprised when she said, 'Let's see how the time goes, shall we? I expect there's enough. And if there's not, you can cut short Alfie's walk. Just down to the corner and back. He'll survive.'

She crossed the room, kissed him fondly and left. In less than a minute, he could hear her banging about in the kitchen. She started to sing.

He plodded along the corridor to the bathroom. It smelled of mildew from grout round the tub that needed cleaning and a shower curtain that needed replacing, and Webberly shoved open the window fully and stood in front of it, breathing in the sodden morning air. It was the heavy, tubercular air of an approaching winter that promised to be long, cold, wet, and grey. He thought of Spain, of Italy, of Greece, of the countless sun-drenched environments round the world that he would never see.

Roughly, he shook off the mental pictures of these places, turning from the window and shedding his pyjamas. He twisted the hot water tap in the tub till the steam rose like an optimist's hope, and when he'd added enough cold water to the mix to make it bearable, he stepped inside and began to work lather vigorously round his body.

He thought of his daughter's reasonable question about insisting that Frances return to the psychiatrist. He asked himself what harm could it do, simply to make the suggestion to his wife. He hadn't mentioned her problem for the past two years. On the twenty-fifth anniversary of their marriage—with retirement looming—how unforgivable would it be to imply that the opportunity for a different life was fast approaching them and in order to have that different life, Frances might want to consider how best to address her problem? We'll want to do some travelling, Frannie, he could tell her. Think of seeing Spain again. Think of Italy. Think of Crete. Why, we could even sell up and move to the country as we once talked of doing.

Her lips would form a smile as he spoke, but her eyes would show the incipient panic. 'Why, Malcolm,' she'd say and her fingers would clutch:

the edge of her apron, the belt of her dressing gown, the cuff of her shirt. 'Why, Malcolm,' she'd say.

Perhaps she'd make the attempt at that point, seeing that he was in earnest. But she'd make the attempt that she'd made two years ago, and it would doubtless end where that attempt had ended: with panic, tears, a phone call by strangers in the street to nine-nine-nine, paramedics and ambulance and police dispatched to Tesco's where she'd taken herself by taxi to *prove* she could do it, darling . . . and afterwards a hospital, a period of sedation, and reinforcement for every terror she felt. She'd forced herself out of the house to please him. It hadn't worked then. It wouldn't work now.

'She has to want to get well,' the psychiatrist had told him. 'Without desire, there is no exigency. And the internal exigency that demands recovery cannot be manufactured.'

So it had been, year after year. The world went on while her world shrank. His world was joined inextricably to her world, and sometimes Webberly thought he would suffocate in its smallness.

He rinsed himself long in the water. He washed his thinning hair. When he was done, he stepped out of the tub into the bone chill of the bathroom where the window still gaped, letting in a last few minutes of the morning air.

Downstairs, he found that Frances had been as good as her word. A full breakfast was laid out on the table as he joined her in the kitchen, where the air was redolent with the scent of bacon and Alfie was sitting at the corner of the cooker, looking hopefully at the frying pan from which Frances was removing the rashers. The table, however, was laid only for one.

'You aren't eating?' Webberly asked his wife.

'I live to serve you.' She gestured with the frying pan. 'One word from you and the eggs go on. When you're ready for them. Any way you want them. Any way you want anything.'

'D'you mean that, Fran?' He pulled out his chair.

'Scrambled, fried, or poached,' she declared. 'I'll even do them devilled for you, if you've a mind for that.'

'If I've a mind for it,' he said.

He didn't feel like eating, but he shoveled the food into his mouth. He chewed and swallowed without tasting much. Only the acidic tang of orange juice made the journey from his tongue to his brain.

Frances chatted. What did he think about Randie's weight? She hated to talk to their daughter about it, but didn't he think she was getting just a bit too chunky for a girl her age? And what of this recent plan of hers to have a year in Turkey? *Turkey*, of all places. She was always coming up with a new plan, so of course one didn't want to get oneself in a dither over something that she might not even do, but a girl her age . . . on her own . . . in Turkey . . . ? It wasn't wise, it wasn't safe, it wasn't sensible, Malcolm. Last month she was talking about a year in Australia, which was bad enough . . . all that distance without her family. But this? No. They had to talk her out of this. And wasn't Helen Lynley looking lovely the other night? She's one of those women who can wear *anything*. Naturally, it's the expense of the clothes that tells the tale. Buy French and you look like a . . . well, just like a countess, Malcolm. And she *can* buy French, can't she? No one's watching to see who she buys from. Not like the poor old dowdy Queen, who's always dressed by some English upholsterer by the look of her. Clothes do so make a woman, don't they?

Chat. Chat. Chat. It filled a silence that might otherwise be used for a conversation too painful to be endured. It simultaneously wore the guise of warmth and of closeness, offering a portrayal of the long married couple breaking their fast *à deux.*

Webberly shoved his chair back abruptly. He scrubbed the paper napkin across his mouth. 'Alfie,' he commanded. 'Come. Let's go.' He grabbed the lead from the hook near the door, and the dog padded after him, through the sitting room and out of the front door.

Alfie came to life as soon as paws hit pavement. His tail began to wag, and his ears perked up. He was all at once on the alert for his sworn enemies— cats—and as he and his master headed down the street, the Alsatian kept an eye out for anything potentially feline at which he could bark. He sat obediently as he always did when they came to Stamford Brook Road. Here, the traffic could be heavy depending upon the time of day, and even a zebra crossing didn't guarantee a driver's seeing a pedestrian.

They crossed and made their way to the garden.

The night's rain had made the place thoroughly sodden. The grass was heavily bent with moisture, tree limbs dripped, and the benches along the perimeter path were shining slickly with water. This didn't matter to Webberly. He didn't want to sit beneath the trees, and he had no interest in the

377

lawn across which Alfie gambolled as soon as Webberly had him off the lead. Instead he took to the perimeter path. He walked determinedly, gravel crunching beneath his soles, but while his body was in the Stamford Brook neighbourhood in which he'd lived for more than twenty years, his mind was centred on Henley-on-Thames.

He'd come this far into his day without thinking once of Eugenie. It seemed something of a miracle to him. She hadn't left his thoughts for an instant during the previous twenty-four hours. He hadn't heard from Eric Leach yet, and he hadn't seen Tommy Lynley at the Yard. He accepted the latter's request for DC Winston Nkata as a sign that progress was being made, but he wanted to know what that progress was because knowing something—anything at this point—was better than being left with nothing but images best forgotten from the past.

Without that contact with his fellow officers, though, the images came to him. Unprotected by the claustrophobic confines of his house, by Frances's chatter, by the duties that faced him once he got to work, he was assailed by mental pictures, pictures so distant now as to be fragments only, pieces of a puzzle he'd not been able to complete.

It was summer, sometime after the Regatta. He and Eugenie were rowing in a boat on the sluggish river.

Hers had not been the first marriage that had not survived the horror of a violent death in the family. It would not be the last that cracked irreparably under the combined weight of investigation-and-trial and the powerful load of guilt attendant on losing a child to someone in whom trust had been mistakenly placed. But Webberly had *felt* more at the dissolution of this particular marriage. It was many months before he admitted why.

After the trial, the tabloids had gone after her with the same rapacity that had driven their stories about Katja Wolff. Where Wolff had been the reincarnation of everyone from Mengele to Himmler, responsible in the eyes of the press for everything from the Holocaust to the Blitz, Eugenie had been the indifferent mother: she who worked outside the home, she who had employed an unskilled girl untutored in English and in the ways of the English to care for a badly disabled child. If Katja Wolff had been vilified in the press—and deservedly so, considering her crime—Eugenie had been pilloried.

She'd accepted this public scourging as her due. 'I'm to blame,' she'd said. 'This is the least I deserve.' She spoke with simple dignity, with neither hope nor desire of being contradicted. Indeed, she would not allow contradiction. 'I just want it to end,' she'd said.

He saw her again, two years after the trial, quite by chance at Paddington Station. He was on his way to a conference in Exeter. She was coming into town, she said, for an engagement with someone she did not name.

'Just coming in?' he'd said. 'You've moved house, then? To the country? That's good for your boy, I expect.'

But no, they hadn't moved to the country. She'd just moved herself, alone.

He'd said, 'Oh. I'm sorry.'

She'd said, 'Thank you, Inspector Webberly.'

He'd said, 'Malcolm. Please, it's plain Malcolm.'

She'd said, 'Plain Malcolm, then,' and her smile was infinitely sad.

He'd said impulsively and in a rush because it was mere minutes before his train left the station, 'Would you give me your number, Eugenie? I'd like to check how you're doing now and then. As a friend. If that's all right with you.'

She'd written it on the newspaper he'd been carrying. She'd said, 'Thank you for your kindness, Inspector.'

'Malcolm,' he'd reminded her.

Summer on the river had been twelve months later and not the first time he'd found an excuse to drive to Henley-on-Thames to check on Eugenie. She was lovely that day, quiet as always but with a sense of peace that he'd not witnessed in her before. He rowed the boat and she leaned back and rested on her side, not trailing her hand in the water in the way some women might have done, hoping for a seductive pose, but merely watching the river's surface as if its depths hid something she was waiting to see. Her face reflected brightness and shadow as they glided along beneath the trees.

He was aware in a rush that he'd fallen in love with her. But they had those twelve months of chaste friendship between them: walks round town, drives in the country, lunches at pubs, the occasional dinner and the warmth of conversation, real conversation about who Eugenie Davies had been and how she'd come to be who she was.

'I believed in God when I was young,' she told him. 'But I lost God along the way to adulthood. I've been a long time without Him now, and I'd like to get Him back if I can.'

'Even after what's happened?'

'Because of what's happened. But I'm afraid he won't have me, Malcolm. My sins are too great.'

'You haven't sinned. You couldn't possibly sin.'

'You of all people can't believe that. Everyone sins.'

But Webberly couldn't see sin in her, no matter what she said about herself. He saw only perfection and—ultimately—what he himself wanted. But to speak of his feelings seemed a betrayal in every direction. He was married and the father of a child. She was fragile and vulnerable. And despite the time that had passed since her daughter's murder, he couldn't bring himself to take advantage of her grief.

So he settled on saying, 'Eugenie, do you know that I'm married?'

She moved her gaze from the water to him. 'I assumed that you were.'

'Why?'

'Your kindness. No woman thinking straight would be foolish enough to let someone like you get away. Would you like to tell me about your wife and family?'

'No.'

'Ah. What does that mean?'

'Marriages end sometimes.'

'Sometimes they do.'

'Yours did.'

'Yes. My marriage ended.' She moved her gaze back to the water. He continued to row and watched her face, feeling as if in a hundred years as a man long blind he would still be able to draw from memory every line and curve of it.

They'd brought a picnic with them and when he

saw the spot he wanted, Webberly bumped the boat into the bank. He said, 'Wait. Stay there. Let me tie it up, Eugenie,' and as he scrambled up the slippery little slope, he lost his footing and slid into the water, where he stood humiliated with the Thames lapping coolly round his thighs. The mooring rope draped over his hand, and the river ooze seeped into his shoes.

Eugenie sat up straight, saying, 'Heavens, Malcolm! Are you all right?'

'I feel a perfect fool. It never happens this way in films.'

'But this way is better,' Eugenie said. And before he could speak again, she scrambled from the boat and joined him in the water.

'The mud—' he began in protest.

'Feels exquisite,' she finished. And she began to laugh. 'You've blushed to the roots of your hair. Why?'

'Because I want everything perfect,' he admitted.

She said, 'Malcolm, everything is.'

He was flustered, wanting and not wanting, sure and unsure. He said nothing more. They clambered from the river onto the bank. He pulled the boat close and took from it the lunch they'd brought with them. They found a spot under a willow that they liked. It was when they sank to the ground that she spoke.

'I'm ready, Malcolm, if you are,' she said.

Thus it began between them.

*   *   *

'So the kid was given up for adoption.' Barbara Havers concluded her recitation by flipping closed

382

her tatty notebook and digging round in her lump of a shoulder bag for a packet of Juicy Fruit which she brought forth and generously offered round Eric Leach's Hampstead office. The DCI took a stick. Lynley and DC Nkata demurred. Havers folded one into her mouth and began to chew vigorously. Her substitute for the weed, Lynley thought. Again, he wondered idly when she'd give up smoking altogether.

For his part, Leach played with the foil interior wrapper of the gum. He folded it into a miniature fan and placed it at the base of a photograph of his daughter. He'd apparently been on the phone to her when the Scotland Yard detectives arrived, and they'd come upon him at the end of a conversation in which he was wearily saying, 'For God's sake, Esmé, this is something you need to discuss with your mum . . . Of *course* she'll listen. She loves you . . . Now you're jumping the gun. No one's getting . . . Esmé, listen to me . . . Yes. Right. Someday she . . . So might I, but that will never mean we don't—' At which point, the girl had apparently hung up on him because he stood behind his desk with his mouth open on what he'd intended to say. He'd replaced the phone in its cradle with undue care and sighed heavily.

Now, he went on. 'That could be what's driving our killer, then. Or our killers. The adopted kid. Wolff didn't put herself in the club without assistance. Let's keep that in mind.'

The four of them continued their exchange of information. A hideous knot of traffic in Westminster had kept the Scotland Yard detectives from Leach's morning meeting with his team in the incident room, so the DCI took notes. At the conclusion of Havers' report on the Convent of the Immaculate Conception, Nkata said, 'Could be the motive we're looking for, this. She wants that kid and no one's giving her any help to find . . . is it him or her, Barb?' As was largely his habit, he hadn't taken a seat in the office. Rather, he stood not far from the doorway, lounging against the wall with one broad shoulder resting next to a framed commendation that Leach had received from the commissioner.

'It's him,' Havers said. 'But I don't think that's the case.'

'Why?'

'According to Sister Cecilia, she gave him up for adoption straightaway. She could have kept him with her for nine months—longer than that if she did time somewhere other than Holloway—but she didn't want to. She didn't even request it and get denied. She just handed him over in the delivery room and never took a look at him.'

Lynley said, 'She wouldn't have wanted to get attached to the infant, Havers. What would be the point, facing a twenty year sentence? It could be an indication of the strength of her maternal feelings for the baby. Had she not had him adopted, he would have spent his life in care.'

'But if she was looking for the kid, why not start with the convent?' Havers asked. 'Sister Cecilia handled the adoption.'

'Could be she's not looking for him at all,' Nkata pointed out. 'Twenty years later? She might know the kid wouldn't likely want to meet his real mum and find out she's a yard bird. And that could be 'xactly why she did the job on Missus Davies in the first place. Maybe she's thinking she wouldn't've *been* a yard bird without Missus Davies. Live with that for twenty years and when you get out, you want to do something about settling the score.'

'I just don't buy that,' Havers insisted. 'Not with this bloke Wiley sitting out there in his book shop, knowing every move Eugenie Davies made. Convenient, wouldn't you say, that he happened to come upon our victim and a mystery man having an argument on the very night she was killed? Who's to say it was an argument at all but just the opposite? And our Major Wiley took some nasty action as a result.'

'We need to track this kid down one way or another,' Leach said. 'Katja Wolff's kid. She might be on his trail and he'll need to be advised. It's messy, but there's no way round it. You handle that, Constable.'

Havers said, 'Sir,' in acquiescence, but she didn't look convinced about the value of the assignment.

Winston Nkata said, 'I say Katja Wolff's the right direction. There's something off with that bird.'

He went on to describe for the others the meeting he'd had with the German woman once he'd returned to Yasmin Edwards' flat on the previous evening. Asked for her whereabouts on the night in question, Katja Wolff had claimed to be at home with Yasmin and Daniel. Watching television, she'd said, although she couldn't name the programme and said they'd channel surfed all evening and she hadn't kept track where they'd touched down. What was the point of having a satellite dish and a remote if you weren't going to use both to entertain yourself?

She'd lit a cigarette as they'd spoken, and from her demeanour it looked as if she hadn't a care in the world. She'd said, 'What's this about, Constable?' in apparent innocence. But her glance flicked to the door before she answered the most important questions, and Nkata had known what that glance meant: She was hiding something from him and wondering if Yasmin Edwards had told a story similar to hers.

'What did the Edwards woman claim?' Lynley asked.

'That Wolff was there. Wouldn't say anything else about it, though.'

'Old lags,' Eric Leach pointed out. 'They're sure as hell not going to finger each other for anything, not on a first go-round with the local rozzers. You need to go after them, Constable. What else have you got?'

Nkata told them of the cracked headlamp on Yasmin Edwards' Fiesta. 'Claimed she didn't know how it happened or when,' he said. 'But Wolff has access. She was driving it yesterday.'

'Colour?' Lynley asked.

'Red gone bad.'

'That's not helpful,' Havers pointed out.

'Any of the neighbours have either one of them leaving the flat the night in question?' Leach asked this as a uniformed female constable came into his office with a sheaf of papers that she handed over. He glanced at them, grunted his thanks, and said, 'Where are we with the Audis, then?'

'Still at it,' she said. 'Nearly two thousand in Brighton, sir.'

'Who would've thought that?' Leach muttered as the constable left them. 'Whatever happened to buy *British*?' He hung on to the papers but didn't refer to them, going back to his previous topic and

386

saying to Nkata, 'The neighbours? What about it?'

'South of the river,' Nkata said with a shrug. 'No one willing to talk, even to me. Just one Bible basher who wanted to bang on 'bout women who live together in sin. Said the residents'd tried to get that baby killer—these're her words, not mine—off the premises with no luck.'

'We've got some more digging to do out there, then,' Leach noted. 'See to it. Edwards might crack if you have a decent go. You said she has a boy, right? Bring him into the picture if you need to. Accessory to murder could get her arse in a sling, so point that out to her. In the meantime,' he rooted through some paperwork on his desk and brought out a photograph, 'Holloway couriered this over last night. It needs to get taken round Henley-on-Thames.' He handed it to Lynley who saw by the line of typing beneath it that it was a photograph of Wolff. The picture wasn't flattering. She was ill-lit, looking haggard and unkempt. Looking, he thought, just like a convicted murderer. 'If she did do the job on the Davies woman,' Leach continued, 'she would have had to begin by tracking her down to Henley. If she did that, someone was bound to see her. Check it out.'

In the meantime, Leach concluded, they'd got a list of all phone calls made into and out of Eugenie Davies' cottage in the past three months. That list was being compared with the names in the dead woman's address book. The names and numbers in the address book were being matched to the calls on her answer machine. A few more hours and they should have some details as to who was last in contact with her.

'And we've got a name for the CellNet number,'

Leach informed them. 'One Ian Staines.'

'That could be her brother,' Lynley said. 'Richard Davies mentioned that she had two brothers, one called Ian.'

Leach jotted this down. He said, 'D'we know our assignments, then, lads and lasses?' as a sign their meeting was at an end.

Havers and Lynley rose. Nkata disengaged from the wall. Leach stopped them before they left the office. He said, 'Speak to Webberly, any of you?'

It was a casual enough question, Lynley thought. But its air of nonchalance didn't feel genuine. 'He wasn't in this morning when we left the Yard,' Lynley said.

'Give him my best when you see him,' Leach said. 'Tell him I'll be in touch very soon.'

'We will. When we see him.'

Out on the street and once Nkata had gone on his way, Havers said to Lynley, 'In touch about what? That's what I want to know.'

'They're old friends.'

'Hmmph. What've you done with those letters?'

'Nothing, as yet.'

'Are you still planning to . . .' Havers peered at him. 'You are, aren't you? Damn it, Inspector, if you'd listen for a minute—'

'I'm listening, Barbara.'

'Good. Hear this: I know you, and I know how you think. "Decent bloke, Webberly. He made a little mistake. But there's no sense letting one little mistake become a catastrophe." Except it has, Inspector. She's dead and those letters just might be why. We've got to face that. We've got to deal with it.'

'Are you arguing that letters more than ten years

388

old would provoke someone to murder?'

'Alone, no. I'm not saying that. But according to Wiley she was going to tell him something important, something *he* thought would change their relationship. So, what if she already told him? Or what if he already knew because he came across those letters? We have only his word that he doesn't know what she had to say.'

'Agreed,' Lynley said. 'But you can't be thinking she wanted to speak to him about Webberly. That's ancient history.'

'Not if they'd resumed their affair. Not if they'd never lost touch. Not if they'd been meeting in . . . say . . . pubs and hotels? That would have to be dealt with. And maybe it was. Only it was dealt with badly and not in the way our principals—Mrs Davies and Webberly—thought it would be.'

'I don't see that happening,' Lynley said. 'And it's far too coincidental for my liking that Eugenie Davies would be killed so soon after Katja Wolff was released from prison.'

'You're jumping on *that* horse?' Havers scoffed. 'It's a non-starter. Depend on it.'

'I'm not jumping on any horse at all,' Lynley replied. 'It's far too early to be doing that. And I suggest you employ the same hesitation with regard to Major Wiley. It gets us nowhere to fix our minds on one possibility and become blind to the others.'

'You're *not* doing that? You haven't decided those letters from Webberly are inconsequential, Inspector?'

'What I've decided is to develop my opinions based on facts, Barbara. We haven't got a lot of them so far. Until we have, we can serve the cause of justice—not to mention pursue the course of wisdom—only by keeping our eyes open and our judgements suspended. Don't you agree?'

Havers fumed. 'Listen to yourself. Bloody hell. I *hate* it when you go all toffs-in-town-for-the-season on me.'

Lynley smiled. 'Do you? Was I? I hope it doesn't provoke you to violence.'

'Just to smoking,' Havers informed him.

'Even worse,' Lynley sighed.

Gideon

8 OCTOBER

Last night I dreamed of her, or of someone like her. But the time and the place were both out of joint because I was on the Eurostar and we were descending beneath the English Channel. It was like going down into a mine.

Everyone was there: Dad, Raphael, my grandparents, and someone shadowy and faceless whom I recognised as my mother. And she was there as well: the German girl, looking much the way she looked in the newspaper photo. And yes, Sarah-Jane Beckett was there, with a picnic basket from which she pulled not a meal but a baby. She offered the baby round like a plate of sandwiches and everyone refused. One can't eat a baby, Granddad instructed her.

Then it was dark outside the windows. Someone said, Oh yes, we're under the water now.

And that's when it happened.

The tunnel walls broke. The water came through. It wasn't black like the inside of the tunnel, though, but rather like the bottom of a riverbed where one might swim and look up through the water at the sun.

And suddenly in that way dreams have of changing, we were no longer in a train at all. The carriage disappeared, and we were out of the water and on the shore of a lake. A picnic basket lay on a blanket, and I wanted to open it because I was famished. But I couldn't unfasten the basket's leather straps and although I asked for someone to open it for me, no one would because they didn't hear me.

They couldn't hear me because they were all on their feet, pointing and crying out about a boat that was floating some distance from the shore. And I became aware suddenly of what they were crying: It was my sister's name. Someone said, She's been left in the boat! We must fetch her! But no one moved.

Then the leather straps from the picnic basket were gone, as if they'd never been. Exultant, relieved, I flung the top open to get at the food, but there was no food inside. There was only the baby. And I somehow knew that the baby was my sister even though I couldn't see her face. She was covered head and shoulders by a veil, the sort you see on statues of the Virgin.

I said in the dream, Sosy's here. She's right here. *But no one on the shore would listen. Instead, they began to swim towards the boat, and I couldn't stop them no matter how I shouted. I picked the baby up from the basket to show them I was telling the truth. I cried out, She's here! Look! Sosy's right here! Come back! There's no one in the boat! But they kept swimming, one by one entering the water in a single line, and one by one disappearing beneath the surface of the lake.*

I was desperate to stop them. I thought that if they

391

could see her face, if I could hold her high enough above my shoulders, they would believe me and come back. So I tore at the veil round my sister's face. But I found another veil beneath it, Dr Rose. And under that another. And under that another. I tore at them till I was weeping and frantic and no one was left on the shore but me. Even Sonia was gone. Then I turned to the picnic basket again to find it filled not with food but with dozens of kites that I kept pulling out and tossing to one side. And as I pulled them out, I felt a desperation like nothing I've ever felt before. Desperation and tremendous fear because everyone was gone and I was alone.

So what did you do, you ask me gently.

I did nothing. Libby woke me. I found I was drenched in sweat, my heart was pounding, and I was actually weeping.

Weeping, Dr Rose. My God, I was weeping over a dream.

I said to Libby, 'There was nothing in the basket. I couldn't make them stop. I had her but they couldn't see I had her, so they went into the lake and didn't come out.'

She said, 'You were only dreaming. Here. Come here. Let me hold you, okay?'

And yes, Dr Rose, she had spent the night, the way she often spends the night. She cooks a meal or I cook a meal, we do the washing up, and we watch the television. That's what I have been reduced to: the television. If Libby notices that we no longer listen to Perlman, Rubenstein, and Menuhin—especially Yehudi, magnificent Yehudi, child of the instrument as I myself was—she does not mention it. Indeed, she's probably grateful for the television. She is, at heart, so much an American.

392

When we run out of programmes to watch, we drift into sleep. We sleep in the same bed and on the same bedclothes that haven't been changed for weeks. But they are not soiled with the mixture of our fluids. No. We have not managed that.

Libby held me while my heart hammered like a miner hewing coal. Her right hand fondled the back of my head while her left hand caressed the length of my spine. From my spine, she worked her way down to my bum till we were pelvis to pelvis with only the thin flannel of my pyjamas and the cotton of her knickers between us. She whispered, 'It's nothing, it's all right, you're fine,' and despite those words which might have been succour under other circumstances, I knew what was supposed to happen next. Blood would rush to my cock, and I would feel the pulse of it. The pulse of it would grow and the organ would ready. I would lift my head to find her mouth or lower my mouth to find her breasts, and I would grind against her, grind against her slowly. I would pin her to the bed beneath us and take her in a silence broken only by our cries of pleasure—like no other pleasure available to men and to women, as you know—when we come. Together, of course. We come together. Anything less than simultaneous orgasm is completely unworthy of my prowess as a male.

Except, of course, that is not what happened. How could it, I being who and what I am?

Which is what? you ask me.

A carapace covering nothing, Dr Rose. No, less even than that. With my music gone I am nothing itself.

Libby doesn't understand this because she can't see that who I was until Wigmore Hall was the music I made. I myself was merely an extension of the instrument, and the instrument was merely the manner in which my being took form.

You say nothing at first when you hear this, Dr Rose. You keep your eyes on me—sometimes I wonder at the discipline it must take to keep your eyes on someone so patently not even in the room with you—and you look thoughtful. But there is something more than consideration in your eyes. Is it pity? Confusion? Doubt? Frustration?

You sit unmoving, in your widow's black. You observe me over the top of your tea cup. What are you crying out in the dream? you say. When Libby wakes you, what are you crying out, Gideon?

Mummy.

But I expect you knew that before you asked.

10 OCTOBER

I can see my mother now because of the newspapers in the Press Association office. I glimpsed her—on the opposite page to Sonia's picture—before I thrust the tabloid out of my sight. I knew it was my mother because she was on my father's arm, because they were on the front step of the Old Bailey, because above them a headline declared Justice for Sonia! in four-inch type.

So now at last I see her where before she was a blur. I see her blonde hair, I see the angles of her face, I see the way her chin is sharp and her lower jaw points to form it like the bottom of a heart. She is wearing black trousers and a soft grey sweater, and she comes to fetch me in the corner of my bedroom where Sarah-Jane and I are having a geography lesson. The Amazon River is what we're studying. How it coils like a snake for four thousand miles,

394

from the Andes, through Peru and Brazil, and into the vast Atlantic Ocean.

Mother tells Sarah-Jane that she must cut short the lesson, and I know that Sarah-Jane doesn't like this because her lips change from lips into an incision in her face although she says, 'Of course, Mrs Davies,' and shuts our books.

I follow Mother. We go downstairs. She takes me into the sitting room, where a man is waiting. He's a big man with lots of ginger hair.

Mother says that he's a policeman, and he wants to ask me some questions, but I'm not to be afraid because she won't leave the room while be talks to me. She sits on the sofa and pats the cushion, right next to her thigh. And when I sit, she puts her arm round my shoulders, and I can feel her trembling as she says, 'Go ahead, Detective Inspector.'

She's probably told me his name, but I can't remember it. What I do remember is that he pulls a chair over close to us and he leans forward with his elbows on his knees and his arms drawn up so that he can rest his chin on his thumbs. When he's close like this, I can smell cigars. The smoke must be in his clothes and his hair. It's not a bad smell, but I'm not used to it, and I shrink back against my mother.

He says, 'Your mum's right, lad. You've no reason to be frightened. No one is going to hurt you.' When be speaks, I twist to gaze up at my mother, and I see that she's looking only at her lap. In her lap lie our hands, hers and mine, because she's taken my hand so that we're connected there as well: by her arm round my shoulders, by our fingers linking. And she squeezes my fingers but makes no reply to what the ginger-haired policeman has said.

He asks me if I know what happened to my sister. I

say I know something bad happened to Sosy. There were lots of people in the house, I tell him, and they took her to hospital.

'Your mum's told you that she's with God now, hasn't she?' he asks.

And I say yes. Sosy's with God.

He asks me if I know what that means, to be with God?

I tell him that it means Sosy died.

'Do you know how she died?' he asks me.

I lower my head. I feel my feet bounce against the front of the sofa. I say that I'm meant to practise my instrument for three hours, that Raphael has told me I must master something—an Allegro, is it?—if I want to meet Mr Stern next month. Mother reaches down and stops my feet bouncing. She says that I'm to try to answer the policeman.

I know the answer. I've heard the tramp of footsteps running up the stairs and into the bathroom. I've been a witness to the cries in the night. I've listened to the whispered conversations. I've walked in on questions being asked and accusations being made. So I know what happened to my little sister.

In the bath, I tell him. Sosy died in the bath.

'Where were you when Sosy died?' he asks me.

Listening to the violin, I say.

Mother speaks then. She says that Raphael has given me some music to listen to twice each day because I'm not playing it as well as I should.

'So you're learning to play the fiddle, are you?' the policeman asks me kindly.

'I'm a violinist, not a fiddler,' I reply.

'Ah,' the policeman says and he smiles. 'A violinist. I stand corrected.' He settles more comfortably into his chair, rests his hands on the tops of his thighs, and

396

says, 'Lad, your mum tells me that she and your dad haven't yet told you exactly how your little sister died.'

In the bath, I repeat. She died in the bath.

'True. But, lad, it wasn't an accident. Someone hurt the little girl. Someone meant to hurt her. Do you know what that means?'

I picture sticks and stones, and that's what I say. Hurt means throwing rocks, I tell him. Hurt means putting out a foot in front of someone, hurt means hitting or pinching or biting. I think of all those things happening to Sosy.

The policeman says, 'That's one kind of hurting. But there's another sort, a sort done by an adult to a child. Do you know what I mean by that?'

Getting spanked, I say.

'More than that.'

And this is when Dad comes into the room. Has he just got home from work? Has he been at work at all? How long after Sonia's death is this? I'm trying to place the recollection in context, but the only context I have right now is that if the police are asking the family questions, it must be before Katja was charged with anything.

Dad sees what's going on and he puts a stop to it. I remember that. And he's angry: both at Mother and at the policeman. He says, 'What's going on here, Eugenie?' as the policeman gets to his feet.

She says, 'The inspector wanted to ask Gideon some questions.'

He says, 'Why?'

The policeman says, 'Everyone must be questioned, Mr Davies.'

Dad says, 'You aren't assuming that Gideon—'

And Mother says his name. She says it in the same way Gran says Jack when she's hoping to forestall an

397

episode.

Dad tells me to go to my room, and the policeman says that he's only prolonging the inevitable. I don't know what that means, but I do as I'm told—as I always do when Dad is the one giving the order—and I leave the room. I hear the inspector say, 'This only makes the situation more frightening for the lad,' and I hear Dad say, 'Now you listen to me—' as Mother says, 'Please, Richard,' in a voice that breaks.

Mother weeping. I should be used to this by now. Wearing grey or black, grey of face as well, she has wept for more than two years, it seems. But weeping or otherwise, she isn't able to alter the circumstances of that day.

From the mezzanine, I see the policeman leave. I see Mother show him to the door. I see him speak to her bent head, watch her intently, reach out to her then withdraw his hand. Then Dad calls out Mother's name and she turns. She doesn't see me as she goes back to him. Dad shouts at her behind the closed door.

Then hands are on my shoulders and I'm pulled back from the railing. I look up to see Sarah-Jane Beckett standing over me. She crouches down. She puts her arm round my shoulders just as my mother did, but neither her arm nor her body is shaking. We stay just like that for several minutes—and all the while Dad's voice is loud and sharp and Mother's is tentative and afraid. '. . . no more of this, Eugenie,' Dad says, 'I won't have it. Do you hear me?'

I sense more than anger in those words. I sense violence, Granddad's kind of violence, violence that is forged on the wheel of a mind collapsing. I am afraid.

I look up at Sarah-Jane, seeking . . . what?

398

Protection? Affirmation of what I'm hearing below? Distraction? Any of it, all of it. But she is rapt by the drawing room door, and her gaze is fixed to its dark panels. She watches that door, unblinking, and her fingers tighten on my shoulder, taking me to the threshold of pain. I whimper and glance down at her hand and see that her fingernails are bitten and torn, with angry hangnails that are chewed and bleeding. But her face is glowing and her breathing is deep and she doesn't move till the conversation below us ceases and footsteps fire against the parquet floor. Then she takes my hand and pulls me along in her wake, up the stairs to the second floor, past the door of the nursery—closed now—and back to my room where the school books have been re-opened to the Amazon River that crawls like a poisonous serpent across a continent.

What's happening between your parents? you ask me.

And the answer seems obvious to me now. Blame.

11 OCTOBER

Sonia's dead and there must be a reckoning. This reckoning must be made not only in a courtroom of the Old Bailey, not only in the courtroom of public opinion, but also in the courtroom of the family itself. For someone must take the burden of responsibility for Sonia: first for her birth—imperfect as she was— then for the scores of medical problems that plagued her short life, and last for her violent and premature death. I know this now although I could not have known it then: There is no surviving what occurred in that bathroom in Kensington Square if blame cannot be assigned somewhere.

399

Dad comes to me. Sarah-Jane and I have finished our lesson, and she's left with James the Lodger. I've watched them from my window as they cross the flagstones at the front of the house and go out through the wrought iron gate. Sarah-Jane has stepped back to let James the Lodger hold the gate open for her, and she's waited for him on the other side and taken his arm. She's leaned into him that way women do, so that he might feel her nearly non-existent breasts press against his arm. But if he's felt them, he's given no sign. Instead he's started walking in the direction of the pub, and she's taken care to match her steps to his.

I've put on a piece of music assigned by Raphael. I'm listening to it when my father joins me. I'm trying to feel the notes as well as to hear them because only if I feel the notes will I be able to find them on my instrument.

Dad searches me out where I sit on the floor in a corner of the room. He squats in front of me and the music swirls round us. We live in the music till the movement is over. Dad turns off the stereo. He says, 'Come here, son,' and he sits on the bed. I go to him and stand before him.

He studies me, and I want to wriggle away, but I don't. He says, 'You live for the music, don't you?' and he smoothes his hand through my hair. 'You concentrate on the music, Gideon. Just on the music and nothing else.'

I can smell the scent of him: lemons and starch, so completely unlike the scent of cigars. I say, 'He asked me how Sosy died.'

Dad draws me to him and holds me. He says, 'She's gone now. No one can harm you.'

He's talking about Katja. I've heard her leave. I've

400

seen her in the company of the nun, so perhaps she's returned to the convent. Her name isn't mentioned within our little world. Neither is Sonia's. Unless the policeman brings one of them up.

I say, 'He said someone hurt Sosy.'

Dad says, 'Think of the music, Gideon. Listen to the music and master it, son. That's all you have to do just now.'

But that turns out not to be the case because the policeman instructs my father to bring me to the station on the Earl's Court Road where we sit in a small, brightly lit room, in the company of a woman who wears a suit like a man and listens watchfully to the questions I'm asked, like a guardian who's there to protect me from something. Asking the questions is Ginger Hair himself.

What he wants to know is something simple, he tells me. 'You know who Katja Wolff is, don't you, lad?' I look from my father to the woman. She wears spectacles and when the light hits them, the lenses reflect it and hide her eyes.

Dad says, 'Of course, he knows who Katja Wolff is. He isn't an idiot. Get to the point.'

The policeman isn't to be hurried. He talks to me as if Dad were not there. He takes me from Sosy's birth, through Katja's coming to live with us, to the care that Sosy received at her hands. Dad protests at this. 'How is an eight-year-old boy supposed to answer these sorts of questions?'

The policeman says that children are observant, that I will be able to tell them more than Dad imagines possible.

I've been given a can of Coke and a biscuit studded with nuts and sultanas, and they sit before me on the table like a three-dimensional exclamation

401

mark. I watch the moisture form its beadwork on the can, and I run my finger through it to shape a treble clef on the curving side. I'm missing my three-hour morning practice to be here in the police station. This makes me restless, anxious, and difficult. I am already quite afraid.

Of what? you ask me.

Of the questions themselves, of giving the wrong answers, of the tension that I sense in my father which, now that I consider it, seems so at odds with my mother's grief. Shouldn't he have been prostrate with sorrow, Dr Rose? Or at least desperate to get to the bottom of what happened to Sonia? But he isn't sorrowful, and if he's desperate, it seems like a feeling born of an urgency that he hasn't explained to anyone.

Do you answer the questions despite your fear? you ask.

I answer them as well as I can. They lead me through the two years that Katja Wolff has lived in our home. For some reason, they seem to focus primarily on her relationship with James the Lodger and Sarah-Jane Beckett. But at long last, they veer to her care of Sosy and to one particular point in that care.

'Did you ever hear Katja shout at your little sister?' the policeman asked.

No, I had not.

'Did you ever see her discipline Sonia if she misbehaved?'

No, I had not.

'Did you ever see her do anything a little bit rough with Sonia? Shake her a bit when she wouldn't stop crying? Smack her bottom when she didn't obey? Pull on her arm to get her attention? Grab her leg to move

402

her about when she changed her nappies?'

Sosy cried a lot, I tell him. Katja got out of bed in the night to take care of Sosy. She talked German to her—'

'In an angry voice?'

—and sometimes she cried as well. I could hear her from my room, and once I got up and looked into the corridor and saw her walking up and down, holding Sosy on her shoulder. Sosy wouldn't stop crying, so Katja put her back in her cot. She took a set of plastic baby keys and jangled them over Sosy's head and I heard her say, Bitte, bitte, bitte' *which is German for* please. *And when the keys didn't make Sosy stop crying, she grabbed the side of the cot and gave it a shake.*

'You saw this?' The policeman leans towards me across the table. 'You saw *Katja do this? Are you certain, lad?'*

And something in his voice tells me I've given an answer that's pleasing. I say I'm certain: Sosy cried and Katja shook the side of the cot.

'I think we're getting somewhere now,' the policeman says.

12 OCTOBER

How much of what a child reports is the stuff of his memory, Dr Rose? How much of what a child reports is the stuff of his dreams? How much of what I say to the detective in those hours in the police station comes from what I actually witnessed? How much grows from sources as diverse as the tension I feel between my father and the policeman and my desire to please them both?

It isn't much of a leap from shaking the side of a

403

cot to shaking a child. And from there, it is the work of a moment to fancy having seen a small arm twisted, a small body jerked upright to put a coat on, a small round face squeezed and pinched when someone spits her food on the floor, a tangle of hair yanked through a comb, and legs wrenched into a pair of pink dungarees.

Ah, you say. Your voice is noncommittal and carefully, scrupulously without judgement, Dr Rose. Your hands, however, rise, pressed together in an attitude that resembles prayer. You place them just beneath your chin. You don't avert your gaze but I avert mine.

I see what you're thinking, and I'm thinking it as well. My answers to that policeman's questions were what sent Katja Wolff to prison.

But I didn't give evidence at her trial, Dr Rose. So if what I said was so important why wasn't I called to give evidence? Anything less than the whole truth sworn to in a court of law was like an article appearing on the front page of a tabloid: something to be taken at face value only, something suggesting that further investigation into the matter by professionals might be required.

If I said that Katja Wolff harmed my sister, all that would have come from that is their looking into the allegation. Isn't that the case? And if corroboration existed for what I told them, they would have found it.

That has to be what happened, Dr Rose.

<u>15 OCTOBER</u>
I might have truly seen it. I might have been a witness to those things which I declared as having occurred between my little sister and her nanny. If so many

sections of my mind are blank when it comes to the past, how illogical is it to assume that somewhere on that vast canvas reside images too painful to be remembered accurately?

Pink dungarees are fairly accurate, you tell me. They come either from memory or from embellishment, Gideon.

How could I embellish with such a detail as the colour of her dungarees if she didn't wear those dungarees?

She was a little girl, you say with a shrug that's not dismissive so much as inconclusive. Little girls often wear pink.

So you're saying I was a liar, Dr Rose? Simultaneously a child prodigy and a liar?

They're not mutually exclusive, you point out.

I reel from this and you see something—anguish, horror, guilt?—on my face.

You say, I'm not labelling you a liar now, Gideon. But you might have been then. Circumstances may have required you to lie.

What sort of circumstances, Dr Rose?

You have no answer to give me other than this: Write what you remember.

17 OCTOBER

Libby found me at the top of Primrose Hill. I was standing before that metal engraving that allows one to identify the buildings and monuments that one can see from the summit, and I was forcing myself to look from the engraving to the view—working from east to west—in order to pick each one out. From the corner of my eye, I saw her coming up the path, dressed in her black leathers. She'd left her helmet elsewhere, and the wind whipped her curls round her face.

She said, 'Saw your car in the square. I thought I'd find you here. No kite?'

'No kite.' I touched the metal surface of the engraving, my fingers resting on St Paul's. I studied the skyline.

'What's up, then? You don't look so great. Aren't you cold? What're you doing out here without a sweater?'

Looking for answers, I thought.

She said, 'Hey! Anyone home? I'm, like, talking to you here.'

I said, 'I needed a walk.'

She said, 'You saw the shrink today, didn't you?'

I wanted to say that I see you even when I don't see you, Dr Rose. But I thought that she would misunderstand and take the comment for a patient's obsession with his doctor, which I do not have.

She came round the engraving to face me, blocking my view. She reached across the sheet of metal and touched her palm to my chest, saying, 'What's wrong, Gid? How can I help?'

Her touch reminded me of all that isn't happening between us—of all that would have been happening between a woman and a normal man—and the weight of this idea was suddenly too much to bear in conjunction with what was already plaguing me. I said, 'I may have sent a woman to prison.'

'What?'

I told her the rest.

When I had finished, she said, 'You were eight years old. A cop was asking questions. You did the best you could in a bad situation. And you might have seen that stuff, too. There've been studies on this, Gid, and they say that kids don't make things up

406

when it comes to abuse. Where there's smoke, there's fire. And anyway someone must have confirmed what you said if you didn't testify in court.'

'That's just it. I'm not so sure that I didn't testify, Libby.'

'But you said—'

'I said I'd managed to remember the policeman, the questions, the station: all of them aspects of a situation that I'd blocked from my mind. What's to say I haven't also blocked from my mind giving evidence at Katja Wolff's trial?'

'Oh. Yeah. I see.' She looked out at the view and tried to tame her hair, sucking in on her lower lip as she thought about what I'd said. Finally, she declared, 'Okay. Let's find out what really went on, then.'

'How?'

'How tough can it be to dig up what happened at a trial that was probably covered by every newspaper in the country?'

19 OCTOBER

We started with Bertram Cresswell-White, the barrister who'd prosecuted Katja Wolff for the Crown. Finding him, as Libby had promised, presented no problem. He had a room in chambers in the Temple, at Number Five Paper Buildings, and he agreed to see me once I managed to get him on the phone. He said, 'I remember the case perfectly. Yes. I'm happy to speak to you about it, Mr Davies.'

Libby insisted on going with me. She said, 'Two heads are better. What you won't think to ask him, I will.'

So we drove to the river and entered the Temple

407

from *Victoria Embankment, where a cobblestone lane ducks beneath an ornate archway, which gives access to the best legal minds in the country. Paper Buildings sits on the east side of a leafy garden within the Temple, and the barristers who have chambers there possess the benefit of views of either the trees or the Thames.*

Bertram Cresswell-White had views of both, and when Libby and I were ushered into his office by a young woman delivering him a set of pink-ribboned briefs, we found him in an alcove behind his desk, taking advantage of the sight of a barge sailing sluggishly in the direction of Waterloo Bridge. When he turned from the window, I felt confident that I'd never seen him before, that there was nothing I'd deliberately or unconsciously wiped from my mind involving him. For surely I would remember so imposing a figure had he questioned me inside a courtroom.

He must be six foot three inches tall, Dr Rose, with the sort of shoulders one gets from rowing. He has the frightening eyebrows of a man over sixty, and when he looked at me, I felt the internal jolt one gets from being pierced by a stare that's used to intimidate witnesses.

He said, 'I never expected to meet you. I heard you play some years ago at the Barbican.' He said to the young woman as she placed the briefs on his desk where already a stack of manila folders lay in the centre, 'Coffee please, Mandy.' And to Libby and me, 'Will you have some?'

I said yes. Libby said, 'Sure. Thanks,' and she looked round the room with her lips forming a small o through which she was blowing air. I know her well enough to see what she was thinking in her California fashion: 'Some joint you got here.' She wasn't wrong.

Cresswell-White's room in chambers was designed to impress: hung with brass chandeliers, lined with bookshelves holding well-bound legal volumes, and heated by a fireplace in which even now was burning a gas fire with a realistic arrangement of artificial coals. He gestured us to a sitting area of leather armchairs that were gathered round a coffee table on a Persian rug. A framed photograph stood on this table. In it, a youngish man dressed in a barrister's wig and gown posed at Cresswell-White's side, his arms crossed and a grin on his face.

'Is this your kid?' Libby said to Cresswell-White. 'There's a big resemblance.'

'That's my son Geoffrey, yes,' the barrister replied, 'at the conclusion of his first case.'

'Looks like he won it,' Libby noted.

'He did. He's just your age, by the way.' This last was said to me with a nod as he set the folders on the coffee table. I saw that Crown Vs. Wolff *was written on each of their tabs. 'You were born a week apart at the same hospital, I discovered. I didn't know that at the time of the trial. But later when I was reading about you somewhere—this would have been when you were a teenager, I suppose—the article included the facts of your birth and there it was: the date, place, and time. It's remarkable, really, how connected we all are.'*

Mandy returned with the coffee then and placed the tray on the table: three cups and three saucers, milk and sugar, but no pot: a subtle omission that seemed designed to determine the length of our stay. We doctored our drinks as she left us.

I said, 'We've come with some specific questions about Katja Wolff's trial.'

'You've not heard from her, have you?' Cresswell-White's tone was sharp.

'Heard from her? No. Once she left our house—when my sister died—I never saw her again. At least . . . I don't think I saw her.'

'You don't think . . . ?' Cresswell-White picked up his cup of coffee and held it on his knee. He was wearing a good suit—grey wool and cut exactly to fit him—and the creases in his trousers looked as if they'd been placed there by royal decree.

'I have no recollection of the trial,' I told him. 'I have no actual clear recollection of that whole period of time. Large areas of my childhood are rather misty, and I've been trying to clarify them.' I didn't tell him why I was making this attempt to recapture the past. I didn't use the word repression, and I couldn't bring myself to reveal anything more.

'I see.' Cresswell-White gave a brief smile that disappeared as quickly as it flashed on his face. To me, the smile seemed both ironic and self-directed, and his next comment reinforced this assumption. 'Gideon, would that we could all drink of the waters of Lethe like you. I, for one, would sleep better at night. May I call you Gideon, by the way? That's how I've always thought of you, although we've never met.'

That was a decisive answer to the main question I'd come with, and the relief I felt at hearing it told me something of how great my fears had been. I said, 'So I didn't give evidence, did I? At her trial? I didn't give evidence against her.'

'Good God, no. I wouldn't put an eight-year-old child through that. Why do you ask?'

'Gideon talked to the cops when his sister died,' Libby said frankly. 'He couldn't remember much about the trial, but he thought his testimony might

410

have been what put Katja Wolff away.'

'Ah. I do see. And now that she's been released, you're wanting to prepare yourself in case—'

'She's been released?' I broke in.

'You didn't know? Neither of your parents informed you? I sent them both letters. She's been out for—' He glanced at some paperwork in one of the folders. 'She's been out for just over a month.'

'No. No. I didn't know.' I felt a sudden pulsing within my skull, and I saw the familiar pattern of bright speckling that always precedes twenty-four hours of pounding. I thought, Oh no. Please. Not here and not now.

'Perhaps they didn't think it necessary.' Cresswell-White said. 'If she's going to approach anyone from that period of time, it's more likely to be one of them, isn't it? Or myself. Or someone who gave damning evidence against her.' He went on to say something more but I couldn't hear because the pulsing in my head was growing louder and the speckling was turning to an arc of light. My body was like an invading army, and I—who should have been its general—was instead its target.

I felt my feet begin a nervous tapping, as if they wanted to carry me from the room. I drew a breath and with the air came the image of that door once again: that blue blue door at the top of the stairs, those two locks upon it, that ring at its centre. I could see it as if I stood before it, and I wanted to open it but I could not raise my hand.

Libby said my name. I heard that much through the pulsing. I held up a hand and signalled her, asking for a moment, just a moment please to recover.

From what? you want to know, and you lean

411

towards me, ever ready for a loop in the yarn into which you can insert your needle. Recover from what? Go back, Gideon.

Go back to what?

To that moment in Bertram Cresswell-White's rooms, to the pulsing in your head, to what led to the pulsing.

All the talk about the trial led to the pulsing.

We've had the trial before now. It's more than that. What are you avoiding?

I'm avoiding nothing . . . *But you're not convinced, are you, Dr Rose? I'm supposed to be writing what I remember, and you've begun to question how trolling through the trial of Katja Wolff is going to take me back to my music. You caution me. You point out that the human mind is strong, that it holds onto its neuroses with a fierce protection, that it possesses the ability to deny and distract, and that this expedition to Paper Buildings might well be a monumental effort on the part of my mind to engage in displacement.*

Then that's how it will have to be, Dr Rose. I do not know how else to go at this thing.

All right, you say. Did your time with Cresswell-White trigger anything else then? Aside from the episode with your head?

Episode. *You choose that word with deliberation, and I know it. But I will not bite at the bait you cast out. I will tell you about Sarah-Jane instead. For this is what I learn from Bertram Cresswell-White: the part that I did not have in Katja Wolff's trial, the part that Sarah-Jane Beckett had.*

19 OCTOBER 9:00 P.M.

'She lived in the house with your family and Wolff, after all,' Bertram Cresswell-White said. He'd taken up the first of the folders with Crown Vs. Wolff *on them, and he'd begun to leaf through the documents inside, reading from time to time when his memory needed to be refreshed. 'She was in a good position to observe what went on.'*

'So did she see something?' Libby asked. She'd moved her chair closer to mine, and she'd placed her hand on the back of my neck as if she knew without my telling her what state my head was in. She kneaded my neck gently, and I wanted to be grateful. But I could sense the displeasure that the barrister felt at this open display of her affection for me, and I tensed because of this displeasure as I always tense when an older man looks on me with a critical eye.

'She saw Wolff being sick in the mornings, every morning for a month before the child was killed,' he said. 'You know she was pregnant, don't you?'

'My father told me as much,' I said.

'Yes. Well. Beckett saw the German girl's patience growing thin. The child—your sister—got her up three or four times each night, so she was short of sleep as well and that, in conjunction with the difficulties of morning sickness, wore her down. She began to leave Sonia too much alone, which was something that Miss Beckett came to realise since she gave you your lessons on the same floor of the house as your sister's nursery. Ultimately, she felt it her duty to report to your parents that Wolff was derelict in her duties. This precipitated a confrontation, which resulted in Wolff being sacked.'

'On the spot?' Libby asked.

Cresswell-White consulted a file for the answer to

413

this, saying, 'No. She was given a month's notice. Your parents were quite generous considering the situation, Gideon.'

'But she never said in court that she saw Katja Wolff abuse my sister?' I asked.

The barrister closed the folder, saying, 'Beckett testified that they'd rowed—the German girl and your parents. She testified that Sonia, over a period of days, was left to cry for as long as an hour in her cot. She said that on the evening in question, she heard the German girl giving Sonia her bath. But she couldn't name the time or the place where she'd witnessed any direct physical abuse.'

'Who did?' Libby asked.

'No one,' the barrister replied.

'God,' I murmured.

Cresswell-White seemed to know what I was thinking because he set the folder back on the coffee table along with his cup and he spoke to me urgently. A case in court is like a mosaic, Gideon. If there's no eye witness to the crime itself—as there wasn't in this situation—then each piece of the case that the Crown presents must ultimately form a pattern from which an entire picture can be seen. The entire picture is what convinces the jury of the defendant's guilt. And that's what happened in Katja Wolff's case.'

'Because there was other testimony against her?' Libby asked.

'Yes, indeed.'

'Whose?' My voice was weak—I could hear *the weakness as well as I could hate it and as fully as I could not remove it from my tone.*

'The police who took her first and only statement, the forensic pathologist who did the post-mortem, the friend with whom Wolff had initially claimed to be

414

on the phone for one minute during which she left your sister alone, your mother, your father, your grandparents. It's less a case of encouraging anyone to say something directly against a defendant than of unfolding for the jury the situation as it existed and allowing them to draw their own conclusions about that situation. So everyone contributed to the overall mosaic. What we ended up with was a twenty-one-year-old German girl who had revelled in the publicity she got when she escaped from her country, who was able to emigrate to England because of the good will of a group of nuns, whose celebrity—which had fed her ego—quickly faded upon her arrival here, who was given a job that included room and board, who got herself pregnant, fell consequently ill, failed to cope, lost her job, and snapped.'

'Sounds like manslaughter, not murder,' Libby said.

'And would probably have gone down as such had she been willing to testify. But she wasn't willing. It was amazingly arrogant, but quite in keeping with her background if it comes down to it, I suppose. She wouldn't testify. And she made matters worse for herself by refusing to speak to the police more than that single time, as well as by refusing to speak to her solicitor, or even her barrister.'

'Why'd she clam up?' Libby asked.

'I couldn't say. But the post-mortem showed there were previously healed fractures on your sister's body that no doctor could account for and no one else was able to explain, Gideon, and the fact that the German girl would say nothing to anyone concerning Sonia made it look as if she wasn't in the dark about those older injuries. And while the jury was instructed—as they were in those days—that Wolff's silence could

not be held against her, juries are only human, aren't they? That silence is going to influence their thinking.'

'So what I said to the police—'

Cresswell-White waved my words away, saying, 'I read your statement. Naturally, it was part of the brief. I re-read it, in fact, when you phoned me. And while I would have taken it into account twenty years ago, believe me I wouldn't have prosecuted Katja Wolff on the strength of it alone.' He smiled. 'After all, you were eight years old, Gideon. I had a son the very same age, so I was well aware of what boys are like. I had to consider the fact that Katja Wolff might have sorted you out about something in the days preceding your sister's death. And if that had been the case, you might have used your imagination for a bit of revenge on her, without knowing where your statement to the police could lead.'

'There you go, Gideon,' Libby said.

'So set your mind at rest if you're feeling guilty about Katja Wolff,' Cresswell-White said, and his words were warm. 'She did herself far more harm than you ever did her.'

20 OCTOBER

So was it revenge or was it memory, Dr Rose? And if it was revenge, what was it for? I can't think of a time that anyone save Raphael sought to discipline me, and the only times he did so were when he made me listen to a piece of music that I wasn't performing to his liking, and that was hardly punishment at all.

Was The Archduke something you listened to? you inquire.

I don't remember. But there were other pieces. The Lalo, compositions by Saint-Saëns and Bruch.

416

*And did you master those other pieces? you ask.
Once you listened to them, Gideon, were you able to
play them?*

Of course. Yes. I played them all.

But not The Archduke?

That piece has always been my bête noire.

Shall we talk about that?

There's nothing to say. The Archduke *exists. I've
never been able to play it well. And now I can't play
the instrument itself. I'm not even close to being able
to play it. So is my father right? Are we wasting our
time? Is what I have just a case of nerves that has
unnerved me and caused me to look elsewhere for a
solution? You know what I mean: Foist the problem
onto someone else's shoulders so that I don't have to
confront it myself. Hand it over to the shrink and see
what she makes of it.*

Do you believe that, Gideon?

I don't know what to believe.

*We drove home from Bertram Cresswell-White. I
could tell that Libby thought we'd found a solution to
my problems because the barrister had given me
absolution from guilt. Her conversation was light—
how she planned to 'put it to Rock the next time he
withholds my wages, the creep'—and when she wasn't
changing gear, she kept her hand on my knee. She'd
been the one to suggest that she drive my car, and I
was only too happy to let her. Cresswell-White's
absolution hadn't obliterated the growing pain in my
head. I was definitely better off not behind the wheel.*

*Once back in Chalcot Square, Libby parked the
car and turned my face to hers. 'Hey,' she said.
'You've got the answers you were looking for, Gideon.
Let's plan a celebration.'*

She leaned towards me and touched her mouth to

417

mine. I felt her tongue against my lips, and I opened them and allowed her to kiss me.

Why? you ask.

Because I wanted to believe what she said: that I had the answers I'd been looking for.

Is that the only reason?

No. Of course not. I wanted to be normal.

And?

All right. I managed a response of sorts. My skull was cracking open, but I reached for her head, held her, and insinuated my fingers into her hair. We stayed like that, our tongues creating that dance of expectation between us. I tasted in her mouth the coffee she'd drunk in Cresswell-White's rooms and I drank of it deeply, with the hope that the sudden thirst I felt would lead to the hunger I'd not experienced in years. I wanted that hunger, Dr Rose, in order to know that I was alive.

One hand still in her hair, holding her to me, I kissed her face and neck. I reached for her breast, and I felt her nipple hardening hardening erect and hardening through the material of her jersey and I squeezed that nipple to bring her both to pain and to pleasure and she moaned. She climbed from her seat onto mine, straddling me, kissing me, unbuttoned my shirt as I squeezed and released and squeezed and released and her mouth was on my chest and her lips were tracing a trail from my neck and I wanted to feel, I wanted to feel, and so I groaned and put my face in her hair.

And there was the scent: fresh mint. From her shampoo, I suppose. But suddenly I was not in the car at all. I was in the back garden of our house in Kensington: in summer and at night. I've picked some mint leaves and I'm rolling them in my palms to

418

release the smell and I hear the sounds before I see the people. They sound like diners smacking their lips over a meal, which is what I think the noise is at first until I pick them out of the darkness at the bottom of the garden where a flash of colour that is her blonde hair attracts my attention.

They are standing against the brick shed where the gardening tools are kept. His back is to me. Her hands cover his head. One of her legs crosses behind him above his arse, holding him to her and they grind together, they grind and grind. Her head is thrown back and he kisses her neck and I can't see who he is but I can see her. It's Katja, my little sister's nanny. It's one of the men from the house.

Not someone else Katja knows? you ask. Not someone from the outside?

Who? Katja knows no one, Dr Rose. She sees no one but the nun from the convent and a girl who comes to call now and then, a girl called Katie. And this isn't Katie out here in the darkness because I remember Katie, God God I remember Katie now because she's fat and she's funny and she dresses with flair and she talks in the kitchen when Katja feeds Sonia and she says that Katja's escape from East Berlin was a metaphor for an organism only it wasn't organism *that she said at all, it was* orgasm, *wasn't it, which is all she ever talks about.*

Gideon, you say to me, who was the man? Look at the shape of him, look at his hair.

Her hands cover his head. He's bent to her anyway. I can't see his hair.

Can't or won't? Which is it, Gideon? Is it can't or won't?

I can't. I can't.

Have you seen the lodger? Your father? Your

419

grandfather? Raphael Robson? Who is it, Gideon?

I DCIN'T KNOW.

And Libby reached for me then, did what a normal woman does when she's aroused and wants to share her arousal. She laughed a breathless sort of laugh, said, 'I can't even believe *we're doing this in your car,' and eased my belt out of its buckle, unfastened it, unbuttoned my trousers, put her fingers on the zipper, brought her mouth back to mine.*

And there was nothing within me, Dr Rose. No hunger, no thirst, no heat, no longing. No pulse of blood to awaken my lust, no throbbing in the veins to harden my cock.

I grabbed Libby's hands. I didn't need to make an excuse or say anything else to her. She may be American—a little loud at times, a little vulgar, a little too casual, too friendly, and too forthright—but she isn't a fool.

She pushed herself off me and got back in her seat. 'It's me, isn't it?' she said. 'I'm too fat for you.'

'Don't be an idiot.'

'Don't call *me an idiot.'*

'Don't act like one.'

She turned to the window. It was steaming up. Light from the square diffracted through the steam and cast a muted glow against her cheek. Round, the cheek looked, and I could see the colour in it, the flush of a peach as it grows and ripens. The despair I felt—for myself, for her, for the two of us together— was what made me continue. 'You're fine, Libby. You're one hundred percent. You're perfect. It isn't you.'

'Then what? Rock? It's Rock. It's that we're still married. It's that you know what he does to me, don't you? You've figured it out.'

I didn't know what she was talking about, and I didn't want to know. I said, 'Libby, if you haven't realised by now that there's something wrong with me—something seriously wrong—'

And at that, she got out of the car. She shoved the door open and slammed it shut, and she did what she never does. She shouted. 'Nothing is wrong with you, Gideon! Do you hear me? Nothing is fucking wrong *with you!'*

I got out as well, and we faced each other over the bonnet of the car. I said, 'You know that you're lying to yourself.'

'I know what's before my eyes. And what's before my eyes is you.'

'You've heard me try to play. You've sat in your flat and heard me. You know.'

'The violin? Is that *what this is all about, Gid? The goddamn cock-sucking violin?' She smashed her fist against the car's bonnet so hard that I started. She cried, 'You are* not *the violin. Playing music is what you do. It is not—and has never been—who you are.'*

'And if I can't play? What happens then?'

'Then you live, all right? You goddamn start living. *How about that for a profound idea?'*

'You don't understand.'

'I understand plenty. I understand that you've got yourself, like, all hooked into being Mr Violin. You've spent so many years scratching at the strings that you don't have any other identity. Why are you doing it? What's it s'posed to prove? Will your dad, maybe, love you *enough if you play till your fingers bleed or something?' She swung away from the car and away from me. 'Like, why am I even* bothering, *Gideon?'*

She began striding towards the house and I followed her, which was when I saw that the front

421

door was open and that someone was standing on the steps and probably had been standing there since Libby had parked the car in the square. She saw him at the same moment that I did and for the first time I caught on her face an expression telling me she held an aversion to him that was as strong as—if not stronger than—the one my father held for her.

'Then perhaps it's time you stopped bothering,' Dad said. His voice was quite pleasant, but his eyes were steel.

Gideon

<u>20 OCTOBER 10:00 P.M.</u>
Dad said, 'Charming girl. Does she always shriek like a fishwife in the square or was that something special this evening?'

'She was upset.'

'That was obvious. As were her feelings about your work, by the way, which is something you might want to consider should you wish to carry on with her.'

I didn't want to discuss Libby with him. He's made his attitude plain from the start. There's no point wasting energy in trying to change it.

We were in the kitchen, where we'd repaired once Libby left us on the steps. She'd said to him, 'Richard, stay out of my way,' and had pushed open the gate to her steps with a clang. She'd pounded down and into her flat, from where the volume of her pop music was now illustrating her state of mind.

'We went to see Bertram Cresswell-White,' I told Dad. 'Do you remember him?'

'I had a look at your garden earlier,' Dad replied,

canting his head towards the back of the house. 'The weeds are starting to go rampant, Gideon. If you aren't careful, they're going to choke out the rest of the plants, what few there are. You know, you can hire a Filipino if you don't like gardening. Have you considered doing that?'

From below in Libby's flat, the pop music blared. She'd opened her windows. Distorted phrases pounded up from the basement: How can your *man* . . . *loves* you . . . slow down, *bay*-bee . . .

I said, 'Dad, I asked you—'

'I've brought you two camellias, by the way.' He walked to the window overlooking the garden .

. . . let him *know* . . . he's *play*ing around!

It was dark outside, so there was nothing to see except Dad's own reflection and mine on the glass. His was clear; mine wavered ghostlike as if affected by either the atmosphere or my inability to manifest strongly.

'I've planted them on either side of the steps,' Dad said. 'They're not quite what I want yet in the way of blooms, but I'm getting close.'

'Dad, I'm asking you—'

'I've weeded both planters, but you're going to have to see to the rest of the garden yourself.'

'Dad!'

. . . a chance to feel . . . free to . . . the feeling grab you, *bay*-bee.

'Or you can always ask your American friend if she wants to make herself useful in ways other than verbally assaulting you in the street or entertaining you with her quaint choice of music.'

'God damn it, Dad. I'm asking you a question.'

He turned from the window. 'I heard the question. And—'

Love him. Love him, baby. Love *him*.

'—if I didn't have to compete with your little American's auditory entertainment, I might actually consider answering it.'

I said loudly, 'Ignore it, then. Ignore Libby as well. You're good at ignoring things you can't be bothered with, aren't you, Dad?'

The music suddenly stopped, as if I'd been heard. The silence following my question created nature's enemy, a vacuum, and I waited to see what would fill it. A moment later Libby's door banged shut. A moment after that the Suzuki fired up in the street. It roared as she angrily revved its motor. Then the sound faded as she spun out of Chalcot Square.

Dad levelled a look at me, his arms crossed. We'd arrived at dangerous territory, the two of us, and I could feel that danger, like a live wire snapping in the air between us. But he said evenly, 'Yes. Yes, I suppose I do that, don't I? I ignore unpleasantness in order to get on with living.'

I sidestepped the implication behind his words. I said slowly as if speaking to someone who did not understand English, 'Do you remember Cresswell-White?'

He sighed and moved away from the window. He walked into the music room. I followed him. He sat near my stereo and racks of CDs. I remained by the door.

'What do you want to know?' he asked me.

I accepted the question as acquiescence, saying, 'I've remembered seeing Katja in the garden. It was night. She was with someone, a man. They were—' I shrugged, feeling heat in my face, aware of the juvenility of that heat, which only made it seem to grow stronger. 'They were together. Intimately. I can't

424

remember who he was. I don't think I saw him
clearly.'

'What's the point of this?'

'You know the point. We've been through it all. You
know what she—what Dr Rose—wants me to do.'

'So tell me, is this particular memory supposed to
relate to your music in some way?'

'I'm trying to remember whatever I can. In
whatever order I can. When I can. One memory
seems to trigger another and if I hook enough of them
together, there's a chance I can get to whatever it is
that's causing the problem with my playing.'

'There is no problem with your playing. There is no
playing.'

'Why won't you just answer? Why won't you help
me? Just tell me who Katja—'

'Are you assuming that I know?' he demanded. 'Or
are you really asking if I was the man with Katja
Wolff in the garden? My relationship with Jill certainly
indicates a predilection for younger women, doesn't
it? And if I have that predilection now, why not then?'

'Are you going to answer?'

'Let me assure you that my current predilection is
recent and directed solely at Jill.'

'So you weren't the man in the garden. The man
with Katja Wolff.'

'I was not.'

I studied him. I wondered if he was telling the
truth. I thought of that picture of Katja and my sister,
of the way she smiled at whoever was taking it, of
what that smile might mean.

He said with a tired gesture towards the racks near
his chair, 'I had the opportunity to look through your
CDs while I was waiting for you, Gideon.'

I waited, wary about this line of talk.

'You've quite a collection. How many are there? Three hundred? Four?'

I made no response.

'A number of different interpretations of the same pieces by different artists as well.'

'I'm sure there's a point in this,' I said at last.

'But not a single copy of The Archduke. Why is that, I wonder?'

'I've never been attracted to that particular piece.'

'Then why were you going to play it at Wigmore Hall?'

'Beth suggested it. Sherrill went along. I had no real objection—'

'To playing a piece of music that doesn't attract you?' he demanded. 'What the hell were you thinking? You're the name, Gideon. Not Beth. Not Sherrill. You call the shots when it comes to a concert. They do not.'

'The concert's not what I want to talk about.'

'I understand that. Believe me, I entirely understand. You haven't wanted to talk about the concert from the beginning. You're seeing this damned psychiatrist, in fact, because you don't want to talk about the concert.'

'That's not true.'

'Joanne heard from Philadelphia today. They wanted to know if you'll be able to make your appearance there. The rumours have travelled to America, Gideon. How much longer do you expect to be able to hold the world at bay?'

'I'm trying to get to the root of this in the only way I know.'

'"Trying to get to the root of this,"' he mocked. 'You're doing nothing but opting for cowardice, and I wouldn't have thought that possible. I only thank

426

God your grandfather didn't live to see this moment.'

'Are you thankful for me or for yourself?'

He drew in a slow breath. One of his hands clenched into a fist. The other hand reached to cradle it. 'What exactly are you saying?'

I couldn't go further. We'd reached one of those moments when it seemed to me that irreparable harm could come from carrying on. And what good could have come from carrying on? What point would be served by forcing my father to turn the mirror from me onto his own childhood? onto his adulthood? onto everything he'd done and been and attempted in order to be acceptable to the man who'd adopted him?

Freaks, freaks, freaks, Granddad had shouted at the son who'd created three of them. Because I too am a freak of nature, Dr Rose. At heart I have always been one.

I said, 'Cresswell-White said everyone gave evidence against Katja Wolff. Everyone from the house, he said.'

Dad watched me through narrowed eyes before he made a comment, and I couldn't tell if his hesitation had to do with my words or with my refusal to answer his question. 'That should hardly have come as a surprise to you in a murder trial,' he finally responded.

'He told me I wasn't called.'

'That's right.'

'I've remembered speaking to the police, though. I've remembered you and my mother arguing about my speaking to the police as well. I've remembered that there were a number of questions about the relationship between Sarah-Jane Beckett and James the Lodger.'

'Pitchford.' Dad's voice was heavier now, weary.

427

James Pitchford was his name.'

'Pitchford. Right. Yes. James Pitchford.' I'd been standing all this time, and now I picked up a chair and moved it to where Dad himself was sitting. I set it in front of him. 'At the trial, someone said that you and my mother rowed with Katja in the days preceding . . . preceding what happened to Sonia.'

'She was pregnant, Gideon. She'd become lax in her responsibilities. Your sister would have been a difficult charge for anyone and—'

'Why?'

'Why?' He rubbed his eyebrows as if trying to stimulate his own memory. When he dropped his hand, he looked up at the ceiling instead of at me, but when he lifted his head, I had time enough to see that his eyes had become red-rimmed. I felt a pang, but I did not stop him when he went on. 'Gideon, I've already recited a litany of your sister's ailments for you. Down's Syndrome was only the tip of the iceberg. She was in and out of hospital for the two years that she was alive, and when she was out of hospital, she had to have someone to attend to her constantly. That someone was Katja.'

'Why didn't you hire a professional nurse?'

He laughed, without humour. 'We hadn't the funds.'

'The Government—'

'State support? Unthinkable.'

And something within me jarred loose at that, my grandfather's words, spoken in a roar over the dinner table: 'We do not lower ourselves to ask for charity, God damn it. A real man supports his family and if he can't do so, he shouldn't produce one in the first place. Keep it in your bloody trousers, Dick, if you can't face the consequences of waving it about. You

428

hear me, boy?'

And to this, Dad added, 'And even if we'd tried for support, how far would we have got once the Government sorted out how much we were already spending to employ Raphael and Sarah-Jane? There was belt-tightening that we could have done. We chose not to do it initially.'

'What about the row with Katja?'

'What about it? We learned from Sarah-Jane that Katja had been lax. We talked to the girl, and during the conversation it came out that she was being sick in the morning. It was a short leap to the fact that she was pregnant. She didn't deny it.'

'So you sacked her on the spot.'

'What else were we supposed to do?'

'Who made her pregnant?'

'She wouldn't say. And we did not sack her because she wouldn't say, all right? That was hardly the issue. We sacked her because she couldn't look after your sister properly. And there were other problems, earlier problems that we'd overlooked because she'd seemed fond of Sonia, and we liked that.'

'What sort of problems?'

'Her clothing, which was never appropriate. We'd asked her to wear either a uniform or a simple, plain skirt and blouse. She wouldn't, no matter how often we instructed her to do so. She felt she had to express herself, she said. Then there were her visitors, who came and went at all hours of the day and night despite our asking her to limit their calls.'

'Who were they?'

'I don't recall them. Good God, this was more than twenty years ago.'

'Katie?'

429

'What?'

'Someone called Katie. She was fat. She wore expensive clothes. I remember Katie.'

'Perhaps there was a Katie. I don't know. They came from the convent. They sat in the kitchen and talked and drank coffee and smoked cigarettes. And several times when Katja went out with them on her evening off, she came back inebriated and overslept in the morning. What I'm trying to tell you is that there were problems before the pregnancy issue came up, Gideon. The pregnancy—as well as the illness that accompanied it—was just the final straw.'

'But you and Mother argued with Katja when you gave her the sack.'

He shoved himself to his feet, walked across the room, and stood looking down at my violin case, closed now as it had been for days, the Guarneri hidden away from my sight so that it might cease to taunt me. 'She didn't want to be sacked, obviously. She was several months pregnant, and she wasn't likely to find anyone else to employ her. So she argued with us. She pleaded to be kept on.'

'Then why not get rid of her baby? Even then, there were places . . . clinics . . .'

'That's not the decision she made, Gideon. I can't tell you why.' He squatted and released the clips on the case. He lifted the top. Inside, the Guarneri lay burnished by the light, and the glow of the wood seemed to make an accusation to which I had no simple reply. 'So we argued. The three of us argued. And the next time Sonia was difficult, which happened the following day, Katja . . . took care of the problem.' He lifted the violin from the case and unclipped the bow. He said and his voice was not unkind and the rims of his eyes were redder than

430

before, 'You know the truth now. Will you play for me, son?'

And I wanted to, Dr Rose. But I knew that there was nothing within me, nothing of what had previously driven the music from my soul through my body to my arms and my fingers.

I said, 'I remember people in the house the night that . . . when Sonia . . . I remember voices, footsteps, my mother calling your name.'

'We were panicked. Everyone was panicked. There were paramedics. Firemen. Your grandparents. Pitchford. Raphael.'

'Raphael was there?'

'He was there.'

'Doing what?'

'I don't recall. Perhaps he was on the phone to Juilliard. He'd been trying for months to come up with a way to convince us it was possible for you to attend. He was set on it, more set than you were.'

'So all this happened round the time of Juilliard?'

Dad lowered his arms, which had been offering me the Guarneri. The violin hung from one hand and the bow from the other, orphans of my egregious impotence. He said, 'Where is this taking us, Gideon? God knows I'm trying to cooperate, but you're not giving me anything to measure with.'

'Measure what?'

'How do I know if there's progress? How do you know if there's progress?'

And I could not answer him, Dr Rose. Because the truth is what he fears and what I dread: I can not tell if this is any good, if the direction I'm heading is the direction that will take me back to the life I once knew and held so dear.

I said, 'The night it happened . . . I was in my

431

room. I've remembered that. I've remembered the shouting and the paramedics—the sound of them rather than the sight of them—and I've remembered Sarah-Jane listening at the door, inside my room with me, saying that she wouldn't be leaving after all. But I don't remember her planning to leave before Sonia . . .'

I could see Dad's right hand tighten on the neck of the Guarneri. Clearly, this wasn't the response he'd been looking for when he'd taken the instrument out of its case. He said, 'A violin like this needs to be played. It also needs to be stored properly. Look at this bow, Gideon. Look at the condition of its hairs. And when was the last time you put a bow away without loosening it? Or don't you think about that sort of thing any longer, now that you're concentrating all your efforts on the past?'

I thought of the day that I'd tried to play, the day Libby had heard me, the day that I'd learned for certain what I'd only felt like a premonition before: that the music was gone, and irretrievably so.

Dad said, 'You never used to do this sort of thing. This instrument wasn't just left lying on the floor. It was stored away from the heat and the cold. It wasn't near a radiator, nor was it within six yards of an open window.'

'If Sarah-Jane was planning to leave before everything happened, why didn't she leave?' I asked.

'The strings haven't been cleaned since Wigmore Hall, have they? When was the last time you failed to clean the strings after a concert, Gideon?'

'There wasn't a concert. I didn't play.'

'And haven't played since. Haven't thought to play. Haven't had the nerve to—'

'Tell me about Sarah-Jane Beckett.'

432

'God damn it! Sarah-Jane Beckett is not the issue.'

'Then why won't you answer?'

'Because there's nothing to say. She was sacked. All right? Sarah-Jane Beckett was sacked as well.'

This was last answer I'd been expecting. I'd thought he would tell me she'd become engaged or found a better position or decided to make a change in career. But that she, too, had been sacked along with Katja Wolff . . . I'd not considered that possibility.

Dad said, 'We'd had to cut back. We couldn't keep Sarah-Jane Beckett and Raphael Robson and have a nursemaid for Sonia as well. So we'd given Sarah-Jane two months' notice.'

'When?'

'Shortly before we discovered Katja Wolff was pregnant.'

'So when Sonia died and Katja left . . .

'Yes. There was no need for Sarah-Jane to go as well.' He turned and replaced the Guarneri in its case. His movements were slow; his scoliosis made him seem like a man in his eighties.

I said, 'Then Sarah-Jane herself might have—'

'She was with Pitchford when your sister was drowned, Gideon. She swore to that and Pitchford confirmed it.' Dad straightened from the case and turned back to me. He looked done in. I felt anguish, guilt, and sorrow surge within me to know that I was forcing him to consider matters he'd buried along with my sister. But I had to continue. It seemed that we were making progress for the first time since I'd had the episode at Wigmore Hall—and yes, I use that word deliberately just as you have done, Dr Rose, an episode—and feeling that progress was being made, I could not back away from it.

433

I said, 'Why didn't she talk?'

'I just said she—'

'Katja Wolff not Sarah-Jane Beckett. Cresswell-White said that she spoke to the police once and never spoke to anyone else. About the crime, that is. About Sonia.'

'I can't answer that question. And—' Here he took up the sheet music that I'd left on the stand when I'd thought to play, and he closed it slowly, seeming to put an end to something that neither one of us wanted to name. 'I can't understand why you're dwelling on this at all. Hasn't Katja Wolff damaged our lives enough?'

'It's not Katja Wolff,' I said. 'It's what happened.'

'You know what happened.'

'I don't know everything.'

'You know enough.'

'I know that when I look over my life, when I write about it or talk about it, all I can remember with accuracy is the music: how I came to it, the exercises that Raphael had me engage in, concerts I gave, orchestras I performed with, conductors, concert masters, journalists who interviewed me, recordings I made.'

'That's been your life. That's who you are.'

But not according to Libby. I could hear her shouting at me once again. I could feel her frustration. I could drown in the wretchedness that flooded her heart.

And I am adrift, Dr Rose. I am a man without a country any longer. I once existed in a world I recognised and was comfortable with, a world with definite borders, peopled by citizens all speaking a language I understood. All that is foreign territory to me now, but it is no less foreign than the land I

434

wander in, without a guide or a map, at your instructions.

CHAPTER ELEVEN

Yasmin Edwards had a busy morning, for which she was grateful. She'd received half a dozen referrals from a women's shelter in Lambeth, and the six women in question all turned up at the shop at once. None of them were needing wigs—these usually went to women undergoing chemo or afflicted with alopecia—but all of them wanted makeovers, and Yasmin was happy to accommodate them. She knew what it felt like to be down and out because of a man, and she wasn't surprised when the women first hung back and spoke in hushed tones about their personal appearance and the changes that they hoped Yasmin Edwards could make for them. So Yasmin started out gently, letting them decide for themselves over magazines, coffee, and biscuits.

'You make me look like this one?' was the question that broke the ice among them. One of the women—who wouldn't see sixty again and who must have tipped the scales at nearly twenty stone—had chosen a picture of a nubile black model with sumptuous breasts and pouting lips.

'You look like that when we done, girl, I'm taking up *residence* in this damn shop,' one of the others said. Soft giggles among them turned to hearty laughter, and everything was easy after that.

Oddly, it was the scent of the cleaning fluid that Yasmin was using on the worktops after the women left that took her back abruptly to the morning. For a moment, she wondered why until she recalled that she'd been cleaning up the few wig hairs that Daniel had missed after his washing chore on the previous night when Katja came into the bathroom to clean her teeth.

'You going in to work today?' Yasmin asked her companion. Daniel had already left for school, so they were free to talk openly for the first time. Or at least they were free to make the attempt.

'Of course,' Katja said. 'Why would I not?'

She still made her w's into v's. Sometimes it seemed to Yasmin that twenty years away from her native language would have been enough to alter even Katja's most deeply rooted habits, but still they remained. There had been a time when Yasmin had found her companion's way of speaking English appealing, but she did not find it so now. She couldn't determine when the charm had diminished for her. Recently, she thought. But she couldn't afford to put an exact date on the change in her feelings.

'He said that you'd missed. Four times in twelve weeks is what he said.' In the mirror above the basin, Katja's blue eyes fixed on Yasmin's. 'You believe that, Yas? He's a copper and you and I are . . . You know what we are to him: fluff and dagger from inside, back in the street. I saw how he looked at us if you didn't. So why should a man like that tell us what really is when lies will serve to put us apart from each other?'

Yasmin couldn't deny that there was some truth in what Katja was saying. In her experience, police couldn't be trusted with anything. Indeed, no one in the whole legal system could be trusted if it came

436

down to it. In the legal system, plods settled on a story and bent the facts to fit it, presenting those facts to magistrates in such a way that bail was deemed foolhardy and a trial in the Old Bailey followed by a lengthy prison sentence was the only cure for what got called a social ill. Like she had been a disease and Roger Edwards had been what she'd infected instead of what each of them had really been: she nineteen and the longtime plaything of stepfathers, stepbrothers, and the friends of both and he a yellow-haired Aussie who'd chased his girlfriend to London where he'd been dumped, with a book of poems tucked under his arm. That was the same book of poems that he'd left at the till at Sainsbury's where she rang up his groceries once a week, a book of poems that made her think he was something better than what she was used to.

And he was, Roger Edwards. He was different and better in so many ways. Just not in the ways that counted.

It was never simple: what brought a man and a woman together. Oh, it looked that way on the surface—hard cock and hot cunt—but it never was. There was no way to explain it: her history and Roger's, her fears and his mighty desperation, their mutual needs and their unspoken beliefs about what each partner should be to the other. There was only what happened. And what happened was a tedious series of accusations that were the children born of his addictions and an even more tedious series of denials that were never enough, not without proof which was in itself a spur to more accusations. And these were flung with a building paranoia that was itself fuelled by the drugs and the

437

drink until she wanted him out of her life, out of their child's life, and out of her flat no matter that their son would go fatherless like so many boys within their community, fatherless despite the promise she'd made to herself that Daniel would not grow up trapped in a web of women.

Roger wouldn't go, though. He fought against going. He really fought. He fought the way a man fights another man, in silence and with strength and closed fists. But she was the one with the weapon, and she used it.

Five years she'd served. She'd been arrested and charged. Because she was six feet tall, she was more than five inches taller than her husband, so gentlemen and ladies of the jury why had this woman felt it was necessary to use a *knife* to stop him when he allegedly became abusive? He'd been what was called under the influence of a foreign substance so most of his punches had gone wide or short or merely grazed her instead of connecting with her dusky flesh, instead of bruising or better yet breaking bones. Yet she used a knife on this unfortunate man, and she managed to connect that knife with his body no less than eight times.

More blood would have been useful in the subsequent investigation by the local police. Her blood, that is, instead of Roger's. As it was, all she had was the story itself in which an attractive bloke on the rebound catches the eye of a girl who's in hiding from the world. He coaxes her out from beneath her rock; she promises him a cool draught of forget. And if he used a little and he drank a lot, what worry was there in that? That was, to her, familiar behaviour. It was the descent into squalor and the demand for her to earn money at night in doorways, in parked cars, or leaning against a tree on the common with her legs spread wide that she hadn't been prepared to accept from Roger Edwards.

'Get out, get *out!*' she'd screamed at him. And it was her screaming and those words that she screamed that the neighbours later remembered.

'Just tell us the story, Mrs Edwards,' the coppers had said to her over her husband's bloodied and very dead body. 'All you need to do is to tell us the story and we'll get all this sorted out straightaway.'

Five years in prison had been the consequence of her telling her story to the police. Five years in prison had been their way of getting things sorted out straightaway. She'd lost those years with her son, she'd come out with nothing, and she'd spent the next five years working, planning, begging and borrowing, making it up to them both. So Katja was right, and Yasmin knew it. Only a fool trusted anything a copper had to say.

But there was more than just the detectives's words about Katja's absences—from work, from the flat, from anywhere at all—that she had to contend with. There was also the car. And no matter whether the black man could be trusted, the car itself could not lie to her.

Yasmin said, 'Headlamp on the car got itself broke, Katja. He looked that over, the plod, last night. He asked how it broke.'

'Are you asking me the same?'

'S'pose.' Vigorously, Yasmin wiped the old bathtub, as if doing so and in such a manner could rub away the spots where the porcelain had worn through to the metal lining beneath it. 'I didn't hit anything that I recall. You?'

439

'Why did he want to know? What business is it of his how a headlamp was broken?' Katja had finished her teeth and she leaned forward into the mirror, inspecting her face as she always did, as Yasmin herself had done for months upon her final release from prison, checking to see that she was really there, in this particular room, guard-less, wall-less, lock-and-key-less, with what was left of her life in front of her and trying not to be completely terrified of that empty, unstructured stretch of years.

Katja washed her face and patted it dry. She turned from the basin and leaned against it, watching Yasmin finish with the tub. When the taps were turned off Katja spoke again. 'What is he after us for, Yas?'

'You,' Yasmin said. 'He's not after me. It's you. How'd that headlamp get busted?'

'I didn't know it was broken,' Katja said. 'I haven't looked . . . Yas, how often do you look at the front of the car? Did you know it was broken before he pointed it out to you? No? It could have been broken for weeks. How badly is it broken? Do the lights still work? Someone probably reversed into it in the car park. Or in the street.'

True, Yasmin thought. But wasn't there something too quick, too anxious to be believed about Katja's words. And why didn't she ask which headlamp? Wouldn't it be logical for her to want to know which of the headlamps it was?

Katja added, 'It could have happened when you were driving it since neither one of us knew it was broken.'

'Yeah,' Yasmin admitted. 'I see that.'

'Then—'

'He wanted to know where you were. He went to where you work and he asked about you.'

'So he says. But if he really talked to them, and if they really told him I'd missed four days, why did he give that information only to you and not to me as well? I was standing there, right in the room with the two of you. Why did he not ask me for my excuse? Think about that. You know what it means: he wants to tear us apart because it'll serve his purposes. And if he manages to do it—to tear us apart—he won't waste much effort putting us back together. Even if he gets what he wants . . . whatever it is.'

'He's investigating something,' Yasmin said. 'Or someone. So . . .' She took a breath that was deep, that hurt. ''S there something you're not telling me, Katja? Something you hiding from me?'

'This is just how it works,' Katja said. 'This is just exactly how he wants it to work.'

'But you're not answering me, are you?'

'Because I've nothing to say. Because I have nothing to hide from you or from anyone else.'

Her eyes held Yasmin's. Her voice was firm. And they both made promises, those eyes and that voice. They also reminded Yasmin of the history between them, the solace that had been offered by one and grasped by the other, and what had finally grown from that solace to sustain them both. But nothing from the heart was indestructible. Experience had taught Yasmin Edwards that. She said, 'Katja, you'd say if . . .'

'If what?'

'If . . .'

Katja knelt on the floor next to the bathtub, next to Yasmin. Gently, she ran her forgers round the

441

curve of Yasmin's ear. 'You waited five years for me to get out,' she said. 'There is no if, Yas.'

They kissed long and tenderly and Yasmin didn't think as she'd thought at first How bloody mad, I'm kissing a woman . . . she's touching me . . . I'm *letting* her touch me . . . Her mouth is here, it's there, it's tasting me where I want to be tasted . . . this is a woman and what she's doing is yes, yes, I want this, yes. All she thought was what it felt like to be with her and what it felt like to be safe and sure.

Now in the wig shop, she packed the make-up back into its case and threw into the rubbish the kitchen towels with which she'd wiped the worktop at which the women had sat, one by one, and allowed her to make them beautiful. She smiled at the pictures she had of them in her mind, all of them laughing, giggling like school girls, given for the morning a chance to be something more than what they'd chosen for themselves. Yasmin Edwards enjoyed her work. When she considered it, she had to shake her head in wonder that a stretch in prison had directed her not only to useful employment but also to a companion and to a life that she loved. She knew that this sort of conclusion to the kind of troubles she'd had was rare.

Behind her, the shop door opened. That would be Mrs Newland's oldest daughter Akisha, coming right on time to pick up Mum's freshly washed wig.

Yasmin turned to the door, offering a smile of welcome.

'Can I have a word?' the black constable said.

*   *   *

Major Ted Wiley was the last person in Henley-on-Thames to whom Lynley and Havers showed the photograph of Katja Wolff. They hadn't planned it that way. In the normal course of events they would have shown him the picture first since, at least from his own account of it as Eugenie Davies' closest companion and neighbour across the street from Doll Cottage, he was the person most likely to have seen Katja Wolff in Henley had the woman come calling. But upon their arrival in Friday Street, they'd found Wiley's Books closed, with a be-right-back sign stating the time of the major's return. So they offered the photograph round every other establishment on Friday Street, having no luck anywhere.

Havers wasn't surprised. 'This is the wrong tree, Inspector,' she informed Lynley.

'It's an institutional picture,' he replied, 'as bad as a passport. It might not even resemble her. Let's try at the Sixty Plus Club before we count her out. If her other visitor waylaid her there, what's to say Katja Wolff didn't do likewise?'

The Sixty Plus Club was reasonably populated even at that hour of the day. Most of the members present were engaged in what looked like a bridge tournament although an intense group of four women were also playing a serious game of Monopoly, with dozens of red hotels and green houses littering the board. Additionally in a narrow room that appeared to be a kitchen three men and two women sat round a table, manila folders open in front of them. The red head of Georgia Ramsbottom bobbed among this latter group, and the sound of her voice rose higher than even the

443

singing of Fred Astaire who was dancing cheek to cheek—or at least claiming to do so—with Ginger Rogers on a television screen in an alcove set up with comfortable armchairs.

'Recruiting internally is *much* more reasonable,' Georgia Ramsbottom was saying. 'We ought to at least try it, Patrick. If someone amongst us wishes to direct the club now that Eugenie's gone—'

One of the women interrupted her, but at a reduced volume.

She countered with, 'I find that highly offensive, Margery. *Someone* has to take the interests of the club to heart. I suggest we set aside our grief and deal with this now. If not today then certainly before more messages stack up to be answered—' Here she gestured with a small fan of Post-Its on which the aforementioned messages were ostensibly written— 'and more bills go asking to be paid.'

There was a rumble of what might have been either assent or disapproval, something that wasn't fully clarified because at that moment, Georgia Ramsbottom descried Lynley and Havers. She excused herself from the table and came to them. The Sixty Plus Club's Executive Committee were in a meeting, she announced, every bit as if the agenda that the committee were following were of national significance. The Sixty Plus Club could not long remain rudderless and directorless, although explaining that a 'suitable period of mourning' for Eugenie Davies did not necessarily obviate the process of replacing her was proving to be *quite* a challenge, Georgia revealed.

'I doubt this will take very long,' Lynley told her. 'We'll just need a few moments alone. With everyone. One at a time. If you'd be so good as to organise that . . .'

'Inspector,' Georgia said and she managed just the appropriate amount of effrontery in her words, 'the members of Henley's Sixty Plus Club are very private, decent, upstanding people. If you've come here thinking that one of them was involved in Eugenie's death—'

'I come here thinking nothing in particular,' Lynley broke in pleasantly, but he didn't miss the third person pronoun that Georgia had used to differentiate between herself and the rest of the club's members. 'So perhaps we can start with you, Mrs Ramsbottom. In Mrs Davies' office . . . ?'

All members' eyes followed them as Georgia stiffly led the way to the office door. It was open today, and Lynley noted as they entered that all items remotely related to Eugenie Davies had already been packed away in a cardboard box that sat forlornly at one side of her desk. He wondered idly what the fearsome Mrs Ramsbottom considered a suitable period of mourning for the club's director. She certainly wasn't letting any grass grow when it came to sweeping the club clean of her.

He wasted no time in small talk once Havers had shut the door and placed herself in front of it, notebook in hand. He took the seat behind the desk, gestured Georgia Ramsbottom into the chair in front of the desk, and brought out the photograph of Katja Wolff. Had Mrs Ramsbottom seen this woman in the vicinity of the Sixty Plus Club or anywhere else in Henley, for that matter, in the weeks preceding Mrs Davies' death?

The production of the photograph seemed to

prompt Georgia to say, 'The killer . . . ?' in the sort of reverential tone that would have done service in an Agatha Christie novel. She was suddenly all helpfulness, perhaps altered by the realisation that the police were not seeking the killer among the over-sixty crowd. She hastened to add, 'I do know it was deliberate, Inspector, and not just an arbitrary hit-and-run. Dear Teddy told me when I rang him last evening.'

Across the room, Havers mouthed *Dear Teddy.* Thwarted love among the ruins, her expression implied. She did some furious scribbling in her notebook. Georgia heard the sound of her pencil *scritching* across the paper. She glanced over her shoulder.

Lynley said, 'If you'd have a look at the photograph, Mrs Ramsbottom . . .'

Georgia did so. She studied the photo. She held it close to her face. She held it at arm's length. She tilted her head. But no, she said at last, she'd never seen the woman in the picture. Not round Henley-on-Thames, at least.

'Somewhere else?' Lynley asked.

No, no. She didn't mean to imply *that.* Of course, she might have seen her in London—a stranger in the street, perhaps?—when she went up to visit her darling grandchildren. But if she had done, she couldn't remember.

'Thank you,' Lynley said, and he prepared to dismiss her.

But he found that Georgia wasn't inclined to be so easily disposed of. She crossed her legs, ran a hand along one of the pleats in her skirt, reached down to smooth her tights, and said, 'You'll want to talk to Teddy, of course, won't you, Inspector?' It sounded more like a suggestion than a question. 'He lives near Eugenie, dear Teddy does—but I expect you already know that, don't you?—and if this woman was hanging about or perhaps paying calls on her, he might well know. Indeed, Eugenie might have told him herself because they were great friends, weren't they, the two of them. So she might have confided in him should this woman have . . .' Then Georgia hesitated, a heavily ringed finger tapping against her cheek. 'But no. Nooo. Perhaps not, after all.'

Lynley sighed inwardly. He wasn't about to engage in the information game with the woman. If she wanted to enjoy the power of playing out what she knew like a fishing line, she was going to have to find someone else to swim in her river. He bluffed her with, 'Thank you, Mrs Ramsbottom,' and nodded at Havers to usher her from the room.

Georgia showed her hand. 'All right. I spoke to dear Teddy,' she confided. 'As I said earlier, I phoned him last night. After all, one does want to offer condolences when someone loses a loved one, even in situations in which the scales of devotion aren't as evenly balanced as one would hope to see in a dear friend's love life.'

'The dear friend being Major Wiley,' Havers clarified with some impatience.

Georgia treated her to another imperious glance. She said to Lynley, 'Inspector, I do feel you might benefit from knowing . . . not that I wish to speak ill of the dead . . . But I don't think we can call it speaking ill, can we, if what I say is simply a fact?'

'What are you getting at, Mrs Ramsbottom?'

'It's just that I'm wondering if I should I tell you

447

something if it may not actually be germane to your case.' She waited for some sort of reply or reassurance. When Lynley said nothing, she was forced to continue. 'But then again, it *may* be germane. It probably is. And if I hold back . . . It's poor dear Teddy I'm thinking of, you see. The thought of something becoming public knowledge, something that might hurt him . . . That's difficult for me to bear.'

Lynley thought that unlikely. He said, 'Mrs Ramsbottom, if you have information about Mrs Davies that might lead to her killer, it's in your best interests to tell us directly.'

It's in our interests as well, Havers' expression said. She looked as if she'd have liked to throttle the maddening woman.

'Otherwise,' Lynley added, 'we have work to do. Constable, if you'll assist Mrs Ramsbottom in organising the others for interviews . . . ?'

'It's about Eugenie, then,' Georgia said hastily. 'I hate to say it. But I will. It's this: She didn't reciprocate, not completely.'

'Reciprocate what?'

'Teddy's feelings. She didn't share the strength of his feelings for her, and he didn't know that.'

'But you did,' Havers said from the door.

'I'm not blind,' Georgia said, over her shoulder to Havers. And then to Lynley, 'I'm also not a fool. There was someone else, and Teddy didn't know. He still doesn't know, poor man.'

'Someone else?'

'Some people might argue that there was something permanently on Eugenie's mind and that's what kept her from getting close to Teddy. But I say it was some*one* on her mind and she hadn't yet got round to dropping the bomb on the poor man.'

'You saw her with someone?' Lynley asked.

'I didn't need to see her with someone,' Georgia said. 'I saw what she did when she was here: the phone calls that she took behind closed doors, the days when she left at half past eleven and never returned. And she drove her car to the club on those days, Inspector, though the rest of the time she walked here from Friday Street. And she wasn't doing her volunteer work at the nursing home on those days she drove, because she volunteered at Quiet Pines on Mondays and Wednesdays.'

'And the days she left at half past eleven?'

'Thursday or Friday. Always. Once a month. Sometimes twice. What does that suggest to you, Inspector? It suggests an assignation to me.'

It could well suggest anything, Lynley thought, from a doctor's appointment to a session with the hairdresser. But while what Georgia Ramsbottom was telling them was coloured by her obvious dislike of Eugenie Davies, Lynley could not ignore the fact that her information matched up with what they'd seen in the dead woman's diary.

After thanking her for her cooperation—no matter how much he'd had to wrest it from her—Lynley sent the woman back to her committee and had Havers assist her in organising the rest of the club members present for individual examinations of the photograph of Katja Wolff. He could tell that everyone wanted to be helpful as he spoke to each of them, but no one was able to attest to having ever seen the pictured woman in the environs of the club.

They headed back to Friday Street, where

449

Lynley had left his car in front of Eugenie Davies' tiny house. As they walked, Havers said, 'Satisfied, Inspector?'

'About what?'

'The Wolff angle. Are you satisfied now?'

'Not entirely.'

'But you can't still be considering her for the killer. Not after that.' This, with a cock of her thumb back in the direction of the Sixty Plus Club. 'If Katja Wolff ran over Eugenie Davies, she would have had to know where she was going that night in the first place, right? Or she would have had to follow her into London from here. Do you agree?'

'That seems obvious.'

'So in either case, she would have had to establish some kind of contact with her once she got out of prison. Now, we may get some joy from those telephone records, and we may find out that Eugenie Davies and Katja Wolff were spending their evenings nattering like schoolgirls on the phone for the last twelve weeks for reasons that're completely obscure. But if we don't get something from those BT records, then what we're left with is someone following her up to town from here. And we both know which someone would have had an easy time of that, don't we?' She indicated the door of the book shop where the be-right-back sign had been removed.

Lynley said, 'Let's see what Major Wiley has to say about things,' and he opened the door.

They found Ted Wiley unpacking a box of new books and arranging them on a table top that bore a hand lettered sign reading *new releases*. He wasn't alone in the shop. At the far end a woman in a paisley headscarf sat in a comfortable armchair, happily sipping from a Thermos top with a book open upon her knees.

'Saw your motor when I got back,' Wiley said in reference to the Bentley as he lifted three books from the box. He dusted each with a cloth before setting it on the table. 'What've you come up with, then?'

The man appeared to have an interesting capacity to direct, order, and demand, Lynley thought. He seemed to assume that the London detectives had come to Henley-on-Thames with the intention of reporting to him. He said, 'It's too early in the investigation to reach a conclusion about anything, Major Wiley.'

'What I know is this,' Wiley said. 'The longer things drag on, the less likely it is that you'll catch the bastard. You must have leads. Suspicions. Something.'

Lynley offered the photograph of Katja Wolff. 'Have you seen this woman? In the neighbourhood, perhaps. Or somewhere else round town.'

Wiley fumbled in the breast pocket of his jacket and brought out a pair of heavy looking horn-rimmed spectacles, which he flipped open with one hand and fixed on his large and florid nose. He squinted at Katja Wolff's likeness for a good fifteen seconds before saying, 'Who is she?'

'She's called Katja Wolff. She's the woman who drowned Eugenie Davies' daughter. Do you recognise her?'

Wiley examined the picture again and it was apparent from his expression that he very much *wanted* to recognise her, possibly to put an end to the anxiety of not knowing who had struck down and killed the woman he loved, possibly for

451

another reason altogether. But ultimately, he shook his head and thrust the picture back at Lynley. 'What about that bloke?' he asked. 'The Audi. He was furious, he was. Bent on hurting someone. I could feel it. And the way he drove off . . . He was just the sort of bastard who blows. Doesn't get what he wants so he makes a statement and the statement is usually a body. Or bodies. You know what I mean. Hungerford. Dunblane.'

'We haven't ruled him out,' Lynley said. 'Constables back in town are working through a list of Audis from Brighton. We should know something at that end soon.'

Wiley grunted and removed his glasses. He shoved them into his jacket pocket.

Lynley said, 'You mentioned that Mrs Davies wanted to talk to you, that she said specifically that she had something to tell you. Have you any idea what that was, Major Wiley?'

'None.' Wiley reached for more books. He checked the dust jackets of these, going so far as to open each one and to run his fingers along the inner flap as if he were looking for imperfections.

As he did so, Lynley reflected upon the fact that a man generally knows when the woman he loves does not reciprocate the emotion. A man also knows—he can't avoid knowing—when the passion within a woman he loves begins to wither. Sometimes he lies to himself about the fact, denying it till the moment comes when he can no longer avoid it or escape it altogether. But he always knows even subconsciously when things aren't right. Openly admitting this is a form of torture, though. And some men can't cope with such torture, so they choose another route to deal

452

with the matter.

Lynley said, 'Major Wiley, you heard the messages on Mrs Davies' answer machine yesterday. You heard the men's voices, so it can't be a surprise to you when I ask if Mrs Davies might have been involved elsewhere besides with you, if that's what she might have wanted to tell you.'

'I've thought about it,' Wiley said quietly. 'Nothing else has been in my mind since . . . Damn. God *damn*.' He shook his head and shoved his hand into his trouser pocket. He brought out a handkerchief and honked into it loudly enough to disturb the reading of the woman in the armchair. She looked round, saw Lynley and Havers, and said, 'Major Wiley? Is everything all right?'

He nodded, raised a hand as if to underscore his assent, and turned his shoulder so she couldn't see his face. She seemed to feel this was answer enough, for she went back to her reading as Wiley said to Lynley, 'I feel a perfect fool.'

Lynley waited for more. Havers tapped her pencil against her notebook and frowned.

Wiley gathered himself together and told them the apparent worst there was for him to tell: about the nights he watched Eugenie Davies' cottage from his upstairs window and about one night in particular when his surveillance had finally been rewarded. 'One a.m.,' he said. 'It was that bloke with the Audi. And the way she touched him . . . Yes. Yes. I loved her and she was involved with someone else. So was that what she wanted to tell me, Inspector? I don't know. I didn't want to know then, and I don't want to know now. What's the point?'

'The point is finding her killer,' Havers said.

'You think it's me?'

'What sort of car do you drive?'

'A Mercedes. It's right there, in front of the shop.'

Havers looked to Lynley for direction, and he nodded. She went outside and the two men watched her giving the car's front end a thorough inspection. It was black, but the colour was inconsequential if there was no damage to report.

'I wouldn't have hurt her,' Wiley said quietly. 'I loved her. I trust you lot understand what that means.'

And what it implies, Lynley thought. But he didn't speak, merely waiting till Havers had completed her inspection and returned to them. It's clean, her eyes told them. Lynley could see she was disappointed.

Wiley read the message. He allowed himself the pleasure of saying, 'I hope that satisfies. Or do you want me on the rack as well?'

'I expect you want us to do our jobs,' Havers pointed out.

Wiley said, 'Then do them. There's a photo gone missing from Eugenie's house.'

'What sort of photo?' Lynley said.

'The only one of the little girl alone.'

'Why didn't you tell us this yesterday?'

'Didn't realise it. Not till this morning. She had them lined up on the kitchen table. Three rows of four. But she had thirteen pictures of those kids in the house—twelve of both of them and one of the girl by herself—and unless she'd taken that one back upstairs, it's gone missing.'

Lynley looked at Havers. She shook her head. There had been no picture in any of the three

454

rooms she'd looked through on the first floor of Doll Cottage.

'When was the last time you saw that photo?' Lynley asked.

'Whenever I was there, I saw all of them. Not like they were yesterday—in the kitchen—but spread round. In the sitting room. And upstairs. On the landing. In her sewing room.'

'P'rhaps she'd taken that one to have a new frame,' Havers said. 'Or thrown it away.'

'She wouldn't have done,' Wiley said, aghast.

'Or given it away or lent it somewhere.'

'A picture of her daughter? Who'd she give it to, then?'

It was a question, Lynley knew, that had to be answered.

*   *   *

Once again on the pavement in Friday Street, Havers offered another possibility. 'She could have posted it somewhere. To the husband, d'you think? Did he have pictures of the girl in his flat when you spoke to him, Inspector?'

'None that I saw. There were only snapshots of Gideon.'

'There you go, then. They'd been speaking, hadn't they? About Gideon's stage fright? Why not about the little girl as well? So he asked Eugenie for a picture of her, and she sent it along. That's easy enough to find out, isn't it?'

'But it's odd that he had no pictures of the daughter already, Havers.'

'Human nature's odd,' Havers said. 'This long on the force, I'd think you'd know that.'

455

Lynley couldn't argue. He said, 'Let's have another look at her house to make sure the photo's not there.'

It was a matter of only a few minutes to double check and to prove Major Wiley right. The twelve photographs in the kitchen were all that were left in the house.

Lynley and Havers were standing in the sitting room mulling this over when Lynley's mobile began to ring. It was Eric Leach phoning from the Hampstead incident room.

'We've got a match,' he told Lynley without preamble. He sounded pleased. 'We've got the Brighton Audi and the CellNet customer rolled into one pretty package.'

'Ian Staines?' Lynley said, recalling the name connected to the CellNet number. 'Her brother?'

'The same.' Leach recited the address and Lynley wrote it down on the back of one of his business cards. 'Get on to him,' Leach said. 'What've you got on Wolff?'

'Nothing.' Lynley reported briefly on their conversations with the Sixty Plus Club's members as well as with Major Wiley, and he went on to tell Leach of the missing photograph.

The DCI offered another interpretation. 'She could have brought it with her to London.'

'To show someone?'

'That takes us back to Pitchley.'

'But why would she want to show him the photo? Or give it to him?'

'There's more to that story than we're hearing, I say,' Leach pointed out. 'Dig up a picture of the Davies woman. There's got to be a snapshot somewhere in her house. Or Wiley'll have one.

Take it to the Valley of Kings and the Comfort Inn. There's a chance that someone remembers her there.'

'With Pitchley?'

'He likes them older, doesn't he?'

*   *   *

When the police departed, Ted Wiley left Mrs Dilday watching over the shop. It had been a slow morning and was shaping up to be a slow afternoon, so he felt no compunction about putting his engrossed customer in charge of things. It was about time that she did something to earn the privilege of reading every bestseller without ever making a purchase other than a greeting card, so he rousted her from her favourite armchair and gave her instructions on working the till. Then he went upstairs to his flat.

There, he found PB snoozing in a patch of weak sunlight. He stepped over the retriever and put himself at Connie's old davenport beneath whose sloping surface he'd stowed the brochures from the forthcoming opera seasons in Vienna, Santa Fe, and Sydney. It had been his hope that one of those seasons would serve as a backdrop to his broadened relationship with Eugenie. They would travel to Austria, America, or Australia and enjoy Rossini, Verdi, or Mozart as they enriched the joy they took in each other's company and deepened the nature of their love. They'd moved slowly towards this destination for three long and careful years together, building a structure comprising tenderness, devotion, affection, and support. They'd told each other that everything else that went with a man and a woman linking themselves together—most particularly sex—would find its way into the equation with time.

It had been a relief for Ted after Connie's death, not to mention after the esurient pursuing by other women to which he'd been exposed, to find himself in the company of a woman who wanted to build a structure first before taking up residence within it. But now after the police had left him, Ted finally forced himself to acknowledge the reality: that Eugenie's hesitation, her gentle and always kind, 'I'm not ready yet, Ted,' were in actuality evidence that she was not ready for *him*. For what else could it mean that a man had phoned and left a message rife with desperation on her answer machine? that a man had left her house at one in the morning? that a man had accosted her in the car park of the Sixty Plus Club and pleaded with her the way a man pleads when everything—and most particularly his heart—is at stake? There was only one answer to these questions, and Ted knew what that answer was.

He'd been such a fool. Instead of being grateful for the blessed respite from sexual performance that Eugenie's reserve had promised him, he should have suspected at once that she was involved elsewhere. But he hadn't because it had been such a relief after Georgia Ramsbottom's carnal demands.

She'd phoned last night. Her, 'Teddy, I'm so sorry. I spoke to the police today and they said that Eugenie . . . Dearest Teddy, is there *anything* I can do?' had barely disguised the enthusiasm with which she'd made the call in the first place. 'I'm coming over straight away,' she'd said. 'No ifs or buts, dear. You're not to be left alone with this.'

He'd not had a chance to protest and he'd not had the courage to decamp prior to her arrival. She'd swept in barely ten minutes later, bearing a baking dish in which she'd made him her speciality, which was shepherd's pie. She whipped off the aluminium foil that covered it, and he saw that the pie was depressingly perfect, with ornate little ridges like waves marking the mashed potatoes. She said, flashing a smile at him, 'It's warmish, but if we pop it into the microwave, it'll be fine. You must eat, Teddy, and I know that you haven't. Have you?' She hadn't waited for an answer. She'd marched to the microwave and shut its door smartly upon the shepherd's pie, whereupon she moved briskly round the kitchen, bringing forth plates and cutlery from cupboards and drawers with the unspoken authority of a woman familiar with a man's domicile.

She said, 'You're devastated. I can see it in your face. I am so sorry. I know what friends you two were. And to lose such a friend as Eugenie . . . You must let yourself feel the sorrow, Teddy.'

Friend, he thought. Not lover. Not wife. Not companion. Not partner. Friend and everything that friend suggested.

He hated Georgia Ramsbottom in that moment. He hated her not only for barging into his solitude like a ship breaking ocean ice but also for the acuity of her perception. She said without saying what he had not allowed himself even to think: His imagination and his longing had created the bond he'd believed he'd had with Eugenie.

Women who were interested in a man showed their interest. They showed it soon, and they

459

showed it unabashedly. They could do no less at an age and in a society in which they so vastly outnumbered available males. He had the proof of this in Georgia herself and in the women who had preceded Georgia in his widowed years. They had their knickers off before a man could reassuringly say to them, 'I'm no Jack the lad.' And if they kept their knickers on, it was only because their hands were busy in his crotch instead. But Eugenie had done none of that, had she? Demure Eugenie. Docile Eugenie. Damned Eugenie.

He'd felt such a swelling of anger that he couldn't reply at first to Georgia's comments. He wanted to pound his fist into something hard. He wanted to break it.

Georgia took his silence for stoicism, the stiff upper lip that was the proud achievement of every upstanding British male. She said, 'I know, I know. And it's ghastly, isn't it? The older we get, the more we have to bear witness to our friends' passing. But what I've discovered is the importance of nurturing the precious friendships that are left to us. So you mustn't cut yourself off from those of us who care deeply about you, Teddy. We won't have that.'

She'd reached across the table and placed on his arm her hand with its encrustation of rings. He'd thought fleetingly of Eugenie's hands and the contrast they made to this red-tipped snatcher. Her hands had been ringless, with the nails clipped short and slivers of moon showing at their bases.

'Don't turn away, Teddy,' Georgia had said and her hand had tightened upon him. 'From any of us. We're here to help you through this. We care for you. Truly and deeply. You'll see.'

Her own brief unhappy past with Ted might not have existed. His failure and the contempt she'd felt being a witness to his failure were banished to a foreign land. The intervening manless years she'd lived through had obviously instructed her in what was important and what was not. She was a changed woman, as he would see once she wormed her way into his life again.

Ted read it all in her gesture and in her tender smile. Bile rose in his throat, and his body burned. He needed air.

He rose abruptly. He said, 'That old dog,' and called out roughly, 'PB? Where've you taken yourself off to? Come.' And to Georgia, 'Sorry. I was about to take the dog for her final nightly when you phoned.'

He'd made his escape that way, without inviting Georgia to accompany him and giving her no chance to make the suggestion herself. He called out once again, 'PB? Come, girl. Time for a walk,' and he was gone before Georgia had the chance to regroup. He knew that she'd assume from his departure that she'd moved too quickly. He also knew that she wouldn't assume anything else. And that was important, Ted realised suddenly. That was crucial: to limit the woman's knowledge about him.

He'd walked rapidly, feeling it all again. Stupid, he told himself, stupid and blind. Hanging about like a schoolboy hoping for a go with the local tart, not seeing her as a tart at all because he was too young, too inexperienced, too eager, too . . . too limp. That's what it was, all right. Too limp.

He'd charged towards the river, dragging the poor dog behind him. He needed to put distance

461

between himself and Georgia, and he wanted to be away from the flat long enough to ensure her departure in his absence. Even Georgia Ramsbottom would not throw all her chances away by playing her trump cards the first evening. She would leave his flat; she would retire for a few days. Then, when she thought that he'd recovered from their initial skirmish, she would be back, offering a renewal of her sympathetic attention. Ted was certain he could depend upon that.

At the corner of Friday Street and the river, he'd turned left. He strode on the town side of the Thames. The lights along the street pooled buttermilk onto the pavement intermittently and the wind blew a heavy mist in sharp waves that felt as if they rose from the river itself. Ted turned up the collar of his waxed jacket and said, 'Come on, girl,' to the dog who was looking longingly at a sapling planted nearby, possibly with the hope of snoozing a while underneath it. 'PB. *Come.*' A jerk on the choke chain did it, as usual. They hurried on.

They were in the churchyard before Ted really thought about it. They were in the churchyard before he recalled the vision he'd had there on the night Eugenie died. PB made for the grass like a horse to its stall before Ted actually knew she was doing so. She squatted wearily and let forth her stream before he had the chance to urge her somewhere else.

Without intending, without thinking, without even considering what the action implied, Ted felt his eyes drift from the dog to the almshouses at the far end of the path. He'd just take a quick glance that way, he told himself, in order to see that the

462

woman who lived in the third house from the right had her curtains closed. If she hadn't and if a light was burning, he'd do her a service and let her know that any stranger passing by could look right in and . . . well, assess her valuables for a burglary.

The light was on. Time to do his good deed for the day. Ted pulled PB away from the tipped gravestone round which she was sniffing and urged her as quickly as he could along the path. It was essential that he get to the almshouse before the woman within it did anything that could embarrass them both. Because if she began to undress as she had the other night, he could hardly knock on her door, caution her about her indiscretion, and thereby admit to having watched her, could he?

'Hurry, PB,' he said to the dog. 'Come along.'

He was just fifteen seconds too late. Five yards from the almshouse and she had begun. And she was quick about it, so very quick that before he had time to avert his eyes, she'd whisked her jersey off, shaken back her hair, and removed her brassiere. She bent to something—was it her shoes? her stockings? her trousers? what?—and her breasts hung heavily downward.

Ted swallowed. He thought two words—*Dear God*—and he felt the first throb of his body's answer to the sight before him. He'd watched her once, he'd stood here once, he'd traced with his eyes those sumptuous full curves. But he couldn't—*couldn't*—allow himself the guilty pleasure of doing so again. She had to be told. She had to be warned. She had to . . . had to know? he wondered. What woman didn't know? What woman had never learned about caution and nighttime windows? What woman threw her

463

clothes off at night in a room fully lit without curtains or blinds without knowing that someone on the other side of those few millimeters of glass was probably watching, longing, fantasising, hardening . . . She knew, Ted realised. She *knew*.

So he'd watched the unknown woman in that almshouse bedroom a second night. He'd stayed longer this time, mesmerised by the sight of her smoothing lotion on her neck and her arms. He heard himself moan like a pre-adolescent having his first glimpse at *Playboy* when she used that same lotion on her succulent breasts.

There in the churchyard, he'd had a surreptitious wank. Beneath his waxed jacket as the rain began to fall, he worked his cock like a man pumping spray onto garden insects. He got about as much satisfaction from the resulting orgasm as one would get from using a garden sprayer and in the aftermath of his release what he felt wasn't exultation. It was bitter shame.

He felt it again now in his sitting room, wave after wave of black humiliation, building and cresting as he sat at Connie's old davenport. He looked at the glossy photo of the Sydney Opera House, moved from it to a picture of the outdoor theatre in Santa Fe where *The Marriage of Figaro* was sung under the stars, set that to one side and picked up a picture of a narrow antique street in Vienna. He stared at this last with a darkness of spirit enveloping him and hearing within him a voice that he recognised as the voice of his mother hovering over him so many years in the past, so eager to judge, even more eager to condemn, if not him then someone else: 'What a waste of time, Teddy. Don't be such a little fool.'

464

But he was, wasn't he? He'd spent so many good hours imagining himself and Eugenie in one location or another, like actors moving on a strip of celluloid that did not allow for a single blemish in either the moment or the individuals. In his mind's eye, there had been no harsh glare of sunlight upon skin that was ageing, no hair out of place, on either of their heads, no breath needing freshening, no sphincter tightening to prevent an embarrassing explosion of intestinal wind at an inopportune time, no thickened toenails, no sagging flesh, and most of all no failure on his part when the time was finally right. He'd pictured the two of them eternally young in each other's vision if not in the world's. And that was all that had mattered to Ted: the way they saw each other.

But for Eugenie, things had been different. He understood that now. Because it wasn't natural for a woman to keep a man at a distance for so many months that bled inexorably into so many years. It also wasn't fair.

She'd used him as a front, he concluded. There was no other explanation for the phone calls she'd received, the visits to her house, and her inexplicable trip to London. She was using him as a front because if their mutual friends and acquaintances in Henley—not to mention the board of directors at the Sixty Plus Club who employed her—believed that she was keeping chaste company with Major Ted Wiley, they'd be far less likely to speculate that she was keeping unchaste company with someone else.

Fool. Fool. Don't be such a little fool. Once burnt, twice shy. I'd've thought you'd know better.

But how did one ever know better? To hope for

that sort of foresight meant never to venture forward at all into the company of another, and Ted didn't want that. His marriage to Connie—happy and fulfilling for so many years—had made him over sanguine. His marriage to Connie had taught him to believe that such a union was possible again, not a rare thing at all but something to be worked for and if not easily achieved, then achieved through an effort that was based on love.

Lies, he thought. Every one of them lies. Lies he'd told to himself and lies that he'd willingly believed as Eugenie had said them. *I'm not ready yet, Ted.* But the reality was that Eugenie hadn't been ready for him.

The sense of betrayal he felt was like an illness coming upon him. It started in his head and began to work oozingly downward. It seemed to him that the only way to defeat it was to beat it from his body, and if he'd had a scourge, he would have used it upon himself and taken satisfaction from the pain. As it was, he had only the brochures on the davenport, those pathetic symbols of his puerile idiocy.

He felt them slick beneath his hand, and his fingers crumpled them first then tore them. His chest bore a weight that might have been his arteries slowly closing but was, he knew, merely the dying of something other and far more necessary to his being than simply his old man's heart.

CHAPTER TWELVE

Entering the shop on the heels of the black constable was Akisha Newland, whose timely arrival gave Yasmin Edwards an opportunity that she would not otherwise have had of ignoring the man altogether. The girl politely hung back, apparently assuming that the man had come on business and was therefore to be given priority. All the Newland kids were like that, well brought up and thoughtful: a rare quality in teenagers.

Yasmin said, 'How's your Mum today?' to the girl, avoiding eye contact with the constable.

Akisha said, 'Doin' fair so far. She had a round of chemo two days back, but she's not taking it's bad as she did the last time. Don't know what that means, but we're hoping the best. You know.'

The best would be five more years of life, which was all the doctors had promised Mrs Newland when they'd first found the tumour in her brain. She could go without treatment and she'd live eighteen months, they'd told her. With treatment she might have five years. But that would be the maximum, barring some miracle, and miracles were in short supply when it came to cancer. Yasmin wondered what it would be like to have seven children to raise with a death sentence hanging over one's head.

She fetched Mrs Newland's wig from the back of the shop and brought it out on its Styrofoam stand. Akisha said, 'That doesn't look like—'

Yasmin interrupted. 'It's a new one. I think she's going t' like the style. You ask if. She doesn't, you

467

bring it back and we'll do the original for her. Right?'

Akisha's dark face gleamed with pleasure. 'That's real nice of you, Mrs Edwards,' she said as she scooped the wig stand under her arm. 'Thanks. Mum'll have a surprise this way.'

She was out in the street, with a bob of her head towards the constable, before Yasmin could do anything to prolong the conversation. When the door shut behind her, Yasmin looked at the man. She found that she couldn't remember his name, which was a delight to her.

She looked round for further employment in the shop, the better to continue ignoring him. Perhaps it was time to catalogue any supplies she now needed in her make-up case after having worked on those six women earlier. She brought the case out again, flipped the catches open, and began sorting through lotions, brushes, sponges, eye colour, lip colour, foundation, blushers, mascaras, and pencils. She laid each item on the counter.

The constable said, 'Could I have a word, Missus Edwards?'

'You had a word last night. More 'an one, as I recall. And who are you, anyway?'

'Metropolitan police.'

'I mean your name. I don't know your name.'

He told her. She found that she was irritated by it. A surname that spoke of his roots was fine. But that Christian name—Winston—displayed such a *grovelling* wish to be English. It was worse than Colin or Nigel or Giles. What were his parents thinking of, naming him Winston like he was going to be a politician or something? Stupid, that was. Stupid, he was.

468

She said, 'I'm working, as I expect you c'n see. I got another appointment coming in in—' She made a pretence of looking at her diary which was, thankfully, out of his range of vision—'ten minutes. What d'you want, then? Make it quick.'

He was big, she noticed. He'd looked big last night, both in the lift and in the flat. But somehow he looked even bigger today in the shop, perhaps because she was alone with him, with no Daniel there to offer a distraction. He seemed to fill the place, all broad shoulders and long-fingered hands and a face that looked friendly—pretended to be friendly because that's what they all did—even with that scar on his cheek.

'Like I said, a word, Missus Edwards.' His voice was scrupulously polite. He kept his distance, the shop counter between them. But instead of going on with the word he wanted, he said, 'Real nice that a new business opened up on a street like this. Always sad, you ask me, to see shop fronts boarded up. It's good to have a business go in, 'stead of some bloke buying up all the properties, bringing in a demolition crew, and putting up a Tescos or something like.'

She gave a mild snort. 'Rent's cheap when you're willing to set up shop in a rubbish tip,' she said, as if it meant nothing to her that she'd managed to actually achieve something she'd only dreamed of during her years in prison.

Nkata half-smiled. 'I 'xpect that's the truth. But the neighbours must feel it a blessing. Gives them hope. What sort of work you do in here, then?' It was more than obvious what sort of work she did. Yasmin didn't trust the question for a second. There were wigs on Styrofoam heads along one wall and a work room in the back where she styled them. He could see both the wigs and the work room from where he stood, so his question was maddening. It was such a blatant attempt to be friendly where friendliness between herself and someone like him was not only impossible but dangerous. Thus, she offered him her scorn, saying, 'What you doing a plod?' with a contemptuous glance that took him in from head to toe.

He shrugged. 'It's a living.'

'At brothers' expense.'

'Only if that's how it plays out.'

He sounded as if he'd resolved the matter of possibly having to arrest one of his own a long time ago. That angered her so she jerked her head at his face, saying, 'Where'd you get that, then?' as if the cicatrix that formed a curve on his cheek was his just reward for abandoning his people.

'Knife fight,' he said. 'Met some blokes in Windmill Gardens when I was fifteen and full of myself. I was lucky.'

'And I s'pose the other bloke wasn't?'

He fingered the scar as if trying to remember. He said, 'Depends on how you think luck works.'

She blew derision from her nostrils and went back to her make-up sorting. She arranged her eye shadows by colour, twisted tubes of lipstick open and did the same to them, flipped open the blushers and powders, and checked the levels on the liquid foundations. She made much of taking notes, writing on an order pad and being so extra scrupulous about her spelling that the lives of her customers might have depended upon the accuracy of her order form.

'I was in a gang, see,' Nkata offered. 'I got out

after that fight. Mostly 'cause of my mum. She took a look at my face when they took me to casualty and dropped to the floor like a stone. Gave herself concussion and ended up in hospital. That was that.'

'So you love your mum.' What rubbish, she thought.

'Know better than not to,' he replied.

She looked up quickly and saw he was smiling, but it seemed directed at himself not at her. He said, 'You got a real nice boy.'

'You stay away from my Daniel!' Her panic surprised her.

'He miss his dad?'

'I said you stay away!'

Nkata came to the counter then. He laid down his hands. He seemed to imply by the action that he was weaponless, but Yasmin knew otherwise. Coppers always had weapons and they knew how to use them. Nkata did so now. He said, 'There's a woman died two nights ago, Missus Edwards. Up in Hampstead. She had a boy, too.'

'What's that to me?'

'She was run down. Three times run over by the same car.'

'I don't know no one in Hampstead. I don't go to Hampstead. I never been to Hampstead. I go there, I stick out like a cactus in Siberia.'

'You would, that.'

She looked at him sharply to catch the sarcasm in his face that she couldn't hear in his voice, but all she saw was a gentleness in his eyes, and she knew exactly what that gentleness meant. It was a gentleness manufactured for the moment that said he'd do her right here in the shop if he could talk

471

her into it, he'd do her if he could get away with it, he'd do her even if he had to scare her into doing it with him, because to do it would prove he had the power to, because she was simply there, like a particularly challenging but nonetheless potentially gratifying mountain he just had to climb.

She said, 'I hear coppers work different to this, I do.'

'What's that?' he asked, managing quite effectively to look perplexed.

'You know what's that. You went to cop school, didn't you? Plods look for lags who're falling back on what they know best. They don't dig in new ground if they don't have to because they know that's a waste of time.'

'I'm not wasting time, far's I see. And I got a feeling you know that, Missus Edwards.'

'I knifed Roger Edwards. I cut him up good. I didn't run him down with a car. Didn't even have a car back then, Roger and me. Sold it, we did, when the money ran out and his little habit needed an urgent seeing to.'

'I'm real sorry about that,' the constable said. 'Must've been a bad time for you.'

'You try five years locked up if you want a bad time.' She turned from him and went on taking her inventory of cosmetics.

He said, 'Missus Edwards, you know it's not you I'm here about.'

'I don't know nothing like that, Mr Constable. But you can leave easy enough, I 'xpect, if it's not me you're wanting to talk to. I'm the only one here and the only one who's going to be here till my next client comes in. Course you might want to have a word with her. She's got cancer in her ovaries but

472

she's a real nice lady, and I expect she'll tell you last time she drove up to Hampstead. That's why you're in this part of town, right? Some black lady was driving in Hampstead and the neighbourhood's all in an uproar about it and you're here trying to suss her out?'

'You know that's not the fact 's well.'

He sounded infinitely patient and Yasmin wondered how far she could push him before he snapped.

She gave him her back. She had no intention of offering him anything, least of all what he apparently was after.

He said, 'What happened to your boy when you were inside, Missus Edwards?'

She swung round so fast that the beads on the ends of her plaits struck her cheeks. 'Don't you talk about him! Don't you try rattling me with Daniel. I didn't do nothing to anyone anywhere and you *bloody* well know it.'

'I 'xpect that's the truth. But what's also the truth is that Katja Wolff knew this lady, Missus Edwards. This lady that got mashed over up in Hampstead. This was two nights back, Missus Edwards, and Katja Wolff used to work for her. Twenty years ago. Back in Kensington Square. She was nanny to her baby. You know the lady I'm talking about?'

Yasmin felt the panic like a swarm of bees attacking her face. She cried out, 'You saw the car. Last night you saw it. You could tell it wasn't in no accident.'

'What I could tell is it had a front headlamp that was broke, with no one able to say how it happened.'

473

'Katja didn't run down no one! No one, you hear? You saying that Katja could run down a lady and only have a *headlamp* get broke?'

He didn't reply, merely letting her question and all that her question implied sing in the silence between them. She saw her mistake. He hadn't directly said that Katja was the person he was looking for. It was Yasmin herself who'd led them to that point.

She was furious with herself for letting panic get the better of her. She went back to the make-up she'd been cataloguing, and she began to slam each article back into the large metal case.

Nkata said, 'I don't think she was home, Missus Edwards. Not when this lady was run down. Happened sometime between ten and midnight. And I think Katja Wolff was gone from your flat just about that time. Maybe she was out for two hours, maybe three or four. Maybe she was gone for the night. But she wasn't there, was she? And neither was the car.'

She wouldn't answer. She wouldn't meet his eyes. She wouldn't acknowledge he was in the shop. Just a counter separated them, so she could almost feel his breath. But she would not allow his presence—or his words—to gain access to her in any way. Still, her heart was slamming against her ribs, and her mind was filled with the image of Katja's face. It was a face that had observed her carefully during suicide watch when she first went inside, a face that studied her through their exercise period and through association later in the day, a face that locked on hers during tea, and ultimately—though she never would have thought it, expected it, or dreamed that she could have

474

wanted it—a face that lingered above hers in the darkness. *Tell me your secrets. I'll tell you mine.*

She knew what had taken Katja inside. Everyone knew though Katja herself had never spoken of it to Yasmin. Whatever had happened in Kensington was not one of the secrets that Katja Wolff had been willing to reveal, and the single time that Yasmin had asked about the crime for which Katja was so much hated that she'd had to guard herself for years from retribution from the other women, Katja had said, 'Do you think I would kill a child, Yasmin? Very well. So be it.' And she had turned from Yasmin and had left her alone.

People didn't understand what it was like to be inside, to face the choice between solitude and companionship, between running the risks that went with solitude and embracing the protection that came with choosing—or allowing oneself to be chosen as—a lover, a partner, and a companion. To be alone was to be imprisoned within the prison, and the desolation that went with that secondary gaol term could break a woman and leave her fit for nothing when she was finally released.

So she'd put aside doubts and embraced the story that Katja's words had implied. Katja Wolff was no killer of babies. Katja Wolff was no killer at all.

'Missus Edwards,' Constable Nkata said in that gentle, trustworthy voice that coppers always used till they saw it wasn't working like they wanted, 'I see the situation you're in. You been together with her for a while. You got loyalty to her from when you were locked up and loyalty's good. But when someone's dead and someone else is lyin''—'

'What do you know 'bout loyalty?' she cried out,

475

swinging round on him. 'What do you know 'bout *anything*, man? You stand there like you think you're God 'cause you made a lucky choice that took you a different route to the rest of us. But you don't know nothing 'bout life, do you? 'Cause your choices always keep you safe but they got nothing in them that make you alive.'

He observed her calmly, and it seemed that there was nothing she could do and nothing she could say to shatter that steady tranquillity of his. And she hated him for the calm front he presented because she knew without having to be told that his serenity went right to the core of who he was.

'Katja was home,' she snapped. 'Just like we said. Now get out of here. I got work to do.'

He said, 'Where d'you 'xpect she went those days she phoned in to the laundry ill, Missus Edwards?'

'She didn't phone in to the laundry. She didn't phone in ill or anything else.'

'She told you that?'

'She didn't need to tell me.'

'You best ask her, then. You best watch her eyes when she answers, too. They fix on you, she's probably lying. They don't look at you at all, she's probably lying as well. 'Course, after twenty years inside, she'll be good at lying. So if she carries on with what she's doing when you ask your question, there's a good enough chance that she's lying as well.'

'I asked you to get out,' Yasmin said. 'I don't 'tend to ask again.'

'Missus Edwards, you're at risk in this situation, but you're not th' only one and you got to know that. You got a boy at risk. You got a fine boy.

Clever and good. I c'n see he loves you 'bove everything on earth, and if anything takes you 'way from him again—'

'Get out!' she cried. 'Get out 'f my shop. If you don't get out right now, I'll . . .' What? *What*, she thought raggedly. What in God's name would she do? Knife him like she'd knifed her husband? Assault him? And then what would they do to her? And to Daniel? What would happen to him? If they took her son from her—put him into care for even a day while they sorted things out the way they *always* did their sorting—she would not be able to bear the burden of responsibility for his pain and confusion.

She lowered her head. She would not give the detective her face. He could see her harsh breathing, he could take note of the beads of sweat that glistened on her neck. But more than that she would not give him. Not for the world, not for her freedom, not for anything else.

Into her line of vision, she suddenly saw his dark hand slide across the counter. She flinched till she realised he didn't mean to touch her. Instead he passed her a business card, then slid his hand away. He said so quietly that it sounded like a prayer, 'You phone me, Missus Edwards. There's my pager number on that card, so you phone me. Day or night. You phone. When you're ready—'

'I got nothing more to say.' But she whispered the words because it hurt her throat too much to do more than that.

'When you're ready,' he repeated. 'Missus Edwards.'

She didn't look up but she didn't need to. His heels sounded sharply against the yellow lino on

477

the floor as he left the shop.

*   *   *

After she and Lynley went their separate ways, Barbara Havers visited the Valley of Kings first. It was filled with swarthy middle eastern waiters. Once they appeared to come to terms with their collective disapproval of a woman wearing mufti instead of a black bed sheet, they studied in turn the snapshot of Eugenie Davies that Barbara and Lynley had managed to unearth from the woman's cottage in Friday Street. She had posed with Ted Wiley on the bridge that served as the gateway to Henley-on-Thames, and the picture had been taken during the Regatta, if the banners, boats, and colourfully dressed crowds along the river in the background were anything to go by. Barbara had carefully folded the photograph to exclude Major Wiley from the composition. No need to muddy the waters of the waiters' memories by showing Eugenie Davies with someone whom the employees of the Valley of Kings might never have seen.

But they shook their heads anyway, one by one. The woman in the photo wasn't anyone that they remembered.

She would have been with a man, Barbara told them helpfully. They would have come in separately but with the intention of meeting each other there, possibly in the bar. They would have seemed interested in each other, interested in a way that leads to sex.

Two of the waiters looked scandalised at this fascinating twist in the information. Another's

478

expression of disgust said that mutual lust played out in public between a man and a woman was just what he'd come to expect from living in the UK's answer to Gomorrah. But the clarification that Barbara had sought to provide through her revelation gained her nothing. Soon enough she was back in the street, and plodding in the direction of the Comfort Inn.

It wasn't, she found, aptly named, but then what affordable hotel in a busy street in their nation's capital ever was? She flashed Eugenie Davies' picture there—for the desk clerk, the maids, and everyone else having contact with the hotel's residents—but she received the same result. The night clerk, however, who would have been the person to see the pictured lady most closely had she ever checked into the hotel with a lover after dining at the Valley of Kings, was not yet on duty, Barbara was told by the hotel manager. So if the constable wanted to return . . . ?

She would have to, Barbara decided. There was no point leaving any stone right side up.

She fetched her car from where she'd left it, illegally parked in front of a cobbled pedestrian path leading into a leafy neighbourhood. She sat inside, shook a fag from her packet of Players, and lit up, cracking open a window against the chill autumn air. She smoked thoughtfully and considered two topics: the lack of damage on Ted Wiley's car and everyone's failure to identify Eugenie Davies in this South Kensington neighbourhood.

On the subject of Wiley's car, the conclusion seemed obvious: Whatever Barbara's earlier thinking in the matter, Ted Wiley hadn't run down

479

the woman he loved. On the subject of everyone's failure to identify Eugenie Davies, however, matters were less defined. One possible conclusion was that Eugenie had no connection with J.W. Pitchley, aka James Pitchford, in the present day despite having had a connection to him in the past and despite the coincidence of her having his address in her possession and dying in the very street where he lived. Another possible conclusion was that a connection did exist between them, but that connection did not extend to a tryst at the Valley of Kings or a bout of mattress bouncing afterwards at the Comfort Inn. A third conclusion was that they'd been longtime lovers who'd been meeting elsewhere prior to the night in question when they were to meet at Pitchley-Pitchford's place, which explained why Eugenie Davies had his address with her. And a fourth conclusion was that, sheer coincidence though it might be, Eugenie Davies had connected through the internet with TongueMan—Barbara shuddered at the name— and had met him like all his other lovers at the Valley of Kings for drinks and dinner, trailing him home afterwards and returning on another night to have some sort of encounter with him.

The fact of those other lovers seemed to be the point, though. If Pitchley-Pitchford was a regular at the restaurant and the hotel, then someone was going to remember his face, if not Eugenie's. So there was a chance that seeing his face next to Eugenie's face would dislodge a memory helpful to the investigation. Thus, Barbara knew that she needed a photo of Pitchley-Pitchford. And there was only one way to get it.

She made the drive to Crediton Hill in forty-five

minutes, wishing not for the first time that she had the talents of a taxi driver who'd passed the Knowledge with highest honours. There wasn't a single parking space in the street when she got there, but the houses had driveways, so Barbara made use of Pitchley's. It was a decent neighbourhood, she saw, lined with houses of a size that suggested no one in this part of the world was hurting for lolly. The area was not yet as trendy as Hampstead itself—with its coffee bars, narrow streets, and bohemian atmosphere—but it was pleasant, a good place for families with children and an unexpected place for a murder.

When she got out of her car, Barbara glanced up and saw a flicker of movement in Pitchley's front window.

She rang the bell. There was no immediate answer, which she considered odd since the room in which she'd seen the movement was no great distance from the front door. She rang a second time and heard a man call out, 'Coming, coming,' and a moment later, the door swung open on a bloke who did not appear at all like the online Lothario Barbara had been imagining. She'd expected someone vaguely oleaginous, decidedly tight-trousered, blatantly open-shirted, and displaying a gold medallion like a prize to be disentangled from the snare of copious hairs on his chest. Instead what she saw in front of her was a grey-eyed whippet of a man, well under six feet tall, possessing rounded cheeks splashed with the sort of natural colour that would have been the bane of his youth. He was wearing blue jeans and a striped cotton shirt with a button-down collar, and this latter garment was closed to the throat. A pair of

481

glasses was tucked into his shirt pocket. He wore expensive looking slip-ons on his feet.

So much for preconceived notions, Barbara thought. It was obviously time to elevate her leisure reading because cheap romance novels were polluting her mind.

She drew out her warrant card and identified herself. 'C'n I have a word?' she asked.

Pitchley's response was immediate as he half-shut the door. 'Not without my solicitor present.'

Barbara put out her hand and stopped the door's progress. 'Look. I need a photo of you, Mr Pitchley. If you have no connection with Eugenie Davies, it's no skin off your arse to hand one over.'

'I've just said—'

'I heard. And what I say is this: I can go through the legal song and dance with everyone from your solicitor to the Lord Chancellor to get the picture I need, but it seems to me that that's not only going to prolong your problems but it's also going to make great entertainment for your neighbours when I show up in a panda with the police photographer. With siren blaring and lights flashing on the roof to get the proper effect, of course.'

'You wouldn't dare.'

'Try me,' she said.

He thought about it, his glance darting along the street. 'I *said* I hadn't seen her in years. I didn't even recognise her when I saw her body. Why won't you lot believe me? I'm telling the truth.'

'Fine. Brilliant. Then let me prove it to everyone interested. I don't know about the rest of the force, but I'm not keen to stick this murder onto someone with no direct claim on the territory.'

He shifted from foot to foot like a schoolboy. He still held onto the door with one hand and his other hand now moved up to grasp the jamb.

It was an interesting reaction, Barbara thought. Despite what she'd said to reassure him, he was responding like a man who was barring the entry. He was acting like a man with something to hide. Barbara wanted to know what that something was. She said, 'Mr Pitchley . . . ? The photo . . . ?'

He said, 'Very well. I'll fetch one. If you'll wait.'

Barbara shouldered her way inside the house, unwilling to give him the chance to add *here* or *on the step,* with or without a courteous *please* attached. She said heartily, 'Thanks very much. Decent of you. I could do with a few minutes out of the cold.'

His nostrils flared with his displeasure, but he said, 'Fine. Wait here. I'll be just a moment,' and he fairly threw himself up the stairs.

Barbara listened hard to his progress. She listened hard to the sounds in the house. He'd admitted to trolling for older ladies on the net, but there was always the chance that he did some trolling where the younger fishies swam as well. If that was the case and if he had the same degree of success with teenagers that he had with the others, he wouldn't risk taking one of them to the Comfort Inn. Any bloke who made I-want-my-solicitor his primary response to any interaction with the police was a bloke who knew his arse from his elbow when it came to doing the deed with an underage girl. If he was bent in that direction, he'd make sure he didn't take the risk in public, but at home.

The fact that she'd seen movement in the room just above the street upon her arrival suggested to

483

Barbara that whatever Pitchley was up to, he was up to it on this floor of the house. So she sauntered to a closed door on her right as Pitchley thrashed about somewhere above her. She swung the door open and found herself in an orderly sitting room furnished with antiques.

The only item that appeared out of place was a tattered waxed jacket that lay over a chair. It seemed an odd place for the neat-as-pins Pitchley to stow a garment of his own. He had that sort of everything-in-its-place look about him.

Barbara took a peek at the jacket, then more than a peek. She lifted it off the chair and held it out at arm's length. Bingo, she thought. Pitchley would have been dwarfed inside it. But so would a teenage girl. Or any woman, for that matter, who wasn't the size of a sumo wrestler.

She replaced the jacket as Pitchley pounded down the stairs and plunged into the sitting room. He said, 'I asked you—' and stopped when he saw her smoothing down the garment's collar. At this, his eyes shifted to a second door in the room, which remained closed. Then they came back to Barbara, and he thrust his hand out. 'This is what you want. The woman's a colleague, by the way.'

Barbara said, 'Thanks,' and took the picture he offered. He'd chosen something flattering, she saw. In it, Pitchley wore black tie and he posed with a stunning brunette on his arm. She wore a sea green form-fitting gown from which balloon-like bosoms threatened to spill. They were patently implants, rising abruptly from her chest like twin domes designed by Sir Christopher Wren. 'Nice looking lady,' Barbara said. 'American, I take it.'

Pitchley looked surprised. 'Yes. From Los

484

Angeles. How did you guess?'

'Elementary deduction,' Barbara said. She stowed the photo away. She went on pleasantly. 'Nice digs. You live here alone?'

His eyes flicked to the jacket. But he said, 'Yes.'

'All this space. You're lucky. I've a place in Chalk Farm. But it's nothing like this. Just a hedgehog hole.' She indicated the second door. 'What's through there?'

His tongue lapped against his lips. 'The dining room. Constable, if there's nothing else . . .'

'Mind if I have a peek? It's always a treat to see how the other half lives.'

'Yes. I do. I mean, see here. You've got what you came for, and I see no need—'

'I think you're hiding something, Mr Pitchley.'

He flushed to the roots of his hair. 'I'm not.'

'No? That's good, then. So I'll have a look at what's behind this door.' She swung it open before he could protest further. He said, 'I haven't given you permission,' as she stepped into the next room.

It was empty, with stylish curtains at the far end drawn back against french windows. As in the sitting room, every article was in its place. Also as in the sitting room, however, one item struck a dissonant note. A cheque book sat on the walnut table. It was open, face down, and a pen lay next to it.

'Paying bills?' Barbara said idly. She took note that the air was tinctured heavily with the scent of male body odour as she advanced on the table.

'I'd like you to leave now, Constable.' Pitchley made a move towards the table but Barbara had the advantage of getting there first. She picked up the cheque book. Pitchley said hotly, 'Hang on.

485

How *dare* you? You have no right to invade my home.'

'Hmm. Yes,' Barbara said. She read the cheque that had gone uncompleted, Pitchley's writing no doubt interrupted by her ringing on his front bell. The amount in question was three thousand pounds. The payee was Robert, and the missing surname marked the moment of Barbara's arrival.

'That's it,' Pitchley said. 'I've cooperated with you. Leave or I'll phone my solicitor.'

'Who's Robert?' she asked. 'Is that his jacket out there and his aftershave in here?'

In reply, Pitchley headed for a swinging door. He said over his shoulder, 'I've finished with your questions.'

But Barbara wasn't finished with him. She was hot on his heels into the kitchen.

He said, 'Keep out of here.'

A gust of cold air answered her as she entered. She saw that the window was open wide. From the garden beyond it, a clatter sounded. Barbara dashed to investigate while Pitchley dived for the phone. As he punched in numbers behind her, Barbara saw the source of the noise outside. A rake that had been leaning against the house near the kitchen window had been knocked over onto the flagstones. And the visitors to Pitchley's home who had done the knocking over were at that moment slip-sliding down a narrow slope that separated the garden from a park behind it.

'Stop right there, you two,' Barbara shouted at the men. They were burly and badly dressed in crusty looking blue jeans and muddy boots. One of them had on a leather bomber jacket. The other wore only a pullover against the cold.

486

Both flashed looks back over their shoulders when they heard Barbara's shout. Pullover grinned and gave her an insolent salute. Bomber Jacket shouted, 'Go for it, Jay,' and both laughed as they slipped in the mud, scrambled back to their feet, and took off at a run across the park.

Barbara said, 'Damn,' and turned back to the kitchen.

Pitchley had his solicitor on the line. He was babbling, 'I want you over here now. I swear, Azoff, if you're not at the house in the next ten minutes—'

Barbara strode to where he stood and snatched the phone from his hand. He said, 'You *bloody* little—'

'Take a stress pill, Pitchley,' Barbara said. She said into the phone, 'Save yourself the trip, Mr Azoff. I'm leaving. I have what I need,' and without waiting to hear the solicitor's reply, she handed the phone back to Pitchley. She said, 'I don't know what you're up to, fast man, but I'm going to find out. And when I do, I'll be back with a warrant and a team to tear this house to shreds. If we find anything that connects you to Eugenie Davies, you're meat on a skewer. *My* skewer. Got it?'

'I have no connection with Eugenie Davies,' he said stiffly although some of the colour was gone from his cheeks and the rest of his face had gone nearly white, 'other than what I've already told Chief Inspector Leach.'

'Fine,' she said. 'So be it, Mr Pitchley. You'd best hope that's what my spade work turns up.'

She strode from the kitchen and made her way to the front door. Once outside, she went straight to her car. There was no point to trying to track down the two blokes; by the time she worked her way round West Hampstead over to the other side of the park, they'd be either long gone or well in hiding.

Barbara fired up the Mini's engine and revved it a few times to let off steam. She'd been ready to go through the motions of taking Pitchley's photo and Eugenie Davies' photo back to the Valley of Kings and the Comfort Inn without the hope of gaining anything from the exercise. Indeed, she'd been nearly ready to dismiss J.W. Pitchley, aka James Pitchford, aka TongueMan from their list of suspects altogether. But now she wondered. He sure as hell wasn't acting like a man with nothing smelly on his conscience. He was acting like a man up to his neck in manure. And with a cheque for three thousand pounds half-written in his dining room and two gorilla size yobbos climbing out of his kitchen window . . . Things no longer looked so cut and dried for Pitchley, Pitchford, TongueMan or whoever the hell he was supposed to be.

Barbara reflected on this final idea as she reversed the Mini into the street. Pitchley, Pitchford, and TongueMan, she thought. There was something in that. She wondered idly if there was another name somewhere that the man from West Hampstead used for something.

She knew exactly how to suss that out.

*   *   *

Lynley found the home of Ian Staines in a quiet street not far from St Ann's Well Gardens. Using the motorways, he'd made the drive down to Brighton from Henley-on-Thames in fairly good time, but the brief daylight of November was fast

488

fading when he pulled up to the correct address.

The door was opened by a woman holding a cat as if it were an infant against her shoulder. The cat was Persian, an insolent looking pedigree who cast baleful blue eyes upon Lynley as he produced his identification. The woman was a striking Eurasian, no longer young and no longer as beautiful as she once might have been, but difficult to look away from all the same because of a subtle hardness beneath her skin.

She took note of Lynley's identification and said, 'Yes,' and nothing more when he asked her if she was Mrs Ian Staines. She waited for whatever was forthcoming from him, although a certain narrowing to her eyes suggested to Lynley that she had little doubt about who the subject of this visit was. He asked if he could have a word, and she stepped back from the doorway and led him to a partially furnished sitting room. Noting the deep impression of furniture feet left on the carpet, he asked if the Staineses were moving house. She said no, they were not moving house, and after the most minute of pauses, she added *yet* in such a way that Lynley felt the undercurrent of her contempt.

She didn't gesture him to one of the two remaining chairs in the sparsely furnished room, both of which were currently occupied with one cat apiece of the same breed as the feline she held. Neither of these was sleeping as one might expect of a cat perched on a comfortable chair. Rather, they were watchful, as if Lynley were a specimen of something in which they might become interested should a sudden burst of energy come upon them.

Mrs Staines set the cat she held onto the floor. Bloomer-legged by fur that shone with careful grooming, he sauntered to one of the chairs, leapt effortlessly to its seat and dispossessed his housemate of it. That cat joined the other and settled down on its haunches.

'They're beautiful animals,' Lynley said. 'Are you a breeder, Mrs Staines?'

She didn't reply. She wasn't very different from the cats themselves: observing, withholding, and palpably hostile.

She walked to a table that stood by itself, next to the carpet impressions of what must have been a sofa. The table held nothing but a tortoiseshell box whose lid Mrs Staines flipped open with one manicured finger. She took a cigarette out and from the pocket of her slender-legged trousers, she scooped up a lighter. She put flame to tobacco, inhaled, and said, 'What's he done?' in the tone of a woman who very much wanted to add *this time* to the question.

There were no newspapers in the room. But their absence didn't mean that the Staineses were unaware of Eugenie Davies' death. Lynley said, 'There's a situation in London that I'd like to speak to your husband about, Mrs Staines. Is he at home or still at work?'

'At work?' She gave a short, breathy laugh before saying, 'London, is it? Ian doesn't like cities, Inspector. He can barely cope with the congestion in Brighton.'

'The traffic?' Lynley asked.

'The people. Misanthropy is one of his less admirable qualities, although he manages to hide it most of the time.' She inhaled from her cigarette in the studied manner of an old film star, her head tilted back so that her hair—thick, stylishly cut, with the occasional strand of grey highlighting it—hung free from her shoulders. She walked to the window in front of which were yet more carpet impressions of furniture now removed. She said, 'He wasn't here when she died. He'd gone to see her. They'd had a row as you must have been told by someone or why else would you have come. But he didn't kill her.'

'You've heard about what happened to Mrs Davies, then.'

'*Daily Mail*,' she said. 'We didn't know about it until this morning.'

'Someone was seen having an argument with Mrs Davies in Henley-on-Thames, someone who took off in an Audi with Brighton number plates. Was that man your husband?'

'Yes,' she said. 'That would be Ian, in the midst of yet another fine plan going awry.'

'A plan?'

'Ian always has plans. And if he hasn't a plan, he has a promise. Plans and promises, promises and plans. All of which generally amount to nothing.'

'That'll do, Lydia.'

The statement, sharply spoken, came from the doorway. Lynley turned to see that they had been joined by a lanky man with the weathered and yellowing skin of a chronic smoker. He did as his wife had done, crossing the room to the tortoiseshell box and taking a cigarette. He jerked his head at his wife. This apparently communicated a desire to her, for in response she brought out her lighter a second time. She passed it to him and he used it, saying to Lynley, 'What can I do for you?'

'He's come about your sister,' Lydia Staines said. 'I told you that you should expect him, Ian.'

491

'Leave us.' He lifted his chin in the direction of the two chairs to indicate the cats, adding, 'And take them with you before they get turned into someone's new coat.'

Lydia Staines threw her cigarette still smouldering into the fireplace. She scooped up a cat in each arm and said, 'Come along Caesar,' to the one who remained. She went on with, 'I'll leave you to your fun, then,' and accompanied by the animals, she left the room.

Staines watched her go, something in his eyes of an animal's hunger as his glance travelled over her body, something round his mouth of a man's loathing for a woman with too much power over him. When he heard a radio clicked on somewhere in the back of the house, he gave his attention to Lynley. He said, 'I saw Eugenie, yes. Twice. In Henley. We had a row. She'd given me her word, her promise, that she'd speak to Gideon—that's her son, but I expect you know that already, don't you?—and I was depending on her to do it. But she said she'd changed her mind, said something had come up that made it impossible for to her to ask him . . . And that was it. I took off out of there in a dead blind rage. But someone saw us, I take it. Saw me. Saw the car.'

'Where is it?' Lynley asked.

'Being serviced.'

'Where?'

'Local dealership. Why?'

'I'll need the address. I'll need to see it, to talk the people at the dealership as well. They do body work there, I expect.'

Staines' cigarette tip glowed, long and bright, as he took in enough smoke to see him through the moment. He said, 'What's your name?'

'DI Lynley. New Scotland Yard:

'I didn't knock down my sister, DI Lynley. I was angry. I was damn well desperate. But running her over wouldn't take me an inch towards what I need, so I planned to wait a few days—a few weeks if it took that and if I could hold out—and try her again.'

'Try her for what?'

Like his wife, he tossed his cigarette into the fireplace. He said, 'Come with me,' and headed out of the sitting room.

Lynley followed him. They went to the first floor of the house, up stairs so well-carpeted that their footfalls were soundless. They walked along a corridor where rectangles of darker paper on the walls indicated paintings or prints had been removed. They entered a darkened room that was set up as an office with a desk holding a computer monitor that glowed with text and numerical information. Lynley examined this and saw that Staines had logged onto the internet, having chosen an online stock broker as his reading or research material.

'You play the market,' Lynley said.

'Abundance.'

'What?'

'Abundance. It's all about thinking and living abundance. Thinking and living abundance *effects* abundance, and that abundance produces more of the same.'

Lynley frowned, trying to piece this together with what he saw on the screen. Staines continued.

'It's all about thinking in the first place. Most people stay stuck in paucity because that's the only

493

thing they know and that's what they've been taught. I was like that myself once. I was damn *bloody* like that.' He came to join Lynley at the desk and laid his hand on a thick book that was open next to his computer's keyboard. This was heavily highlighted in a variety of colours, as if the reader had studied it for years and had taken something new from each perusal of its words. It looked like a text—Lynley thought of vaguely of economics—but Staines' words sounded more like a new age philosophy. The man continued in a low, intense voice.

'We attract to our lives that which closely resembles our thoughts,' he said insistently. 'Think beauty, and we're beautiful. Think ugliness, and we're ugly. Think success, and we become successful.'

'Think mastery of the international market, and we have it?' Lynley said.

'Yes. *Yes.* If you spend your life contemplating your limits, you can expect no freedom from limitation.' Staines' eyes fixed on the glowing monitor. In its light, Lynley saw that his left eye was milky with a cataract, and the skin was puffy beneath it. He went on. 'I used to live only within my limits. I was bound by drugs, by drink, by horses, by cards. If it wasn't one thing, it was another. I lost everything that way—my wife, my children, my home—but that'll not happen to me again. I swear it. Abundance will come. I *live* abundance.'

Lynley was beginning to get the picture. He said, 'It's a risky sort of business, playing the market, isn't it, Mr Staines? A great deal of money can be made. Or lost.'

'There is no risk, with faith, right action, and belief. Right thought produces the result that's intended by God, Who is Himself goodness and Who wants goodness for His children. If we are one with Him and part of Him, we are part of the good. We must tap into it.' As he spoke, he stared intently at the screen. It was divided in such a way that the continually altering prices on a stock exchange somewhere flickered in a band along the bottom. Staines looked mesmerised by this band, as if its moving figures were coded directions to find the Holy Grail.

'But isn't the good open to interpretation?' Lynley asked. 'And isn't it the case that man's timeline and God's timeline to reaching the good may be running on different calendars?'

'It's *abundance*,' Staines said, and he spoke through his teeth. 'We define it and it *comes*.'

'And if it doesn't, we're in debt,' Lynley said.

Abruptly, Staines reached forward and pressed a button on the monitor. The screen faded. He directed his words to it, and his tone underscored a rage that he held at bay. 'I hadn't seen her for years. I hadn't bothered her for years. I never *asked* her for a God damn thing. All those years with the drugs, the drink, the horses, I never asked. I usually went to Doug and he helped me when he could. But this last time he said, "Can't do it, old man. Have a look at the cheque book if you don't believe me." So what was I supposed to do?'

'You asked your sister for money to pay down your debt. What's it from, Mr Staines? Selling short? Day trading? Buying futures? What?'

Staines swung away from the monitor, as if the sight of it now offended him. He said, 'We've sold

495

what we can. We have only a bed left in our room. We're eating from a card table in the kitchen. The silver's gone. Lydia's lost her jewellery. And all I need is a decent break, which she could have helped me to get, which she *promised* to help me to get. I told her I'd pay her back. I'd pay him back. He's got thousands, millions. He *has* to have.'

'Gideon. Your nephew.'

'I trusted her to speak to him. She changed her mind. Something's come up, she said. She couldn't ask him for money.'

'Did she tell you this the other night when you saw her?'

'That's when she told me.'

'Not earlier?'

'No.'

'Did she tell you what the "something" was?'

'We argued like hell. I begged. Begged my own sister, but . . . no. She didn't tell me.'

Lynley wondered why the man was admitting so much. Addicts, he knew from personal experience, were masters of manipulation. His own brother had demonstrated that for years. But Lynley was no intimate of Ian Staines, not a close relative whose overpowering sense of responsibility for something that was not in fact his responsibility was nevertheless going to compel him to hand over— even metaphorically—the cash that was needed 'just this once'. Yet he knew with the assurance of long experience that Staines was saying nothing without being fully aware of what it was.

Lynley said, 'Where did you go when you left your sister, Mr Staines?'

'Drove round till half past one in the morning, till I knew Lydia would be asleep when I got home.'

'Is there anyone who can confirm that? Did you stop for petrol somewhere?'

'Didn't need to.'

'I'll ask you to take me to the dealership where your car's being serviced, then.'

'I didn't run Eugenie down. I didn't kill her. That would have gained me nothing.'

'It's routine, Mr Staines.'

'She said she'd talk to him. I just needed a break.'

What he needed, Lynley thought, was a cure for his delusions.

CHAPTER THIRTEEN

Libby Neale took the corner into Chalcot Square so sharply that she had to put out a foot to prevent the Suzuki from going into a skid. She'd decided to take a break from her delivery route by scoring an English version of a BLT at a Pret a Manger on Victoria Street, and while she'd been munching at one of the stand-up counters, she'd spied a newspaper that a previous customer had left lying by an empty Evian bottle. She'd flipped it over to see that it was the *Sun*, the paper she loathed most due to the taunting presence of the Page Three Girl who served as a daily reminder to Libby Neale of all she was not. She was about to shove it to one side when the headline grabbed her attention. *Virtuoso's Mother Murdered* took up about four inches of space. Beneath it was a grainy picture that was dated by the hairstyle and the clothing of the woman in it: Gideon's mother.

497

Libby snatched up the paper and read it as she ate. She made the jump to page four where the story continued, and what she saw on that page made her mouthful of sandwich begin to taste like wood shavings. The entire spread covered not the death of Gideon's mother—about which only a limited amount of information was currently available—but another death entirely.

Shit, Libby thought. The Fleet Street dickheads were digging *everything* up all over again. And tabloids being what they were, it was only a matter of time before they started hounding Gideon himself. In fact, they probably were *already* hounding him. A side bar about Gideon blowing his concert at Wigmore Hall was a feature just begging for further exploration. And as if the poor dude didn't have enough messing up his mind, the paper looked like it was trying to make some sort of connection between Gideon's tough time at that concert and the hit and run in West Hampstead!

As *if*, Libby thought contemptuously. Like Gideon would even *recognise* his mother if he'd seen her on the street or something?

Uncharacteristically, she'd thrown half her sandwich away and stuffed the tabloid down the front of her leathers. She had another two deliveries to make, but to hell with that noise. She needed to see Gideon.

In Chalcot Square, she roared counterclockwise around the street and skidded to a stop right in front of the house. She pulled the motorcycle onto the sidewalk without bothering to chain it to the railing. Up the front steps in three strides, she banged on the door, then followed that with a long ring on the bell. He didn't answer, so she looked around the square to see if she could spy his Mitsubishi. She picked it out in front of a yellow house a few doors down on the right. He was at home. So come on, she thought, answer the door.

Within the house, she heard his telephone begin ringing. Four rings and it was abruptly cut off, which made her think he was at home and just not answering the door, but then a distant disembodied voice that she couldn't recognise told her that Gideon's answering machine was taking a message.

'Damn,' she muttered. He must have gone off somewhere. He must have learned that the papers were digging up everything about his sister's death and decided to split for a while. She couldn't blame him. Most people had to live through shit only once. But it looked like he was going to have to live through everything connected with her murder a second time.

She went down to her flat. The day's post lay on the mat, and she picked this up, unlocked her door, and looked through the letters as she stepped inside. Among the BT bill, a bank statement showing that her account was in dire need of an emergency transfusion, and a circular for a home alarm system, there was also a legal sized envelope from her mother, which Libby dreaded opening because of the possibility of being confronted with yet another of her sister's success stories. But she tore the end off it anyway, and as she removed her helmet with one hand, with the other she shook out the single sheet of purple paper that her mother had sent.

Have What You Want . . . Be Everything You Dream ran in heavy black script across the page. It seemed that Equality Neale—CEO of Neale

499

Publicity and recently featured on the cover of *Money* magazine—was giving a seminar in Boston on the topic of Self-Assertion and Achievement in Business, which she would follow with another appearance in Amsterdam. Mrs Neale had written in the precise hand that would have done proud the nuns who'd taught her, *Wouldn't it be nice if the two of you could get together? Ali could arrange for a stopover on her way back. How far is Amsterdam from London?*

Not far enough, Libby thought, and she balled up the announcement. Still, the very idea of Ali and everything so righteously irritating about her that *made* her Ali caused Libby to bypass the refrigerator where she'd normally have headed after being thwarted in her intentions to see Gideon. Instead she poured herself a virtuous glass of highland water in lieu of the six cheddar *quesadillas* she was feeling like scarfing down. As she drank it, she looked out of the window. Against the wall that marked the side boundary of Gideon's backyard stood his kite-making shed, and its door was ajar, a light within throwing a wedge of illumination onto the ground in front of it.

She set her water glass on the counter and ducked outside, bounding up steps that were grey-green with lichen. She called out, 'Hey, Gideon!' as she strode down the path in his direction. 'You in there?'

There was no response, which gave Libby a qualm and slowed her steps for a moment. She hadn't seen Richard Davies' Granada out in the square, but she hadn't been looking for it. He might've come calling for another one of those pain-in-the-butt father/son talks of his that he appeared to be addicted to. And if he'd managed to piss off Gideon just enough, Gideon might've left on foot and Richard might right now be getting even by wrecking Gideon's kites. That would be just like him, Libby thought. The one thing Gid did that wasn't connected to that stupid violin and his father wouldn't hesitate a second to smash it to smithereens. He'd even come up with a good excuse afterwards. 'It was taking you away from your music, son.'

As *if*, Libby thought scornfully. Giedeon's kites weren't what needed wrecking.

Richard continued, if only in her head, 'I accepted it as a hobby before, Gideon, but I can't accept it now. We've got to get you well. We've got to get you playing. You've concerts scheduled, recordings to make, and a public waiting.'

Fuck *off*, Libby told Richard Davies. He's got a life. He's got a good life. Why don't you think about getting one, too?

The thought of actually going to the mat with Richard for once—of actually telling him off without Gideon there to stop her—renewed Libby's energetic surge along the path. She reached the shed and knocked the door the rest of the way open.

Gideon was there, no Richard with him. He was sitting at his makeshift design table. A large piece of paper was taped on the working surface before him, and he sat staring at it like it had something to say to him if he only listened to it long and hard enough.

Libby said, 'Gid? Hi. I saw the light.'

He didn't act like he'd heard her. He kept his gaze on the paper in front of him. The only change

501

in him was that he began to squint as he looked it over.

Libby said, 'I knocked on the door upstairs. I rang the doorbell too. I saw your car in the square, so I figured you were home. Then when I saw the light out here . . .' She heard her own words die off, like a plant that's wilting without its necessary water.

He said, his eyes still fixed on the paper, 'You're back from work early.'

'I got my deliveries better organised today so I wouldn't be backtracking all over the place for once.' She was surprised at her aptitude for hasty lying. Something of Rock was rubbing off on her.

'I'm surprised your husband didn't want you to stay on anyway.'

'He doesn't know, and I'm sure as hell not telling him.' She shivered. A small electric heater stood on the floor near him, but Gideon didn't have it on. She said, 'Aren't you cold without a sweater or something?'

'I hadn't actually noticed.'

'Been out here long?'

'A few hours, I think.'

'So what're you doing? Another kite?'

'Something to fly,' he said. 'Higher than the others.'

'Sounds cool.' She went to stand behind him, eager to see his latest design. She said, 'You could do this professionally. No one makes kites like you do, Gid. They're incredible. They're—'

The sight of the design paper stopped her. What he'd produced was an elaborate mass of smudges where he'd drawn and then erased what he'd drawn. They covered the paper, with some of the erasures tearing through it.

Gideon turned to look at her when she didn't complete her remarks. He turned so quickly that she didn't have time to arrange her face.

He said, 'I've lost this as well, it seems.'

She said, 'No, you haven't. Don't be dumb. You're just . . . blocked or stopped up or something. This is a creative thing, right? Making kites is creative. Anything creative gets stopped up now and then.'

He read her face and apparently saw on it what she hadn't said. He shook his head. He looked the worst she'd seen him look in all the time since he'd been unable to play his music. He looked worse even than he'd looked just the previous night when he'd come to tell her that his mother was dead. His light hair lay flat and unwashed against his skull, his eyes seemed sunken, and his lips were so chapped that they looked like scales were growing on them. It all seemed so *extreme*, she thought. Hell, he hadn't even seen his mother in years, and he hadn't exactly been tied to her when she was alive, had he? Not like he was tied to his dad.

As if he knew her thoughts and wanted to respond to correct them, he said, 'I saw her, Libby.'

He said, 'I saw her, and I *forgot* that I saw her.'

'Your mom?' Libby asked. 'You *saw* your mom?'

'I don't know how I'd forgotten that I saw her. I don't know how it works when you forget, but that's what happened.'

He was looking at Libby but she could tell he wasn't seeing her, and he seemed to be talking to himself. He sounded so filled with self-loathing that she hastened to reassure him. She said, 'Maybe you didn't know who she was. It'd been . . .

what . . . years and years . . . since you were a kid that you last saw her. And you don't have any pictures of her, do you? So how would you even remember what she looked like?'

'She was there,' he said dully. 'She said my name. "Do you remember me, Gideon?" And she wanted money.'

'Money?'

'I turned away from her. I am too important, you see, and I have important concerts to give. So I turned away. Because I didn't know who she was. But I'm at fault for that, no matter what I knew or when I knew it.'

'Shit,' Libby murmured as she began to realise what he was implying. 'Gid, heck. You're not thinking you're, like, responsible for what's happened to your mom, are you?'

'I don't think,' he said. 'I know.' And he moved his gaze away from her, fixing it on the open doorway, where the daylight had faded and what remained of it were shadows that created great wells of darkness.

She said, 'That's bullshit. If you'd known who she was when she came to you, you would've helped her out. I know you, Gideon. You're good. You're decent. If your mother was on the ropes or something, if she needed cash, you wouldn't've ever let her go under. Yeah, she ran out on you. Yeah, she kept away from you for years. But she was your mom and you aren't the kind of guy who holds grudges against anyone, least of all your mom. You're not like Rock Peters.' Libby gave a humourless laugh at the thought of what her estranged husband might have done had his mother shown up in his life asking for money after

504

a twenty year absence. He'd've given her a piece of his mind, Libby thought. He'd've given her *more* than a piece of his mind. Mother or not, he'd've probably given her the sort of smacking around that he reserved for women who righteously pissed him off. And he would've been righteously pissed off at that: having a deserting mom show up on his doorstep asking for money without so much as a how've-you-been-son first. In fact, he might've been so pissed off that—

Libby put the brakes on her runaway thoughts. She told herself that the whole idea that Gideon Davies of all people would lift a hand to harm even a spider was plain idiotic. He was an artist, after all, and an artist wasn't the type of man who would run down someone in the street and expect to keep his creative flow flowing afterwards. Except that here he was with the kites, unable to do what he'd earlier been able to do with ease.

She said, although her mouth was dry, 'Did you hear from her, Gid? I mean after she asked you for money. Did you hear from her again?'

'I didn't know who she was,' Gideon repeated. 'I didn't know what she wanted, Libby, so I didn't understand what she was talking about.'

Libby took that for negation because she didn't want to take it as anything else. She said, 'Listen, why don't we go inside? I'll make you some tea. It's freezing in this place. You gotta be an ice cube if you've been out here a while.'

She took his arm and he allowed himself to be helped to his feet. She switched out the light and together they felt their way through the gloom to the door. He seemed like a heavy burden to Libby, leaning against her as if all his strength had been

505

depleted in the hours he'd spent trying to design a simple kite.

'I don't know what I'm going to do,' he said. 'She would have helped me, and now she's gone.'

'What you're going to do is have a cup of tea,' Libby told him. 'I'll throw in a teacake on the side.'

'I can't eat,' he said. 'I can't sleep.'

'Then sleep with me tonight. You're always able to sleep with me.' They didn't do anything else, she thought, that was for sure. For the first time she wondered if he was a virgin, if he'd lost the ability to be close to a woman once his mother deserted him. She knew next to nothing about psychology, but it seemed like a reasonable explanation for Gideon's apparent aversion to sex. How could he take the chance that a woman he grew to love might actually abandon him again?

Libby led him down the steps to her kitchen, where she discovered that she didn't have any of the teacakes she'd promised him. She didn't have anything to toast at all, but she bet that he did, so she hustled him up to his own part of the house and sat him at the kitchen table while she filled the kettle and rustled through his cupboards for tea and something edible that would go with it.

He sat looking like the living dead . . . although Libby winced when she came up with the analogy. She chatted about her day in an attempt to distract him and she found herself putting so much energy into the effort that she built up a sweat beneath her leathers. Without a thought, she unzipped the top and started to work her way out of it as she talked.

The newspaper she'd stuffed inside fell out. Just like a piece of buttered bread, it fell with the part she wouldn't wish to find face up exactly that: face up. The screaming headline managed what screaming headlines always seek to do: It got Gideon's attention and he bent from his chair and pulled the paper to him as Libby made a grab for it herself.

She said, 'Don't. It'll just make things worse.'

He looked up at her. 'What things?'

'Why put yourself through more shit?' she asked him, her fingers closing over one side of the paper as his fingers closed over the other. 'All it does is dig everything up all over again. You don't need that.'

But Gideon's fingers were as insistent as hers and she knew that she could either let him have the paper or they would rip it in half between them like two women fighting over a dress at a Nordstrom's sale. She released her half, mentally kicking her butt for having brought the paper with her in the first place and for having forgotten she had it in the second place.

Gideon read the article much as she had done. And just the same, he made the jump to the double spread of pages four and five. There, he saw the pictures that the paper had disinterred from its morgue: his sister, his mom and his dad, his own eight-year-old self, and the other parties involved. It must have been one hell of a slow news day, Libby thought bitterly.

She said, 'Hey. Gideon. I forgot to say. Someone phoned when I was banging on your door. I heard a voice on the answering machine. You want to listen? You want me to play it back for you?'

'That can wait,' he said.

'Could've been your dad. Might've been about Jill. How d' you feel about that anyway? You never

507

said. It must be so weird to be going to have a little brother or sister when you're old enough to have a kid yourself. Do they know what it's going to be?'

'A girl,' he said, although she could tell his mind was elsewhere. Jill had the tests. It's going to be a girl.'

'Cool. A little sister. What a trip for you. You'll be, like, so totally excellent a big brother.'

He got to his feet abruptly. 'I can't cope with any more nightmares. I don't sleep for hours when I go to bed. I lie there and I listen and I watch the ceiling. When I finally fall asleep, there're the dreams. The dreams and the dreams. I can't *cope* with the dreams.'

The kettle clicked off behind her. Libby wanted to see to the tea, but there was something in his face, something so wild and despairing in his face . . . She hadn't seen such an expression before, and she told herself that she was mesmerised by it, drawn in to it in such a powerful way that any action other than looking at him was completely impossible. Better that, she thought, than go in any other direction . . . like wondering if his mother's death had pushed Gideon over the edge.

That couldn't be the case because what reason was there? Why would a man like him wig out if his mom died? If his mother whom he hadn't seen or heard from in years just died? Okay, so he saw her once, so she asked him for money, so he didn't know who she was and refused . . . Was that something to totally lose it over? Libby didn't think so. But she knew that she was distinctly glad that Gideon was seeing a psychiatrist.

She said, ' 'd you tell your shrink about the dreams? They're supposed to know what they mean, aren't they? I mean, what else are you paying them for if not to tell you what your dreams mean so that you can stop having them. Right?'

'I've stopped seeing her.'

Libby frowned. 'The shrink? When?'

'I cancelled my appointment today. She can't help me get back to the violin. I've been wasting my time.'

'But I thought you liked her.'

'What does it mean that I *liked* her? If she can't help me, what the hell's the point? She wanted me to remember and I've remembered and what's been the result of that. Look at me. Look at this. Look. *Look.* Do you actually think I can play like this?'

He held out his hands, and she saw something she'd not noticed before, something she knew hadn't been there twenty-four hours ago when he'd first come to her and told her of his mother's death. His hands were shaking. They were shaking bad, like her grandpa's hands shook before his Parkinson's medication kicked in.

One part of her wanted to celebrate what it meant that Gideon had stopped seeing the psychiatrist: He was beginning to define himself as more than a violinist, which was definitely good. But another part of her felt a prickling of unease at what he was saying. Without the violin, he could discover who he was but he had to *want* to make the discovery, and he didn't much sound or look like a man willing to embark on a journey of self-actualisation.

Still, she said gently, 'Not playing's not the end of the world, Gideon.'

'It's the end of my world,' he told her.

509

He went into the music room. She heard him stumble, hit against something, and curse. A light switched on and as Libby saw to the tea Gideon listened to the message that had come in while he'd been trying to work in the shed.

'This is Detective Inspector Thomas Lynley,' a plush costume-drama baritone informed them. 'I'm on the way up to London from Brighton. Will you phone me on my mobile when you get this message? I need to speak to you regarding your uncle.'

An *uncle* now? Libby wondered as the detective recited his cell phone number. What next? How much more was going to be heaped on Gideon and when would he finally shout, 'Enough!'

She was about to say, 'Wait till tomorrow, Gid. Sleep with me tonight. I'll make you not have nightmares. I promise,' when she heard Gideon punching in numbers on his telephone. A moment later he began to speak. She tried to sound busy with the tea, but she listened all the same, in Gideon's best interests.

'Gideon Davies here,' he said. 'I got your message . . . Thanks . . . Yes, it was a shock.' He listened long to something that the detective was telling him. He finally said, 'I'd prefer it on the phone, if it's all the same to you.'

Score one for our side, Libby thought. We'll have a quiet night and then we'll sleep. But as she took their tea cups to the table, Gideon went on, after another pause to listen to the cop.

'Very well, then. If there's no other way.' He recited his address. 'I'll be here, Inspector.' And he hung up.

He came back to the kitchen. Libby tried to look

as if she hadn't been eavesdropping. She went to a cupboard and opened it, searching for something to go with their tea. She settled on a bag of Japanese crackers. She ripped it open and dumped its contents into a bowl, searching out two peas and popping them into her mouth as she carried it back to the table.

'One of the detectives,' Gideon said unnecessarily. 'He wants to talk to me about my uncle.'

'Something happen to your uncle, too?' Libby scooped a spoonful of sugar into her cup. She didn't really want the tea, but as she'd been the one to suggest it, she didn't see a way to get out of drinking it.

'I don't know,' Gideon told her.

'Think you should call him before the cops get here, then? Check out what's going on?'

'I've no idea where he is.'

'Brighton?' Libby felt her face get hot. 'I overheard that guy say he was coming in from Brighton. On his message. When you played it.'

'It could be Brighton. But I didn't think to ask his name.'

'Whose?'

'My uncle's.'

'You don't *know* . . .? Oh. Well. Never mind, I guess.' It was just another twist in his family history, Libby thought. Lots of people didn't know their relatives. As her father would have said, it was a sign of the times. 'You couldn't put him off till tomorrow?'

'I didn't want to put him off. I want to know what's happening.'

'Oh. Sure.' She was disappointed, seeing herself

511

ministering to him throughout the long evening, figuring inanely that ministering to him now that he was at his lowest might lead to something more between them, making a final breakthrough somehow. She said, 'If you can trust him, I guess.'

'Trust him how?'

'Trust him to tell you the truth. He's a cop, after all.' She shrugged and scooped up a handful of the Japanese mix.

Gideon sat. He pulled his teacup towards him, but he didn't drink. 'It doesn't matter one way or another.'

'What doesn't?'

'Whether he tells me the truth or not.'

'No? Why not?' Libby asked.

Gideon looked her square in the face when he delivered the blow. 'Because I can't trust anyone with the truth. I didn't know that before. But I know that now.'

*   *   *

Things were moving from bad to worse.

J.W. Pitchley, aka TongueMan, aka James Pitchford logged off the internet, stared at the blank screen, and cursed it to hell. He'd finally managed to get CreamPants on the net for some cybertalk, but despite a good half hour of reasoning with her, she wasn't going to cooperate. All she had to do was walk into the Hampstead police station and have a five minute conversation with DCI Leach and she wouldn't do it. She merely needed to confirm that she and a man she knew only as TongueMan had spent the evening together, first in a South Kensington restaurant and then in a claustrophobic little room above Cromwell Road where the ceaseless traffic noise disguised the frantic creaking of bedsprings and the cries of pleasures that he coaxed from her when he performed the services implied by his moniker. But no, she couldn't do that for him. No matter that he'd brought her off six times in under two hours, no matter that he'd held off taking his own satisfaction till she was weak, sodden, and limp with having taken hers, no matter that he'd fulfilled her every seamy fantasy about the rewards of anonymous sex. She wasn't going to step forward and 'face the humiliation of having a complete stranger know the sort of woman I can be under certain unusual circumstances'.

I'm a bloody stranger, you filthy bitch! Pitchley had roared, if only in his head. You didn't think twice about letting me know what you like to get up to when you're panting for it.

She'd seemed to know what he was thinking, though, despite the fact that he didn't communicate it on the screen. She'd written *They'd want my name, you see. I can't have that, Tongue. Not my name. Not with tabloids being what they are. I'm sorry, but you understand that, don't you?*

Which was how he'd come to realise that she wasn't divorced. She wasn't a woman in her declining years who was desperate for a man to prove she still had It. She was a woman in her declining years who was looking for a thrill to balance against the tedium of marriage.

That marriage had to be a longtime covenant, one made not with an Everyman or an Anyman but with a Somebody, an important Somebody, a politician, perhaps, or an entertainer, or a

513

successful and well-known entrepreneur. And if she gave her name to DCI Leach, it would quickly leak through the porous substance that was the hierarchy of power at the police station. Having leaked through that, it would find its way to the ears of an informant from within, a snout who accepted cash from a journalist eager to make his name by outing someone on the front page of his filthy scandal sheet.

Bitch, Pitchley thought. Bitch, bitch, bitch. She might have thought of that before she'd met him at the Valley of Kings, Mrs Butter-Wouldn't-Melt-If-You-Put-It-On-Coals. She might have thought of all the potential consequences before she walked in, dressed to be seen as Mrs Demure, Mrs Out-Of-Style, Mrs I've-Got-No-Experience-With-Men, Mrs Please-Please-Show-Me-I'm-Still-Desirable-Because-I've-Been-So-Low-On-Myself-For-So-Long. She might have thought it could actually come to having to say Okay, I was there in the Valley of Kings, having drinks and then dinner with an utter stranger whom I met online in a chat room where people hide their identities while sharing their fantasies about wild, wet, and lubricious sex. She might have thought she could be asked to admit to hours lying splayed on a thin-mattressed bed above the South Kensington traffic, naked on that bed with a man whose name she didn't know, didn't ask to know, and didn't want to know. She might have *thought*, the rotten little cow.

Pitchley pushed himself away from his computer and sank his elbows onto his knees. He took his forehead into his hands and dug into it with his fingertips. She could have helped. She wouldn't have been the complete solution to his problem—

514

there was still that long period between the Comfort Inn and his arrival in Crediton Hill to be accounted for—but she would have been a bloody good start. As it was, he had only his story, his willingness to stick to his story, the unlikely possibility that the evening clerk at the Comfort Inn would confirm his presence two nights ago without confusing that night with the dozens of other nights he'd passed the requisite cash across the counter, and the hope that his face was guileless enough to convince the police to believe his story.

It didn't help matters that he knew the woman who'd died in his street in possession of his address. And it truly didn't help matters one iota that he'd once been involved—no matter how peripherally—with a heinous crime that had taken place when he'd lived under her roof.

He'd heard the shrieking that evening and he'd come running because he'd recognised who was crying out. When he'd got there, everyone else was there as well: the child's father and mother, the grandfather, the brother, Sarah-Jane Beckett, and Katja. 'I do not leave her for more than a minute,' she shrieked, frantically laying this information in front of everyone milling round the closed bathroom door. 'I swear. I do not leave her for more than a minute!' And then looming behind her was Robson, the violin master, who grasped her by the shoulders and pulled her away. 'You must believe me,' she cried and continued to cry as he pulled her with him down the stairs and out of sight.

He hadn't known at first what was going on. He hadn't wanted to know and couldn't afford to know. He'd heard the argument between her and the parents, she'd told him she'd been sacked, and the last thing he wanted to consider was whether the argument, the sacking, and the reason for the sacking—which he suspected but could not bear to contemplate—were in any way related to what lay behind that bathroom door.

'James, what's going *on*?' Sarah-Jane Beckett's hand had slipped into his, clutching at him as she breathed the whisper. 'Oh God, something hasn't happened to Sonia, has it?'

He'd looked at her and saw that her eyes were glittering, despite her sombre tone. But he hadn't wondered what that glitter meant. He'd only wondered how he could manage to get away from her and go to Katja.

'Take the boy,' Richard Davies had instructed Sarah-Jane. 'For God's sake, get Gideon out of here, Sarah.'

She'd done as he commanded, taking the little white-faced boy into his bedroom where music was playing, issuing blithely forth as if nothing terrible was going on in the house.

He himself went seeking Katja and he found her in the kitchen, where Robson was forcing a glass of brandy on her. She was trying to refuse, crying, 'No. No. I cannot drink it,' looking wild-haired, wild-eyed, and completely wrong for the part of loving, protective nanny to a child who was . . . what? He was afraid to ask, afraid because he already knew but didn't want to face it because of what it might mean in his *own* small life if what he thought and dreaded proved to be true.

'Drink this,' Robson was saying. 'Katja. For the love of God, pull yourself together. The paramedics will be here in a moment and you can't afford to be seen like this.'

'I did not, I did not!' She swung round in her chair and grabbed onto his shirt, the collar of which she grasped and twisted. 'You must *say*, Raphael! Say to them that I did not leave her.'

'You're getting hysterical. It may be nothing.'

But that did not prove to be the case.

He should have gone to her then, but he hadn't because he'd been afraid. The mere thought that something might have happened to that child, might have happened to *any* child within a house in which he was a resident, had paralysed him. And then later, when he could have talked to her and when he tried to talk to her, in order to declare himself the friend she needed and clearly did not have, she would not speak to him. It was as if the subtle flaying she was taking in the press in the immediate aftermath of Sonia's death had driven her into a corner and the only way she could survive was to become tiny and silent, like a pebble on a path. Every story about the unfolding drama in Kensington Square began with the reminder that Sonia Davies' nanny was the German whose famed escape from East Germany—previously considered laudable and miraculous—had cost a vital young man his life, and that the luxurious environment in which she found herself in England was a dire and bleak contrast to the situation to which her ostentatious asylum seeking had condemned the rest of her family. Everything about her that was remotely questionable or potentially interpretable was dug up by the press. And anyone close to her was liable to the same treatment. So he'd kept his distance, till it was too late.

517

When she was finally charged and brought to trial, the van that had taken her from Holloway to the Old Bailey had been pelted with eggs and with rotten fruit, and shouts of 'baby killer' greeted her when that same van returned her to the prison at night and she had to make the few yards' walk to the prison's door. Public passion was aroused by the crime she had allegedly committed: because the victim was a child, because the child was handicapped, and because—although no one would say it directly—her putative killer was German.

And now he was back in it all, Pitchley thought as he rubbed his forehead. He was mixed up in it as effectively as if he'd never managed to put twenty years between himself and what had happened in that miserable house. He'd changed his name, he'd switched jobs five times, but all his best efforts to remake himself were going to be brought to nothing if he couldn't get CreamPants to see that her statement was crucial to his survival.

Not that CreamPants' statement was the only thing he needed to put his house in order. He also needed to deal with Robbie and Brent, those two loose cannons who were about to fire.

He'd assumed they wanted money again when they'd shown up a second time in Crediton Hill. No matter that he'd already given them a cheque, he knew them well enough to realise there was a decent possibility that Robbie had been inspired by the sight of a Ladbrokes to deposit those funds not in a bank account but on the head of a horse whose name he rather fancied. This assumption on Pitchley's part was ratified when Robbie said, 'Show 'im, Brent,' not five minutes after the two of them had hulked through his front door, carrying with them the stench of their poor bathing habits. Accepting the instruction, Brent brought forth from his jacket a copy of *The Source*, which he opened like someone shaking out bed sheets.

'Look who it was got mashed on your doorstep, Jay,' Brent said with a grin as he showed the scabrous paper's front page. And of course it would be *The Source*, Pitchley thought. God forbid that either Brent or Robbie would elevate their taste to something less sensational.

He couldn't avoid seeing what Brent dangled in front of him: the garish headline, the photograph of Eugenie Davies, the inset photograph of the street in which he himself lived, and the second inset photograph of the boy no longer a boy but a man now and a celebrity. It was all down to him that this death was taking up newsprint at all, Pitchley thought bitterly. If Gideon Davies hadn't achieved fame, fortune, and success in a world that increasingly valued those accomplishments, then the papers wouldn't even be covering this situation. It would simply be an unfortunate hit-and-run that the police were in the process of investigating. Full stop and end of story.

Robbie said, ' 'Course, we di'n't know when we was here yesterday. Mind 'f I unload this, Jay?' And he'd shrugged his way out of his heavy waxed jacket and lobbed it onto the back of a chair. He made a circuit of the room and a point of examining everything in it. He said, 'Nice gaff, this. You done good for yourself, Jay. I expect you got a big name in the City, least 'mong the people who count. That right, Jay? You massage their money and presto amazo, it makes more money and they trust you to do that, don't they?'

Pitchley said, 'Just say what you want. I'm rather pressed for time.'

'Don't see why,' Robbie said. 'Shoot. In New York . . .' He snapped his fingers in the direction of his companion. 'Brent. Time in New York?'

Brent looked at his watch obediently. His lips moved as he did the maths. He frowned and employed the fingers of one hand. He finally said, 'Early.'

Robbie said, 'Right. Early, Jay. Th' market's not closed yet in New York. You got plenty of time to make a few more quid before the day's over. Even with this little confab of ours.'

Pitchley sighed. The only way to get rid of the two men would be to make it look as though he was playing Rob's game. He said, 'You're right, of course,' and nothing more. He merely walked to a bureau near the window that overlooked the street, and from inside he brought out his cheque book and a biro that he clicked open officially. He carried the cheque book into the dining room, where he pulled out a chair, sat, and began to write. He started with the amount: three thousand pounds. He couldn't imagine that Rob would ask for less.

Rob strode into the dining room. Brent, as always, followed his brother. Rob said, 'That's what you think, is it, Jay? Us two show up and it's all about money?'

'What else?' Pitchley filled in the date and began to write the other man's name.

Robbie's hand smacked down on the dining room table. 'Hey! You stop that and look at me.' And for good measure, he knocked the biro from

520

Pitchley's hand. 'You think this is about *money*, Jay? Me and Brent trot round—all this way up to Hampstead, mind you—with business waiting to be tended to out there—'this with a jerk of his head back in the direction of the sitting room, by which Pitchley took that he meant the street—'with us losing dosh by the bucketful just to stand here and bunny with you for ten minutes and you think we come about money? Hell, man.' And to the other, 'What d'you think of that, Brent?'

Brent joined them at the table, *The Source* still dangling from his fingers. He wouldn't know what to do with the paper till Robbie gave him his next set of instructions. As for now, it gave him something to occupy his hands.

The poor oaf was pathetic, Pitchley thought. It was a wonder he'd ever learned to tie his shoes. He said, 'All right. Fine,' and sat back in his chair. 'So why don't you tell me why you've come, Rob?'

'Can't just be a friendly visit, that it?'

'That's not exactly our history.'

'Yeah? Well, you *think* about history. 'Cause it's ripe to come back and pay a call on you, Jay.' Robbie flicked his thumb at *The Source*. Cooperatively, Brent held it higher, like a schoolboy displaying his primitive artwork. 'Slow going on the news front last few days. No Royals misbehaving, no MP getting caught with his dick in a school girl's hole. The papers're going to start digging, Jay. And me and Brent come to see you to lay our plans.'

'Plans.' Pitchley repeated the word with a great deal of care.

'Sure. We took care of things once. We c'n do it again. Situation's bound to heat up fast once the coppers suss out who you really are and when they give the word to the press like they always do—'

'They know,' Pitchley said, in the hope that he could head Robbie off, that he could bluff him with a partial truth that the man might take as a full admission. 'I've already told them.'

But Rob wasn't swallowing that tale. He said, 'No way, Jay. 'Cause if you did, they'd feed you to the sharks soon 's they need something to make it look like they been working hard. You know that. So I 'xpect you told them something, true. But 'f I know you, you didn't tell them all.' He eyed Pitchley shrewdly and seemed to like what he read on his face. He said, 'Right. Good. So me and Brent here figger we got to lay some plans. You'll be wanting protection and we know how to give it.'

And then I'll owe you forever, Pitchley thought. Double what I already owe you because it'll be twice in my life that you've played at keeping the hounds at bay.

'You need us, Jay,' Robbie said. 'And me and Brent? We don't turn our backs when we know we're needed. Some people do, but that's not our way.'

Pitchley could only imagine how it would play out: Robbie and Brent doing battle for him, strong-arming the press in the same ineffectual manner that they'd employed in the past.

He was about to tell them to go home to their wives, to their fading inadequate ill-managed business washing waxing buffing the cars of the rich among whom they would never be able to mix. He was about to tell them to piss off permanently because he was tired of being drained like a bath tub and played like a badly tuned piano. Indeed, he

522

opened his mouth to say all of it but that was when the doorbell rang, when he walked to the window and saw who it was, when he said, 'Stay here,' to Robbie and Brent and closed the dining room doors upon them.

And now, he thought miserably as he sat at his computer and tried and failed to come up with a way to bend the will of CreamPants to his own, he would owe them more. He would owe them more for Rob's quick thinking, the thinking that got him and Brent out of the house and into the park before the dumpy female detective constable was able to put her mitts on them when they'd hidden in the kitchen. No matter that what they might have told her would have added nothing harmful in his present situation. Robbie and Brent would not see it that way. They would see their actions as protecting him, and they would come calling when they thought it was time for him to pay.

*   *   *

Lynley made the drive to London in fairly good time after paying a visit to the Audi dealership that was working on the car owned by Ian Staines. He'd taken Staines with him as a safeguard against the man making any phone calls in an attempt to direct the course of Lynley's inquiries, and once they'd pulled to a stop in front of the showroom, he'd told the man to wait in the Bentley while he went inside for a chat.

There, he corroborated much of what Eugenie Davies' brother had told him. The car was indeed being serviced; it had been brought in at eight that morning. An appointment for the work had been scheduled on the previous Thursday, and nothing irregular—like a request for body work—had been noted in the computer when the service secretary had taken the call.

When Lynley asked to see the car, that presented no problem either. The service representative walked him out to it, chatting away about the great strides that Audi had made in craftsmanship, manoeuvrability, and design. If he was curious as to why a policeman had come round asking about a particular car, he gave no evidence of this. A potential customer was, after all, a potential customer.

The Audi in question stood in one of the service bays, raised some six feet on a hydraulic lift. Its position gave Lynley the opportunity to examine its undercarriage as well as the chance to scrutinise its front end and both of its wings for damage. The front end was fine, but there were scratches and a dent on the car's left wing that looked intriguing. They looked fresh as well.

'Any chance a smashed bumper was replaced before you got the car?' Lynley asked the mechanic who was working on it.

'Always a chance of that, mate,' the man replied. 'Bloke don't need to drop money at the dealership if he knows how to shop.'

So despite the verification provided by the Audi's general condition and its presence just where Staines said it would be, there was still the chance that those scratches and that small dent meant something more than poor driving skills. Staines couldn't be crossed off the list, despite his claim that the scratches and dent were a mystery to him, that 'bloody Lydia uses the car as well,

524

Inspector'.

Lynley dropped the man at a bus stop and told him not to disappear from Brighton. 'If you move house, phone me,' he said to Staines, handing over his card. 'I'll want to know.'

Then he headed for London. Northeast of Regent's Park, Chalcot Square was yet another area of town that was undergoing gentrification. If the scaffolding on the front of several of the buildings hadn't told Lynley this much when he pulled into the square, the freshly painted façades of the rest of the residences would have filled him in on the information. The neighbourhood reminded him of Notting Hill. Here was the same bright paint in a variety of cheerful colours fronting the buildings along the streets.

Gideon Davies' house stood tucked into a corner of the square. It was bright blue in colour with a white front door. It possessed a narrow first floor balcony along which ran a low white balustrade, and the french windows beyond that balcony were brightly lit.

His knock on the door was answered quickly, as if the house's owner had been waiting on the bottom step just beyond the entrance. Gideon Davies said quietly, 'DI Lynley?' and when Lynley nodded, he added 'Come upstairs,' and led the way. He took him to the first floor, up a staircase whose walls displayed the framed hallmarks of his career, and he led him into the room that Lynley had seen from the street, where a CD system occupied one wall and comfortable furniture scattered across the floor was punctuated by tables and music stands. Sheet music stood on these stands and lay on the table tops, but none of it was open.

Davies said, 'I've never met my uncle, Inspector Lynley. I don't know how much help I'll be to you.'

Lynley had read the stories in the newspaper after the violinist had walked out on his concert at Wigmore Hall. He'd thought—probably like most of the public interested in the tale—that it was another instance of someone who had been too feather-bedded for too many years getting his knickers in a twist about something. He'd seen the subsequent explanations put forth by the young man's publicity machine: exhaustion after a killing schedule of concerts in the spring. And he'd dismissed the entire subject as a three-day wonder that the papers needed to fill column inches at a slow time of year.

But now he saw that the virtuoso looked ill. Lynley thought immediately of Parkinson's— Davies' walk was unsteady and his hands trembled—and of what that disease could do to finish his career. That would be something that the young man's publicity machine would indeed want to keep from the public for as long as possible, calling it everything from exhaustion to nerves until it was impossible for them to call it anything else.

Davies gestured to three overstuffed armchairs that formed a group near the fireplace. He himself sat nearest the fire itself: artificial coals between which blue and orange flames rhythmically lapped like a visual soporific. Despite his sickly appearance, Lynley could see the strong resemblance between the violinist and Richard Davies. They shared much the same body type, with an emphasis on bones and stringy muscles. The younger Davies had no spinal curvature, however, although the manner in which he kept his

526

legs locked together and his clenched fists pressed into his stomach suggested that he had other physical problems.

Lynley said, 'How old were you when your parents divorced, Mr Davies?'

'When they divorced?' The violinist had to think about the question before he answered it. 'I was about nine when my mother left, but they didn't divorce immediately. Well, they couldn't have done, not with the law being what it is. So it must have taken them what . . . four years? I don't actually know, now I think of it, Inspector. The subject never came up.'

'The subject of their divorce or the subject of her leaving?'

'Either. She was just gone one day.'

'You never asked why?'

'I didn't like to. We never talked much about personal things in my family. There was a lot of . . . I suppose you could call it reticence amongst us. It wasn't just the three of us in the house, you see. There were my grandparents, my teacher, and a lodger as well. Something of a crowd. I suppose it was a way to have privacy: by letting everyone have a personal life that no one else ever mentioned. Everyone kept their thoughts and their feelings to themselves. Well, that was the fashion anyway, wasn't it.'

'And during the time of your sister's death?'

At that, Davies moved his gaze off Lynley and fixed it on the fire but the rest of his body remained motionless. 'What about my sister's death?'

'Did everyone keep their thoughts and feelings to themselves when she was murdered? And during the trial that followed?'

527

Davies' legs tightened against each other as if they would defend him from the question. Still, he answered frankly despite the picture he painted of his family by doing so. 'No one ever talked about it. "Best to forget" was like a family motto, Inspector, and we lived by it.' He raised his face towards the ceiling. He swallowed and said, 'God. I expect that's why my mother finally left us. No one would ever talk about what desperately *needed* talking about in that house, and she just couldn't cope with it any longer.'

'When was the last time you saw her, Mr Davies?'

'Then,' he said.

'When you were nine years old?'

'Dad and I left for a tour in Austria. When we returned, she was gone.'

'You've not heard from her since?'

'I've not heard from her since.'

'She never contacted you in the last several months?'

'No. Why?'

'Your uncle says she intended to see you. She intended to borrow money from you. He says that she told him something came up to prevent her from asking you for money. I'm wondering if you know what that something was.'

Davies looked guarded at that, as if a barrier had come down like a thin shield of steel to cover his eyes. 'I've had . . . I suppose you could call it some trouble with my playing.' He let Lynley fill in the rest: A mother anxious about her son's well-being was unlikely to petition him for funds, either for herself or for a ne'er-do-well brother.

That supposition didn't conflict with what

528

Richard Davies had told Lynley about his former wife phoning him to learn more about their son's condition. But the timing was off if the musician's condition was supposed to be what had kept his mother from making her request for funds. Indeed, it was off by several months. For Gideon Davies had undergone his trauma at Wigmore Hall in July. It was now November. And according to Ian Staines, his sister's change of heart concerning asking her son for money had occurred in the more immediate past than had Gideon's musical difficulties.

'Your father tells me she'd been phoning him regularly about you, so she did know that something was wrong,' Lynley said in agreement. 'But he made no mention of her wanting to see you or asking to see you. You're certain she didn't contact you directly?'

'I think I'd remember my own mother contacting me, Inspector. She didn't, and she couldn't have done. My number's ex-directory, so the only way she had to contact me would have been through my agent, through Dad, or by turning up at a concert and sending a note back stage.'

'She did none of those things?'

'She did none of those things.'

'And she passed no message to you through your father?'

'She passed no message,' Davies said. 'So perhaps my uncle's lying to you about my mother's intention of seeing me to ask for money. Or perhaps my mother lied to my uncle *about* her intention of seeing me to ask for money. Or perhaps my father's lying to you about her phone calls to him in the first place. But that last is unlikely.'

'You sound sure of that. Why?'

'Because Dad himself wanted us to meet. He thought she could help me out.'

'With what?'

'The trouble I've had with my playing. He thought she could . . .' Here, Davies went back to looking at the fire, his assurance of a moment before quite gone. His legs trembled. He said, more to the fire than to Lynley, 'I don't really believe that she could have helped me, though. I don't believe anyone can help me at this point. But I was willing to try. Before she was killed. I was willing to try anything.'

An artist, Lynley thought, who was being kept from his art due to fear. The violinist would be looking for a talisman of some sort. He would want to believe his mother was the charm that could get him back to his instrument. Lynley said to make certain, 'How, Mr Davies?'

'What?'

'How could your mother have helped you?'

'By agreeing with Dad.'

'Agreeing? About what?'

Davies considered the question, and when he answered, he told Lynley volumes about the difference between what was going on in his professional life and what the public was being told about it. 'Agreeing that there's nothing wrong with me. Agreeing that my head's playing me for a fool. That's what Dad wanted her to do. He has to have her agree with him, you see. Anything else is unthinkable. Now, unspeakable would be par for the course in my family. But unthinkable . . .? That would take too much effort.' He laughed weakly, a brief note that was as humourless as it was bitter. 'I'd have seen her, though. And I'd have tried to believe her.'

So he would have reason to want his mother alive, not dead. Especially if he held fast to the conviction that she was the cure for what ailed his playing. Nonetheless, Lynley said, 'This is routine, Mr Davies, but I need to ask it: Where were you two nights ago when your mother was killed? This would have been between ten and midnight.'

'Here,' Davies said. 'In bed. Alone.'

'And since he left your home, have you had contact with a man called James Pitchford?'

Davies looked honestly surprised. 'James the Lodger? No. Why?' The question seemed ingenuous enough.

'Your mother was on her way to see him when she was killed.'

'On her way to see James? That doesn't make sense.'

'No,' Lynley said. 'It doesn't.'

Nor, he thought, did some of her other actions. Lynley wondered which of them had led to her death.